"Old-timey dialogue, newly minted, rhetorical stretches, and whopping good humor right out of Twain."
— *Kirkus Reviews* on *The Smiling Country*

"Elmer Kelton is a Texas treasure. . . . Kelton truly deserves to be made one of the immortals of literature."
— *El Paso Herald-Post*

"A wonderfully humorous book with just enough evil in a few of the characters to keep realism alive and well. All this, and the most delightful narrator since Huck Finn."
— *Amarillo News-Globe* on *Cloudy in the West*

"This latest Kelton masterpiece is difficult to put down. The story was more important to finish than sleep. . . . I could easily summarize Kelton's story, but it is too good and too entertaining to take away the surprises that await readers. . . . It is a great story from a superb storyteller."
— *San Angelo Standard Times* (Texas) on *Cloudy in the West*

"The San Angelo author, whose nonfiction works stands right up there with his novels, again displays his talents as a superb storyteller and his great knowledge of the American West of yesteryear. His fiction always rings true because he has made such a thorough study of what we fondly call the Old West. . . . Kelton continues to be a master at capturing the spirit of the West of the nation's past."
— *Reporter-News* (Abilene, Texas) on *The Pumpkin Rollers*

"Elmer Kelton does not write Westerns. He writes fine novels set in the West—like *The Pumpkin Rollers*. Here a reader meets flesh-and-blood people of an earlier time, in a story that will grab and hold you from the first to the last page."
— Dee Brown, author of the *New York Times* bestseller *Bury My Heart at Wounded Knee*

D0043083

Other Books by Elmer Kelton

Barbed Wire

Shadow of a Star

Buffalo Wagons

Hot Iron

The Texas Rifles

Donovan

The Pumpkin Rollers

Cloudy in the West

The Smiling Country

The Buckskin Line*

The Good Old Boys

The Time It Never Rained

The Day the Cowboys Quit

Captain's Rangers

*forthcoming

THE DAY THE COWBOYS QUIT

Elmer Kelton

A TOM DOHERTY ASSOCIATES BOOK
NEW YORK

NOTE: If you purchased this book without a cover you should be aware that this book is stolen property. It was reported as "unsold and destroyed" to the publisher, and neither the author nor the publisher has received any payment for this "stripped book."

This is a work of fiction. All the characters and events portrayed in this book are either products of the author's imagination or are used fictitiously.

THE DAY THE COWBOYS QUIT

Copyright © 1971 by Elmer Kelton

All rights reserved, including the right to reproduce this book, or portions thereof, in any form.

A Forge Book
Published by Tom Doherty Associates, Inc.
175 Fifth Avenue
New York, NY 10010

Forge® is a registered trademark of Tom Doherty Associates, Inc.

ISBN: 0-812-57450-8

First Forge edition: April 1999

Printed in the United States of America

0 9 8 7 6 5 4 3 2 1

Dedicated
to those fine chroniclers of the West Texas cowboy:

J. EVETTS HALEY

BOB BEVERLY

LAURA V. HAMNER

PAUL PATTERSON

I

IN LATER YEARS PEOPLE OFTEN ASKED HUGH Hitchcock about the Canadian River cowboy strike of 1883. If they were strangers he looked them over carefully before he answered, and sometimes he did not answer at all; he figured there was no way of explaining it to anyone who did not understand the nature of the old-time cowboy.

It irritated him like a prickly pear thorn imbedded under his hide that some people seemed to think cowboys spent their time loping around aimlessly on horseback and firing their pistols. Many of the men he had known in the Texas Panhandle never owned a pistol, and probably half the cowboys between the Canadian and the Pecos could not have shot themselves in the foot if they had tried. What they did most in those days was work, from before they could see in the morning until they could no longer see in the evening.

Those days, Hitch always said, a man proved himself with horsemanship. A rider a cut above average was looked up to, even by the sourest wagon cook. If a man's saddle did

not have a shine to it, they knew nothing good would come
of him.

Next to his way with a horse, a cowboy was proudest of
his independence. He worked for other men, but they owned
nothing of him except his time. He was a free soul. He could
ride from the Rio Grande to the Powder River and seldom
see a fence. He could start that ride with five dollars in his
pocket and have three left when he finished, if that was the
way he wanted to travel. Money did not rule him.

The Canadian River region of Texas then was less than
ten years settled, the sandy-bottomed river cutting a deep,
rough gash across the heart of that uplifted tableland known
to the Spanish as *Llano Estacado*, the Staked Plains. It was
a grand plateau, larger than some Eastern states, a vast tree-
less ocean of grass often flat to the eye but gently rolling
when a man tested it in a wagon, finding himself alternately
easing downward or putting forth extra effort to climb. A
decade before, this prairie had teemed with grazing buffalo,
fleet white-rumped antelope and the roving packs of gray
wolves which lived among them, pulling down the halt and
the lame. Across this unmapped sunny land had roamed the
Comanche and the Kiowa, brothers to the wolf. They had
known its hidden watering places, its changing seasons, its
hunger, its bounty, its angry storms, and its quiet peace.

Now the buffalo were gone, and with them the Indian.
White men's cattle by the hundreds of thousands had plod-
ded and bawled up the long trails from South Texas, and
down through Raton Pass from Colorado, spreading out over
these seemingly infinite miles of open grasslands, finding
water in occasional creeks and streams fringed with cottonwood and hackberry and black walnut, almost the only timber from the eastern caprock to the New Mexico breaks.
Out in open country, wood was so rare that men gathered
dry buffalo and cow chips for fuel wherever they found
them, hoarding them in sagging cowhides lashed loosely
beneath their wagonboxes.

Now most of the plains grass was claimed by right of
occupancy, and already the more observant cowboys could

see that it grew less tall. Dust stirred easier now, a sign of overgrazing because these great herds of longhorned cattle did not migrate with the rains and the changing seasons as had their wild and shaggy predecessors. Already men in their eagerness for gain foreshadowed their own defeat by demanding more from the land than it could produce. And those in a position to hire demanded more of other men.

Hugh Hitchcock always said cowboy independence triggered the cowboy strike. There came a time that some men decided independence was too costly when the wrong people had it, so they tried to mold others to a pattern of their own cutting. And when you crowd a man too far, he may do something in self defense that is not sensible either.

Old cowboys in later years argued no end over the causes of the strike, and the starting of it. To each it began in a different place and a different way. To Hugh Hitchcock, looking back, it started the day Rascal McGinty and the Figure 4 rep went to their guns over ownership of a roan cow.

He always remembered the kind of day it was—the sun bright over the gentle roll of the open plains, the sky blue as a pretty woman's eyes, the brown winter grass starting to show tinges of springtime green, the first prairie flowers bursting scarlet and yellow and white. He remembered Rascal McGinty and that red face of his and red hair and a temper to match them both. Rascal was riding Sweetheart, an ill-named mustang bay he had traded for, a long-tailed pony ugly as a mud fence but able to stay with a man to the last crossing—an honest horse that would work his heart out, but only after he had done his damnedest to bust the rider first. That bay was a lot like Rascal.

Hitch always recalled that Dayton Brumley was riding a Figure 4 sorrel called Blaze for the crooked streak that ran from forelock down to a snip nose. Blaze had fox ears and three stocking feet and an R Slash branded on his left hip, and moved with as smooth a saddle gait as Hitch ever saw.

He forgot in later years just what Dayton Brumley looked

like. After all that time a man couldn't be expected to remember details.

She wasn't much of a cow; she had seen too many hard
winters, and the scrubby calf punching its long nose futilely
at her near-dry udder showed she had been less than choosy
in the bull she associated with. But to a syndicate outfit like
the Figure 4, its bookkeepers dreading each encounter with
the Kansas City board of directors, every calf branded meant
dollars of capital gain on the ledger. To a wage-working
cowboy like Rascal McGinty or his brother Law, trying to
build a shirttail herd for themselves, even a crippled cow or
a blind one was of value so long as she could yet conceive
and deliver. When Dayton Brumley rode into the "stray"
herd and called the cow's brand a Figure 4, Rascal stood
straight up in his stirrups. His voice carried halfway across
the gather.

"The hell you say! That cow's an LR, sure as ever was."

Hugh Hitchcock heard, and the voice was a warning flag.
Hitch was wagon boss on the W's "river division," that
part of the ranch which lay nearest the Canadian, and the
McGinty brothers worked under him. He knew Rascal's
emotions lay always near the surface, the volatile cowboy
quick to laugh or quick to explode like the Sharps Big Fifty
that had cleared these plains and river breaks of buffalo. No
one could ever judge which direction Rascal would jump.

A cowboy came spurring. "Hitch, you better git over
yonder. There's apt to be trouble." Instinctively they always
looked to Hugh Hitchcock; that was why he was wagon
boss.

Dayton Brumley ignored Rascal and again called the pair
as property of the Figure 4. On open range before barbed
wire cut all of Texas into pastures, cattle of many brands
mixed together. Boundary lines were an invisible thing; the
cattle drifted wherever they found the grass green and the
water good. At roundup time the big ranches sent their
chuckwagons and teams of men to the various divisions, and
they sent cowboy representatives to neighboring outfits'

wagons, each to watch out for the interests of the brand that paid him. The calves were branded according to the marks of ownership on their mothers, and when a calf became weaned and still had no brand, it was by custom considered a maverick, belonging to the man on whose range it was found. In practice it more often belonged to the man whose loop caught it first. One purpose of the roundup, then, was to leave as few mavericks as possible for the quick-loop men.

Identification of the cow was usually easy, for a cowboy who couldn't read his own name soon learned the brands of the ranches around him. But sometimes a brand healed poorly or haired over heavily. That was a time for negotiation, and failing agreement it was a time when someone must arbitrarily play the role of judge and declare ownership by reasoning, instinct or favor.

Rascal McGinty's nose was slightly flattened. He always claimed the damage had been done by a horse, but Hugh Hitchcock had long suspected it happened in a fistfight.

"Go slow, Rascal," Hitch said quietly as he pushed his gray horse between the two men. A young W rider named Joe Sands had a rope around the calf's neck and was waiting for Hitchcock's judgment before he dragged the animal out to the men afoot by the branding fire. The roan cow was bawling and making as much fuss over her offspring as if it had been blueblooded Durham stock brought down from the east.

Hitch expected to find Rascal crackling in anger; instead the unpredictable cowboy was grinning like a possum. "The Figure 4s need to buy ol' Dayton a set of eyeglasses, Hitch." Nobody ever called Hitchcock *Hugh* except his mother. "I know that old cow," Rascal claimed. "I can recollect the color of every calf she's given to me and Law."

Hitch's natural inclination was to accept Rascal's word because they had been friends so long, but he knew that was not the right and proper way. "Let's have a look at her." He rode slowly around the cow, frowning at the earmarks.

She had more than one. He leaned from the saddle for a close look at the brand. "Somebody done a bad job with the iron. Way it's haired over, she could be either one or neither one. I been tellin' you, Rascal, your LR brand is too much like the Figure 4."

"Tell *them*," Rascal grinned. "Me and Law, we had our brand first. Let the Figure 4 change theirs." The thought pleased him because the Figure 4 outfit was reputed to own forty or fifty thousand head.

Dayton Brumley, crowding forty, was an employee too far removed from policy-making to comment. Stubbornly he said, "I call her a Figure 4."

Another cowboy trotted up on a nervous-eyed dun. Law McGinty, four or five years younger than Rascal, demanded, "What is it, Rascal? That rich damnyankee outfit tryin' to steal our cow?"

Brumley colored. At least Rascal hadn't accused him of stealing. "Boy . . ." he said threateningly.

Rascal made a placating gesture to his brother. "Don't bust your cinch, button. Hitch is fixin' to set things straight."

Hitch had an uncomfortable feeling Rascal was taking advantage of friendship, putting Hitch in a position where he must stand up for a preconceived judgment. He said, "We'll stretch her and take a good look." He dropped his loop over her horns and took up the slack, then motioned for Law to catch her hind feet. They laid her down helpless on the ground, and Hitch dismounted. He depended on the gray, Walking Jack, to keep the rope taut. He purposely had put Law on the heels because that obliged the cowboy to stay in his saddle and out of trouble; if Law allowed any slack on the heels, the cow could kick loose from the rope and get up. She would not be in good humor.

On his knees Hitch carefully ran his fingers over the brand, trying to feel through the hair any scar that didn't show to the eye. This was complicated by the fact that he was missing the tip of one finger, pinched off between a rope and a saddlehorn a long time ago. A missing finger or a gimpy leg were marks of a working cowboy. He shook his head. "Still can't tell."

Rascal stepped from his saddle, fishing in his shirt pocket. "I said I know that old cow, and I'll prove it." He brought out a pair of tweezers and began plucking hair.

Hitch came near smiling despite the potential seriousness of the matter. Probably not another man on the roundup was so certain of argument that he would carry tweezers. Though Rascal was a W cowhand, he was also an owner of sorts whose nature called for him to protect his interests with whatever degree of belligerence seemed appropriate.

It bothered Hitch, assuming responsibility for a dispute like this. No court could consider him completely neutral. He and Rascal and Law McGinty had known each other before they had come to the Panhandle. They had helped Charlie Waide bring his W herd up here from cattle-poor South Texas brush country in the late '70s. At thirty, Hitch was a little younger than Rascal, older than Law. Rascal was as good a roper as Hitch and unquestionably a better bronc rider. Yet Rascal had evidenced no hard feelings when Charlie Waide set Hitch up as second in command only to himself. Rascal had seemed to accept it as proper, for there was an indefinable character in Hugh Hitchcock that caused cowboys—even better ones—instinctively to follow him. Law McGinty, then a kid of eighteen or so, had taken a sour view of Rascal's being passed by and temporarily fell out with Hitch over it, but Rascal had told him flatly, "Charlie knows what he's doin'."

Dayton Brumley hunched over Rascal, critically watching his work with the tweezers. If he saved them a hundred such cows the Figure 4 would not raise his wages a dollar, but he had an old-time cowboy loyalty: when you worked for a ranch and accepted its pay, you stood up for it to the turn of the final card. If you couldn't be loyal to an outfit, you called for your time and rode away.

Rascal's tweezers caused a definite outline to begin showing through the hair. "Like I told you, Hitch, she's comin' up an LR, plain as the tobacco in ol' Dayton's *mus*-tache."

Brumley grunted angrily. "Because *he*'s got the tweezers."

Hitch could tell the thing was still dangerous. "Settle down, boys. One cow ain't worth a fight." –

In his saddle, Law McGinty said, "Not to an outfit that's got fifty thousand like her. But to a little man grindin' himself to the bone for thirty dollars a month she's worth a fight. You ought to know."

Hitch knew; he had a brand too. Many of the cowboys who had first come north onto these plains had established small herds of their own to run on the free grass with those of the men they worked for. Charlie Waide had been so nearly broke when he came here that he had been able to keep only those men willing to take pay in calves instead of cash. Hitch had owned two shirts and one pair of ragged britches then; he hadn't even had enough money to get a blacksmith to make a branding iron for him. So he had taken Charlie's W iron, branded it, then turned it upside down and stamped it again to make a combination he called the Two Diamonds. Now he had a little one-section claim over on a creek where he had built a dugout he almost never used. He had a hundred and thirty or forty Two Diamond cows and their calves grazing the red clay breaks and the short-grass prairies. Most of it was still state land, the grass belonging to the man whose cow happened to eat it.

Hitch decided Rascal had picked long enough. He ran his fingers over the brand and was seventy-five percent sure. "Dayton, it looks like an LR to me."

He saw triumph in the McGinty brothers' faces. But Brumley was adamant. "It looked like a Figure 4 till he took the tweezers to it. If I'd of had the tweezers it'd still be a Figure 4."

Rascal's hands knotted into fists. "You callin' me a cheat?" Brumley didn't say so out loud, but the answer lay plain in his eyes. Rascal took a step toward him, and Law swung a leg over the cantle.

Hitch moved quickly. "Law, you stay up there and keep

that rope tight. Rascal, you and Dayton go cool off. In opposite directions. We got work to do here.''

Rascal gave no ground. ''Whichaway you callin' that calf?''

Hitch thought he had made it plain enough. He saw a heavyish man riding around the herd toward them, and he felt relief. ''Yonder comes Charlie. We'll have him confirm it, then we'll hear no more about this cow.''

Solemn-faced, Charlie Waide climbed down from the saddle. He took his time as if he were older even than his late fifties. He was careful in bringing his left hand from the saddlehorn, for his arm had been stiff since a Yankee saber had slashed it in the war. There hadn't been a day in eighteen years that it hadn't brought him pain. ''I come in after ridin' twenty miles from the eastern division and find somebody pawin' sand,'' he said irritably. ''What in hell's the matter here?''

''No trouble, Charlie.'' Hitch wanted to spare him worry; Charlie had enough of that. ''Just been a little question come up over the brand of this cow.''

Charlie Waide glanced impatiently at Rascal and Brumley, then knelt and ran his fingers over the brand. ''I'd call her an LR.''

The red-haired cowboy laughed. Rascal could afford to, now that the judgment had gone his way. But Hitch took no chances. ''Rascal, I'll see that the calf is branded for you. I want you to go to the wagon and find out how much Trump lacks havin' dinner ready.''

It was a useless errand, for Trump Tatum always had dinner ready at straight-up noon and would be cussing if he didn't see cowboys on the way. But Rascal took the order without question. He rode off, his back straight, his hat cocked a little to one side, a picture of justice triumphant.

Dissatisfied, Brumley said, ''Charlie, I'll have to talk to the company about this.''

Waide's eyes narrowed. He had been boss too long to be crossed. ''You do that.''

''It ain't the cow, Charlie, it's the principle.'' Brumley

rode into the herd to seek out Figure 4 cattle that had strayed into W country. Waide stared after him balefully, running a big rough hand through hair that had turned gray years too early. "One damned cow," he grumbled. "The Figure 4s will lose more than that between the barn and the haylot."

"He could get himself killed someday," Hitch said. "Reckon they know it?"

Waide shook his head. "He's just a name on the payroll."

Hitch nodded at the cowboy who still held the calf on the far end of the rope. "Tell them to put an LR on him, Joe." Hitch waited for Charlie to get to his horse, then he took the rope off the cow's horns. She would come up looking for a fight, and he didn't want Charlie caught on the ground. Hitch's own father had not come home from the war. Charlie was as near a father as he had had since.

Law McGinty gave slack on the rope, and the cow shook her heels loose. She got up rump first, slinging her head and trying to choose between several targets. But her calf blatted in fear as it was dragged unceremoniously toward the branding fire, and her motherly instincts sent her trotting and bawling in its dusty wake.

Charlie paid no attention to the cow. He still watched Brumley.

Hitch said, "He'll cool off; so'll Rascal."

Charlie's bewildered face was furrowed. "Ain't nothin' like it was, Hitch. This was a cowman's country once. A cowman gave his word and another cowman took it. Now it's a different breed . . . syndicates, Yankee bankers, English money and all that. Ain't enough anymore just to know the cow."

Charlie Waide knew the cow. But he found himself ill at ease among a new kind of ranchers who knew cows as figures on a ledger rather than flesh and blood creatures of leg and long horn; who thought of a herd of cattle as a large sum written in black at the bottom of a page rather than as a teeming mass of bawling beasts, strung majestically across a mile or more of God's green grass, the brown dust rising and swirling above them like some living thing, the air sharp

with the bite of hoof-flung dirt and the mingled smells of
trampled green grass and calves' milky breath and fresh ma-
nure.

Hitch had accompanied Charlie last year on a trip to Kansas City to try to float a loan. Charlie had been in a cold
sweat the whole time, going from bank to bank with a new
white hat crushed awkwardly in his big hands, trying to talk
the language of men he couldn't understand, men measuring
him for what he owned and not for what he knew or what
he was. Charlie had finally obtained an expansion loan,
smaller than he wanted, and he had to sign over everything
but his own blood to get it.

Charlie Waide had always been strict about liquor; he
didn't allow the cowboys to drink on the place. But he
stayed drunk all the way home, downing whisky as a pur-
gative to cleanse away the stain of humiliation. He told
Hitch at the time, "I felt like a crippled horse penned up
amongst a pack of gray lobo wolves. I was fishin' in deep
waters against that crew." Hitch had felt that Charlie's time
in Kansas City had scarred him deeper than his encounter
with the Yankee saber. The Yankees at least had been an
enemy he could see and understand and shoot at. To Charlie
Waide—at heart basically still a cowboy—the world of fi-
nance was the Tower of Babel. But he was in it to the gray
tips of his mustache. To remain a cowman of major pro-
portions these days, a man had to be.

The roan cow was the only one that day whose ownership
caused any dispute. Most cows in the gather clearly showed
the W brand. A few carried small-owner brands like the Two
Diamonds of Hugh Hitchcock, or the LR of Rascal and Law
McGinty. Some carried the syndicate's Figure 4. When one
appeared questionable, Dayton Brumley took a careful look
for the benefit of the company he worked for, but earmarks
or a quick clipping of hair were enough to establish ownership. Hitch made it a main-order of business to be sure
the McGinty brothers and Brumley were kept far apart. He
hoped by dark they would be too tired to do anything more
about their grudge.

Late in the afternoon Law McGinty asked Hitch if it would be all right for him to drop out and ride over into the breaks to see his wife. "I'd be much obliged, Hitch. I'll be back by daylight. Her bein' in a family way and all, I like to look in on her pretty regular."

That suited Hitch fine, for, it got Law out of the way awhile. "I wisht you'd take Rascal with you."

Law made a weak smile. He had never been open and easy with Hitch the way Rascal was. "If you was married, Hitch, you'd know not to ask a man a thing like that."

Law rode away without supper. Kate McGinty would cook him a better meal than he would get at the chuckwagon. Watching, Hitch pictured the loving reception Law would receive from his handsome young bride, and the thought brought him an empty feeling of something missed. Kate McGinty was a farm girl happy to live in a rude dugout on the small claim her husband and brother-in-law had made, for never in her life had she known anything better. On the contrary, this might be the best home she had ever had.

If ever I have a woman of my own, I'd want to give her something better than that, Hitch thought. His chance of having such a woman was slim; they were scarce. This was a man's country.

Trump Tatum's chin was fuzzy, but he had more hair on one joint of his index finger than on all of his head. He had been Charlie Waide's wagon cook fifteen years or so. Before that he had cowboyed while Charlie was struggling to rebuild a South Texas ranch that had gone to ruin during the time they were all off trying to save the South for Jefferson Davis. Bad horses had forced Trump to hang up his saddle in favor of the pots and Dutch ovens. Except for broken bones that precipitated the change, it wasn't necessarily a bad thing; a wagon cook drew a better wage than a working cowboy; and he ruled his tiny domain with an autocracy that not even a ranch owner often challenged. Trump Tatum had his rules, and the cowboys either knew them or learned them damned quick. A minor infraction could spark sarcasm bitter as gypwater, and a major breach could send Trump into a glorious case of the "rings" that would spoil coffee for three or four days.

At the same time, he had a protective feeling for the cowboys whose digestion he was slowly ruining. He seemed to sense the tension resulting over the roan cow, and a benevolent gleam shone in his wrinkle-edged eyes like the welcome glow of a lantern to a man lost at night on the open prairie. "Boys," he said, "I figured this evenin' would be a good time to use up that dried fruit Miz Waide brung to the wagon. I fixed you-all a nice cobbler for supper."

Cobbler pie was an infrequent treat in a plains cowcamp, for there wasn't a decently bearing fruit tree in perhaps two hundred miles. Beef and beans were the mainstays, and it was little wonder that now and again the average cowboy developed a painful case of boils. In such events it was usually Trump Tatum who lanced them, which was only proper because his cooking had helped create them in the first place. His chuckbox was a combination commissary and medicine chest, carrying some remedy for everything from hemorrhoids to snake-bite.

Trump grinned at Rascal. "I know how partial you are to cobbler."

Suspiciously Rascal said, "If you're tryin' to sweet-do me into draggin' you up some firewood . . ."

"You know I never had no such notion."

"The hell you didn't." Rascal was pleased as he looked at the cobbler in the deep Dutch oven.

Why shouldn't he be pleased? Hitch asked himself. Rascal had won his dispute. Hitch felt almost a resentment against his friend, for he harbored a nagging suspicion he had been used. He disliked having to feel even a twinge of guilt toward Dayton Brumley and the Figure 4, for he had no particular respect for the outfit. But that, he supposed, was what a man put up with to earn the extra twenty dollars a month as wagon boss instead of being a straight cowboy. Sometimes he wished he had stayed where he used to be, for it had been more fun and no worry. Sometimes responsibility had an uncomfortable fit, like a right boot on a left foot. But men delegated responsibility to Hitch whether he wanted it or not.

Dayton Brumley still brooded over the roan cow. As rep for the Figure 4 he enjoyed the privileges—such as they were—of the regular W cowboys, as did reps for the other brands. But tonight he kept to himself, taking a long time unsaddling his horse. He waited until the W men and the other company reps had all filled their plates before he went to the chuckbox and got one for himself. Spooning into it quietly, he strode out to his bedroll and squatted down alone.

Trump Tatum leaned his thin old frame against the wagonwheel, his uneasy gaze touching Brumley first, then Rascal. In contrast to Brumley's somber mien, Rascal was laughing and talking as if no roan cow had ever been born. Rascal had always loved to talk.

It was not customary for a wagon cook to carry food to anybody; a man came to the fire and helped himself or by God did without. But when the rest of the men were through, Trump took the Dutch oven to Brumley. "Wouldn't want it said the W wagon didn't feed its neighbors."

"The Ws is all right," Brumley said. "It's just one or two of them that works for it who bother me some."

Rascal was too busy talking to hear.

Supper done, Trump began rattling the tin plates and cups in his washtub, then dropping them into a second tub of scalding hot water. A kid horse jingler—low man of the outfit—fished them out gingerly with his fingers and dried them to put them back into the chuckbox. He caught some caustic comment from Trump when he let a hot one drop to the sand at his feet.

Charlie Waide walked away from the wagon, out where the night horses had been staked. He stood a long time staring into the starlight, his hand reaching up and rubbing his bad left arm. Hitch finished his coffee and joined him. "Arm hurtin' you tonight, Charlie?"

"Arm hurts me every night. Nothin' new about that."

"You got somethin' else on your mind, then."

"There's always worries enough to go around. That damned roan cow is apt to bring trouble to camp even yet; been better if she'd died last winter. Then, I owe enough to break two Kansas City banks. And finally, there's ugly talk goin' around some of the wagons."

"Talk?"

"Discontent. I can't find out enough to get to the guts of it. Heard any talk around this wagon, Hitch?"

"Only about horses and cattle and women."

Charlie Waide frowned. "I hope it stays that way."

For an hour or two before they crawled into their blankets, the cowboys usually sat near the campfire, feeding it just enough to keep it from dying. By turns they told yarns, sometimes of things which had happened on drive that day, more often of things from other years, other outfits. Times they talked of badmen like Billy the Kid, who had stolen cows up and down this Canadian River country and was hardly more than a year in his grave. Times they talked of other cowboys they had known, or of women encountered in the cowtowns and at the railheads. Most often the conversation centered around horses, for to the cowboy the horse was more than a tool of the trade, he was a friend; a servant, yet something of a god; an occasional tormentor, yet a creature deserving admiration that bordered on deification. The cowboy was prone to invest the horse with a super intelligence it never really had, and a code of honor invented in the mind of the rider. Small wonder, then, that a man was judged more on his horsemanship than on whatever personal vices or virtues he might possess. The most notorious cow thief in the Panhandle since passing of the Kid was a man named Cato Bramlett. In speaking of him the cowboys gave less attention to his being a rogue than to the fact that he handled a horse unusually well.

Charlie Waide drifted to the fire, listening, and finally he seated himself in the circle. It was not an accustomed place to him anymore, for in the pressure of the times he seemed to have lost the gift of laughter. The younger men who had not known Charlie in an olden day stood a little in awe of him, and perhaps a little afraid. But for a while then Charlie was not an owner, he was another cowboy reaching back into memory. For a while the hunch seemed gone from his shoulders, and he was as young as any man here.

It pleasured Hitch to see this rare transformation in Charlie Waide, to see him for a little while the way he had been in another time when he wasn't big and struggling to become bigger, when he ran two hundred cows instead of twenty thousand. It seemed a pity, in a way, that he had ever changed. Charlie began telling fondly about a bay horse he once had traded from a Mexican and had ridden off to war, only to lose him in battle. "Many's the good horse I've ridden before and after," he said wistfully, "but never one I thought more of than that bay. When the war was over I went lookin' for the Mexican, thinkin' he might have some more horses of the same blood. But he'd got himself killed in some war down in Mexico, so I reckon the blood was scattered and lost. They sure had good horses in them days, the likes we'll never see again."

Rascal McGinty fidgeted to talk, and the moment Charlie finished, Rascal grabbed his chance. He told about a horse he had gotten once from a Mexican. Stolen; no, *stolen* wasn't the word for it because down in that Rio Grande country in those days you didn't steal when you took from a Mexican, you only exacted vengeance for the Alamo and other atrocities. So, for that matter, did the Mexican when he stole from you. Thieving took on the aura of patriotism. The way Rascal told it, that horse could do almost anything except count cattle. Upshot of the story was that the Mexican was a lowdown scoundrel who came one night in the dark of the moon and stole the horse back. "We'd of hung that thief if we could've caught him," Rascal laughed, "but the horse was so fast that nothin' we had could get close enough to give us the smell of his dust."

From the distance came the sound of a horse-drawn vehicle bouncing across the tufted prairie grass. Trump Tatum lifted the lantern from the chuckbox lid up onto the top, so it might better serve as a guide. Hitch pushed to his feet and dropped extra wood on the fire so it would blaze up. The cowboys had to move away from its heat. He heard the driver curse this God-forsaken country as a wheel dropped into a hole, and he knew the voice. He frowned at Rascal, then at Dayton Brumley. The general manager and major stockholder of the Figure 4 was coming; Hitch could have done without him very well.

He had no inclination to walk out and meet the man, but Charlie Waide arose stiffly, grunting a complaint against arthritis, and stepped forward to extend the hand of hospitality from one owner to another. Brumley went too, for this man was his boss.

Prosper Selkirk was not by birth or training a range man, but he had been in cow country long enough that he knew better than to ride up into the wagon cook's domain and raise dust. He stopped at the edge of the firelight. A saddled horse was tied to the rear of the buckboard. Charlie Waide stuck out his hand. "You're travelin' late, Prosper. But Trump's still got some supper left."

Selkirk nodded, leaving any thank-yous implied rather than spoken, and perhaps none were even thought of. He jerked a thumb toward three sleek greyhounds tied in the back of the buckboard. "Take care of the hounds, Brumley." He did no more than glance at the man, the way he might glance at a company horse. To Charlie he said, "The dogs ran themselves down chasing loboes, and dark caught us. I'm just making a visit to all the neighbors' wagons in the interest of the Figure 4."

Charlie Waide was never at ease in the company of Prosper Selkirk, for he considered him one of the Kansas City crowd. But he made a show of hospitality. "Everybody gets treated fair and square at the Ws." He motioned toward Hitch. "You know my wagon boss, Hugh Hitchcock."

Selkirk said simply, "Nice to see you again, Hitchcock."

Hitch felt a nudge of resentment. Selkirk didn't offer to shake hands. He knew Hitch well enough to address him as

Hugh or Hitch if he had chosen, and he hadn't enough respect to call him Mister Hitchcock. So, it was just Hitchcock. Hitch thought, *The hell with him.*

If this had been some luckless cowboy stumbling in late, Trump Tatum would have chewed him up and spit him out, but he deferred to Selkirk. "Biscuits is cold, Mister Selkirk, and the steak is apt to be a little greasy now."

Selkirk's offhand reply was made without thought to the way it might sound to Tatum. "I never count on much around these chuck-wagons. I'll survive until I get home to something better."

Tatum had fetched a plate and utensils out of wooden drawers for him, but now he left them sitting on the chuckbox lid and jerked his thumb toward the wagon. "Cups is in yonder," he said and turned his back.

Selkirk hit him with another unconscious insult. "I suppose the leftovers would be good enough for the dogs?"

Tatum neither turned nor tried to answer. He stalked off toward his bedroll in angry silence. It wasn't enough having to take this treatment from Selkirk; he would catch hell for the next week from the cowboys, for they would hurrah him until he crowned somebody with a skillet or starved them into submission.

Selkirk was in his late forties, basically an indoor man whose aptitude at figures in a banking institution had earned him the confidence of men owning substantial fortunes and wanting more. Selkirk knew how to make money for them, and incidentally for himself as well. The Figure 4 to him was a beef factory, little different from a shoe factory or a plant for the manufacture of farm implements. The Figure 4 was basically a set of ledgers that must always show a comfortable figure in black at the bottom of every page. Under his direction it usually did. The neighboring ranches were regarded as competitors for the beef buyers' dollar, and the cowboys were names on a payroll book that seemed always to show too much money paid out for the services rendered.

Hitch knew Dayton Brumley was still fretting over that

roan cow. He watched Brumley talking as Selkirk ate the cold supper without enthusiasm. In the muffled conversation he heard his own name and stood up, glancing at Charlie and finding Charlie watching him. Charlie motioned for Hitch to join him beside Selkirk.

Charlie told the Figure 4 manager, "You know Hitch is a good man with cattle. He called that brand an LR and so did I."

Selkirk stopped chewing and frowned at Hitch, measuring him. "Charles, if you say she was an LR, I'll accept that as the word of one gentleman to another."

Charlie seemed to want to settle it beyond any question. "She belonged to Rascal and Law McGinty; they been cowboyin' for me a long time. They're as honest as the day is long."

Selkirk put down his plate and took a long sip of black coffee, face creasing in the dislike of it. "Never seems civilized to take it without cream," he remarked. "Pity with all these cattle there is never any milk." He seemed inclined to throw the coffee out but didn't. "Charles, that brings up a point I've wanted to talk to you about, that you let some of your men run cattle of their own."

"I always have."

"It's a bad practice. We don't allow it at the Figure 4."

"So I've heard."

"Have you ever thought what such a practice can lead to?"

"It leads to me bein' able to keep good men here when some outfits have to scratch to find men that know which end of the cow eats grass."

"There are always men looking for jobs. We can hire all the cowhands we ever need at twenty-five dollars a month and turn others away. We don't have to grant special favors."

Charlie said, "There was a time I couldn't pay twenty-five dollars. I gave my men cattle."

"An expedient of the time. When times change, a business enterprise should change with them. Has it ever occurred to you, Charles, how easy it would be for some of your men to brand your cattle with their own irons? And when one of them finds an unbranded maverick out on your range, how do you know he puts your brand on it and not his own? You can't watch them everywhere they go.''

''I hire men I can trust.''

''No man can be trusted if the stakes are high enough. I've heard rumors, Charles, even about your men.''

Charlie Waide began to anger. ''If rumors was cattle, this whole country would be overstocked and the grass grazed down to the roots.'' He didn't look at Selkirk, nor did he glance at Hitch.

Hitch had sat still as long as he could. ''Charlie's right, Mister Selkirk. Treat a man fair and you can trust him.''

Selkirk had not asked for Hitch's opinion. ''You have some cattle in a brand of your own, don't you, Hitchcock?''

Hitch's teeth ground together. He didn't know whether the man was implying anything or not; Selkirk had an unfortunate habit of saying a thing in its worst possible way. ''Charlie Waide has personally watched me brand most every cow I own.''

''I wasn't singling you out, Hitchcock. I was only pointing out that your position might prevent your being altogether the best judge of what I consider to be a bad practice.'' He switched his attention to Charlie. ''I've been in conference with some other major owners. Most of us agree it would be a healthy thing on this range if we made a blanket order that no man employed for wages be allowed to own cattle.''

By now every cowboy was listening. Even Trump Tatum had come back from his bedroll, barefoot and in his underwear.

Charlie Waide said, ''Some of these men stuck with me through cruel hard times, and they been years buildin' up a shirttail outfit of their own. What kind of a man would take that away from them?''

''I'm not suggesting you take anything away, Charles.

Nobody advocates cheating any man out of his rightful due. We would all agree to buy such cattle at a fair market price and vent the brands to our own. Then, after a specified date no man on a ranch payroll would be allowed to own cattle. That would take away the incentive for brand changing and maverick chasing and all these other evils that stand in the way of sound business practices on these ranches.''

Charlie Waide stood up and rubbed his bad arm where the night air had brought the ache again. "You do as you please on the Figure 4s. This here is the Ws.''

"You're not alone on this range. You owe the rest of us something, too.''

Charlie scowled. "I don't know how you figure that. Was you here helpin' me when my herd was dyin' of the Texas fever? No, you wasn't. Was you here when the Indians kept comin' back off the reservations and cuttin' across this country, takin' cattle, shootin' at whoever got in their way? No, you wasn't. But there's men here that was, like Hitch and the McGintys and some of the others. I don't take nothin' away from them and they won't take nothin' away from me.''

Selkirk retreated a little. "Perhaps you're right; perhaps no one in your employ would take cattle from you. But they might not be so scrupulous in respecting the property rights of the rest of us. How do you know, for instance, that they would not take Figure 4 cattle if the opportunity presented itself? And on a range as large as this one, there is always opportunity.''

Dayton Brumley took a stick and began to sketch in the sand. "Like that cow this mornin', Charlie. You and Hitch called her an LR, and maybe you was right. But can you say for sure she was *always* an LR?'' Brumley drew a Figure 4 brand in the sand. It was open-topped for easy healing.

4

"Now looky here," he said. "All a man has to do is add a little at the top and bottom. He's got an LR."

𐭣𝐑

Rascal McGinty came around the fire in a rush. Before Brumley could get to his feet, Rascal hit him. Brumley staggered and fell on his back. Cursing, Rascal grabbed him and tried to pull him to his feet. Hitch threw his arms around McGinty and wrenched him loose. "Rascal . . ."

Rascal fought free. "Ain't no boot-lickin' Figure 4 puncher goin' to call me a thief!" His eyes wide, he ran for the chuckbox.

Trump Tatum said hoarsely, "I got a pistol in there!"

Dayton Brumley scurried desperately for his bedroll and rammed his hand down into his canvas warbag. Hitch knew he kept a .45. Hitch ran for Rascal. As Rascal fished the cook's pistol out of the chuckbox, Hitch grabbed his arm. "Rascal, let go of it!"

"He called me a thief."

"I want that gun, Rascal, before somebody gets killed."

They struggled for possession. Hitch lunged forward, jamming Rascal against the wagonwheel and trying to bend him backward over it. He had a tight grip on Rascal's wrist and tried to slam it against the corner of the chuckbox. The cowboys scattered like quail. Resisting, Rascal pulled the trigger. The pistol went off with a roar like a cannon. Glass shattered from the lantern atop the chuckbox. The lantern tumbled to the ground, spilling coal oil into the sand and setting it ablaze. Rascal tried to step away from the flames at his feet, and as he did, Hitch wrenched the pistol from his hand. Turning quickly, he saw Dayton Brumley crouched by his bedroll, pistol ready.

Prosper Selkirk's voice was crisp with authority. "Put it back, Brumley. There'll be no fight."

Brumley seemed not to hear until Selkirk spoke again, sharper. Seeing that Hitch had the other pistol, Brumley slowly let his own sag and finally placed it back into the canvas sack. He was on hands and knees.

Most of the cowboys had hit the ground on their bellies. Now some pushed to their feet, but others lay still. The kid horse jingler called querulously, "Is it all over, Hitch?"

"It's over," Hitch said, shaking a little. "You can get up." He moved partway to Brumley. "Dayton, you owe Rascal an apology."

Brumley was in no mood to apologize. Hitch thought it probable the man couldn't even speak. Selkirk spoke for him. "He apologizes. It wasn't meant the way your man took it; it was only meant to show what *could* happen."

Hitch knew better. Brumley *had* meant it, but it would be foolish to say so in this atmosphere.

Charlie Waide found his voice. "And you, Prosper, you've seen what can happen, too. Better go slow in makin' implications against a man."

Selkirk turned to his rep. "Brumley, it's best you leave this wagon tonight . . . *now*. Gather your things and go over to our east wagon; send Estep to rep for us here."

The cowboys went quietly to their blankets, though nobody would sleep much. Rascal sat by himself on the wagon tongue, trembling in delayed reaction. Old Trump Tatum scratched himself through the long underwear. "Hitch, maybe we ought to go talk to him."

"And say what? Best thing is to leave him alone."

Trump picked up the shattered lantern. It was beyond repair. He stepped gingerly, trying to avoid broken glass with his bare feet. "Hell of a note, is all I can say. I'm glad it's over with."

Is it over? Hitch asked himself.

Prosper Selkirk stood beside Charlie Waide. "If this doesn't change your mind, Charles, I'll find something that will. You've got to be with us; we won't have you against us."

Charlie gave Selkirk a long, harsh frown. "Goodnight, Prosper."

As the Figure 4 manager moved toward his buckboard

and the bedroll he carried there, Charlie Waide walked stiffly to Trump's chuckbox. He reached deep into it and came out with a bottle Tatum kept for medicinal purposes. He walked around to the wagon tongue, nudged Rascal and without saying anything handed him the bottle. Rascal looked up at him, blinking in surprise. He uncorked the bottle and took a long double swallow, draining much of the whisky.

Charlie retrieved the bottle, took a swig that finished it, then growled, "Go to bed now, Rascal. Go to bed before I haul off and kick your butt!"

II

HITCH SLEPT LITTLE. WHEN TRUMP TATUM got up grumbling to start breakfast, Hitch got up too. He hunkered on the far side of Trump's stingy little wood-saving fire to nurse the coffeepot along, and Trump fussed about his being in the way.

Trump always kept two lanterns, one over his pots and one over the chuckbox. Because Rascal had shot up one of them, Trump had to make do by carrying the other back and forth. He complained so much that Hitch promised to find him another the first chance he got. Hitch could always predict Trump Tatum's mood because it was almost always the same: irritable.

Hitch worried, "That thing last night could've turned out a lot worse. I keep wonderin' if there was somethin' I ought to've done different."

Trump said, "You done your job the way you seen it; you wasn't partial to no man. Don't fret over what you can't change. Take things as they come and stay cheerful, I always say."

By the time the water boiled, Rascal was up. He came silently to the fire, nodding at Trump and Hitch and glancing to see if the coffee was ready yet. His sleepy eyes showed he hadn't slept. Rascal furtively rubbed his right hand.

"Hurt?" Hitch asked.

"A little. You gave it a right smart of a wrench."

"Had to."

Rascal nodded soberly. "I know." He squatted on his heels and stared into the flames. "A man ought to have better control of himself. I might've killed Dayton Brumley if you hadn't stopped me."

"Or he might've killed you."

"We're a pair of damn fools, him and me. The hell of it is, I know I'd do the same thing again."

Hitch frowned, knowing that was true. "Well, he's gone."

"But his boss ain't. Dayton only said out loud what Selkirk was thinkin'."

The cowboys began getting up from their soogans before Tatum ever called "Chuck!" Law McGinty rode in about the time the horse jingler brought the remuda for the men to catch their morning mounts. Law turned his horse loose among them and went to the wagon for a plate. He knew nothing of what had happened here last night, and Hitch had as soon somebody else told him. He was mostly concerned that Law was late getting his breakfast. The other cowboys were ready for their horses.

Law said, "I'll be there, Hitch, before they get mounted."

Hitch nodded. "How was Kate?"

Law blinked. "Kate? Oh, she's fine. Gettin' along fine." He wolfed down a biscuit and some steak while Trump Tatum watched sourly. Trump hated to see his cooking taken for granted.

Hitch said, "She oughtn't to stay there by herself much longer. You ought to send her someplace, or get somebody to go stay with her."

"It ain't that time yet. Kate'll do fine."

Prosper Selkirk was up and out of his bedroll, finally. The

Figure 4 manager was not given to such early hours. Even Hitch wondered sometimes why everybody got up so early in a cowcamp. Often he would ride many miles, then sit idly and smoke cigarettes waiting for the morning to turn light enough that he could see what he was supposed to do. Custom, he guessed. It was considered slothful of a man to let sunrise catch him in bed.

Selkirk's greyhounds had been tied to the buckboard wheels all night. Now he turned them loose to allow them to stray out of camp and attend to the pressures of nature. The thin-bodied dogs moved cautiously around the remuda, watchful of the hoofs. Most of the horses were unacquainted with dogs but knew the wolf; they watched with ears pointed warily forward.

The cowboys formed a circle around the horses in the thin light of approaching dawn, stationing themselves twenty feet apart and holding ropes up between them to fashion an improvised corral. It would not have held any horse determined to get away, but the horses had been con-ditioned by training to respect the rope. It was as impene-trable to them as if it had been ten feet high and of solid oak.

It would be chaotic for so many cowboys to try to rope out their own horses. Custom had delegated this responsi-bility to two or three individuals, Hugh Hitchcock chief among them.

"Catch me ol' Quanah," Rascal told him. Hitch, afoot inside the loosely held rope corral, shook out a large loop and spotted Rascal's horse about three deep in the milling bunch. He brought the loop up, gave it a backhand twist and sent it sailing forward into the horses. It fell over the head and neck he had aimed for. The horse dropped its head, hoping to shake off the loop, but Hitch pulled up the slack. Once caught, Quanah came out of the remuda without re-sistance. He had learned through hard experience that it was useless to fight the rope.

In a few minutes horses were caught for very man. The rope corral fell, each man recoiling his own part of it. The

remaining horses were turned back to the jingler to be loose-
herded on grass until needed for another change when the
morning's drive was finished and the day's gather brought
into a single herd for working. The cowboys saddled their
horses. Each moved hurriedly to be able to watch the show,
for in every man's string were some green broncs, and on
any given morning one or more were sure to buck.

It would not have been much of a show had it not been
for Selkirk's greyhounds. One black horse crowhopped, and
that was all of it until Selkirk realized his dogs were out of
sight and became uneasy. He whistled. They came in a run,
too close to a wild-eyed bronc whose back was still humped
under Joe Sands. The bronc bawled in fright and went
straight up. When he came down from the third jump he
fell hard on his side. The horse struggled to its feet, but Joe
Sands didn't get up. He lay grinding his teeth and writhing,
trying not to cry out in pain.

Hitch hit the ground and flipped his reins back for Law
McGinty to catch. Sands tried to pull up and couldn't. He
cursed fervently. "My leg, Hitch. I think that Goddamned
crowbait busted my leg."

As other cowboys gathered around, Hitch felt of the leg.
Sands cried out. Hitch found Charlie Waide standing there,
his face grave. "It's sure as hell broke, Charlie. We better
get him to town."

Waide nodded. "You take him, Hitch. We'll throw the
stuff out of the hoodlum wagon."

Hitch looked around for Selkirk. "Prosper Selkirk has got
his buckboard here. It'd be faster and easier."

Waide turned to the Figure 4 manager. "If it wouldn't be
no imposition . . ." The way he put it made it a statement
of expectation.

Selkirk was momentarily taken aback. "I had
planned . . ." He bit off the words. The cowboys plainly
held him responsible. "I suppose it's the least I can do."

Rascal McGinty put in, "Hitch, me and Law got a light
spring wagon over at our claim. Wouldn't be out of your
way none to haul Joe by there. Then you could take our

wagon and let Mister Selkirk go on about his business.''
Rascal's resentment was plain.

Selkirk said, ''Anything you want.'' He seemed relieved
that he might get away from here with no more responsibility than that.

The cowboys put Selkirk's team to the buckboard and
brought it around. They fetched Joe Sands's blankets and
tarp, spreading them in the bed of the vehicle. Carefully they
lifted the groaning man and covered him with a blanket
Trump Tatum spared.

The bedroll took up most of the room. Selkirk looked
back worriedly. ''Where'll I put the dogs?''

Hitch had a quick answer but didn't use it. ''They got
four legs,'' he said curtly. He clucked the team into movement, Selkirk's saddle-horse tied behind. Selkirk hadn't had
time for breakfast, and Hitch didn't give a damn.

They rode in silence, Hitch devoting his attention to finding the smoothest ground and bouncing Sands as little as
possible. He looked ahead, too, borrowing all the problems
he might encounter down the road. Foremost would be to
find a team that could pull the McGinty wagon. The
McGintys had a pair of horses, but they might be grazing
miles from the unfenced camp. Hitch made up his mind that
if he didn't find them close by, he would keep Selkirk's.
Selkirk could either go to town with him or stay at the
McGinty camp.

Selkirk finally decided to talk. ''Where is this place we're
going?''

''The McGinty's claim. Law McGinty's wife lives there
in a dugout.''

''A dugout?'' Selkirk showed disapproval. ''I can imagine what kind of woman she must be to tolerate that. Probably looks like some hard-used scullery maid.''

''She's a good woman, Mister Selkirk, and pretty as a
spring day.''

Selkirk grunted in disbelief and changed the subject.
''You tell the doctor that whatever the cost is, I'll pay it.

Since my dogs precipitated the incident, I think it is only proper.''

Hitch hadn't expected that. The man came up a notch in his estimation, but only a notch. ''What if it turns out the leg won't heal straight? What if Joe winds up crippled? You goin' to guarantee him a job the rest of his life?''

''I couldn't promise a thing like that.''

''Charlie Waide would. Trump Tatum'd still be cow-boyin', likely, if one of Charlie's horses hadn't boogered him up. Charlie'll see to it that Trump's never hungry the rest of his life.''

''No man can expect to be insulated from all risk. If I invest my entire fortune in a bad venture and lose it, nobody guarantees to take care of me the rest of my life. When a man gets on one of those bad horses he knows the risks; he implies his willingness to accept that risk when he agrees to the job.''

''He accepts the job because he's partial to eatin'.''

''The same reason I take a risk and invest capital.''

''There's a difference between a man's limbs and his money.''

''Not basically. Your cowboy offers his skill in the mar-ketplace; he sells the service of his hands, his arms, his legs. That is his equivalent of capital. I sell my capital and the service of my brain. We all sell something; we all risk what-ever we sell. We're all at the mercy of chance.''

''Looks to me like you got more chance, though, than Joe has.''

Hitch decided it was fruitless to argue viewpoints with Prosper Selkirk; they were the products of two different types of world. Neither would understand the other and per-haps they were never meant to. Anyway, understanding the other man made it more difficult to reject his ideas, and Hitch did not feel like putting up with any such complica-tions. In his view Selkirk was wrong, so why talk about it and cloud up a clear picture?

They dropped into the rough country that broke away to the river. Hitch pointed. ''Yonder's the place.''

Selkirk had to look hard before he was able to find the dugout, set into a hillside and almost hidden unless a person knew what to look for. The earthen roof and the sod front made it blend into the ground from which it came. The pole corrals were easier to see, cut from the cedar and hackberry and other small timber native to these breaks and the riverbottom. To his relief Hitch saw a couple of horses grazing down the draw . . . the McGinty team.

A woman stood by the well, drawing up a bucket of water on the windlass. Her plain gray dress fluttered in the breeze as she heard the buckboard and turned to look, raising her hand to shade her eyes.

Selkirk said, disappointed, "I thought you told me she was pretty."

"She is."

Selkirk shook his head. "I suppose it depends on what one is accustomed to. I never could reconcile myself to these rawboned, sunburned country women down here, living in a hovel like that."

"A hovel?" Hitch had never regarded it that way. True, it wasn't fancy, but hundreds of hardy women were living in the same type of dwelling all over the Texas Panhandle, raising kids, standing by their men while they either made their fortunes or lost the little they had. Hitch said, "The house you live in don't matter so much; it's your feelin's that count. Kate, now, she thinks that cowboy hung the moon. Fixin' to bear him a child pretty soon. She come from a farmin' family that scratched the hard earth for every bite they ate and every stitch of clothes they wore. She wouldn't call this a hovel."

"When you burrow into a hillside like a badger, I'd call that a hovel."

Like most settlers, the McGintys had a dog. It came bouncing out barking to meet the buckboard. Selkirk had to call back his hounds. Kate McGinty stepped away from the well, her hand still over her eyes. She was by nature a slender woman, though anyone with eyes to see would know she was carrying.

Hitch saw apprehension in her face and said, "No, it ain't Law."

As the buckboard came up even with her she looked anxiously at the hurt cowboy. "Joe Sands. What happened to him?"

Hitch told her. "I need the borrow of your wagon, Kate."

She nodded quickly and told him what he had already seen, that the horses were grazing in the draw. Her eyes glistened with sympathy. "Anything I can do for him, Hitch?"

He had always been drawn to this girl; she had compassion. She had known hardship all her life, so anyone else's trouble was her trouble too. He said, "Joe's pained considerable. If Law's got a bottle stashed someplace . . ."

"In the house," she said, and hurried down the hewn-log steps to floor level of the dugout.

Selkirk exclaimed in surprise, "She called that a *house*."

"You judge a person by his heart, not by his house. Kate has a heart as big as a door."

Selkirk observed the canvas flap through which Kate disappeared. "She hasn't even *got* a door."

Hitch pulled the Selkirk buckboard up beside the spring wagon that belonged to the McGintys. Selkirk had to speak roughly to the dogs to keep them away from the shaggy black one of Kate's. The two men carefully got their arms beneath the blankets and lifted Joe Sands from one vehicle across to the other. Selkirk was stronger than Hitch had thought, looking at him. Joe sucked breath between his teeth, and when they set him down he cursed vigorously. Then he said, "I hope Kate didn't hear that."

Hitch shook his head. "She'd of understood." He turned to Selkirk. "I'll borrow your horse and go fetch that team. You can wait here or in the dugout. Maybe Kate has got some coffee."

Selkirk eyed the dugout disapprovingly. "I'll go fetch the team. She's a friend of yours; you visit with her."

As Selkirk swung into the saddle, Kate came out with a whisky bottle. Selkirk touched a hand to his hatbrim in deference to her, which Hitch noted with satisfaction. If Selkirk did not particularly respect cowboys, at least he respected their women. Or perhaps pitied them.

Hitch held up the whisky bottle. "Bourbon?"

Kate shook her head. "Land sakes, I wouldn't know one kind from the other."

"No matter. Anything'll help." He took the cork out and raised Joe's head so the cowboy could drink. Joe accepted the whisky almost desperately. "Thanks, Miss Kate. Thanks."

"You're welcome. It helps my conscience anyway."

"How's that?" Hitch asked.

"For a minute there I was glad it was Joe instead of Law. I'm ashamed of the thought."

Joe said, "We're even. I wish it was Law instead of me."

Hitch watched Selkirk move down the draw and hoped the man knew enough about horses to bring them back rather than run them off. He turned to the woman. "You're lookin' fine, Kate, real fine."

"Thank you, Hitch. In all my life I've never felt this good." She touched a hand to her stomach. "It's movin' now; it's alive." She colored. "I don't reckon a man would understand."

Hitch could only imagine that he did. He didn't know what else to say, so he repeated, "You're sure lookin' fine."

He remembered when Kate's father had moved his family here from some failure down in Central Texas. He had picked a level piece of ground to squat on and had violated the virgin prairie with his plow. All the old man seemed able to raise was kids, and those half hungry much of the time. He was of a hard-luck breed Hitch had seen everywhere he went, the kind who always sought new places and started new projects but never carried them quite to completion, always stopping shy of success and turning away in failure, leaving what he had begun for someone else to pick up and turn into prosperity. The old man had worked himself into his grave, leaving the family to scatter like brown leaves in a winter wind. Hitch had seen Kate when she was fourteen or fifteen, a skinny freckled-nosed kid whose large blue eyes sparkled with life and promise. He had seen her at eighteen and had been much taken by her, for then she was a woman grown, a gentle but enduring woman who could take the worst punishment this raw land could give her. But Hugh Hitchcock had made the mistake of admiring in silence, while Law McGinty had moved in fast and claimed her.

Hitch said, "I was tellin' Law he ought to get somebody to stay with you, or maybe you ought to go to your mother. She still in town?"

"She washes for people and does cookin' for the *ho*-tel when they need it. I got no business in town, Hitch. This is home."

"You'll be needin' help."

"I'll have it when the time comes. There's a few other women up and down the river. There'll be somebody come." He could tell she wasn't worried. Her mother had borne many a child, one or two of them alone. She said, "I sure wish Law could come home once in a while, though."

Surprised, he asked, "You haven't seen him?"

"Not in maybe three weeks. He's all right, isn't he?"

"He's fine," Hitch said looking away to hide the suspicion in his face. "He's real fine." He had been on the verge of telling her Law had left the wagon to come here last night. Obviously, wherever Law had gone, it hadn't been home. Hitch fished for words. "Kate, you and Law are gettin' along all right, aren't you?"

"Sure, Hitch, why wouldn't we?"

He forced away his frown. "No reason. He's a good boy, that Law. I'll give him a couple days off soon and make sure he gets home."

She gripped his arm in gratitude, and the unexpected touch of her fingers startled him. "Thanks, Hitch," she said. "You're a friend." She waved her arm toward the dugout. "Law says after the baby is big enough, we'll expand the house, build another room. Says it won't be much longer till we'll have enough cattle so he can quit workin' for the other man; he can come home and stay here with me. We'll live like the rich folks in town do. That'll sure be fine, won't it?''

"It'll be real fine." Hitch turned to look for Selkirk and the team. He could see them coming up out of the draw. But his mind was on Law McGinty. Where had Law gone last night?

The thought that came was an ugly one. He never had pictured Law as unfaithful, but maybe in her condition Kate was less attractive to him and he was seeking companionship elsewhere. Like Kate had said, other women lived up and down the river. Perhaps somewhere Law had found one young and pretty, and not pregnant.

Hitch pulled the gate shut as Selkirk brought the horses into the corral. The horses turned to eye him balefully. They hadn't been used in a while, and they liked it that way. Hitch figured he would have to keep a firm hand on the reins the first few miles till they settled down to the notion of working for a living. He made a point of catching them without a rope, though that took longer, for he didn't want to spoil them. Kate would need to catch them herself occasionally, and it was unlikely she was good with a loop; few women were.

Selkirk helped put the team to the McGinty wagon. "I meant what I said, Hitchcock." Hitch glanced at him. "About what?"

"About paying this man's doctor bills. I'm not as cold and conscienceless as you think."

"I never said nothin' against you, Mister Selkirk."

"You don't like me, though."

"I just don't understand you, is all."

"I've watched you, Hitchcock. You're sure of yourself; you have an easy way of leading men. I think I understand you better than you understand me. If ever you get tired of working for Charles Waide, come to see me."

Hitch doubted he would tire of Charlie; if he did, it was unlikely he would willingly turn in Selkirk's direction.

Selkirk said, "It would be strictly business. You don't

have to like a man to do business with him.''

It damn sure helps, Hitch thought, though he didn't say so. He glanced at Kate. ''I'll let you know how things go with Joe Sands.'' He flipped the reins, and the fresh team highstepped out of the yard.

He had to fight the horses a while till they settled down. He heard Joe say, ''Hitch?''

''Hurtin' you bad, Joe?''

Joe Sands took a draw on the bottle. ''It ain't that. I was thinkin'. I heard what Kate said about not seein' Law. You reckon he's cheatin' on that girl?''

''I wouldn't know, Joe.''

''I'll stomp on him, is what I'll do.''

Hitch smiled. ''It'll be a long time before you stomp anybody.''

III

BY THE TIME HE HAD HELPED THE DOCTOR set Joe's leg, all the black coffee Hitch had downed was turning over and trying to come up. The doctor assured him that the leg would heal properly, for cowboys were a tough lot. But Hitch knew from experience that cowboys were not usually as tough as they looked to a man in town. They were flesh, blood and bone like everybody else, and subject to a great deal more breakage than most.

"You don't reckon this'll leave him crippled?" Hitch fretted.

"If whisky'll cure him, he's a cinch."

"Joe don't normally drink thisaway. Charlie don't allow it at the ranch. I bet Joe ain't been drunk three times in his whole life."

Hitch was defending not only Joe Sands but all the cowboys, for the face the townspeople saw when the hands got their rare trips to town was not the one they wore the other twenty-nine days of the month. The doctor said, "Maybe not, but when he wakes up it'll be hard to tell which hurts

him the most . . . his leg or his head.'' He paused thoughtfully. ''You need to leave him here in town where I can
look in on him.''

"I'd figured on it. I'll go now and hunt him a place to
stay."

He walked from the small frame house, grateful to be
outside. He looked up and down the dusty street past flat-
topped adobes and picket shacks and square-fronted clap-
board houses like the doctor's. A dry smile came as he
mused that these were the people Kate McGinty considered
rich. When the winter blue northers howled down off Can-
ada's snowfields and lashed across these wide-open plains,
there probably wasn't a house in town half as snug and
warm as the dugout she lived in. Yet he knew there was not
a woman on the Staked Plains who had not rather freeze to
death in an unsealed twelve-by-twelve box cabin than spend
the winter cozy in a soddy or a dugout. It was a matter of
vanity, of prestige.

Well, it wasn't winter now, and he had to find Joe Sands
a bed. But even more pressing for the moment was his own
need for a drink to blunt the ordeal of setting Joe's leg. He
brought the wagon about, walking the team down into that
section locally known as Hogtown, where dwelled those
people who took it as their mission in life to make the working cowboy feel like a king, until he ran out of funds and
had to abdicate. Hitch stopped before a brown adobe structure of questionable architecture whose vertical sign over
the front door said COWBOY BAR.

Fant Gossett made sure his place lived up to its name. He
catered to the cowboys and small shirttail ranchers who
scratched for a living up and down the river. A man like
Prosper Selkirk or even Charlie Waide was unlikely to let
his shadow fall across Fant's door, and that suited Fant just
as well. He knew which end of the wick burned for him. He
said loudly and often that he had rather have ten fun-
seeking cowpunchers spend a dollar apiece over his bar than
for one demanding rich man to spend ten. Fant Gossett had
never earned a dollar in his life punching cows himself, but

folks who ought to know said he had built a small fortune
catering to the riders who did.

He greeted the W wagon boss at the wide-open door as
if Hitch was a long-lost brother come home from out west,
though Hitch suspected that Fant had to fish a minute to
remember his name. "How do, Hitch? Come in this house!"
Fant swung his heavy arms open in a big gesture of welcome, displaying in rotund grandeur a broad middle that two
gold watchchains couldn't reach across. He had the whitest
teeth Hitch had ever seen, locked into a perennial grin beneath a black mustache, generous in size. "How's everything out at the Ws? How's that cranky old Charlie Waide?"
Gossett demanded as if he had been waiting a month to hear.
He didn't give Hitch time to answer, though. He said, "Seen
you haulin' somebody to town in a wagon. Got a man
hurt?"

Hitch told him about Joe Sands. Gossett's brow creased
in studied concern, though Hitch would bet even money
Fant couldn't have picked Joe Sands out of a crowd. Downing a shot of bourbon and pouring a second to sip slower,
Hitch said, "I got to find Joe a place to lay up. Was wonderin' if you got a spare room with a cot in it, or know
where there's one to be had? And I'd need somebody to
fetch Joe his meals."

Fant frowned in thought. Hitch added, "Prosper Selkirk's
payin' for it."

Fant's interest stirred. "Selkirk? You mean that tight-
fisted dude is goin' to turn loose of a little Kansas City
money in this town?" Hitch could almost see the man's
mind totting up figures. Fant said, "Just so happens I got a
little house I been rentin' out, and right now there ain't no
girl . . . no renter in it. It'd be a jimdandy place for Joe. My
good little ol' wife would be plumb tickled to fix extry at
mealtime for a stoveup cowboy."

"Just because Selkirk's payin' for it don't mean I'd want
it costin' no more than was fair."

"The farthest thing from my mind! I wouldn't ask no
more than was right. A dollar a day . . . no, better say a

dollar and a half when you figure how extravagant my wife gets with her cookin' if it's for sick folks. She's got a heart as big as her rump is broad, and that's considerable.'' His eyes narrowed slyly. ''I bet I could find a girl who'd be glad to look in on that cowboy and be sure he don't die from lonesome.''

''Remember, Fant, he's got a broken leg.''

''A happy spirit helps heal the body.''

''Selkirk might frown on payin' for the extras.''

''No charge, just a bonus throwed in with the room and the chuck.'' His smile began to fade. ''It'd be only fitten that I get my hands on a little Selkirk money. You know he's made it awful hard against the Figure 4 cowboys drinkin' any liquor at any place and any time. They come to town damned seldom. Figures to starve this little ol' town to death, is the way I see it.''

As Hitch saw it, this ''little ol' town'' had no more than a toenail hold on survival at best, and its passing might solve as many problems as it created. But he wouldn't say so and insult a man in his own place of business.

He heard a scuffling of hoofs in the street and the squeak of saddle leather as a man swung to the ground, spurs jingling. A cowboy walked through the open door, slapping his dusty clothes with a hat. He had a stubble of whiskers and a ragged brown mustache grayed considerably by a coat of dust. ''Rye, Fant,'' he growled before he reached the bar. He downed the glass in one quick gulp, then coughed as if everything inside him was coming out. ''Damn,'' he rasped, ''that stuff clunks when it hits the belly, like a horseshoe dropped into a bucket. Ought to be agin the law to sell whisky that bad.''

He tapped the empty glass impatiently against the bar. ''More!'' Gossett had held the bottle open and tilted as if knowing one drink wouldn't reach all the way. He refilled the glass.

Hunching over the bar, the cowboy demanded, ''How much?''

''Fifty cents. Two bits a shot.''

"Two bits?" The cowboy stared in protest, his mouth hanging open. "Ain't enough to poison a man, you got to rob him, too. When did it go up?"

"It's always been two bits, Asher. You just forgot."

The cowboy grumbled, "Then it's always been too damned high. Always some son of a bitch tryin' to squeeze a nickel out of a cowboy's sweat and blood."

"You sure came in with a burr under your blanket," the barman said. "Horse step on your foot or somethin'?"

"I quit the Snaketracks, that's what I done. I up and quit. I hope lightnin' strikes the whole damned outfit and kills everything but the lobo wolves and rattlesnakes, and I hope they multiply."

Hitch turned his head to smile. He had worked with Asher Cottingham, and he couldn't remember that anything had ever suited that cowpuncher. Cottingham had been born protesting, and thirty-odd years of experience had only shown him what a great variety of things the world held for him to detest.

Cottingham turned his attention from Gossett. "Hitch, you still nursemaidin' that ol' tightwad Charlie Waide?" He didn't give Hitch a chance to answer. He demanded, "Ol' Charlie given you-all the law yet?"

Hitch didn't know what he was talking about. Cottingham pulled a folded paper from his shirt pocket and slammed it against the bar with the palm of his hand. "This here is what I mean. Read that if you want to see how low and mean an outfit can get." His eyes snapped like the popper on a whip. "They tacked this on our bunkhouse door."

Fant Gossett stared in curiosity as Hitch unfolded the paper and glanced at it, then handed it to him. Fant said, "I been hearin' about these, but this is the first I seen."

Hitch had recognized it. The Nine Bars had posted the same set of rules a while back. A Nine Bar rep had brought a copy to the W wagon, and the cowboys passed it around to snicker over. They burned it to keep Charlie from seeing it and getting ideas. The majority were commonsense rules long observed but never formally written. One forbade

drinking, card playing or gambling of any sort and required
"proper decorum" about camp; forbade use of the rope on
cattle except in actual need; forbade abuse of horses. A man
couldn't make much quarrel against these.

Many would object, though, to rules which forbade use
of a company horse on any private business and forbade the
keeping of individually owned horses without the express
permission of the manager, which in effect could set the
cowboy afoot except when he was working; forbade
"tramps and idlers" more than one night's stay in a camp,
a sharp departure from traditional range hospitality and a
direct move to eliminate the unemployed chuckline riders
who if down on their luck could pass the winter free by
spending a few days as guests in one camp, a few days in
another; forbade employees' owning cattle in their own
brand less than two fences away from the ranch where they
worked, which in the Panhandle's open range country ef-
fectively canceled out their right to own cattle anywhere.

Hitch said, "A little extreme, some of them. But if a man
don't like the rules he's free to go and work someplace
else."

Asher Cottingham said bitterly, "Pretty soon there won't
be noplace to go unless we stop these big outfits before they
get any bigger."

"What do you mean, stop them?"

"They're teamin' up against us, Hitch. I'm sayin' it's
time the cowboys done a little teamin' up of their own."

"Seems to me like the people that own a place have got
a right to run it as they please."

"Not if they're goin' to step on us. Not if we was to call
a halt. Ever occur to you, Hitch, that if all the cowboys was
to quit at the same time, them ranchers would go to their
knees in a week? Their money wouldn't save them; nothin'
would move if we didn't do their dirty work. We'd have
them by the short hair."

Hitch blinked incredulously. "You're talkin' about a
strike!"

"Your damned right. There's a bunch of them been talkin' about it."

Hitch took another drink, a big one. It came to him now why Charlie Waide had been trying to find out from him about talk around the wagon. "I've heard of factory strikes and miners' strikes, but I never heard of a cowboy strike."

"Nobody ever heard of the United States, either, till George Washington and some of them boys decided to show the Englishmen whichaway the river forked. We're not tow-headed schoolboys to be treated like this, we're men, and *white* men at that." His eyes slitted. "There's a sight more cowboys than there is owners, Hitch. We'd have them beggin' us."

Hitch stared into his glass. The liquor had somehow gone sour. This kind of talk made him uneasy; it went against all his tradition of loyalty to the brand a man worked for, made him feel even a little guilty as if by listening to this he was somehow condoning treason. He tried to change the subject. "Been any rain over on the Snaketracks?"

Fant Gossett didn't let the subject shift. "Asher's got a point, Hitch. Them big outfits are out to run this country and ruin this town. Now, you know as well as I do that they control the politics. Half the counties you see on the map ain't organized; the ranchers don't *want* them organized. And them that is, they're under the ranchers' thumbs. The owners make sure the cowboys vote their way, and there ain't enough dissident votes to swing an election agin them. Now they've taken it in their heads they're goin' to squeeze everybody off of the range but themselves. They been meetin' with one another, figurin' how to divide it all up."

Hitch shook his head. "Some of them old boys have fought each other over grass and water till one hates the ground the other walks on. They wouldn't agree to what time it is."

"You been tendin' ol' Charlie's cows and ain't had time to see it, Hitch. They're tryin' for one thing to fix it so there don't no workin' man run any stock of his own."

Hitch conceded that. "Selkirk tried to push that idea on Charlie. Charlie didn't bite."

"He will when they show him where it touches his pocketbook. Another thing, they been tryin' to buy out or push out all the little outfits they can, especially the Mexican sheepmen. There was Mexicans here with sheep when the Comanches still had this country. Me, I got no particular love for a Mexican, but his money spends as good as anybody's. Selkirk goes up and down the *plazas* with a sackful of money and shoves it at them Mexicans, lettin' them know that if they don't take what he gives them and move, they'll get moved anyway. Soon's he gets their names or their X on the paper, he burns their houses so they can't tarry. Been a bunch of them already trailed their flocks back over into New Mexico. Thing like that hurts this town."

"They got paid."

"Paid ain't enough. Selkirk could offer me fifty dollars for a bottle of cheap rotgut and I wouldn't sell it to him if he didn't treat me white." Fant shook a thick, stubby finger near Hitch's nose. "It was little men that built this town, and without them it'll die. You think them big outfits give a tinker's damn for us? They can buy everything out of Dodge City or Kansas City or someplace that don't even need their money, and they can starve this town to death. They don't want no town here because a town means families, and families means kids, and kids means schools, and that takes taxes. Ever see a big rancher that didn't choke into a conniption fit over the thought of payin' taxes?"

Hitch didn't reply though he kept thinking that what Fant Gossett paid in taxes would probably starve a field mouse. He looked first at Cottingham, then at Fant. "Fellers, you're talkin' crazy. There won't be no strike in this country."

"Why not?"

He tried to think of an answer. "It just ain't done, that's all."

Cottingham glowered. "It'll *be* done if they don't change their ways."

Hitch had intended to stay and rest awhile in the cool

quiet of Gossett's adobe walls, but he disliked the turn of the talk. In his view you didn't accept a man's pay and cuss him; if you couldn't stand up for him you left. Which was just what Cottingham had done, though Hitch would bet a paint pony that Asher had been talking rebellion while still on the payroll. He set his glass on the bar. "Fant, the liquor's good. You get that house ready; I'll have Joe brought over when the doctor says to."

Gossett nodded. He waited until Hitch was almost at the door, then called, "Hitch! It occurs to me that Asher here is out of a job, and you-all at the Ws are short-handed since Joe busted his leg."

Hitch gritted his teeth. If a man wanted a job he ought to ask for it himself. Hitch said, "We're not short enough to hurt us."

Cottingham grunted. "Let the other men work a little harder so ol' Charlie won't be out no extry wages, is that it?"

The pair were beginning to irritate Hitch like gravel in his boots. "Charlie Waide alway treats a man fair."

Cottingham said, "I don't know as I'd want the job noway. How much they payin' at the Ws?"

"Thirty and found. It's as good as there is."

"Thirty dollars a month." Cottingham's mouth turned downward. "Hell of a lot for a poor man riskin' life and limb to make some rich man richer. Keep your job, Hitch. I don't want it."

"I never offered," Hitch said stiffly, knowing he ought to go instead of letting the argument run on. But he had to add, "I wouldn't want you out there agitatin' the men."

Cottingham looked surprised. "Me? I never agitated nobody in my whole life."

IV

ASHER COTTINGHAM HAD ENJOYED HARD
luck all his life; people had always conspired against him.
When he was about fourteen his father had told him he was
old enough to go out and work for wages. Very low wages
they had been, too, to hear him tell it. Nothing made him
happier than to have somebody listen to all his sad stories.
That day must have been one of the happiest of his life.

Cottingham said he intended to go visit some friends at
one of the Figure 4 wagons and would like to ride partway
with Hitch. Hitch figured what he was after was a few days
of free chuck at Selkirk's expense, but that was Selkirk's
problem. The cowboy invited himself to tie his horse behind
the wagon and climb up into the seat. Hitch was not thrilled
by all that company.

"Look at this," Cottingham said, waving his arm, "all
this land claimed by the Figure 4s. Ought to be a law against
companies like that in the first place. A workin' man ought
to be able to stand up face to face with the man he works
for, like in the old days. Tryin' to talk to a company is like

fightin' your way through a tangle of spider webs; you never can get to the heart of things, if it's even got a heart. I say no man ought to be allowed to own more than he can personally take care of."

"If that was the case," Hitch asked dryly, "who would you work for?"

Cottingham deliberated. "I don't know, but there ought to be a law."

It was a time of grand relief to Hitch when they came finally to a fork in the trail and Asher Cottingham climbed down from the wagon. Hitch had listened to all he could stand; Asher was one of those people always advocating tearing down whatever he disliked but having no idea how to build back something better in its place.

Asher said, "Well, I reckon I'll have to let you make the rest of the trip by yourself."

"I'll miss you."

The solitude afterward gave him time to think, to ponder whether trouble was indeed coming to the Canadian River country and to assure himself that there was no reason it had to involve the W. He didn't know a man in the outfit who was sore at Charlie Waide.

As he came onto W land, Hitch began pulling out of the trail to inspect every grazing bunch of cattle he saw. The cattle would raise their heads warily at the approach of the wagon, and many would hightail it across the prairie. But the vehicle itself was an object of curiosity because the cattle saw few of them, and the horses had no men astride to suggest the trouble which cattle associated with riders. Many cattle would run a little way, then turn to look. This was an area over which the roundup crew had already worked. The calves bore fresh brands just now in the process of healing.

At length Hitch came upon a group of cattle that kept pulling away, maintaining a respectable distance between themselves and the wagon. But they were not so far that he did not find himself staring in disbelief. "Slick-ears," he said aloud, as if the team knew what he was talking about. "I swear, there's slick-eared calves in that bunch."

He tried to maneuver the wagon around the cattle, but they kept edging away from him. Finally he had to unhitch one of the horses, get on it bareback and kick it bareheeled into a trot that took it around the cattle. Bringing them to a halt, he counted twenty cows and fourteen calves.

Slick, all right, he thought, looking at their unmarked ears. *Ain't but two branded calves in the bunch.* Those two were W calves, following W cows. The rest of the cows were Figure 4s plus one Snaketrack, and not one of their calves carried a brand.

Can't hardly see how we missed them in the roundup; we worked this strip like a fine-tooth comb.

But there they were. Puzzling, Hitch decided the Figure 4 cows must have drifted over onto this part of the W in a bunch, perhaps pressed by the roundup crews on the Figure 4. Some spooky cattle always had a tendency to keep moving out in front of the roundup, avoiding capture as long as they could. But these cattle, though shy, didn't seem inclined to break and run once he had circled them.

Well, he would tell the Figure 4 rep and let him take them back to the range where they belonged. It would have to be done before long, for once the cows began kicking off these calves and weaning them, the calves would be considered mavericks. Sure would cripple the Figure 4, he thought sarcastically, to lose a dozen calves to a maverick hunter.

In late afternoon he heard the bawling of the day's gather before he reached the roundup ground. The branding crew was sweaty and dirty and moving with the slowness that indicated a day's work was nearly done. Recognizing his own team and wagon, Law McGinty rode out from his position on the perimeter of the herd. "See you got back," the young cowboy said needlessly.

Hitch watched him with suspicion. "Thought about takin' your wagon by your place and leavin' it, then decided you'd rather take it back yourself. Give you a chance to see your wife." He paused, considering whether to say more. "Law, there been trouble between you and Kate?"

Law seemed surprised. "Why?"

"You left here the other night sayin' you was goin' home. Yesterday she told me it'd been a spell since you was there. Now, maybe it's none of my business, but I think you owe Kate better treatment."

Color rose in Law's face. He offered no explanation.

Hitch said, "You take this wagon home tonight and act like a husband. Be back here by daylight."

Law was solemn. "All right, Hitch. Want me to start now?"

"I think that would be a dandy idea."

Law tied his horse behind the wagon so he would have a way to return to camp. Hitch climbed down, carrying a new lantern he had bought for Trump Tatum, and handed the lines to Law. He watched Law turn the team and start across the prairie, skirting the bawling herd. Hitch turned his attention to the cattle a moment, but he was afoot and would be no help at the herd. He could go to the branding fire, but it looked as if they were about done anyway. He walked to the chuckwagon and poured a cup of coffee. Be-whiskered Trump Tatum eyed the lantern with no words of gratitude, as if it were no more than his due. He made some comment to the effect that supper wasn't ready yet and that a boss set a poor example showing up at the wagon ahead of his men, the sun still an hour high. Hitch ignored him, which annoyed Trump even more.

Charlie Waide rode in from the herd directly. This surprised Hitch a little; he expected Charlie to have moved on to another wagon by now. Charlie kept close watch on them all. The rancher fetched coffee and sat down on a bedroll, his shoulders hunched, the bad arm plainly hurting him. He tried to avoid letting Hitch see the pain in his face, but Hitch caught it anyhow. Charlie asked, "How'd you leave Joe Sands?"

"He'll mend."

"Didn't happen to run onto another hand to take his place awhile?"

"I saw Asher Cottingham. I didn't hire him."

"Good. His jaw works like a gate-hinge. Anyway, last I heard he was at the Snaketracks."

"He quit." Hitch considered a moment, then decided to tell him about the Snaketrack posting the new company rules.

Charlie nodded gravely. "Not a bad set of rules, though, the most of them. They make sense."

"You seen them, Charlie?"

"Weeks ago. The owners been passin' them around."

It struck Hitch funny now, remembering that the cowboys had taken pains to burn the rules from the Nine Bar to keep Charlie from seeing them. They should have known he was always a jump or two ahead.

Hitch found his coffee cold. He sloshed it around in the cup, not wanting to drink it but too frugal to throw it out; he could remember times when there hadn't been any. "You wasn't thinkin' about postin' them rules yourself, was you, Charlie?"

"What do you think of them?"

"The good ones are understood without you havin' to write them down on paper and makin' men look like boys that need to be told to wipe their nose. The bad ones . . ." He left the rest unsaid.

"Maybe times change."

"You ain't changed, Charlie; neither have these men. You don't need to post rules like that; these men won't let you down."

Charlie's eyes were tried and worried. "I had company today. Owner of the Nine Bars was by to see me. Said there's some ugly talk amongst cowboys around the country. You hear anything in town?"

"Just Asher Cottingham bellyachin'; nothin' I'd take stock in. I get the notion some of the boys resent the new rules, but that's nothin' to concern yourself about. It's outfits like the Figure 4s and the Snaketracks and the Nine Bars that'll have the trouble if any comes."

"So, it's true, then, about the strike talk?"

"Ain't been none of it around this wagon, and there won't be. I'll guarantee you that."

"Can you, Hitch? Can anybody guarantee anything anymore?"

The roundup progressed methodically the next several days. Charlie Waide left to spend a while at his other wagons. A couple more cows showed up whose brands were impossible to identify definitely as either a Figure 4 or an LR, so Hitch arbitrarily called one for the McGintys, one for Selkirk. He sensed Law was a little sore about it, but Rascal accepted it in good grace. By now a new Figure 4 rep had replaced Dayton Brumley. To Hitch's relief he seemed disinclined to make any fuss. On the contrary, when Hitch called one of the cows a Figure 4, the lanky rep said, "You sure, Hitch? If there's any question I'd rather the McGintys got her. Selkirk and his crowd won't starve to death."

Hitch appreciated harmony in camp, but on the other hand he respected a man who stood up for the outfit that paid him. He made a mental resolution that if this cowboy ever came looking for a place on the W payroll, he wouldn't get it. Hitch's feeling was reinforced that night at supper when he heard the cowboy relating his grudges against the ranch he worked for.

"I sure was glad to come to the W wagon," the man said. "I'd about had me a bellyful of ol' Selkirk and his crowd treatin' us like we was English servants, or like maybe we owed them money. Selkirk seems to think everybody is tryin' to cheat him out of somethin'. Guilty conscience, I'll bet; he's done to other people and he don't want nobody doin' it to him. It'd serve him and the Figure 4s right if some of the New Mexico cow thieves was to come over and sack them out."

Rascal McGinty chimed in, "Boys, them big outfits are tryin' to get a stranglehold on this country and everybody in it."

The trend of the talk irritated Hitch. "What do you know about it, Rascal? Charlie Waide's the only man you've worked for. He ever treat you less than fair?''

"I wasn't pointin' at Charlie.''

"Well, be damned sure you don't.''

Hitch loosened a little. Maybe he had jumped on Rascal a little too hard. He said, a little more evenly this time, ''Rascal, whatever the other outfits do, the Ws has always treated a man right. It always will.''

"Always is a long time, Hitch. People been known to change, even people like Charlie.''

"The day Charlie Waide ever let us down, you can all get up and leave here, Rascal. I'll be out there in front, leadin' you.''

Law McGinty's eyes narrowed. "I'll remember you said that, Hitch. If things ever come to dividin' up the blankets, we'll hold you to it.''

Hitch shook his head. "I'll bet all my chips on Charlie.''

The day Charlie Waide came back, Prosper Selkirk showed up in his buckboard. He didn't have the greyhounds with him. The Figure 4 rep saw Selkirk's rig when it came over the hill, and Hitch grinned as the cowboy craftily contrived to get busy on the far side of the herd, trying to keep out of his boss's sight and hopefully off of his mind. Charlie Waide walked his horse around the herd and jerked his head at Hitch, indicating he wanted Hitch to ride down to the wagon with him. Hitch said, "You don't need me, Charlie.''

"I don't care to talk to him by myself. Anyway, he may want to go over your tallies. Quicker we satisfy him, the quicker he'll get the hell away from here. If he spends the night that rep will stay out with the wild bunch and go hungry.''

At the wagon Charlie offered coffee and the other amenities, while Trump Tatum offered nothing but an acid stare. Selkirk seemed agitated and in no mood to socialize. "Charlie, has there been any talk among your men?''

Charlie asked innocently, "Talk about what?'' though Charlie had to know very well what Selkirk meant.

"Rebellion. It's spreading across these ranches like the plague.''

Blandly Charlie said, "I've heard no talk, except that some of the boys ain't keen on the rules certain outfits have posted."

Selkirk's voice was critical. "I don't believe you've recognized the seriousness of the problem in which we find ourselves, Charles."

"I ain't got no problem. I ain't posted the rules."

"If it comes to us, it'll come to you. This kind of thing is a contagious disease. We have to cut it off before it becomes worse."

"You figurin' on shootin' a few cowboys?"

"You know better than that. But I do intend to root out the troublemakers and get them off of this range."

"You go right ahead and do what suits you, Prosper. It's no problem of mine."

"It *is*, can't you see that? This problem must be faced by every substantial rancher on the plains, and the only way is to band together, to meet this trouble with our combined strength. It is becoming a contest of wills, Charles. We have far too much invested here to be thwarted by troublemakers and lazy malcontents."

Charlie Waide frowned. "You ever try to just sit down and talk man-to-man with the hands that work for you?"

"How could I do that? From the first I found they were mocking me. Behind my back they called me a dude, a damnyankee, and worse. No, I don't talk *with* them, I talk to them. That's the only way you can treat men of that type, with authority."

Hitch was surprised to find himself seeing Selkirk's side of it, a little. He doubted Selkirk had ever tried very diligently to communicate with his cowboys on any congenial plane, but he knew that even a good effort might have failed. As a group, cowboys—like the ranchers they worked for—had a tendency to be intolerant of men whose ways and values were different from their own. In particular they resented what Selkirk stood for . . . Yankee money, generally considered to have been squeezed from the flesh and blood of the South. Though the Civil War was long since over and the men who had fought in it were now middle-aged or older, the sectional bitterness was still much alive.

Charlie said, "You-all just don't understand one another."

"They understand me. I won't be bullied or threatened."

"We've got law here," Charlie pointed out. "The ranches control it, and I'd think the county sheriffs can take care of any trouble."

"The law can't stop all this talk, and it can't control a range overrun with all sorts of undesirable people. That is where we can give the law some assistance. I've called several of the owners and managers over to my place tomorrow for a talk."

"War conference, you mean?"

"Call it what you wish. I want you there, Charles."

Charlie was ill at ease. "I don't see where I got any part in this."

Selkirk stood up. Anger hardened the set of his jaw. "Charles, we are rapidly reaching a point where those who are not with us must be considered to be against us. I have no intention of letting you be against us."

Charlie was on his feet too. "I ain't against nobody, but I intend to run my outfit and let you run yours."

Selkirk stared at him with hard, ungiving eyes. "I hate to hold this over your head, but I will if I have to. You have a large loan on this ranch, and it's with a Kansas City bank, is it not?"

"Why ask me? You seem to know all about it."

"Would you care to guess who is a member of that bank's board of directors?"

Charlie swallowed, stunned.

Selkirk said, "I'll see you tomorrow, Charles." He dropped his cup into Trump Tatum's washtub, climbed into the buckboard and left without looking back.

V

CHARLIE WAS RINGIER THAN A WAGON COOK after Selkirk left. He bawled out the kid jingler for herding the remuda too tightly and not giving the horses a chance to graze. Rascal McGinty caught thunder for trying to brand a calf with an iron not hot enough. Charlie raised cain with Trump Tatum because half an oven of biscuits was left over, and that was wasteful of flour. He said if Trump did not learn to be sparing and help keep the costs down, he would find his employer bankrupt and himself working for some Kansas City bank . . . if he was working at all.

Rascal grumbled, "I don't like Charlie goin' to that meetin'."

"He's got to," Hitch said.

"Charlie's fought Indians and he's fought Yankee soldiers, but he never could stand up to Selkirk's brand of thimbleriggers."

"Nobody'll make Charlie do somethin' he don't think is right."

"They'll crowd hell out of him. If he was to agree to that

rule against a cowboy owin' livestock, it'd ruin us, Hitch. Me and Law, we ain't got so many cattle that we could make a decent livin' for us and Law's wife and that youngun comin'.''

"I'll guarantee Charlie."

Law McGinty demanded, "How much is that guarantee worth, Hitch?"

"Meanin' what?"

"Meanin' if Charlie was to weaken, what would you do about it?''

Hitch kept arguing for faith in Charlie, but Law relentlessly pressed him for an answer, and Rascal backed his brother. At length Hitch said, "If Charlie ever did turn his back on us, I'd roll up my bed and leave here."

Rascal glanced at Law, then back to Hitch. "And let the rest of us come with you?"

"And let the rest of you come with me."

"That's the kind of guarantee we wanted, Hitch."

"That's how much faith I got in Charlie."

Charlie made no move to join the cowboys around the fire. He kept to himself, which—considering the mood he was in—suited everybody. He called Hitch over. "Hitch, you're goin' with me."

Hitch argued, "Them ranchers don't want me. My little bunch of cows don't make me an owner in their eyes. I'd be like salt in their wounds."

"If it itches them, let them scratch."

"Likely I'd be a hindrance to you."

"Damned if I'm goin' over there by myself. I want somebody with me who talks the same language I do, who can keep that Yankee highbinder from tyin' me in a knot with fast talk."

"I'd sooner get stomped by an outlawed stud."

"So had I. But we're both goin'."

Hitch had not been to the Figure 4 headquarters since the syndicate had bought its much smaller forerunner from a buffalo hunter who had stayed to traffic in cattle after the

heavy guns had killed out the shaggy herds. He saw not a
trace of the soddies that had been here before. He saw frame
buildings, the management house and the office sitting along
one end of a big open yard that lacked only a flagpole and
some cavalry to make it look like a military quadrangle. The
cookshack and the long bunkhouse sat at the opposite end,
the barns and corrals set in almost perfect straight lines, all
buildings and fences coming to neat ninety-degree angles.
It had the look of having been designed on a drafting table
in Kansas City and set down here without an inch of devi-
ation from plan. There was not a hint of decoration anywhere, nothing that did not serve some utilitarian purpose.

"Like an Army post," said Charlie Waide.

"Or a prison," Hitch replied.

Buckboards and wagons and horses stood around the office building. "Guess we're not the first ones here," Hitch
said.

Charlie shook his head. "And I don't intend to be the
last to leave."

They dismounted in shade at a hitching rack near the office. Hitch loosened the cinch to make the horse easier during what could be a considerable wait. Charlie frowned at
the open door, dreading, then squared his shoulders and
strode in. Hitch looked back regretfully toward the barn
where he could see a few cowboys working, then followed
Charlie.

A dozen or fifteen men sat in a cramped room that served
as an office. Hitch surmised that the rest of the building was
sleeping quarters for a city-raised bookkeeper who wouldn't
feel at home in the bunkhouse with the cowboys. He knew
most of the faces and names; these men were ranch owners
and managers. He noted no representation from the small
outfits and nester-type operations. These men counted cattle
by the thousands and tens of thousands. It struck him that
this was probably the first time so many had ever met in a
group. Some had become enemies through competition for
land. He saw gray-bearded, hawk-eyed old John Torrington
of the Snaketrack and Allie Clay of the Nine Bar, bitter

rivals who once had been so near killing each other over a
few sections of second-rate grazing land that when one went
to town he sent a couple of men ahead to make sure the
other was not there. Now they were brought together in an
uneasy alliance, but no nearer together than they had to be.
Torrington sat in one corner, Clay in another.

Selkirk stood at the front of the room, one hand on a
rolltop desk that had dozens of rolled-up papers sticking out
of convenient little pigeonholes. A thin and fleeting smile
crossed his face as he paused in his talk to acknowledge
Charlie.

"I doubt, gentlemen, there is anyone in this room who is
not acquainted with Charles Waide. Charles, I'm glad you
could come."

Charlie said stiffly, "Don't recall that I was given any
option." He took up two or three minutes of Selkirk's time
working through the room shaking hands with friends and
acquaintances. He was warm to some, coolly businesslike
with others. A few were old-line cowboy-ranchers of his
own stripe, who had battled their way up despite drouth and
flood, fire and storm, Indians and Texas fever. John Torrington, for an example, was one of the fire-eating breed
who had fought Mexicans on the border, Indians on the
plains; he had been fighting somebody all his life. More of
the men, though, were of the newer corporate breed, trans-
planted from the board room of a bank or a mercantile firm.
Many had been easy learners in the ranch business, hiring
dependable men who could take care of the cowcamp details
while they concentrated on the broader aspects. After all,
they did not have to be cowboys; they could hire plenty of
men to do the horseback work. Their own task was planning
and high-level decisions, and this the majority had learned
to do well. That they might not know or at least might not
particularly appreciate the traditions which had grown up
among cowboys and old shortgrass ranchers was to be expected. Traditions did not produce beef, nor did they retire
a loan.

For that matter, many of the old-line ranchers themselves

had discarded practices and outlooks that once had been their hallmark. New times called for new ways.

Done with hand-shaking, Charlie turned toward Hitch. "Fellers, I brought my wagon boss; most of you know Hugh Hitchcock."

Some spoke to Hitch, some didn't. Selkirk said, "Nice you could come, Hitchcock. I think you'll find coffee down at the cookshack, and some cowboys to talk to."

Charlie Waide put in, "He can drink coffee at the Ws. I brought him to take part in this thing with me."

Selkirk rubbed his hands uncomfortably. "As you wish, Charles. I thought he might not feel that he fits in."

"Hell," rasped Charlie, "I don't fit in either, but I'm here. Let's get on with it. I want to be back at the wagon tonight."

Whatever Selkirk's line of talk had been, Charlie had thrown him offstride. "Charles, these men here already know, but you probably have not heard. Most of the work force left the Snaketrack yesterday. The Nine Bar has lost two-thirds of its hands, too."

Charlie glanced at Hitch in surprise. Hitch felt a chill. Somehow he hadn't believed when he had listened to the angry talk in Fant Gossett's saloon that it would ever get past the jawing stage.

"You see now," Selkirk continued, "the problem we're up against. It will probably come to the rest of us shortly; a thing of this sort tends to become epidemic. Now, I realize there are some among us who have had differences of opinion in the past—even violent differences. But we have to put that behind us and face this threat united. Struggling along separately we can be hurt like a crippled animal caught by the wolves apart from the herd. But together, with our combined strength, we can snuff out this insurrection with a minimum of damage. And cost." He paused as if to give this latter element its proper emphasis. "Now, as to strategy: I think from the experience of the Snaketrack and the Nine Bar that most of us have some men who will not join the strike, either for fear of losing their jobs, for apathy, or for lack of courage.''

Charlie suggested, ''They might just be *loyal*.''

Selkirk nodded and went on. ''The point is that we'll have these men as a crutch until we can hire others. And make no mistake, there *will* be other men we can hire. We do not have to let ourselves be panicked by a few malcontents and their followers.

''We all know this trouble goes deeper than just the hired hands on these ranches. We know some of these men are thieves, and that other men who may not be thieves themselves nevertheless condone them because they hate us for our success. Up and down the river are small squatters and that sort who dignify their position by calling themselves ranchers; in reality they are maverick runners and cattle thieves. Then in these miserable nesterments that pass themselves off as towns are people who agitate against us. In short, gentlemen, we stand against a motley array of ragtag enemies who represent a threat to the growth and security of this entire region. Whatever we do has to be calculated to clear the range once and for all of this obstructionist element. Until we, the substantial owners who have a bonafide investment in the future of this region, can control it and shut out these undesirables, there will be no security for us or for our property.''

Bearded old John Torrington of the Snaketrack squinted his flinty eyes and spoke out angrily, ''Hell, looks to me like the thing to do is to find out who these troublemakers are and go stretch a little rope. That'll by God put an end to it.''

Selkirk seemed embarrassed. ''Gentlemen, the idea has some merit, and perhaps a few years ago it would have been the best way. But now the law of Texas will not stand for it. They would have the Rangers on us in a week. We have to accomplish the same thing by more subtle methods and with as little violence or bloodshed as possible. We don't have to choke a man to death with a rope. In the business world we can choke him off financially by refusing him a loan or other support.'' He looked directly at Charlie. ''With these cowboys, all we have to do is refuse them jobs, until they spend whatever they have in their pockets. Then they have no choice but to leave this country.''

A murmur of argument began to rise. Torrington declared, ''The hell with the state law; it's none of their business. We control the county law around here, and there ain't much anybody can do if we run our own courts. I say let's stretch some rope!''

Selkirk waved his hands, trying to get order back into the meeting. Charlie Waide and John Torrington stood toe to toe, arguing angrily. They had argued before over land Charlie used and Torrington wanted. ''Gentlemen!'' Selkirk pleaded. ''Gentlemen!'' In a minute the men had settled enough that Selkirk was able to take the floor again. ''I must say I agree with the spirit of John Torrington's argument, though the application of it under today's civilized conditions might bring us more problems than it would solve.''

Torrington declared, ''Charlie Waide, I know for a certain fact that you once dispatched a thief without the benefit of a judge. No use you turnin' squeamish over it now.''

Charlie said, ''Not once, John, *twice*. There was a time you didn't even know about. But it was different then; we didn't have law, so we made our own. Now we got law.''

''And it's ours,'' Torrington said. ''I say if we help it along with a little summary judgment and save the county the expense of some trials, we'll throw the fear of God into the rest of them maverick chasers and brand burners and strike agitators. It'll clean this country like a grassfire.''

Charlie said tightly, ''If they was to hang all the maverick runners, John, me and you would be the first to go. You know that neither one of us had a seat in our britches till we'd mavericked us a herd.''

''That was a long time ago. Times change.''

''Exactly what I'm tryin' to tell you.''

Selkirk said, ''Gentlemen, we're arguing needlessly over a moot point. There'll be no wholesale hanging, so we're wasting time talking about it. Our immediate problem is this strike.''

Charlie Waide said, ''I ain't clear in my own mind what set it off. Maybe if we was to just give them boys a little raise in pay . . .''

Selkirk shook his head. ''Out of the question. None of us will stand for being blackmailed or bullied. If the situation merited more wages we would have given them without having a pistol put to our heads. Wages, gentlemen, are set the same way cattle prices are set, by supply and demand in the marketplace. We cannot set our own cattle prices; we take what the market will bear. So long as there are men all over the country willing to work for twenty-five dollars a month, it would be folly on our part to pay more.'' He eyed Charlie levelly. ''Charles, since you bring this up, I should comment on one of your practices that has contributed to our problems. Too often a cowboy who does not like what he earns on the Figure 4 has gone to you at the W and received more pay than I was giving him. This creates dissatisfaction among the other men and undermines the position of other ranch operators. We could eliminate this by cooperating closer with one another.''

Charlie said, ''Cattle are sellin' higher this year. I figure if I can do it, you-all can do it too.''

Selkirk argued, ''Charles, the only place you can find money to pay more wages is out of your profit margin, and I have reason to know it is as thin as paper already. I say this: that if a man is not willing to work for what an employer is willing to pay him, he ought to go somewhere else.''

Charlie said, ''I got men who came here with me from South Texas and went through hell with me. We was like partners then. Without them I'd of gasped and gone under. I figure I owe them.''

''How long will you owe them, Charles, the rest of your life? They've eaten your food and taken your wages for years. You've treated them well and paid them all that you ever agreed to. Certainly, we appreciate what these men went through years ago. Many of us went through the great war on one side or the other, but we do not expect to live on the country's gratitude all our lives. A man makes his way on what he does *now*, not on what he once did. We cannot let what happened years ago stand in the way of progress. This is a raw frontier no longer. It is a modern, civilized country, and we are in a position to build it on a sound business basis without false sentimentality and without clinging to outmoded customs and attitudes.

"I have been a banker long enough to know that the one object of anyone in any business venture is to show a profitable return on investment. Without this, the nation would collapse; there would be hunger all over the land. We strive to make this region prosperous and healthy for business, and in doing so we do the entire nation a service. We cannot jeopardize this great purpose by lack of unity or by sentimentality toward a few cowhands long since amply repaid.

"Now, there have been objections to the adoption of the rules we have set up, but they are sensible rules that simply establish an order of conduct. Anyone who objects is probably a misfit anyway. As I see it, we in this room face the same type of pressures as these cowboys do except that ours are multiplied many times over. Each of us has financial backers, partners or whatever, who look at us as coldly and objectively as we must look at our employees. If we fail to perform, we are discarded with no hesitation. I do not see that the workmen who accept our wages are entitled to more consideration than those of us who bear the burden of responsibility."

Worriedly watching Charlie, Hitch thought he could see at least partial acceptance in the old rancher's leathery face. Selkirk made an effective argument for his case, Hitch conceded.

Selkirk evidently thought he was gaining ground, for he pressed the attack, looking directly at Charlie Waide. "The crux of this matter is the allowing of some men on our payrolls to own cattle. Most of us know we are sustaining losses we cannot pinpoint. Some come from outlaw bands raiding out of New Mexico who hit us and run away with cattle when they find the way clear; the death of Billy the Kid did not stop all of it. But far more serious, I believe, is the slow attrition of our herds due to dishonest people on our payrolls and to scurvy pilfering by some so-called ranchers who squat among us on starvation claims. Losses of this size can be compounded into ruin if we stand by and do nothing.

"We cannot afford to subsidize this dishonesty any longer. We must agree together to stop this custom of allowing our people to own cattle. This will remove the incentive for a majority of the stealing. Then if we can find effective means to remove these marginal operators who only survive by robbing us, we will have the way clear to make this region efficient and profitable without the eternal vigilance now required of us."

He paused, watching Charlie Waide. "Charles, the majority of us have agreed to impose the cattle rule. How about you?"

The other ranchers turned their attention to Charlie, who fidgeted and looked at Hitch. Hitch watched him uneasily, feeling the pressure of these other men heavy against him.

Selkirk pressed, "Well, Charles?"

An old rawhide rancher who had come out of the brush country said, "I ain't among them, Charlie. If you say no, you ain't by yourself."

That rancher didn't have any money borrowed from Selkirk's bank. Looking nervously at the others, Charlie got carefully to his feet. "I'll answer you thisaway, Prosper." He motioned toward Hitch. "You-all know Hugh Hitchcock," he told the crowd. "He's the caliber of man I got workin' at the Ws. I'd trust Hitch to the moon and back with everything I own. I feel the same way about the rest of my hands. Now, I can see your argument about the cattle rule. If I didn't have men like Hitch I might be easy convinced. But I don't want Hitch to lose his cattle, or the other men like him. If I was to go along with you-all it'd be like tellin' the men I didn't trust them nomore. I won't do that."

Selkirk said narrowly, "You put a lot of trust in men you may not know as well as you think you do."

"I know them."

"But what if you're wrong? What if one day you find some of them *have* betrayed you?"

Blinking, Charlie glanced at Hitch as if wondering whether Selkirk knew something Charlie didn't. "I'd stake all I got on my men."

Selkirk's voice carried a hard threat. "You *are* staking all you've got."

Charlie stared at him, hating the power Selkirk represented, hating Selkirk because he envied him, a damnyankee. "You want to spell that out to me in English?" he demanded.

Selkirk said, "I don't think I have to."

Flushed, Charlie pushed through the men and out the door. Hitch followed, glancing back in concern at the angry Selkirk. Outside, Charlie cursed vigorously a moment. Then he said in misery, "Hitch, the son of a bitch can fair gut me if he takes a notion."

Hitch saw Charlie weakening. Selkirk had hit him where he was vulnerable.

Charlie was so unsettled that he forgot to tighten the cinch before he tried to mount, and Hitch caught him to save him from a fall. Charlie cursed and fought his way free. "Dammit, I can make it myself!"

When Charlie was like that, the best thing was to leave him alone. The older he got, the more true this had become. Hitch silently tightened his own cinch and swung into the saddle. He noticed that when Charlie mounted, he did so slowly. He was wearing out, for it had been a long ride over here. But Hitch didn't mention it, for that would have invited a cussing. Hitch rode in silence, letting Charlie simmer. At length Charlie settled enough to start paying attention to the cattle they passed, and at one point he stopped to look at three horses that watched curiously beside the trail. After a long time Charlie declared, "There's truth in some of what Selkirk says."

"He's wrong about the W cowboys."

"There ain't a man on the Ws would steal from me, is there?"

"You know those men better than that."

"Always thought I did. But times change. Things ain't what they was, and maybe people ain't either."

They rode slowly, sparing horses that already had put in a long day. Once in a while Hitch looked uneasily at Charlie, seeing weariness grind the old rancher down. They hadn't come prepared to camp, but they needed to. Hitch couldn't afford to suggest it directly, for Charlie would ride all the way to the wagon out of pure stubbornness.

Hitch said, "Charlie, I been thinkin' these horses need water, and I could sure stand some coffee. Wouldn't be far out of our way to go by the McGinty place."

"I'm doin' fine," Charlie said pridefully, "and I don't think the horses are sufferin' any. But if you're that weak . . ."

Hitch smiled thinly.

Approaching the McGinty claim, Charlie said, "I ain't seen that girl Kate in a long time. She close to deliverin'?"

"Lookin' at her, I'd say she was."

"And that boy's leavin' her out here all by herself?"

"I've tried to get him to send her to town. She don't want to go."

The sun was low, and Hitch hoped for Charlie's sake that Kate would talk the old man into staying for supper. By that time it would be getting on toward dark and Charlie would probably agree to stay the night. He needed the rest.

A tall, slender woman stood in front of the dugout, peering curiously at them from under the protection of a big slat bonnet. This, Hitch knew at a glance, couldn't be Kate McGinty, but the bonnet hid her face. He finally recognized Kate's mother.

"Howdy, Miz Fallon. Didn't figure to see you here."

The gaunt woman studied him with no great friendliness. She had little use for people so much more fortunate than herself. "Where's that fiddlefooted husband of hers? Why didn't you bring him?"

Concerned, Hitch asked, "Somethin' the matter with Kate?"

"No, she's fine, but it's no credit to him. He ought to be here seein' after her. He ought to know a young woman ain't no heifer to be left to calve by herself."

Charlie Waide leaned forward in the saddle, hunched in his weariness. "I was just fixin' to tell Hitch, we could take and send her up to W headquarters till she's delivered."

"No need," the woman said, "though I reckon it's civil of you to be askin'. I'm here with her now, and I'll stand by her. It pleasures me anyway, gettin' to stay in a place as nice as this." She waved her hand toward the low-slung dugout, and Hitch thought at first she was being bitter. It occurred to him then that she meant it; this was better than most of the places she had ever lived.

Hitch dismounted, stiff from the ride. He walked a little to exercise his legs. "We thought we'd stop and see about Kate, and water the horses. Thought maybe, too, we might be lucky enough to beg us a cup of coffee."

Kate McGinty spoke from the dugout opening. "We'd be tickled, Hitch. You-all come on in." She held the canvas flap open. He stared a moment, distressed by the splotched color in her face. He hadn't been around women much in this stage of the game; he didn't know if this appearance was normal or if possibly something was wrong with her. All he knew was that she didn't look quite right for Kate.

"Charlie," Hitch said, "I'll take and water the horses. Why don't you go set a spell?"

Charlie gave him no argument, a fact which bore witness to his fatigue. Mrs. Fallon went into the dugout ahead of Charlie. Kate stood in the doorway, holding the flap and watching as Hitch swung back into the saddle, leading Charlie's horse. After watering them he turned them loose in a corral to roll and rest.

Kate McGinty walked heavily down to meet him. "There's a little grain in the shed." He thanked her and fed the horses sparingly. "It's late," she said. "You-all ought to spend the night."

"That'd be up to Charlie. Sure it wouldn't put you out none?"

"We'd be tickled." That expression, often repeated, seemed to sum up Kate's attitude toward almost everything. She was so used to adversity that she appeared immune.

He said, "You ought to be in the house, restin' too."

"Exercise is good for a woman in my condition, or don't you know?"

"That kind of experience is out of my line."

"It shouldn't be. You ought to find you a woman, Hitch. She'd be good for you, and I know you'd be good for her."

He couldn't tell her he had long wished he had claimed her before Law McGinty did. And he could not tell her he was waiting until he could provide a woman something better than this, for it would seem he was downgrading what Law had given her. "A cowpuncher like me is always too busy, seems like. I'm in no hurry. The Lord always provides."

"He provides for them that helps theirselves."

It seemed to Hitch that Law McGinty wasn't helping himself much, letting a handsome little woman like this sit alone while he prowled the river looking for something else. Granted, she wasn't at her best right now, but she wouldn't be in this condition much longer. A man ought to be willing to wait. "I sent Law home with the wagon the other night," he said.

"I thank you, Hitch. He should've come on his own."

Hitch felt obliged to make excuses. "Law's a man, Kate, but he's still got a little of the boy left in him. Maybe he don't realize yet the way you feel about him, the way you need him."

"I'm grateful you sent him. Even if it was just for an hour or two, I'm glad you made him come."

An hour or two. Hitch remembered that Law hadn't come back to camp till about daylight.

"It'll be better someday," Kate said hopefully. "When

the place is bigger and we got more cattle, he'll have time then to stay.''

Hitch turned away to hide the anger that gnawed him. *Damn that Law; somebody ought to take a horsewhip to him.*

By the time Kate and her mother got the coffee made, Charlie had relaxed and was an easy mark for an invitation to stay for supper. By the time supper was done, it was dark outside. Kate asked them to stay; the horses needed a rest anyway, she argued, and there were plenty of blankets in the dugout which Rascal McGinty had built for himself, well apart from this one he had given up for Law and Kate. In his weariness Charlie was not hard to persuade. They sat around in lamplight awhile, talking of all manner of things. By Fallon and McGinty standards, Charlie Waide was a rich man, but he had known these same privations in his earlier years. He didn't seem out of place here.

The men finally said their goodnights. They would be up at three in the morning without awakening the women; they could make the wagon by breakfast. In Rascal's dugout Charlie took the lone bed. Hitch spread a blanket on the hard-packed dirt floor, wrapping it over him. Charlie was quickly snoring, but Hitch lay awake looking up at the low roof, unaccustomed to the musty, earthy smell of the place. He thought back on the meeting at the Figure 4, on the trouble that had come to the river country, wondering if the W would be lucky enough to see it pass by.

They rode sleepy-headed by starlight, stomachs lank. Charlie was hunched. The long ride yesterday had been hard on him, and the short night had not given him enough rest. Maybe today Charlie would have the good judgment to stay at the wagon.

Charlie said, ''That's a sweet little woman Law has got. Takes me back a long ways.'' He lapsed into silence, re-membering. ''I don't see that bein' short one more man would cripple us. You send Law home to stay with her till she's through her time.''

'"He needs the money, Charlie."

"Hell, I didn't mean to take him off of the payroll. I'll work his butt off later and make up for the lost time. You send him home, Hitch."

"I'd be tickled."

"And Hitch..." Charlie paused until Hitch prompted him with "What?"

"Hitch, if ever you see another little woman like that, don't you stand off next time. You grab her."

VI

IT WAS STILL DARK WHEN THEY CAME UPON
the horse jingler and rode into camp with him and the remuda. The jingler was uneasy, remembering how he had
been chewed on. He kept edging away from Charlie like a
colt shying away from some mean old stud.

The cowboys, gathered around the fire eating their breakfast, did not notice that the jingler brought company. Hitch
heard a familiar voice talking loudly.

Charlie rubbed a big hand across his mustache and started
to curse. "Asher Cottingham! Get rid of him, Hitch. I'd
sooner have smallpox in camp." Charlie turned back toward
the remuda.

Hitch walked closer to the fire and stopped to listen. Cottingham was talking small treason and didn't realize Hitch
was there. "Like I was tellin' you boys last night, I'm of-
ferin' you a chance to come along and join the strike. I'm
goin' on to some more wagons today. Any of you wants to
come along, you're welcome." He launched into a tirade
against rich old misers and greedy damnyankees getting

richer off of other men's hard labor. He declared that all the cowboys had to do was stand together and the ranchers would come begging.

Funny, Hitch thought, oddly detached from it all for a moment, how sometimes both sides of an argument will tend to sound the same. In a way, what Asher Cottingham said was akin to what Prosper Selkirk was saying in the ranchers' meeting except he had the gun pointed the other way. The blind striking out at the blind. What they both needed was a deep blue bruise across the breadth of the butt.

Hitch demanded, "Asher, you about finished your breakfast?"

Cottingham almost dropped his coffee in surprise. "Just about, I reckon."

Hitch clenched his fists. "Then finish it and let's see how fast you can get yourself out of this camp."

"Now looky here, Hitch, this ain't bein' hospitable."

"You got a lot of nerve to talk about hospitality after you come and eat a man's chuck and sleep in his camp and try to turn his friends against him. I've changed my mind; you ain't even finishin' that breakfast. You get yourself up and catch your horse."

Cottingham pushed to his feet, grumbling. "High-handed damned outfit if you ask me. I ain't done a thing to bother you, Hitch."

"Whatever hurts Charlie Waide hurts the Ws, and whatever hurts the Ws bothers the hell out of me. Clear out, Asher! Don't let me catch you on the Ws again."

Cottingham dropped his plate into Trump Tatum's washtub and stood by the wagonwheel a moment, trying to muster a show of defiance but unable to bring it off. "All right, I'm goin'. Any of you boys got any sense, you'll go with me." He received no response, and he added, "Everybody else is doin' it. If you don't want to work for thirty a month the rest of your lives, you better go with me."

Hitch took a couple of strides toward him. "I said move, Asher. Go while you can still ride a-horseback, else they'll have to come fetch you in a wagon."

With the jingler's help Cottingham caught his horse out of the remuda and rode away from camp. Law McGinty frowned critically at Hitch. "Treated ol' Asher a little rough, didn't you?"

"You want to go with him?" Hitch demanded. Law shook his head.

Charlie Waide walked up to the wagon, cursing softly. "In my own camp! I didn't think it'd come to my own camp."

"Nobody followed him," Hitch pointed out.

He ate breakfast and began to rope out horses for the cowboys. Law McGinty asked for a sorrel named Redfish. Instead Hitch perversely caught him a black. "You ain't rode ol' Stepper in a while; he needs a little work." Hitch's voice was testy as he watched Law bridle the horse, plainly biting back a retort. Hitch said, "Me and Charlie spent the night in Rascal's dugout. Kate's all right; her mother's with her."

That surprised Law.

Hitch said, "You should've known. In fact, you ought to've taken the old lady out there yourself. It's dangerous, Kate bein' alone."

"Wasn't much I could do, us bein' so busy here and all."

"This afternoon when we get through you take your stuff and go stay with her till the baby comes."

Doubt showed in Law's face. Hitch told him, "Don't worry; you'll stay on the payroll."

At the wagon Charlie watched Law top off the black, which seldom failed to pitch in the cool of the morning. He walked out to Hitch. "Thought you was lettin' Law go home."

"This evenin'. We can use him all day and still get him home by dark."

Charlie studied Hitch curiously. "You act like you're mad at him."

Hitch shook his head, not wanting to tell Charlie his suspicions. "Seemed to me like he was spurrin' that horse a little hard, is all."

Charlie seemed to sense that wasn't the real reason. "Have patience. He's young; he don't know how he's supposed to treat a woman."

He's old enough to use her, Hitch thought harshly. *He ought to be old enough to do her right.*

When they got through working cattle that afternoon, Law McGinty caught a horse that belonged to him rather than the company and tied his bedroll behind his saddle. Charlie Waide watched him, a little of a smile lifting his heavy gray mustache. "You take good care of that little woman now, Law."

"You bet I will, Charlie." Law rode away.

Watching him narrowly, Hitch rode to the wagon on his favorite gray horse. "Trump," he said to the bald cook, "you got any cold biscuits you was goin' to throw out, and maybe a can of tomatoes? I got a trip to make. May be a little while comin' back."

Puzzled, Charlie Waide asked, "What's up, Hitch?"

Hitch shrugged, wishing Charlie wasn't there.

"It's somethin' I can't tell you about, Charlie. Maybe there's nothin' to it. You'll just have to trust me."

"I've always trusted you, Hitch. But I think I ought to know."

"When I get back. Please, Charlie, this is one time you got to ask me no questions." Hitch took a quick cup of black coffee, accepted the sack Trump handed him and rode off in the direction Law had taken.

He took his time, not wanting to push too fast and unexpectedly ride up on the cowboy. He would have a hard time explaining himself. It was easy enough to follow Law's horsetracks, and Hitch had to be content with that awhile. It might be that Law would want to go home first to get shed of the bedroll and the other things he had brought. Yet on the other hand if he had come home to stay until the baby arrived, what excuse could he give to ride away almost immediately? No, the more Hitch thought about it the more likely it seemed that Law would go visit his woman friend first. Somewhere down the line Law would change direction.

Hitch intended to follow him till he found out who he was dallying with, then walk in and stomp salvation into him.

At dusk he began pushing, knowing that after a while the tracks would be difficult to follow, and he might lose Law. The tracks took a sudden turn to the left. Hitch missed them and had to ride back and hunt. He could tell by their depth that Law had started moving in a slow lope, making up time. Hitch touched spurs to Walking Jack. At length he could see Law in front of him, and he slowed. Law moved in an easy trot now, looking carefully from side to side as if searching for something. That struck Hitch as odd, for Law wouldn't find a woman out here. This was Figure 4 country.

At almost darkness he saw Law move to the left. Hitch swung down from the saddle to avoid being seen. In a few minutes Law moved into an easy lope and disappeared into a wash. He came out three hundred yards farther on, pushing a little bunch of cattle. In the poor light Hitch could not tell, but he guessed Law had fifteen or twenty head. Puzzled, he watched Law bring the cattle to a stop and ride around them gently, looking them over. Law started pushing the cattle back in the direction from which he had come.

He'll see me now if I don't be careful, Hitch thought. Walking, he led the gray down the lee side of a rise and ground-hitched him; the horse was trained to stay as if he had been securely tied. Hitch worked his way up the rise far enough that he could watch. The cowboy had the cattle moving now. Gently he rode in among them to push out one cow and calf, then drove the others away. The cow tried to rejoin the bunch, but Law gave chase in a run, throwing her and the calf so far back that she abandoned the effort.

Hitch remained still a long time, waiting for Law to get well past him. He rode back to look at the cow and calf Law had left behind. The cow wore Charlie Waide's W brand.

In the darkness Hitch could follow within fifty to a hundred yards. That was close enough to smell the dust, to hear the plodding hoofs, the occasional lift of Law's voice as he urged a tired calf into movement. They walked a long time, and gradually Hitch's suspicions began building to conviction, for he remembered the unaccountable unbranded calves he had found days ago. He resisted a growing impulse to confront Law. No, he had come this far; he would see it through.

By the stars he knew they were into the early hours of the morning when Law reined to a stop. The cattle drifted on, not realizing they no longer were being pushed. They were now well within the W lands, in an area over which Hitch's roundup crew had passed several days ago, an area that would not be worked intensively again until fall.

Law slouched in the saddle, leisurely rolling himself a cigarette. He raised his leg and laid it across the saddlehorn, showing he didn't intend to drive the cattle any farther. He sat there smoking, watching the cattle disappear in the moonlight.

Well, Hitch thought, *now is as good a time as any*. He pushed forward. Law didn't hear him until he was almost there. Instantly Law's leg came down from the horn and he whirled around, reaching for a pistol he didn't have. If he had brought it, he had it tied in his warbag.

"Stand easy," Hitch said. "It's me."

"Hitch!" Law said shakily. "What the hell you doin' out here?"

"Same question I was fixin' to ask you."

"I don't suppose you'd believe me if I said I was enjoyin' the night air?"

"I'd say you was enjoyin' the smell of unbranded calves a lot more."

"How long you been behind me, Hitch?"

"Long enough. I've trailed you since you left the wagon."

"And you seen me drivin' a little bunch of cattle that had strayed from home. That's what Charlie pays me for."

"I seen you cut out a W cow and her calf and leave them. I'm guessin' them other cows you brought was wearin' the Figure 4 brand, and maybe others. You wasn't bringin' them home; you was bringin' them off of their own range and onto Charlie's. You're sleeperin' them cattle, Law. You threwed them onto country that has already been worked. You count on them calves bein' weaned by their mammies this summer so they won't be followin' a branded cow. Then you can safely brand them with your LR.''

''A maverick's fair game, Hitch.''

''Not when you create them yourself.''

''You ain't seen me break no law. You didn't see me take them cattle to my own land. You didn't even see what brand them cows carried; for all you know, they're LRs, every one. You didn't see me lay a hand on one, brand anything or alter an earmark, did you?''

''No, I didn't.''

''So when you take tally, you didn't see a damned thing, Hitch. Looks to me like the best thing you can do is forget you ever followed me.'' He stared in curiosity. ''Why did you?''

''Suspicious.''

''Why?''

''I knew you hadn't been goin' home every time you said you was. I figured you was visitin' some woman.''

Law's eyes narrowed. ''When I got Kate? You must be crazy.''

''I thought you was. I figured I'd catch you with that woman and beat you within an inch of your life.''

''Damn you, Hitch, you ought to know I ain't low enough to cheat on Kate.''

''Wouldn't you call a man low when he steals off of people who trust him?''

''I've never stole from Charlie, not one time. I've made it a point to never take no W cows. Time or two I've picked up W cows in the dark, and when I seen my mistake I went ahead and put a W on their calves. But I sure ain't got no compunction about puttin' an LR on the rest of them. Big outfits like the Figure 4s and the Snaketracks, they don't own the land nomore than I do. A lot of them got their start maverickin' cattle; now they don't want nobody else to do it.''

"Brandin' an honest maverick is one thing; makin' a maverick out of another man's calf is somethin' else. There's no excuse for what you done, Law. Don't go tryin' to make up one."

"It's no skin off of your nose, Hitch. I don't see you got any call to give a damn."

"There's a lot you don't see, Law. But I think you know that I got to let you go from the Ws."

"Why, Hitch? I'll take a paralyzed oath that I ain't never took from Charlie. For Kate's sake if not for mine, you got to forget tonight."

"Forget what I seen with my own eyes?"

"You know me and Rascal ain't got enough cows yet to make a livin' for Kate, much less for the youngun comin'. Give me a little more time and I'll have enough cows that I don't need the Ws; I won't need *no*-body. But right now I got to have that job."

"You ought to've thought about that before. There's people who would hang you for no more than I've seen tonight. All I'll do is take you off of the payroll."

Law seemed to realize there was no use in pleading; he had too much pride for it anyway. "What you goin' to tell Charlie?"

"What you told me, and what I've seen."

"What'll I tell Kate?"

"Start with the truth."

"If the word gets out, there won't nobody in this country hire me."

"Somethin' else you ought to've thought about."

Resentfully Law said, "I always suspicioned you'd turn out this-away, Hitch, when the chips was down. Charlie gave you the boss job when by rights it ought to've gone to Rascal, or even to me; we'd been with him longer. You was always a little better than the rest of us, or thought you was. But there was one thing you didn't get."

"What do you mean?"

"You didn't get Kate. I could tell you wanted her, and I

made up my mind I'd get *something* that you couldn't have. I got busy and won her.''

''You married her out of spite?''

''That's how it started, only the joke was on me, Hitch. I come to love her. Why else you think I been sleeperin' these cattle, tryin' to build us a herd of cows so big that there couldn't nobody touch us or hurt us? It's *cows* that make a man big in this country, and I aim to have enough that Kate and the baby will have everything they ever need.''

Gravely Hitch said, ''What she really needs, you can't buy or steal. Go home to her, Law.''

Law nodded. Crisply he said, ''Don't be comin' around, Hitch. You won't be welcome.''

Hitch sat and smoked while he listened to hoofbeats trailing away. Anger had drained, leaving him a heavy sense of sorrow and disappointment. He almost wished he *had* caught Law with another woman. He thought of Kate, and he wondered what Law would tell her. Probably not the truth, not all of it. Whatever Law told her would probably be turned in such a manner as to be unfavorable to Hitch. Well, maybe that was best; she was Law's wife. A little twisting of the story might hurt her less than the unvarnished truth.

He reached the wagon a while before Trump Tatum was due to get up and start breakfast. He flopped on his bedroll, not bothering even to take off his spurs. He lay sleepless, staring at the morning star. When Trump got up, Hitch did too. The cook eyed him suspiciously but seemed to sense it was best to ask no questions. Hitch haunted the coffeepot until it came to a full boil. He poured in cold water to settle the grounds, then dipped out a cup and began to drink it, disregarding its scalding heat.

Pinching off sourdough in biscuit-sized chunks and putting it into a greased Dutch oven, Trump said, ''You look ready to challenge a wildcat to barehanded battle.''

''I already did.''

''Lose?''

"Everybody lost."

Trump ached with curiosity, but Hitch gave him no satisfaction. Presently Charlie Waide got up. He was usually the first to the coffeepot. He looked a moment at Hitch as he dipped his cup into the simmering brew and brought it out brimful. "I see you're back."

Hitch nodded.

"Want to tell me about it?"

"No, but I'll have have to sooner or later."

"You trailed after Law, didn't you?"

"Yep."

"Find the woman?"

Hitch glanced at him in surprise, for he had no idea the same suspicion had come to Charlie. Charlie said, "Hell, Hitch, I could read it in your face. A young feller like that, he gets to itchin'. I ain't so old but what I can remember how it was. I hope you kicked him good and proper."

Hitch studied his cup. "We was both wrong, Charlie. It wasn't a woman." Reluctantly, the words coming slowly like a calf dragged out of a herd at the end of a rope, he told what he had found. Charlie's cup sagged and the coffee spilled between his feet, but he was oblivious of it. His face fell; he took it harder even than Hitch had expected. Finally he asked, "What did you do to him?"

"Told him not to come back."

Charlie turned away in painful silence. Hitch waited a little, then said, "He swore he never branded none of your W cattle."

"Do you believe him?"

"I want to believe him."

Charlie rubbed his face. "That boy has worked for me since . . . Hell, I can't hardly remember when he *didn't* work for me. I just can't see what could've got into him . . ." He noticed that his coffee cup was all but empty. Stiffly he walked back to the pot, refilled the cup, then moved out away from the firelight, out into the darkness. Hitch looked down at his boots, wishing he hadn't followed Law, wishing he'd never had to find out.

The jingler came in with the horses, and the cowboys arose for breakfast. Charlie came back into the edge of the firelight but didn't take a plate. He stood silent and depressed, watching the men. When they started toward the remuda he told Hitch, "Don't catch me a horse. Ol' shoulder's hurtin' me some. I think I'll stay at the wagon this mornin' and rest."

Hitch nodded. "Sure, Charlie." He paused once on the way to the remuda and glanced back frowning. He hadn't liked the look in Charlie's face. The old man was not well.

The horses caught and the pitching ones topped off, the cowboys followed Hitch as he led them out on the morning drive. Rascal pulled in beside Hitch. "Charlie don't look good," he declared. "Somethin's chewin' on him. Meetin' go bad the other day?"

"He sure didn't enjoy it none."

"He didn't give in to them, did he?"

"You know Charlie better than that."

"I know he wants to be as big as the rest of them. I think it kind of gets his goat sometimes that them city-raised dudes are bigger than he is. If he was in enough of a tight, he might throw in with them."

Hitch rode a while trying to think what to say. "It ain't Charlie you better worry about, Rascal; it's Law." He watched Rascal's face for some sign that Rascal might know what he was talking about. He saw only puzzlement.

"What about Law?"

Hitch told him. Rascal's mouth dropped open. "There's bound to be a mistake someplace."

"There is. Law's the one that made it."

With Rascal, there was never any telling how he would react. His first response was an angry, "I ought to whip you!"

Hitch said evenly, "I'd sooner you didn't."

Rascal simmered down a little as the full gravity of the matter soaked in on him. "I didn't know about it, Hitch. I swear I didn't."

"I never thought you did."

"What'll we do now, Hitch? I can't make a livin' for the three of us—four, pretty soon—on the thirty dollars a month I'm gettin' here. You reckon Charlie'd pay a little more?"

"It's Law's mistake. You can't expect to carry the whole burden by yourself."

"Maybe if Charlie paid a little more we could still make it, Law takin' care of the place, me bringin' in money from the outside work."

"Charlie's already payin' as much as anybody in the country."

"But it ain't enough, thirty dollars a month."

"There's more cowboys gettin' twenty-five dollars than there is thirty."

"That don't make it right; it ain't right by a damn sight. Cows worth what they're worth today, we ought to be gettin' more."

"Charlie's always paid as much as the best."

"But them ranchers always work together. They keep the workin' man down."

Rascal was whipping himself into anger because of what had happened to Law and, perhaps without realizing it, was trying to twist the whole thing around to blame Charlie Waide for it. Hitch said, "Rascal, you and me and Charlie have always been friends."

"We was friends when Charlie didn't have nothin'. But when a man starts to get into big money he's apt to let old friendships go. Charlie's gettin' big, Hitch. Sure, I'll grant you that what Law done was wrong. But he done it on account of Kate and that kid. The few cows he might've took from the big outfits didn't hurt them; hell, the wolves will get ten times that many."

"It's still wrong."

"After this thing with Law, Charlie may not want me around nomore either. He may not trust me."

"I trust you. And if I do, then Charlie will."

"I don't know. I don't know nothin' no more."

Rascal pulled back to brood alone, and Hitch decided the best thing was to let him go.

VII

When the cowboys brought the day's gather to the roundup grounds at noon and went to the wagon in relays to eat, Charlie Waide stayed out of their way. He sat by himself in the shade of the wagon, his back against the wheel, his head down.

Hitch eyed him uncertainly a while, then finally went to him. "You sick, Charlie?"

Charlie never looked up, but his voice was wicked. "Hell yes, I'm sick. Sick of bein' bothered. Go on and eat your dinner. If I need you, I'll send for you."

Hitch retreated, looking back.

Trump Tatum spoke quietly, taking care to keep his back turned so Charlie wouldn't see his lips moving. "Hitch, if he'd done all the walkin' in a straight line this mornin' instead of around and around that wagon, he'd be halfway back to South Texas. You'd as well of shot Charlie in the gut as to've told him about Law."

Defensively Hitch said, "He had to know."

"Wisht you'd learn that there's times when a little lie or

two is head and shoulders above the truth. I'm glad I ain't cursed with bein' overhonest.''

Charlie watched the cowboys, his eyes half closed so nobody could read what was going on behind them. When the hands turned their horses loose at sundown, Charlie was still there, sitting against the wagonwheel. Hitch walked to him, stopped and waited to see if Charlie would speak. Charlie didn't.

Hitch asked, ''Want to see the day's tally?''

''Wrote it in the book, didn't you?''

Hitch nodded. Charlie said, ''Then I'll see it when I'm damned good and ready.'' Hitch could tell that was going to be the extent of the conversation. He went to the fire to see if Trump had coffee ready.

Trump rubbed his hands on a sack that he wore for an apron, and he grumbled, ''Next time you give him a jolt like that, I hope you take him with you instead of leavin' him on my hands.''

''He don't look any better than he did at dinner. Has he talked any?''

''Some.''

''About what?''

Trump shrugged. ''Ain't my place to say. He'll say it for himself in his own good time, I expect.'' Hitch didn't like the implication in Trump's eyes. He pressed for more, but the cook limped back to his work at the chuckbox. All Hitch would get out of him would be coffee.

After a while Trump called ''Chuck!'' The cowboys got their cups and plates and filed by the Dutch ovens and the coffee pot. Hitch waited till Charlie came, then followed the old man. Charlie took his plate and returned to his station by the wagonwheel. He gave Hitch no invitation, so Hitch went to his bedroll and sat there to keep an eye on the rancher. Charlie dabbled at his food a little, then gave it up and set the plate on the ground. He sipped his coffee, head slowly turning from one side to the other, eyes moving from one man to another and another and another.

Hitch suspected he could read Charlie's thought: *Which one next?*

The cowboys were uneasily aware of Charlie's quiet scrutiny, for by now the word had gotten around about Law. One by one they finished and dropped their plates noisily into the tub. When all were through, Charlie pushed to his feet. In an unusual breach of cowcamp etiquette he left his full plate and his cup lying in the boot-flattened grass. "Boys," he said gravely, "I got somethin' to say to you . . . all of you."

Hitch glanced at Trump Tatum. The old cook quickly turned to his chuckbox. With a sense of foreboding, Hitch joined the circle of men around the fire. Charlie was inside the ring, pacing a little and rubbing his shoulder. He kept it up a while after all the men gathered, as if dreading what he was about to say. He stopped, looking into the fire, his hand still on the bad arm. "Boys . . ." He paused to clear his throat. "Boys, durin' the war a Yankee officer damn near cut my arm off with a saber. I'd rather have had him cut off both arms than go on with what I'm about to say, but I'm forced to say it."

In the firelight Hitch could see cold anger in the old rancher's face, and he shivered.

Charlie said, "I always tried to treat every man right and to pay a fair wage. I always told everybody who would listen to me that I had me the best bunch of cowboys in the state of Texas. I said I could trust them to the ends of the earth, and I think I still could, with most of you. But by now you've all heard what happened last night.

"I know every one of you is different. I take it on faith that what Law done, he done by himself. I'll take it on faith that he spoke the truth when he said he never stole from me. But he did steal from neighbors after I promised them they had nothin' to fear from any man on the Ws. In doin' that he betrayed me as much as if he'd stolen my cattle. He compromised my word. You-all know the other ranches have put pressure on me to make me post the same rules they've got. I held off because I didn't think we needed them. Now Law has pushed me into a hole I can't climb out of. You-all know what the rules are. You can consider that from now on they're posted for the Ws!''

Hitch swallowed. ''All of them?'' He sensed a stir of disbelief among the cowboys, and of displeasure.

''All of them!''

''Not the cattle-ownership rule, Charlie.''

''That one most of all. If I'd of had it in the first place, we wouldn't of had this mess.'' Charlie looked at the men one at a time. ''Boys, I didn't think anybody would ever do to me what Law done. I've bent over backwards to let you-all run your own cattle, them of you who wanted to. We've even branded them for you and kept your tallies. But times change, and we all got to change with them.'' He seemed now to see anger stirring among the men. ''There won't no man get hurt. I'll pay fair market. I'll buy your brands right now at a fair figure and accept the book tally for the count. Or if you'd rather, you can go out and get you a bonafide bid from anybody else and I'll give you five dollars a head above his best offer. I want to be fair.'' He looked at Hitch. ''That is a fair way to price them, ain't it?''

''Charlie, most of us look on them cattle as a hedge against the future. How can a man put a price on his future?''

Half a dozen voices came up in quick and angry agreement. Hitch felt a sudden fear for Charlie's safety and moved protectively toward him, to help him if it came to that.

Rascal McGinty grabbed Hitch's arm. ''See there, Hitch, me and Law was tellin' you this was liable to happen. You promised it never would. Now you better see that he changes his mind!''

Hitch said, ''Charlie, let's back off and think about this.''

''I been thinkin' about it since mornin'. I ain't eaten all day for thinkin' about it. I keep comin' back to this; it's the only way it can be.''

''Charlie, there was promises made a long time ago.''

''And they been kept, every one, till Law broke his.''

Rascal McGinty flared. "We been loyal to you, Charlie. You're forgettin' what some of us went through to put you where you're at today."

"And you had *my* loyalty every month, when I paid you." Charlie's voice was gritty. "No, I ain't forgotten a thing. Maybe that's been the trouble: maybe I've remembered too long." What he said then was an echo of the argument Prosper Selkirk had used against him. "I've paid you a hundred times over for all that, Rascal. Don't keep hangin' it over my head."

Rascal leaned into Charlie's face. "You know we can't stand still for this. You better think on it some more."

"I've done my thinkin' and had my say. Anybody wants to sell me his cattle, I'll buy them. Anybody wants to leave, I'll pay him." Charlie pushed through the cowboys and walked back to the wagon. He fished in the chuckbox but found no whisky. He poured a fresh cup of coffee and carried it out into the darkness.

Hitch stared in numbed disbelief. A door which had stood open for fifteen years had been slammed shut in his face; it might never open again. Rascal grabbed Hitch's arm. "I been tellin' you, Hitch! See what you got us into? What you fixin' to do now?"

Defensively Hitch said, "I didn't get you into nothin'."

"If you'd kept your mouth shut about Law this wouldn't of happened."

"That wouldn't of been right."

"You call this right?"

"Give Charlie time. He's hurt and he's mad. Give him time."

Rascal demanded, "How much time is he givin' *us?* Wouldn't surprise me if he's wanted to do this all along and just waited for an excuse. He wants to be as big as them other ranchers—wants it so bad he can taste it. Think he'd let a bunch of two-bit cowboys stand in his way? Not when it comes down to the tawline he won't. The old Charlie we used to know is dead and buried . . . buried in ten years of cattle tallies."

Hitch trembled in anger. He found Rascal's grip so tight that it hurt his arm. "Turn me loose, Rascal."

Rascal dropped his hand but not his voice. "Asher Cottingham called it right. Them boys that've gone on strike, they're the smart ones."

"That's enough. I won't listen to no more of that talk."

Rascal pointed a finger in Hitch's face. "You *will* listen to it. A few days ago I told you I was afraid Charlie would sell us out. You said he wouldn't, and if he ever did you'd be the first to leave. I'm holdin' you to that, Hitch."

Hitch all but lost his breath. "You can't mean it."

"You're the one that said it. Now either you change Charlie's mind or you go out of here with us to join them boys on strike."

Hitch looked from Rascal to the other men, trying to assess this as flash anger that would pass. "You-all ain't serious."

Rascal looked around for support. "You see any other way? Be damned if we'll take this lyin' down."

"It'd be a mistake to leave here."

"It'd be a worse one to take this like a whipped dog."

"Give me time to talk to Charlie."

"Do it fast. Him nor nobody else is takin' me and Law's cows."

The angry rise of other voices convinced Hitch that at that moment the cowboys were stirred enough to follow Rascal McGinty into anything he took a notion to do. Maybe if Hitch could hold things together until the air stilled, something could be worked out. Hitch walked past them to the chuckbox and stared uncertainly into the darkness where Charlie had gone. Trump Tatum watched him sorrowfully.

"Hitch, don't you let Rascal stampede you."

Hitch turned to the crippled cook. "Trump, what'm I goin' to do?"

"I don't know. But whatever you do, take it slow."

"Reckon I can talk Charlie out of this?"

Tatum shook his head. "I watched it build all day, watched him whip himself into it. You know Charlie when

he's made up his mind; you ain't got the chance of a snow-
ball in hell to change it."

"If I don't, Rascal is fixin' to take the boys out of here."

"Don't you let Rascal rimfire you into somethin' you'll
wish you hadn't done."

"I *did* give Rascal my word; I counted on Charlie."

"Makin' a promise for somebody else was one mistake.
Don't compound it with another."

"I take it that if the boys went on strike, you'd stay
here."

Tatum grimaced. "I'm old and I'm boogered up in the
legs. I got no cattle, but I do have a job. If I lose what I
got here, I wouldn't have nothin'. Maybe Charlie's wrong,
but that don't mean he ain't my friend nomore, and it don't
mean the strike would work. Times are changin', Hitch;
nothin' stands still. Me and you, we're seein' the sun go
down on the old free times for the man on horseback.
Nothin'll stop that, not a strike or anything else. The old-
time cowboy is goin' the way of the buffalo. The big
ranches are marked, too, only they don't know it yet. That's
why a strike is useless. Win, lose or draw, we've all had
our day. The ranches . . . the cowboy . . . we're all fixin' to
go down together under all them planters, and all that wire.
I say hang onto what we can and be thankful we was here
to see it while it lasted."

"Looks like you've studied on this a right smart,
Trump."

"Kneadin' dough and boilin' beans leaves a man lots of
time to think. We're comin' into a time when the individual
don't count for much, Hitch. You'd just as well get used to
the idea."

Hitch grunted. "Stand back and take it like a sheep? No,
Trump, even if we lose, we need to fight and kick all the
way to the slaughterhouse." He caught sight of Charlie
standing alone beyond the wagon. Reluctantly he walked out
and stood beside the rancher a long time without speaking.
The silence between them was oppressive. Charlie said,
"Hitch, I didn't mean to include you in the cattle rule. Bein'

my wagon boss . . . my manager, even . . . you're high enough up that I can make an exception for you. Keep your cattle.''

''I been with these boys too long to accept a right they couldn't share in.''

Charlie said, ''Maybe some kind of workin' partnership, then.''

''That'd be the same, Charlie. It wouldn't be fair to the others.''

''There comes a time when a man has got to take care of himself. You better be doin' it.''

Hitch started to say, *Like you, Charlie?* but bit it off unsaid. He tried rolling a smoke and found his hands so nervous he spilled most of the tobacco. ''Charlie, you told me you wouldn't ever do this. I believed you. I put so much faith in you that I went and gave the boys my word. I went and promised them that if ever it happened on the Ws, I'd leave here with them.''

''You oughtn't to've told them that.''

''I gave my word, and I'm stuck with it.''

''Tell them you've changed your mind.''

Hitch shook his head. ''I keep *my* promises, Charlie.'' Instantly he wished he hadn't said it.

Moonlight revealed hurt in the rancher's deep-furrowed face. ''I'm protectin' my ranch. I've done what I had to do. Now, Hitch, I reckon you'll do what you think *you* have to. I'm sorry.''

Defeated, Hitch returned to the chuckbox. He got a fresh cup out of the drawer and poured himself more coffee. It was half grounds, but he gave little heed. He sipped it, aware that the cowboys were silently gathering around him. Rascal McGinty stood in the firelight, waiting for Hitch to speak. In time he gave up. ''Well, Hitch, didn't change him none, did you?''

Hitch shook his head.

Bitterly Rascal said, ''When a man gets money, he don't need old friends.''

Hitch warned, "Go easy on Charlie; I won't have you talkin' him down."

"How about it, Hitch? You takin' us on strike like you promised?"

Only then did Hitch notice the heavy grounds in his cup. For a moment he thought he would choke. His voice sounded unnatural to him. "Boys, I can tell that some of you have already made your minds up. For them that haven't, let me say this: the whole idea of this strike goes against my nature. Another thing, there's a damned big chance it won't work. If you lose the strike, you lose everything; there won't be nothin' left to salvage.

"Now, havin' said that, and sayin' that I think any man who goes on this strike is a droolin' idiot, I'll say one thing more: if you still want to go, I've given my word and I won't back down. I'll ride with those who want to go."

Rascal declared, "Well, *I* sure do, and I think everybody else does."

Rascal was overconfident. About half the cowboys quickly came to his side. To Hitch's surprise and somewhat to his satisfaction, the rest held back. Talking it was one thing, but actually rolling up their beds and leaving was something else.

Rascal began to browbeat the men who hesitated. He grabbed a cowboy's arm and tried to pull him into the group with the others. Hitch laid a heavy hand on Rascal's shoulder, half threatening, half cajoling. "Hush up, Rascal. Let every man decide for himself. I don't want no man goin' on this strike with me that ain't doin' it of his own free will."

In the end only a little more than half the crew decided to go, including the kid jingler. To those Hitch said, "One last time, this could turn out to be a fool's errand, and you may cuss the man who took you. Are you dead sure you want to do it?"

No one backed out. Hitch half hoped they would. He turned to the men who had elected to stay. "No hard feelin's. To be honest, I think you're the only smart ones in the bunch. You-all stand by Charlie. He'll be needin' you.''

He could see Charlie in the edge of darkness: the old rancher had worked back closer to the fire to listen. Throat tight, Hitch said, ''I wish it had never come to this.''

Charlie made no reply.

VIII

TO HITCH THE LONG RIDE TO TOWN WAS LIKE
going to a funeral. It was as if he were on his way to bury
an old friend, as if he had come to a bend in the road and
knew there would be no going back, ever.

He thought it a wonder that the jewsharp had not caused
men to be murdered. The kid horse jingler was twanging on
one as he rode, and it made Hitch wish Trump Tatum had
done him the bodily harm he had always threatened. Some
of the cowboys joked and cut up and watched their shadows
like happy buttons on their way to a big drunk at the end
of roundup. They were young, most of them, brimming and
busting in the pride of their new manhood.

Hitch took the lead and held it, for he had no wish to mix
with that funning crew. Walking Jack eased himself into a
trot that he could maintain all day without a misstep. Hitch's
eyes stayed on the gentle roll of the horizon line, but his
mind was on everything he had left behind him, on all that
lay wrecked by the damnfool stubbornness of other men,

dragging him into a vague cause for which he felt no particular allegiance.

A familiar voice said behind him, "Cheer up, Hitch; there'll be better days." Rascal McGinty shoved a whisky bottle at him.

"Where'd you get that?" Hitch demanded.

"Never been a day a man couldn't find a little whisky on the Ws if he really needed some."

"Charlie's always forbidden it."

"Charlie never was hurt by anything he didn't know. Drink up, Hitch; you look like a pallbearer."

"I feel like one." Hitch turned away. Rascal kept awkwardly pushing the bottle at him, then pulled back and left him alone. If anything, the offer of whisky made Hitch angrier than he already was. He felt like stopping Walking Jack and telling Rascal and the others they could go to hell in a handbasket for all he cared, that he was riding back to the W and Charlie Waide. But he didn't do it.

Once you make up your mind to something, Charlie had told him more than once, *stick by it and don't drive yourself crazy wondering if it's right. You'll find you're right more often than you're wrong, and a man who ain't wrong once in a while ought not to be trusted noway.*

Hitch had already chopped down the bridge. No use tugging over it like a cat trying to spark fight out of a dead mouse. But a black mood settled over him, a feeling that in a moment of pinched pride he had thrown away something he could never regain. He wondered if the same thoughts tormented Charlie Waide. Hitch was haunted by a notion that if he had held things off for another day or two, he and Charlie might have come to some agreement and avoided all this. He beat the palm of his hand against the saddlehorn, angry at Rascal and the cowboys, angry at Charlie, angriest of all at himself.

He wished it were a hundred miles to town; he dreaded getting there. But in time he could see the ugly spread of it along the red sandy banks of the river, and he saw two chuckwagons camped on a little hill at the near side of the settlement, the cookfires sending up curls of gray smoke. Large groups of men idled in the shade of tall old trees. Horses stood staked or hobbled on the grass. He didn't count, but he guessed there must be fifty or sixty head, at least, scattered for a quarter mile up and down the river. Some of the cowboys got to their feet and left the shade, moving forward to meet the newcomers.

Rascal McGinty gave a long loud yell and spurred into a lope. He waved his battered old felt hat over his head as he passed Hitch, like some Rebel soldier galloping into his first battle before he had time to learn what it was really all about. Most of the other W hands took after him, yelping like coyotes. Hitch pulled on the reins and ate dust. Walking Jack acted as if he too wanted to move faster. Hitch felt they would get there too soon as it was.

He didn't know exactly what a strike was supposed to look like, for he had never seen one, but he had not expected to see it resemble a Fourth of July celebration; he had pictured it more as an angry funeral. Everybody here seemed to be laughing and talking at the same time; it was like a horserace where everybody had won. Men he had never seen before shoved their hands at him. One big red-faced boy perhaps a year off of the plow declared, "The more the merrier. We'll have them big outfits beggin' us to come back inside of a week."

Hitch felt like a fool, but he decided the easiest thing was to agree. "Sure, a week." He listened to the whooping and shouting, and the thing he wanted to do most was to climb on top of a chuckwagon and yell louder than anybody, "Ain't there a man here that understands what he's done?"

There was no use dwelling on it; if they were fools, he was perhaps the biggest one, for he, at least, had some notion where all this might lead. He started looking for familiar faces. He saw Dan Truman of the Nine Bar; Hitch had had some pleasant set-tos of poker and had shared good whisky with him. Then there was Edson Biggs, one of the wagon bosses from the Snaketrack. Seeing them surprised him a little. He had considered them unlikely to get mixed up in

a short-deck game. Edson especially. Edson was a smart
fellow from Chicago or one of those other Eastern cities
where the money grew, and he had a tolerable amount of
schooling. He was a poor relation who had come out here
to keep books for a wealthy uncle and learn the ranch business. He and his uncle had come to a parting of the ways,
as kinfolks will, but not before Edson had rounded out his
education and had become a pretty fair practical cow man.
Some folks said if things went on the way they had started,
he would own his uncle's ranch someday and the uncle
would be working for him. Perhaps the uncle figured that
out for himself, which could be why Edson was on the
Snaketrack payroll when the strike came.

Guess Edson ain't any smarter than I am, Hitch consoled
himself.

He saw sadness in Edson Biggs's eyes. Edson was a man
who habitually shaved his chin clean every day of the world;
right now he had a three-or four-day stubble and didn't seem
to care. Edson said, "Can't say I'm glad to see you, Hitch.
I hoped the W would manage to stay out of it."

"So did I," Hitch told him, sober as a hanging judge.
"But I reckon we're all in it. Looks like some of the boys
are havin' themselves a time."

"Like raw recruits just joining the Army," Edson said.
He was a few years older than Hitch and could remember
the war from a soldier's point of view. Hitch always suspected Edson had worn the blue, but he never said and Hitch
saw no gain in asking him. Edson added, "The first shot
hasn't even been fired yet."

Dan Truman obviously shared Edson's misgivings. He
said, "It's a holiday to most of the boys. It ain't really sunk
in yet that they're out of a job and got no money comin'
in. They been paid off and got coin in their pockets. They
feel like they got the ranchers by the tail and they're fixin'
to tie a knot in it."

Hitch heard the shrill laugh of a woman. A cowboy—
stranger to him—came to meet the W riders, a whisky bottle

in one hand, a saloon girl in the other. It was easy to tell the pair of them had thrown the cork away.

Hitch didn't like it and said so. Dan told him, "Wait till night. There'll be a bunch of women up here from Gossett's and some of the other joints, or half the boys'll be down in town huntin' for them."

"It don't look like a strike to me," Hitch said. "Looks more like a spree."

"It is," Edson observed. "Most of the boys haven't figured out yet that there is a difference."

"How come you here, Edson?"

"Had a little cow herd started from when I was with my uncle. The company didn't give me any choice except to sell or leave. If there had been any alternative short of letting them have my cows, I wouldn't be here." He kicked angrily at a rock and sent it sailing. "I'll bet you-all are hungry. Come on over and we'll find you something at the Snaketrack wagon."

Hitch couldn't feature old John Torrington letting the Snaketrack cowboys use his wagon in a strike against him. Edson said he didn't, intentionally. When the trouble came the Snaketrack west division was camped not far from town, and every man in the crew decided to strike, including the cook. They couldn't go off and leave a good wagon deserted on the prairie. "He'll miss it by and by," Edson said. "Till then, we had just as well make use of it."

The other wagon belonged to a small rancher from north of the river. Beleaguered by big neighbors who made him feel as welcome on the range as a frog in a sourdough jar, he supported the cowboys and lent them his wagon to use as long as they needed it. "When this thing is over," Edson said, "we'll probably all be out there dogging him for a job."

This made Hitch feel no easier. "You don't sound confident."

Edson shook his head. "Are you?"

Word drifted down into town that the W cowboys had come. A while after Hitch ate, half a dozen men rode up on

horseback, flanking a big man in a buggy. Hitch knew Fant
Gossett by his bulk and by the wink of sunlight on his long
gold watchchain. That chain, Hitch always figured, gave the
cowboys a second look at their money.

Fant grinned like a possum. "Howdy, boys. Howdy,
Hitch. My, it's good to see you W boys come in thisaway.
Makes a man feel like all his good efforts ain't been in vain.
I wanted to come out and personally welcome every one of
you to town."

Hitch had gone to see a stage show that time he went to
Kansas City with Charlie Waide. The actors had used the
same broad gestures Fant Gossett did; Hitch wondered if
Fant had seen the show. The saloonkeeper shook hands all
around, teeth shining. "Brought you boys a little welcome-
to-town gift," he said, and reached into the buggy to fetch
out half a dozen whisky bottles. Some of his cheapest stuff,
but a cowboy never looked at a gift horse's teeth.

Fant's coat swept back, and he shoved his big hands into
the pockets of that broad vest. His voice went suddenly
grave. "Boys, I'm sorry it's come to this. You-all got a just
grievance here. You can be sure that ol' Fant Gossett is back
of you all the way. Anything you need, anything us folks
in town can do, just call on me and I'll see that you get it.
In the meantime my saloon is open to you any time of day
or night. If you find it closed, just come kick on my door.
Man my age don't need much sleep. We'll all stand together
shoulder to shoulder; we'll show these dollar-grubbin' big
outfits that it's *men* who'll run this country, not money.
They ain't goin' to buffalo you boys and they ain't goin' to
buffalo this town. Ain't nothin' we can't do if we all stick
together."

Dan and Edson didn't seem as impressed as the W cowboys. They had heard the speech before.

One of the horsemen with Fant was Asher Cottingham.
He looked like somebody had lighted all his candles. "Glad
you W boys done some thinkin' on what I told you. Even
ol' Hugh Hitchcock. Must've took a big lever to prize you

loose, Hitch. Bet ol' Charlie got a hankerin' after your little herd of cows, didn't he?''

Hitch knew no satisfactory way of answering him except by hitting him in the mouth, which seemed a pretty good idea the more he thought about it. Rascal sensed Hitch's mood and warned, ''Go easy, Asher.''

Cottingham went on, ''Too bad you-all didn't bring along a W wagon. We could've used it, as many men as we got to feed here. But I don't reckon ol' Charlie would cotton to feedin' a bunch of men that had done quit him. He'll cotton to it a lot less when we make him start payin' us a decent wage.''

''Us?'' Hitch bristled. ''You never worked for him, Asher. He don't owe you *any* wage. Come to think of it, you didn't have a job with anybody. Just who *are* you strikin' against?''

Cottingham gave him a glare that would wilt cotton. ''By God, I'm strikin' agin *all* of them!''

Hitch, Edson and Dan Truman sat at the Snaketrack wagon awhile talking about horses, about cows, about everything except what was really on their minds. After a time Hitch decided he couldn't shove that off anymore. ''I never been on a strike before. What're we supposed to do?''

Dan and Edson glanced at each other. ''Do?'' Dan asked. ''Are we supposed to *do* anything?''

''Well, it looks to me like we got reasons for bein' here, things we want. Shouldn't we be figgerin' out just what it is we *do* want so we can tell the ranchers what it'll take to get this thing over with?''

Edson studied a while. ''That's the way it ought to be done, only we haven't had anybody yet take the bit in his teeth and start.''

Dan Truman made a weak grin. ''Maybe what we been waitin' for is somebody to show us the way. You're the one to do it, Hitch.''

Hitch didn't want the responsibility, but he could tell that if somebody didn't start things moving they could be here till Christmas. They called in the men who were around

close and asked them to go out and fetch the others. After
a while they had perhaps seventy or eighty men.

Edson Biggs had a way with words, so Hitch and Dan
talked him into starting the discussion. "Boys," Edson said,
"some of us have been here several days already; others are
just now getting in. We've been at loose ends, and some of
us think it's time we tied everything together. We think we
should decide among ourselves just what kind of presenta-
tion we ought to put to the ranchers and then be about it so
this affair doesn't drag on any longer than necessary. We've
never all sat down and decided just what we want to ask
for."

What happened then should have been predictable, Hitch
decided, if he had stopped to think on it. Every man in the
bunch tried to talk at the same time. Every man wanted
everybody else to hear him out. The sudden rise of agitated
voices caused two tied horses to break their reins and trot
away. It seemed to Hitch the only men there who knew what
they were doing were the two who went to catch the horses.

The hubbub didn't settle, and Edson Biggs became flustered. Sitting down, he told Hitch impatiently, "You wrestle
with them."

Hitch had always been able to handle men at work, on
the roundup or around headquarters, but he had never tried
to handle a large group like this which included many men
he didn't know. It took him a few minutes to get them quieted down to listen to him. Most of them seemed to be
trying to convince the ones around them that they had the
whole problem figured out.

"Boys," Hitch said when he thought they could hear him,
"let's do first things first. We don't know how long we're
goin' to be here, and we don't want any man hungry. We
better pool some resources and build up a fund to feed ourselves." He thought this down-to-earth matter might pull
them together awhile. He knew that up to now nothing had
been done to organize a commissary. A bunch of the men,
he was told, had chipped in various amounts, and a few
people in town had brought out food. "Now," he said, "it

ain't fair for some to carry the heavy load. Most of us are goin' to eat pretty much the same, and everybody in the strike ought to put in the same. How about ten dollars apiece for a chuck fund? Ain't hardly no way a man can eat ten dollars worth of food in less than a couple of weeks.''

He felt that if they didn't take up that collection pretty soon, some cowboys might not have ten dollars left. The town was full of people who spent their lives seeing to it that a fool and his money were not long a burden to each other.

Most of the cowboys knew Edson Biggs, and it was quickly decided that he should take charge of the chuck fund. It could be locked in a safe in town and tapped as needed to keep the outfit in beef and beans.

That done, they went back to the first question, what to ask of the ranchers. For what they accomplished, they had just as well have been out racing horses on a grass flat. It seemed that almost every cowboy put in his two cents' worth, and a few like Asher Cottingham made it nearer a dollar-and-a-half. The wrangle went on for a couple of hours and seemed nowhere near a solution.

Hitch listened, frowning deeply. He had given up trying to talk. It became increasingly evident to him that many of the men were not even sure why they were here. They were dissatisfied, but the reasons for that dissatisfaction were so many and so varied that it was difficult to boil them down to a few clear and negotiable points. In frustration it was understandable that the men dwelt more and more upon the one point common to them all: a desire for more money.

Many tired of the argument and quietly slipped away until less than half the original crowd remained. The question was no nearer settlement. Hitch said finally, ''Let's quit for tonight. Let's think it over amongst ourselves and make a fresh run at it tomorrow. Maybe we'll be thinkin' straighter.''

That turned out to be a forlorn hope, for when the cowboys gathered after breakfast it was largely a repetition of what had already been said. Some had spent the night in town and were none too clearheaded. But gradually most of the loudest got themselves talked out and became more inclined to listen, or at least to keep quiet. Complaints against the ranchers boiled down mainly to two: wages and the written rules of conduct.

Rascal McGinty had had himself a royal time in town all night, and his eyes matched his uncombed red hair. "Boys," he said, his voice rough-edged from celebration, "there's more to it than just money." Asher Cottingham said money was the main thing *he* was after and pressed Rascal to be specific. Rascal couldn't put his feelings into words. "They're changin' things too much," he said. "They're changin' things that ought to've been left alone."

Some of the cowboys kept pushing him, and Rascal rubbed his hand across his face and his broken nose, trying to think clearly. "Well, now, you take that cattle rule. Main thing to me is they don't want no workin' cowboy to accumulate anything that would make him independent. Them owners, they got their pile made, and they want to keep the rest of us down to where we'll always have to work for them. I'd go on workin' for the wages I been gettin' if I knowed they'd let me keep ownin' cattle."

That roused a storm of argument. Asher Cottingham declared, "Damn it, Rascal, that's no more than I ought to've expected from you. Give an ordinary cowhand a few head of cattle and already he's thinkin' like an owner. You'd be willin' to take less money, and you'd hold down the rest of us who ain't lucky enough to own any cattle like you do."

Rascal's face reddened, but Asher Cottingham didn't let that faze him. "I can see where you rich fellers with cattle might be upset, but most of us here ain't got no cattle and don't ever expect to have no cattle. For us the big problem is money. That's what we're goin' to ask them ranchers for, is more money."

Rascal got awfully redheaded for a minute or two after Cottingham accused him of selfishness. It looked as if Hitch might have to step in and break up a fight.

The wrangle went on a long time. In the end the cattle

rule somehow got lost in the dust and the smoke. There simply were not enough cattle owners among the cowboys. Those like Hitch and Rascal considered themselves poor, but to the men who had no cattle at all, they were too rich to be concerned about.

Edson Biggs said, "Asher, a little while back you yourself said there was more to it than money. There was the whole set of rules and of rancher attitude toward employees . . . there was the question of respect."

"By God," Cottingham declared, "when they have to pay us enough, they'll respect us."

The fevered discussion finally got down to a question of how much the strikers should ask for. Asher Cottingham said, "A hundred dollars a month!" That sounded good, and others took up the cry.

Edson Biggs had a bookkeeper's mind; he argued against that figure. "Boys, it's not realistic. It takes three cows to bring a hundred dollars, and there's never been a time a cowboy's labor was worth three cows a month."

Cottingham declared, "Maybe it's been worth that much; we just never had guts enough to ask for it before."

Biggs said, "Asher, you're supposed to shear the sheep, not skin it. If we break these ranchers, who will we work for?"

"I don't give a damn," Cottingham said. "There ought to be a law against them havin' so much anyway. If I was runnin' this country there couldn't no man have more than ten cows apiece. Then maybe we'd all have a chance."

Cooler men began to speak up, and some cowboys who had initially backed Cottingham seemed inclined to scale down the asking price. It settled awhile at a sullen seventy-five. Hitch saw they were angering at Edson, so he took up the argument in Edson's stead and convinced most of them that seventy-five was still too much to hope for. Somebody suggested a compromise on fifty. A lot of the cowboys seemed to regard that figure as satisfactory. Hitch thought it unrealistic.

He said, "Most outfits in this country are payin' hands

twenty-five. A few pay thirty. We'll have snow three feet deep the Fourth of July before any of these ranches'll agree to double a man's salary. It's one thing to take a firm stand for somethin' reasonable; it's another to ask for somethin' plumb out of sight.''

Cottingham was not convinced they couldn't get more. ''We got them ranchers where the hair is short. We can get anything we want if we'll all stick together.''

Hitch cleared his throat and spat. ''Use your head for somethin' besides that hat, Asher. A good many cowboys didn't come with us; they're still workin'. Soon's the word gets out there'll be more men comin' into the country lookin' for the jobs we left behind. We ain't got *that* much leverage. Best thing is to get ourselves a settlement and go back to work before too many job hunters come driftin' in.''

Cottingham clenched his fists. ''We can go out to them ranches and make them other boys wish they *had* come with us. We can patrol the roads and throw back anybody who tries to come in from outside. If we bloody a few heads, folks'll sit up and take notice.''

Hitch spat again. ''For a man who talks all the time about his own freedom, you don't seem to give a damn for anybody else's.''

''I say there's nobody else gives a damn about us; we got to take care of ourselves.''

''There's always two sides to an argument. I figure if we've got a right to strike, other people have got a right not to strike.''

''The other man ain't *got* no side when we're in a fight. The hell with *him*; the only thing that matters is to win.''

Fifty dollars was as low as the majority was willing to go. Hitch had a cold feeling in the pit of his stomach; they would never get it. But perhaps the ranchers would make a counter offer and somehow reason would prevail to get this wagon out of the mud. A vote was taken and the decision was almost unanimous: fifty dollars.

Edson Biggs was given the task of tailoring the demand into good legal terms that would seem to give the whole thing a courthouse flavor and perhaps impress upon the ranchers that they were not dealing with a bunch of naïve, unschooled cowpunchers. He wrote:

> We the undersigned cowboys of Canadian River do by these presents agree to bind ourselves into the following obligation, vis—First that we will not work for less than $50 pr. mo. and we furthermore agree no one shall work for less than $50 pr mo. after 31 of Mch. Second. Good cooks shall also receive $50 pr mo. Third. Anyone running an outfit shall not work for less than $75 pr. mo. Those not having funds to pay board after Mch 31 will be provided for for 30 days.

Reading over Edson's shoulder, Hitch said, "It's too much money; it's just too damned much."

Edson Biggs laid down his pencil and flexed his writing hand, frowning at some of the cowboys who lay in the shade of the trees, or hunched over a game of poker on a saddle-blanket. "I'll grant you, most of these men have been underpaid for their work and the hell they go through. But if you paid every man just what he's worth, there are a few who wouldn't be making twenty dollars."

"And they," Hitch said, looking for Asher Cottingham, "are generally the ones that holler the loudest."

He studied Edson's handiwork and decided it said what the cowboys had voted to say. But it said nothing about the underlying causes aside from money that had brought the conflict to the surface. It said nothing about the fact that the cowboy considered himself something unique, a breed apart and perhaps a little above the common man. He considered himself the instrument which had brought this country up from the buffalo range and made it flourish. The document said nothing about dignity, about pride, about respect. It said nothing about unwritten traditions and the unspoken trust which seemed violated when ranch owners felt it necessary to start writing down guidelines for a cowboy's conduct and slapping him in the face by posting them on a wall, making him seem irresponsible and less than a man, making him appear somehow unworthy of trust. But maybe these were things you couldn't adequately put into words, couldn't hope to capture on paper.

One by one as they got around to it the cowboys came and affixed their names. Somehow then, with all those signatures on it, the thing seemed more like a real legal document. In its own small way it was sort of a declaration of independence.

It was up to Edson to sit down and make enough copies by hand to go around to all the ranchers. While he did that, Hitch went to town to make a duty call on cowboy Joe Sands, still recuperating from his broken leg in a shack Fant Gossett was furnishing, for a fee.

He lay on a cot, the splinted leg propped. He shoved his hand at Hitch. They howdied and shook and swapped yarns awhile. Some of the W hands had been in to see Joe already, and they had thoughtfully carried him some whisky which still sat on a table unopened. Joe Sands was not much inclined in that direction.

When Hitch got through telling him about all the friends he hadn't seen, and about the horses he had left behind, Joe said, "I don't know much about this strike thing, Hitch, but if you'd like me to join up with you I will. Can a man strike with a broken leg?"

"You've got no cattle, Joe. Are you sore at Charlie Waide?"

Joe shook his head. "Charlie's always been a friend to me."

"Then you stay right where you're at. Stay on the payroll; don't be tippin' over the chili pot. You need Charlie and he needs you."

As Hitch stood up to go, Joe said, "Hitch, there's an awful lot happenin' these days that I don't understand."

Hitch frowned. "Neither do I."

Edson Biggs had finished making all the copies when Hitch returned to the campground. His right hand was so stiff from writing that he couldn't hold a coffee cup with it.

A group from each outfit got together and decided who would take a copy to each ranch owner or manager. It was important that they choose men the ranchers might respect. Charlie Waide was Hitch's responsibility.

Hitch had rather take a rawhiding, but he went. First stop was Trump Tatum's chuckwagon, where cowboys told him Charlie had gone on to another camp. Some of the men from the other two divisions had left their wagons to join the strikers in town, so Charlie had regrouped what men he had left into only two divisions, both sadly short-handed.

"How is Charlie?" Hitch asked Trump Tatum.

The old cook was cool. In his view Hitch had betrayed Charlie. Perhaps even worse, Hitch had asked for Trump's advice and then had not followed it. He answered curtly by repeating Hitch's own question. "How is Charlie always? Same as ever, only more of it." Whatever that meant. Hitch looked regretfully at Trump, knowing he had lost a friend.

He knew he would lose other friends before this was over.

He found Charlie with the second roundup crew in the midst of the herd and cutting out cattle, something he hadn't done much in recent years. He had let younger men do it, for a cutting horse could move swiftly and shift direction in the batting of an eye, spilling a rider. Charlie saw Hitch, but he didn't quit until he had finished pairing up cows and calves to his satisfaction. He let Hitch wait on horseback at the edge of the herd for the better part of an hour.

He rode out slowly and raised his hand in a half-hearted salute. He appeared sad, much the way Hitch felt. They looked at each other, a strain between them. Charlie said, "You come back to work?"

"No, Charlie, I come to deliver this." Hitch handed him the strike declaration, careful so the paper flapping in the breeze wouldn't booger Charlie's horse and perhaps cause him to be thrown. At Charlie's age he didn't need that. Charlie held it at arm's length, face furrowed. He rubbed a hand across his big gray mustache and complained that it didn't seem like anybody could write worth a damn anymore, that a letter was no good if written in such a poor hand that a man couldn't read it. He would not have admitted that the trouble was his eyes. "You'll have to tell me what's in it."

Hitch told him.

"Wisht I could read it," Charlie said, "but it wouldn't make no difference anyway. The ranchers have all agreed they won't treat with any of the strikers; every cowboy who went on strike is fired for good. We've agreed that none of us will ever hire any man who took part, whether he was from our outfit or another. We're through with all of them."

Hitch had more or less expected that, but it hit him a little.

Charlie said, "Hitch, I'll make one exception, *you*. If you'll come back, you still got a job. And you can keep your cows."

The temptation was strong to grab Charlie's hand. Hitch said, "I never did want to leave here in the first place. Between you on one side and Rascal and them on the other, I found myself in a bind to where I couldn't do anything else."

"Will you come on back?"

Hitch wanted to shout *yes*. He came so near doing it, he didn't know exactly what stopped him. But something did. "Charlie, would you extend the same offer to the other boys?"

"I can't."

"I'd never be satisfied in my own mind if I took somethin' the other boys couldn't have."

"I've made my agreement with the ranchers."

The pain then was heavy; Hitch wished he hadn't come. "And I've made mine with the boys, Charlie. Looks like we're both stuck with somethin' we didn't want."

When Hitch returned to the strike camp, he recognized the old spring wagon, the tongue dropped slantwise in the badly beaten grass. Rascal McGinty strode out to meet him, all grin. "Looky who's joined up with us, Hitch."

Law McGinty didn't hump himself any to come forward.

He hadn't unbent in his feelings about Hitch firing him from the W. Because Law didn't offer his hand, Hitch didn't risk embarrassment to himself by trying to push his own hand forward. Hitch said, "Law," and Law said, "Hitch."

Rascal repeated, "He's come to join up with us."

Hitch had heard him; he wished he hadn't. "You think you ought to?" he asked Law. "Seems to me like you should be stayin' out yonder with Kate till she's delivered."

"Kate's had herself a boy."

Rascal laughed. "You hear that, Hitch? A boy! Law says it's the spittin' image of its daddy. That makes me an uncle, Hitch."

Hitch looked dubiously at Law. "She's doin' all right, is she?"

"Her mother is goin' to stay awhile, and you know how hard that old lady is to get along with. I felt like I could come over here and join up with the boys. The more there are of us, the stronger we'll be."

Hitch couldn't think of a thing that had gone right, and it wasn't getting any better. "Law, I ain't sure you got any place here. You were out of a job before the strike ever commenced. You can't strike against somebody you wasn't even workin' for."

"Your fault, Hitch. I figure my place is here with the boys. I'm payin' my way; even brought a beef." He jerked his thumb toward two halves of a beef hanging from a tree limb, one uncovered, the other wrapped in a bloodstained tarp.

Hitch had an uneasy feeling. "One of your own?"

"Was when I finished skinnin' him. I don't reckon ol' Selkirk will starve because of one beef. Especially when this one had a broken leg."

"How'd he break it?"

"When I roped him."

Hitch felt he ought to hit Law, but he didn't see how it would do anybody any good easing his own feelings a little. He turned to Rascal, thinking Rascal should be able to see the wrong in this for himself, but Rascal simply grinned. He turned back to Law. Sharply he said, "Right or wrong, we're into this strike with all we got. You bein' here puts a cloud over the whole bunch of us. Bringin' a stolen beef makes it worse. They're *wantin'* to call us thieves, some of them."

"The beef is here now. We can't just put the hide back on that critter and turn it out on the grass again."

It never did set well with Hitch to see meat go to waste; in the early days before the bonepickers scavenged the prairies, it had hurt him to look at the scattered buffalo bones and think of all the meat rotted there years ago because a man had a market for the shaggy hides. He said, "But if we're goin' to eat it, we're goin' to pay for it. Since you killed it, it's your place to pass the hat and take up a collection to pay Selkirk for it."

He reached up and took Law's hat from his head and handed it to him. Law hurled it to the ground. "The hell I will!"

Hitch picked it up and handed it back to him, crown down. "That's the way to hold it. The money stays in better." He dropped in a four-bit piece for a starter.

Law seemed likely at first to fight, but Rascal McGinty dropped a couple of coins in the hat, by that silently telling his brother to get moving. Sullen, Law moved among the cowboys, and most dug into their pockets. Presently he was back, eyes still angry. He shoved the hat at Hitch. "That ought to be enough."

"Law, you done right well." Hitch spilled the coins onto a blanket spread on the ground and handed Law's hat back. Counting, he found almost thirty dollars. Hitch decided to make up the difference from the chuck fund and turn it in for a check that they could send the Figure 4. He wondered which would have given Selkirk the most satisfaction, getting the money or not getting it and thereby proving to his own satisfaction that the cowboys were the motley thieves he had been telling himself they were.

IX

MOST OF THOSE OLD-TIME RANCHERS LIVED by the adage that idle hands were the devil's workshop and saw to it that the devil had very little show with their cowboys. It pinched old John Torrington, not having all the help he wanted; it galled him to see so many men idle when he had work that needed doing.

Idle they were. As time became heavy on their hands, some cowboys spent most of the day and night down in town, keeping the cash flowing into Fant Gossett's till, and those of the red-lantern places in Hogtown.

The strike notice carried to John Torrington by two of his former cowboys was like a sharp goad used against an angry bull. He beat them back to town to wring out the sheriff, raising hell and putting a chunk under it. He could not see why the law did not arrest the whole bunch and throw them in jail. The sheriff, cowed by the fire in those sharp eyes, tried to explain that the jail had not been built that large; the county had been trying to keep taxes down for the ranchers. Anyway, he had to wait until the cowboys broke a law.

"They're vagrants," old Torrington stormed for everybody in town to hear. "A man don't have a job, he's a vagrant. You go up there and arrest them or you'll be huntin' a new job too!"

A rumor had already gotten out that the sheriff was considering getting himself some long heavy chains and locking the cowboys to them, but he couldn't find that many handcuffs if he requisitioned from every Ranger west of the state capital.

Given no satisfaction by the sheriff, John Torrington rode up the hill with saddlegun in his lap to hurl the challenge where it belonged. It was said he had once ridden boldly into a Comanche camp to recover stolen horses; age had not dulled his sharp edge. He was flanked by four loyal cowboys, all pushing to keep up with him. He demanded fiercely, "Who's in charge of this heathen outfit?"

Hugh Hitchcock had seen him coming and had drifted down partway to meet him. "Nobody, Mister Torrington, and everybody. These are all free men." Torrington's narrowed eyes swept the crowd in contempt. "Free of work, free of responsibility. Bunch of damned thieves and radicals."

Hitch studied the four cowboys. Next to Torrington sat Slant Unger, whose nickname came from a misshapen shoulder; people said he had suffered it when a horse was shot from under him in a Mexican border battle fought for John Torrington. Two other cowboys Hitch knew by sight but not by name. Beside Unger sat Tobe Ferris, a Negro cowboy whose mother Torrington had owned before the war. Some people claimed they could see a resemblance to Torrington in some features of Tobe's dark face. Hitch had always regarded that as overactive imagination.

Torrington's hard gaze cut into Hitch. "Well, Hitchcock, Charlie Waide was sure as hell wrong about you."

Hitch said, "Somethin' you wanted, Mister Torrington?"

"Damned right! I want all you loafers down off of this hill, and I want you off in a hell of a hurry. This is my land you're squattin' on, and I won't have it. It's all my land, right up to where the town starts. If I'd had any sense I'd of never let them put the town there either.''

Hitch wanted to avoid provocation. ''As I remember it, Mister Torrington, this here land still belongs to the state. You just been usin' it for your cattle. You got no more claim on it than anybody else.''

''I claim it by right of first possession. Wasn't nobody here when I come but a few Mexican sheepherders and a remnant of Indians with the butt end out of their britches. I took it and I'm keepin' it. I want you off.''

Hitch made his voice sound calm, though he was much less than that. ''I take it you've already talked to the sheriff. What does he say?''

''Never mind the sheriff; he's just a county employee. I do my own talkin'.''

Hitch looked around to be sure of his support. He could tell by the strikers' faces that he had it. ''Then I reckon we'll just have to tell you *no*, Mister Torrington. Respectfully, of course, but *no*. Anything else you wanted?''

Torrington pointed. ''You got a Snaketrack chuckwagon up here. It belongs to me, and I'm takin' it.''

''We been keepin' it for you. You're welcome to it. You'll find some supplies gone from it. We'll pay you for those.''

That threw the old man off for a moment; he hadn't expected it. His sharp eyes searched the crowd, fastening briefly on each striking Snaketrack hand he saw. ''There was a team of mules with that wagon. Where they at?''

''Grazin' along the river. They'll be easy to find.''

''Some of these men rode in here on company horses. I'm gatherin' up every Snaketrack horse I lay my eyes on.''

''They're yours, Mister Torrington.''

The old man seemed somehow disappointed. Perhaps, Hitch thought, he had hoped for physical opposition that would give him an excuse to cut the dogs loose. He turned to the cowboys on either side of him. ''Go get the stock.''

Hitch said, ''Like to step down and have some coffee while you wait?''

Torrington's gray beard seemed to bristle. "Amongst *this* crowd? I wouldn't touch it."

He sat there alone and defiant in the midst of the opposing men while his cowboys spurred down the river and began working through the scattering of horses. It was evident he meant his presence to be a challenge; he seemed to hope someone would make a move against him. He wore an old six-shooter on his right hip, and he continued to hold the saddlegun ready.

The crowd of striking cowboys stayed, staring expectantly at Torrington or talking quietly among themselves. In a little while Unger and Ferris brought the mules. The other two men remained on the river, holding the horses they had gathered.

The striking Snaketrack cook moved to help harness the team, but Torrington shouted at him, "You ain't workin' for us no more; you keep your grubby hands off of them mules!"

When the mules were hitched to the wagon, the Negro tied his horse on back and climbed up into the seat, ready to move. Slant Unger took his place beside Torrington, his eyes making a blanket challenge for any in the crowd to contest him.

Torrington looked back at Hitch. "I'm tellin' you, Hitchcock, I want all of you down off of this hill."

Law McGinty had walked up behind Hitch. Law said, "You heard what Hitch told you, so you just chase yourself up a stump, old man. There ain't nobody here afraid of you."

Hitch warned Law, "Stand easy."

Torrington's gray whiskers worked up and down. His eyes narrowed dangerously. "Seems to me I know you, cowboy, but I can't quite call your name."

"It's Law McGinty."

Torrington's gaze was so severe that Law flinched. "Oh, yes," the old man said, "you was the one caught sleeperin' cattle. I remember you now. And·I'll keep on rememberin' you." He looked back at Hitch. "You're in bad company,

Hitchcock. But I reckon it's of your own choosin'." His voice came up. "Now listen to me, every one of you! If the sheriff won't do nothin' about you, there's other ways. There's men left over from the Lincoln County war in New Mexico that'll do anything for hire. I bet it wouldn't take more than five-six of them to chase the whole damned bunch of you clear into Indian Territory. You think on it now, do you hear? You think on it!"

As Torrington rode away and the chuckwagon trailed dust down the hill, Dan Truman and Edson Biggs moved to Hitch's side. Biggs said worriedly, "That old cougar means what he says, Hitch."

A chill played up Hitch's back. "Even if he does, it'll take him time." At the edge of camp he saw a woman a cowboy had brought up with him. Hitch said, "It may not take guns to bust up this outfit. Hard whisky and easy women will undo more cowboys than Torrington ever could."

Turning, he noticed a man talking to Law McGinty and Asher Cottingham. He looked like another cowboy—the working clothes, the battered felt hat, the boots and spurs—but Hitch knew he was not one of the striking group. "Edson," Hitch asked urgently, "is that who I'm afraid it is?"

Edson frowned. "That's Cato Bramlett."

Hitch cursed. Cato Bramlett carried the reputation of being the worst cow thief in the Texas Panhandle, working between here and the sanctuary of the New Mexico line. Hitch started to move toward him. Dan Truman caught his arm. "You better watch him; he's dangerous."

"In more ways than one."

Law and Cottingham watched Hitch curiously, but Hitch's eyes were on the thief. "Bramlett, I want to talk to you."

Bramlett's eyes showed instant challenge. "Talk away."

"You don't belong in this camp."

"I got friends here."

"If old Torrington saw you—and them sharp eyes see everything—you know what he must've thought."

Bramlett began to stiffen. "Maybe you'd like to tell me what he thought."

Hitch angered, for he sensed that Bramlett was playing with him. "Torrington wants to believe we're a band of thieves. You bein' here makes that easy."

"You callin' me a thief?"

"You got that reputation."

Bramlett took a step forward, then stopped. Dan and Edson had moved up on either side of Hitch, and other cowboys silently came in behind him. Bramlett blustered, glancing back at Law and Cottingham. "This the man in charge up here?"

Nobody said anything, so Bramlett surmised the answer himself. "Well," he said, "then you boys are worse off than I thought." He got on his horse and rode down the hill.

Law McGinty turned angrily. "Now, Hitch, what did you go and do that for?"

"If you don't know, then it won't do no good for me to tell you."

Two men had been appointed to deliver the strike declaration to Prosper Selkirk at the Figure 4. They returned with the paper still in their hands. Angrily they related that they had ridden out to Figure 4 headquarters and had been met at the office door by Selkirk, bolstered on both sides by cowboys who had remained with him. Selkirk had refused to touch the declaration or allow the messengers to read it to him. Face red and voice embittered, he declared, "I will not treat with saddle tramps and chuckline riders who try to justify their idleness by calling it a strike, with men who demand more than a day's work is honestly due. It is the employer's duty and right to affix wages and conditions of work. Any employee dissatisfied with the terms is always free to leave. And you men . . . if you're ever seen on Figure 4 land again you will be considered trespassers and may very well be shot!"

Selkirk sent four men with rifles to escort them off the property in a fast trot.

The news spread through the strike camp like a grass fire. Hitch listened to the sullen messengers with Dan Truman and Edson Biggs. "It's no more than we ought to've expected," he said. "We didn't figure Selkirk would invite them in for a drink."

One of the messengers said, "They got some new hands out there. I seen men I never seen before."

Asher Cottingham jabbed his finger at Hitch. "I been tellin' you we ought to cut off the roads."

Rascal McGinty smacked his right fist into the palm of his left hand. "It's an insult, Hitch. It's a rotten insult to every cowboy that ever lent life and limb to these ranches. We're welcome as rain when they can use us and throwed off like old socks when they can't."

Hitch saw the ugly mood and tried to temper it gently. "You never worked for the Figure 4s a day in your life, Rascal."

Rascal was not to be placated. "Him and his kind . . . it ought to be open season on them big-city highbinders like on rattlesnakes and centipedes. They ought to be hung up by the thumbs."

Hitch kept trying to pour cold water on the threatening talk. "We didn't none of us expect them to take this strike and like it. In Selkirk's place we'd kink our tails a little bit ourselves."

Cottingham declared, "I told you the day you come here, Hitch, they'd be hirin' new hands to take our place. I say we ought to go patrol this country and throw all them stray cowboys out. Time we splash a little blood around, they'll stop comin' in."

Curtly Hitch told him, "The man who tries that is goin' to have to whip me first. Them others, they got rights too."

Cottingham cursed vigorously. "God damn a man's who's always talkin' about somebody else's rights! Hard to tell half the time whose side you're on, Hitch. It's *us* we got to worry about. Everybody else can go to hell!"

The atmosphere in camp became so thick it was a relief that night when Rascal and Law and a sizable bunch of men decided to go down into town to look for refreshment. "Time they've bought a few rounds at Fant Gossett's," Hitch told Edson Biggs, "they'll have more to worry about than cussin' Prosper Selkirk. I'm goin' to hit the soogans and catch some sleep while it's quiet around here."

He figured when they came in they would make enough noise to rouse Boothill, but he never heard a thing. He slept through till the rising sun hit him in the eyes. Pushing the blankets back, he raised up, put on his hat, then his shirt and his britches, and finally started feeling under the edge of the tarp for his boots, where he had stuck them to keep them from being wet by the dew.

Edson Biggs blinked the sleep out of his eyes and yawned. "Boys was sure quiet comin' in last night."

Looking around, Hitch saw a lot of empty bedrolls; they hadn't been slept in. "They didn't come in at all." It wasn't unheard of for some of the boys to drink so much that they went to sleep in the alleys, and a few had been finding beds down there, and somebody to share them. But this struck Hitch as being too many missing men. He couldn't feature Rascal snoring in an alley. He couldn't feature Law Mc-Ginty laid up in the arms of some wheeligo girl when he had a wife and new baby waiting for him out yonder at the claim, though on second thought Hitch realized it hadn't been long since he had suspected him of just that.

Dan Truman was up walking around worriedly and sharing Hitch's thoughts. "Reckon we better go down and hunt for them, Hitch? Could be they've went and got themselves throwed in jail."

That wouldn't surprise Hitch, knowing where the sheriff's loyalties lay. He took time for breakfast first, figuring the men were probably asleep anyway, wherever they were. Then he, Dan and Edson rode down from the hill. They made Hogtown first, riding out the streets and alleys. They found a couple of cowboys, but not the ones they were looking for.

They put off the crackerbox of a jail until last. When they didn't find the men anywhere else, they decided there was

nowhere left. The sheriff was sleeping in the tiny front office, and it took him a while to come fully awake. He sat
on the edge of his steel cot, bare feet on the earthen floor,
his red underwear half unbuttoned. He yawned, a gold tooth
shining, and he scratched under his armpits. He had probably been up a big part of the night nervously riding herd
on cowpunchers who could, when the mood struck them, be
to a town of this caliber like a bull set loose in a glass
factory. Considering that, plus the pressure the sheriff was
getting from the ranchers, Hitch saw no cause to envy him.
The man had originally been a Torrington cowboy, not really good enough with livestock to keep on the ranch but
too tractable to lose altogether.

"Yeah," the lawman said sleepily, "I got some cowpunchers in here. Say, ain't there anybody in charge up there
at you-all's camp? Ain't there anybody got authority to tell
some of these yahoos when it's time to quit? *Strike!* Hell,
the whole damned bunch of you had ought to be in jail, is
the way I see it."

Hitch nodded, knowing all that anyway. "Could we see
about your prisoners, Sheriff?"

The lawman started to get up and changed his mind.
"Hell's bells, go see them for yourself. You don't need to
bother me about it. Take them with you if you've got a mind
to; they probably ain't got any money left to pay a fine
noway."

Only three men were in the cell, and it was plain they
weren't going anywhere for a while. Hitch didn't disturb
them. He backed out, and Edson said, "Wrong men. Sorry
we bothered you, Sheriff."

The lawman looked like a bobcat with a foot caught in a
trap. "Think nothin' of it. I enjoy bein' up most of the night
quietin' down cowpunchers, then gettin' woke up at the
crack of dawn. Makes me feel like I'm doin' somethin'
worthwhile."

The three climbed back into their saddles and looked at
each other uneasily. Dan Truman spoke the thought the
other two had been afraid to express. "You reckon they rode

off someplace?'' When they didn't answer, he knew they were thinking the same. ''Selkirk's.''

Edson said, ''We better go bring them back before they get in trouble.''

Dread was like a cold hand against the middle of Hitch's back. ''Whatever trouble they had in mind, I'm afraid it's too late now to stop them. They're already in it.''

They rode through the scattered horses. Hitch didn't see Rascal's bay Sweetheart, and Edson and Dan missed some they knew belonged to men from their outfits. The three looked at each other in knowing silence and returned helplessly to camp.

A couple of hours later they heard horses plodding along. The riders slouched in their saddles, wearied and half asleep. They rode into camp without fuss and slipped out of the saddles. Rascal McGinty leaned against his bay horse to support his rubbery legs till the circulation got going. He took off his hat and ran his hand through his tangle of red hair. His eyes were watery and bloodshot. He looked at Hitch like a schoolboy caught turning over an outhouse. ''Want to know where we been at, Hitch?''

''I'm afraid to ask you.''

''We went out to hooraw ol' Selkirk a little and show him how the wolf went over the hill.''

''Figured you did.'' Hitch looked past Rascal and saw frustration in Law McGinty's face. It struck Hitch that maybe they hadn't gotten anything done, which could have been a blessing. ''I hope you-all didn't wind up in no trouble.''

Rascal still held his hat in his hand. He rubbed it roughly across his stubbled face as if he itched. He pulled a bottle from his pocket, found it empty and tossed it away. ''One thing you got to give ol' Selkirk, he's a cold, gutty bastard. I didn't think he had it in him. He stood up there like a man and told us exactly what he thought about us, which was considerable. You ain't been properly cussed till you've had it done to you by a damnyankee banker, Hitch. He purely knows the words. And you remember Dayton Brumley, that used to rep for him at the W wagon, the one I come near shootin' over that roan cow? He stood right by Selkirk. They got more guts than I gave them credit for.''

''For God's sake, Rascal, I hope you didn't hurt anybody.''

Rascal shook his head. ''How could we, them standin' there on the gallery with all them guns pointed straight at us? Damn it, Hitch, you never seen so much cannon in all your life. Looked like enough to've shot their way through the battle of Bull Run.''

Law's voice was brittle. ''There wasn't but four guns. I kept tellin' you, Rascal, we could've took them.''

''Could've got your fool head blowed off,'' Rascal snapped back. ''You was too drunk to know how close you come to bein' killed. Damn fool button, I hope that baby boy don't take after you when it comes to sense; he'll never make it to be grown.''

Hitch glanced at Edson and Dan and let out a long breath he had held as if it were the last he would ever have. ''I'm glad, Rascal, there wasn't nobody hurt.''

''We could've took them,'' Law said again, ''if Rascal would've let us. We didn't have to stand there and take that cussin'.''

''Better a cussin' than a funeral,'' Rascal said.

Law's jaw jutted. ''At least it'll be a while before ol' Selkirk chases wolves with them hounds of his and gets some other cowboy's leg broke like he done Joe Sands.''

Hitch caught that breath again. He saw a shamed look in Rascal's face. ''What did you do?''

Law said, ''I rode by the dog pen as we left. I shot them dogs.''

Hitch hit him. Law staggered and went down on his rump. Hitch spat, ''Goddamn you, Law, get up from there!'' When Law did, Hitch knocked him down again. Law waved his arms in surprise and reached to his hip for a pistol he didn't have.

Rascal stood and blinked, glancing at his brother but making no move to help him to his feet. He spoke mildly,

"Hitch, I had sort of intended to do that myself."

"Why the hell didn't you?"

"I tried, but I kept missin' him."

Law was on his feet again, swaying a little. Hitch knocked him down a third time. "I didn't miss him. Get him out of my sight, Rascal. Keep him out of my sight till you're both sober."

That time Hitch went down to town and bought a bottle at Fant Gossett's saloon. He took it over to the shack where Joe Sands stayed and let Joe watch while Hitch drank most of it.

Joe said, "You're goin' to hate yourself."

"I think I already do."

Looking back later, Hitch could see that from that point things went downhill. It would be hard to say the strike ended on any particular day, or even in a particular week, for it just dragged on and died away gradually in painful gasps. Some cowboys began straggling off, a few to seek jobs at their old outfits. They didn't find them.

A Nine Bar hand Hitch had known a long time came back cheerless and tired from a ride out to the ranch. "They wouldn't even talk to me, Hitch. I offered to work for the same wage I was gettin', and they're so short-handed it hurts to watch them. But they got themselves a blacklist . . . got all our names on it. There won't none of them ranchers give a job to one of us."

It was as Charlie Waide had said. The ranches would suffer in the short run, but new hands would keep drifting into the country and hiring on at the same wages the ranchers had been paying before the strike, or perhaps five dollars a month more. In that respect the strike would help some cowboys, but not the ones who had participated in it.

After the affair out at Selkirk's, Rascal McGinty stayed sober. He was good help, finally, when it was too late for help to matter much. Holding the strike together was like trying to grab a handful of water; it leaked out between all fingers.

Edson Biggs came to Hitch one day, expression dark. "We spent the last of the chuck fund today, and there ain't enough flour and coffee to go past tomorrow noon. We'll be out of beef pretty quick."

Hitch could feel the ground slowly sliding from beneath his feet. "We'll make another assessment. How much you figure we'll need?"

"We've already lost between a third and a half of the men. We'll lose the rest before long, I expect. Five dollars ought to do it. There might be enough left at the end for us to hold a wake."

They went among the cowboys. Some dug into their pockets without complaint. A few of the cautious ones declined. One said, "Hitch, I was figurin' on leavin' here in the mornin' anyway. Thought I might find somethin' over east, over in the Clarendon country or the Palo Duro."

Some turned their pockets wrongside out and found nothing. Some gave a dollar, some two dollars, all they had. When Hitch and Rascal and the other collectors turned the money over to Edson, it counted out to only enough for four or five more days. A few people in town might still contribute money or grub, but by now they knew what most of the cowboys did: the strike was a failure. The heart beat feebly, but the illness was terminal.

Fant Gossett came in his buggy, his weight mashing the spring seat way down. That fine broad smile he had used at first was gone now. He pointed a big stubby finger like a pistol. "Hitch, I need to be talkin' to you."

The tone was like a hoof rasp going to the quick. "Nothin' ever stopped you yet."

"Now, Hitch, you know that when you-all started this strike I told you it was all right with me, I was back of you all the way. I didn't think it was much of an idea; I always talked against it, but if you-all wanted to strike I told you you had ol' Fant Gossett's support. I always told you that, didn't I?" He paused, waiting for Hitch to agree. Hitch said nothing. Gossett went on, "Well, Hitch, I've always been a generous man; I'd give the shirt off of my back if it would help some poor soul to his feet. But on the other hand I ain't operatin' no charity institution down there. Now, there's three or four of them cowboys been givin' me a mite of grief, been comin' down there thinkin' because they'd spent all their money I ought to give them whisky on credit. You know credit's poison to a businessman. It's cash on the barrelhead, I always say.

"Now I don't want them boys troublin' me no more. If they do I'll have to call the sheriff into it. He's lookin' for an excuse to jail all you boys he can anyway. So you tell them boys for me, Hitch, if they ain't got the money to spend, don't be a-comin' down to the place and botherin' me for whisky. You do that, and it'll save us all a right smart of grief."

Hitch figured Fant Gossett had made enough money out of these cowboys to buy a quarter interest in the Figure 4 ranch if he had a mind to. "I'll tell them, Fant. And in return I want you to do *me* a favor."

"Anything reasonable, Hitch. You know I'll be tickled to."

"If I ever again show my face in your place of business, I want you to kick me out the front door."

Quickly Gossett was smooth as warm butter. "Now, Hitch, you know you're welcome down there any time, just any time atall. What I said about them others . . . I just got to take care of my business, is all."

"Then you go on and see about your business, Fant. I don't want to detain you none."

X

HITCH TOLD EDSON AND DAN HE WAS PLAN-
ning to leave come daylight. "The wise man realizes when
he's whipped. He wipes his nose, picks up his hat and leaves
while he can still walk. I don't aim to be the last one out."

Edson Biggs stared past Hitch toward the main part of
camp, his eyes sober. "At least you have somewhere to go,
Hitch. Many an old boy here doesn't have that, or the money
to take him there if he had."

Hitch bent down to buckle his big-roweled spurs to his
boots. "They're not all broke, Edson. There's some of these
cowboys that sat on their money like they was tryin' to
make it hatch. There'll always be the thrifty kind among
us."

Edson said, "But there'll always be some of that other
kind who can't see past tonight's poker game, who'll spend
their last dime to pinch some emptyheaded girl on the cheek,
front or rear. Give one man a hundred dollars and pretty
soon he'll have two hundred. Give another man a hundred
and pretty soon he'll come back to you looking for more."

Dan Truman said sourly, "I been askin' myself a hundred times, where'd we go wrong? Where'd we come apart?"

Edson Biggs punched at the campfire, where a can of coffee was slowly coming to a boil. He glanced at Hitch, then back to Dan Truman, putting together what he wanted to say. "We lost it before we started. We lost it, for one thing, because we struck for the wrong reasons. We cheapened ourselves . . . we cheapened what we stood for when all we could agree to ask for was higher wages. We should have talked about dignity and freedom; those things count for more than money. Money's soon spent, and when it's gone it leaves no mark. But when a man loses dignity, that leaves a mark on him that stays. We didn't come apart; we never were really together."

Hitch said, "There didn't have to be a strike. Both sides had some right and some wrong. If we'd all been willin' to talk to each other, maybe we could've got around it. But the wrong people always seem to grab hold of things and holler instead of listen. I've never understood why it's always easier to fight than it is to talk."

Edson said, "Not many people can see more than one side to an argument. You have that gift, Hitch, if it is a gift; I'm inclined to think it's a handicap. You'll be miserable all your life because you see both sides. The man at peace with himself is the one who sees nothing but his own."

Much of what Edson was saying went over Dan Truman's head. Dan said, "All I know is that we lost and the ranchers won."

Edson shook his head. "We lost, but they didn't win. In the end they'll find out that they've lost too."

Dan said, "Damned if I see how you figure that."

"You will, in time. Hitch, where you goin' when you leave here?"

"I got a little money saved back that I can buy the necessaries with. I got me a section of deeded land and a little bunch of cows. I can plant me a garden, and I can hunt. I can live awhile on a little of nothin'. They'll play hell starvin' me to death."

Edson glanced at Dan. "Same goes for you, too. It goes for a lot of these men. The big ranches figure on them leaving the country, but they won't. They have a toenail hold here, and they'll stay. What's more, they're mad, and anything the ranches do to squeeze them out will make them dig in a little deeper. There are probably fifteen-twenty men who came to this strike as working cowboys and will leave it as small ranchers, mad at the big outfits and determined to stay. Some cowboys will find themselves a place in town, and the town itself is more against the outfits now than it ever was. The ranches will find out that instead of clearing this country they've broken a hornet's nest around their ears. They won't be able to control elections; they'll find people voting taxes on them like they've never paid before. They won't run this sheriff's office much longer, and they won't run the court."

He burned his hand on the coffee can and let it go. "I've had time to do a lot of thinking since we've been here. The old-time cowboy is finished, but the days of the big ranches are numbered, too. This is going to be a little man's country, and the little man is going to need himself a bank he can go to with dignity and trust. I think I know some money men back home who will listen to me. I'll get the backing and open a bank here that will serve men like you, Hitch, and you, Dan. A bank too small for the Figure 4 or the W or the Snaketrack but able to lend a man money to buy a section of land or fifty cows or groceries to help him survive till spring in a dugout winter camp. A lot of state land here is for sale if people can raise the money. I'll help them raise it. We'll crowd these big ranches off of the free range. Then we'll see who has lost and who has won."

Rascal McGinty had come up to listen. His jaw was working a little, though he wasn't saying anything aloud. Farther down in camp, Law McGinty and Asher Cottingham were still talking strike. But Rascal knew.

Hitch said, "Rascal, maybe it's time you was takin' Law home."

"Past time. He don't mean no harm, but seems like he

causes it just the same. I wisht you could talk to him, Hitch.''

''I'm done talkin' to him. From now on, Rascal, I reckon you'll have to do that yourself.''

Rascal and Law and Cottingham were hunched over a coffeepot next morning as Hitch swung into the saddle at good daylight. Cottingham squatted on his spurs, nursing a hot cup in his hands and watching resentfully. ''Desertin' us, are you, Hitch?''

Hitch considered some kind of answer but decided against it. Rascal muttered something to Cottingham.

Cottingham persisted. ''It's your fault, Hitch. If they'd of listened to me instead of to you, we'd of given them ranchers hell. If you hadn't acted like some scared old woman . . .''

Rascal grabbed Cottingham's collar and jerked him backward. Caught by surprise, Cottingham landed on his back. He rolled over on his side, frantically trying to brush away the hot, wet coffee he had splashed all over himself. Rascal said impatiently, ''Asher, I told you to shut up.'' He looked then at Hitch. ''Take care of yourself.''

''I will.'' Hitch glanced at Law to see if the younger McGinty had anything to say. Law simply stared. Hitch spoke no more as he rode out of camp. But seeing Law set him to wondering about Kate.

It was not out of the way for him to go by the McGinty place; it lay only a few miles from his own. They had originally planned it that way, he and Rascal and Law, in a happier day when they had all been confident they would someday be rich and build fine mansions and have cows roaming over a thousand hills. It would be nice in their old age, they had thought, to be able to ride over and play cards and talk about the good old days when they were poor as a whip-poor-will.

Hitch led a dun packhorse he had bought as an extra animal to spell Walking Jack at the work. He had it loaded with supplies he would be needing. But he headed for the McGinty place instead of his own.

Kate stood beneath a clothesline she had strung between the corner post of a fence and a wooden cross post she had set up near the front of the dugout. Flapping clothes had always been a worry to Walking Jack, so Hitch dismounted and tied him a little way from the line. Hat in his hands, he walked up to Kate.

She was surprised. "Strike over, Hitch? Did we win?"

"It's over. We didn't win."

She was slender and small again like she used to be. He said, "You look real fine, Kate. Hope you been all right."

"Just fine. I want you to see my baby boy. He's in the house with Mother."

He remembered how astonished Selkirk had been to hear her call that dugout "house."

She said, "I'm sorry about the strike. What'll you do now?"

"Work for myself. I'm out of a job."

"Then I reckon everybody is . . . Law, Rascal . . . everybody." She frowned. It seemed to Hitch she looked pleasant even when she let her face wrinkle that way. Maybe Selkirk had not considered her pretty, but Hitch thought she was. She asked, "Law and Rascal, they behind you?"

"I expect they'll be comin' along. If not today, pretty soon. Not everybody's given up yet."

"I'm sorry, Hitch. But come on, let me show you the boy."

He followed her into the dugout. It was small and crowded but much cleaner than the name would imply. The floor was packed hard from people walking on it all the time, almost like cement, and a good housekeeper like Kate would sweep it clean a time or two every day, clearing up the dust that always seemed to filter down from the sodded-over roof. Kate's mother sat there, a time-worn, worry-torn woman aged beyond her years, embittered to the point that she trusted no one. That, Hitch feared, could be Kate by the time she was forty if life did not improve for her. It would be a pity.

Babies had always appeared pretty much alike to him, one

and then another, but he bragged about this one being real special and already having its legs bowed to fit a horse as soon as it was a couple of months older and had its balance. This, of course, was an exaggeration. Most ranch boys didn't get put in the saddle till they were walking good.

Kate wouldn't let Hitch go until she had fed him, and he didn't really want to leave anyway on an empty stomach. He knew what it would be like, batching on his own place. But by and by there was no excuse to tarry longer. Kate followed him out to the horses. He must have looked worried, for she made a weak smile. "You'll do fine, Hitch. You've always been one to do fine. I hope you'll come over real often."

He hadn't told her about the unpleasantness between him and Law. He said, "I doubt there'll be much time, Kate; I'll have a right smart of work to do fixin' up the place. Besides, here lately since I had to let him go from the Ws, Law ain't been none too friendly with me."

"That'll pass," she said confidently. "You've always been good friends; anything wrong now, it'll pass."

"I hope so. I'm worried about you-all tryin' to make a livin' on a little place like this."

"Things always work out for people who have faith. I have faith in Law and Rascal." She made it sound cheerful, but in her eyes he saw a shade of doubt. She had seen many dreams go to dust in her father's time.

"Goodbye, Kate. If ever you need help, you know where I'm at."

"I'll remember." After he had ridden a long way he turned in the saddle to look back. She was still watching him.

He had told her he would have lots to do, but he hadn't realized how much there was. Working on the W, he had had to let his cattle more or less take care of themselves. He had done very little toward building corrals to handle them in, or a dugout for him to live in. He had a small one, built for an overnight camp and hardly big enough for a man to stretch his legs. Even that little one was half caved in from last winter's rains. The more he looked at it, the more it seemed he would be better off to let it fall and build a new one. Meantime he slept outside and hoped it didn't rain more than was needful.

He decided to build what was known as a half-human, a dugout half under the ground and half above it. That was one step up in civilization, lying somewhere between a cave-type dugout and a frame shack in respectability. It took much pick and shovel work, which was a good thing because he brought up all the grievances of recent weeks and worked them out on the brown earth. By the time he had planted the garden and finished the dugout, he had pretty well rid himself of the pent-up angers. Spring was moving well along into summer. The rains came about as they were supposed to, the grass rising green and the cattle licking themselves, a sign they were doing well. The garden thrived, which pleased him in view of the fact that he had done little farming in his life. He had decided that until he had himself established financially, he would raise whatever he needed beyond coffee, flour and the like, and if he couldn't raise it he would do without it. That way he could conserve that tiny bankroll.

Rascal came by Hitch's place a few times. He still tried to be his old redheaded, grinning self, though he was more serious now. When Hitch looked for it he could see trouble lying behind the forced laughter in Rascal's eyes. Rascal was out hunting for work where he could get it, pitching in as day labor when one of the smaller ranchers needed help, one of the little men who had not been a party to either side in the strike and didn't give a damn about the blacklist. Most of these greasy-sack outfits weren't recognized at the big ones' roundups and couldn't send reps to watch out for their interests. They took care of themselves the best way they could. Rascal's travels kept him posted on the gossip. He knew where most of the striking cowboys had gone. As Edson Biggs had predicted, a majority were still somewhere around. Some had found work with small ranches not in the inner circle. The pay was small because these little ranchers didn't have the money. A number of cowboys stayed in town, some working, some showing no visible means of support.

A few cowboys simply squatted on open range and went to mavericking, trying to build themselves a herd. This was dangerous now, for the big outfits had outlawed it, though enforcement was difficult in a country so broad and open. A man who kept his eyes peeled could brand cattle under the noses of the big outfits' cowpunchers and not get caught at it. It was not illegal except in the eyes of the big ranches. An unbranded animal not following a branded mother was considered the property of the man on whose range it grazed. Since the big outfits did not own or pay leases on much of the grass they used, a man could make out a case that they had no solid claim on the mavericks. Any time Hitch came upon a maverick and felt to his own satisfaction that it did not rightfully belong to Charlie Waide, he shook his rope down and built a little fire to heat the cinch ring he carried in the pocket of his chaps. By summer his little herd of Two Diamonds was bigger than before the strike.

He made it a point to ride out the country diligently and keep his cattle thrown back close to their own home range. If a Two Diamond cow and calf were gathered in some big ranch's roundup, the cowboys were not likely to appropriate his calf, for that would be stealing; but on the other hand they would not brand it for him, either. They would simply throw the cow and unbranded calf back onto the open range. If Hitch did not happen to come upon them before the calf was weaned, it would be a maverick subject to branding by the first man who threw a loop on it. He supported the right of a man to maverick cattle, but he wanted to be sure none of them were his.

One day he saw a cowboy riding a horse that looked familiar. The cowboy was a stranger, but Hitch remembered the horse, a little W mustang named Chicken that Law McGinty used to ride. Hitch and the cowboy howdied and shook and introduced themselves. The name Hugh Hitch-

cock meant nothing to the young rider, though he worked
for Charlie Waide and the W now. Hitch asked him how
Charlie was and found the rancher was all right except, the
cowboy said, grouchy as an old he-coon with the colic.

Seemed the cowboy had come up from South Texas with
two dollars in his pockets. He had heard about the strike
and the ranch jobs open. To him thirty dollars a month
seemed a gold mine. Looking back on it, Hitch could see
how futile it had been for the strikers to think they could
bend the ranchers backward very long; too many needy people all over the country were ready and willing to take their
jobs.

"Thirty dollars a month," the boy exclaimed, like it was
a million. "I can't see what all them fellers went on strike
for. Just got too big for their britches, I reckon."

"I reckon."

The cowboy went on to say they had been having trouble
with maverickers and the like, and Hitch promised to keep
his eyes open. Before he left, the cowboy said, "Them boys
that lost the strike, I hear they're a desperate bunch that had
as soon shoot a man as to look at him. I'm sure watchin'
out that I don't run into none of them."

"You do that," Hitch told him.

He almost rode into one himself a few days later. He had
finished looking through a string of cattle to see if any Two
Diamonds were among them, or any mavericks. They
weren't. He found several Snaketrack and Figure 4 cows
with calves, and one weaned heifer yearling carrying a fairly
fresh Figure 4 brand. Hitch wished he had found her before
the Figure 4 men did, but that was water under the bridge.

Riding away through a clump of brush, he heard a stirring
of hoofs and looked back. Another horseman had ridden
among the same cattle, checking them over just as Hitch
had done. He evidently had not seen Hitch. Out of curiosity,
Hitch dismounted and watched him. The horseman shook
down his rope, eased the heifer yearling away from the other
cattle and threw a loop over her stubby horns. Then he put

spurs to the horse and dragged the heifer jumping and bawling into the brush. Hitch could not see now, but he could
tell from the popping of limbs and the angry bawling that
the cowboy jerked the heifer down and tied her. Directly he
caught a faint smell of burning wood, though the fire was
kept so small that he never saw smoke. The tenor of the
heifer's bawling changed; Hitch knew the horseman was
burning a new brand on her hide.

Hitch swung onto Walking Jack and worked through the
brush, coming up behind the man on the ground. The cowboy had a heated cinch ring and was changing the Figure 4
brand into an LR.

"Law," Hitch said, "if I was a Figure 4 man, I could
kill you right now."

Law McGinty whirled, dropping the cinch ring and grab-
bing at a pistol on his hip. It was half out of the holster
before he recognized Hitch. Breathing hard, face pale, he let
the pistol slip back into leather. "Hitch, you got an awful
bad habit of slippin' up on a man."

"You got a bad habit of makin' a man need to."

Law was trembling now. "You oughtn't to ever ride up
on a man like that. It can get you killed."

Coldly Hitch said, "You killin' people now, Law?"

"You know better than that."

"Not necessarily. You've moved up from sleeperin' cattle
to changin' brands. Why not move on up a little farther and
kill somebody? Keep up this kind of business and sooner or
later you'll have to. Can't you find enough honest mavericks
to suit you?"

Law picked up the cinch ring from the dirt. It had cooled,
and he dropped it back into his tiny fire to reheat. Defensively he said, "You throwin' in on the big companies' side
now?"

"I got no side except my own, but I got eyes. That heifer
had a Figure 4 brand on her before you got here."

"Ol' Selkirk ain't goin' to miss one now and again."

"Is it just one now and again, or are you changin' brands
as fast as you can get around to them? Kate wouldn't be

proud if she knew what you're doin'. Neither would Rascal.''

"You figurin' on tellin' them?"

"It's not my place to."

"It ain't your place to tell *me* anything, either. We might've won that strike if we'd used stronger measures. You wouldn't stand for them, and we lost it.''

"The strike's got nothin' to do with you changin' brands on somebody else's stock. We had some justice on our side in that strike. You got none with you in this."

"Justice is a useless word in this part of the country. What matters is how many cows you got. The LR is goin' to have plenty of them before I'm through."

"Even if you have to steal them?"

"You figure ol' John Torrington come by all his cattle honest, or Selkirk all his money? You can bet that anytime they got the chance, they just reached out and grabbed. Well, I'm grabbin' too." He frowned darkly. "Now, Hitch, suppose you just ride on out of here. You ain't seen nothin' and you ain't tellin' nothin'.''

"I've seen," Hitch said, heavily disappointed, "but nothin' I'll ever want to tell."

One thing Hitch badly needed was a better set of corrals. He had only a couple of small working pens, and when he threw cattle into them he found some of the calves crawling out because the spaces at the bottom were too large. He didn't want to spend money on lumber that could better be spent on land or cattle, so he carried an ax down into the creekbottom and chopped brush. It took him all the time he could spare for some weeks, chopping and hauling trunks and branches big enough and long enough to serve as posts and fencing. He laid out the pattern on the ground, then set the posts in pairs, just enough space between them to wedge the branches in lengthwise, solid from the ground to a height of about five feet. This required a lot of digging and a lot of chopping; it was something a man could not do a-horseback, and it set him to longing for the good days on

the W when he was never afoot except around the bunkhouse or the chuckwagon. It was hard to find dignity in
work like this, at least dignity by cowboy standards.

He was chopping branches to fit the fence when he saw
a buggy approaching from the west, two people on the seat.
One was a woman, he could tell by the scarf flying in the
breeze. The man he soon recognized as Joe Sands. Joe
reined the trotting team to a stop by Hitch's half-finished
fence. Hitch dusted his hands on his torn-knee britches and
walked out to meet him. Joe extended his hand without trying to get down from the buggy. "Hitch, you probably don't
know Maggie. This here is Maggie Horn, from town."

Hitch knew the buggy and team now; he had seen the
saloonkeeper Fant Gossett use them several times. Though
he didn't know the woman, he judged that Fant Gossett had
probably used *her* a few times, too. Hitch said awkwardly,
"Good to have you visit, Miss Horn." He touched the brim
of his hat; he knew that if he took it off the sweat would
immediately roll down into his eyes. "Joe," he said,
"how's the leg?"

"Better, but I can't climb up and down from this buggy
without help. That's how come I brought Maggie with me."

Hitch raised his hands. "I'll help you down."

Joe shook his head. "No time, Hitch. I come to warn
you."

Hitch dropped his hands. "Warn me?"

"Bunch of the big ranchers are meetin' in town with the
county commissioners' court. John Torrington and Prosper
Selkirk and some of them others, they've drawed up a list
of what they call 'maverick brands.' The county court is
goin' to order them seized and held."

"They can't do that; it ain't legal."

"Anything is legal if you're big enough, and if you own
the court and the sheriff. Hitch, they got your name and
brand at the top of the list."

"Why me?"

"They look on you as one of the leaders of that strike.
The ranchers figured when the strike was over the trouble

would be over, but it's only just started. They thought all
the strikers would leave the county, but the biggest part are
still around pesterin' them ranchers like horseflies, chasin'
mavericks, runnin' brands . . . things like that. Them big outfits are like a snake mad enough to bite itself. They want to
put all the maverick men out of business, and they consider
you one.''

"I never stole a cow in my life."

"They're fixin' to steal *yours*, Hitch, if you don't get the
jump on them. They got the McGintys on their list and a
bunch of others."

"We could get us a lawyer . . ."

"And fight them in their own court? It'd be like a banty
hen fightin' a chickenhawk. You got to take care of your
ownself, Hitch. Charlie Waide said he tried to head them
off, but he was swimmin' upstream."

Hopefully Hitch asked, "Did Charlie tell you to come
and warn me?"

Joe shook his head. "Not exactly, he didn't." He saw the
disappointment in Hitch's face. "But he must of knowed I
would, else he wouldn't of gone to the trouble of tellin' me
about it."

"I don't know what to do, Joe. I can't fight the law, even
their law."

"That's what I told Charlie. He said if he had a friend in
that fix, he'd tell him this is a county court and it's got no
jurisdiction anywhere else. Said he'd tell him that if he
rounded up his cattle and pushed them across the county
line, they couldn't touch him. At least not unless they got
to the next county to do the same thing." Joe paused.
"Mind you, if anybody was to ever ask, I couldn't tell them
that Charlie told me to tell you that. He just said if he had
a friend in that fix, that's what he'd say."

"Thanks, Joe. I reckon I'd best get busy."

"Wisht I could help you round them up, Hitch, but this
leg won't let me get on a horse yet, and ol' Fant's buggy
won't hardly operate off of a road."

"I'll do for myself." Hitch stepped back, then thought of

one thing more. "You're goin' over to tell Rascal and Law, ain't you?"

"Hadn't figured on it."

"I'd take it as a personal kindness if you would."

Joe Sands considered soberly. "I been hearin' some things about Law . . ." He broke off. "All right, Hitch, I'll go."

After Joe left, Hitch stood around a few minutes trying to reason out what steps he should take. They couldn't do this to him, yet he knew Joe was right; legal or not, they *would* do it. It was a hard week's horseback ride from here to the state capital. The law here was whatever the big outfits chose to say it was.

He quickly gathered up a few necessaries such as coffee and cold bread and jerked beef and wrapped them in a sack, then caught and saddled Walking Jack. He rode north first, making a circle over that side of his claim and over open range well beyond, picking up what Two Diamond cows he found and pushing them southward. Giving them a long start, he rode off in another circle and made a second drag, picking up more cattle. They moved sluggishly, for the grass here was good, and they had no inclination to leave it. Whenever he let up pushing them, they slowed and began grazing again. When he finally had them strung out on a southerly course, he left them and went back to the first gathering. He found these no longer moving but spread and grazing. He bunched them, shouting and bullying them into a trot. After a long time he managed to join them with the other cattle. A quick count showed he had perhaps two-thirds of his herd. The rest were scattered to Kingdom Come. Frustration gnawed at him; if only he had a little help he could hunt while someone else pushed the cattle. He felt that in every swag, every creekbottom and brush motte he was missing a few, if only he could go get them. But whenever he left this herd it would quit moving forward and begin scattering to graze. It was better to save this many than to try for the rest and possibly lose them all. If he got these across the county line, he could come back for more.

The new calves quickly tired and fell to the rear of the herd. Anxious mothers missed them and dropped back bawling for their offspring. Hitch shook his rope loose from the hornstring and used it like a whip, sending it stinging across the hips of the cows. But he could do little about the calves. They were too young to be properly fearful of him, too tired to run even if they had been scared. One by one he began to let the smallest of the calves drop out, and he cut their mothers to stay with them. By late afternoon he had left ten or twelve pairs strung across the prairie as he bullied the rest of the herd along, shouting, charging them on the running horse, whipping them with the rope.

The county line was imaginary, not based on any geographical feature such as a creek or a river. It was a straight line arbitrarily drawn on some map years and years ago. Hitch thought he knew about where it was, and he felt some relief when he pushed the cattle over and beyond it. He let them slow a little, but he was not confident enough to allow them to stop. Safety lay in distance; the more he could get of it, the better. There was always a chance some of the cattle might try to return to accustomed ground, though as a general rule in this part of the country cattle drifted south, following the prevailing winds.

Dusk was upon him when he began to think of stopping and fixing some supper. This was open range just as in his own county, only a minor part of it yet deeded to individual owners. This county also knew cattle of the W and the Figure 4 and the Snaketrack brands, as well as those of other ranches big and small which headquartered south of here. Hitch's cattle had as much right to graze this grass as anyone's did, wherever he chose to turn them loose.

This, he decided, was as good a place as any. He stepped down from Walking Jack at a tiny creek where he found dead mesquite that would make firewood for his supper. He watered the horse, built a small fire in a sheltered spot where it could not spread out into the grass, and put a small can of coffee on to boil. Standing up from these exertions, he saw half a dozen riders bearing down upon him from the north.

Hitch was unarmed except for the saddlegun in its scabbard on his saddle. Not once did he even think of going for it. He stood uneasily and watched the riders approach. The one in front made a circular motion with his arm, and four men spurred out around Hitch's cattle. The remaining two rode up to Hitch. One was the sheriff he knew from town.

"Howdy, Hitchcock. Hope you're fixin' enough coffee to go around. I sure do need me some."

Hitch said, "You're welcome to coffee, Sheriff. But if you've come for my cattle, you can forget about it. I'm well over the county line."

The sheriff looked at his companion, the Torrington cowboy Slant Unger. "Slant, did you see anything back yonder markin' a county line?"

Unger gravely shook his head.

The sheriff turned again to Hitch. "Afraid you're mistaken, Hitchcock. Far as I know I'm still in my county. I got an order here from the commissioner's court that says I'm supposed to take custody of all cattle in the Two Diamonds herd and brand, among others. Them cattle you got yonder is all wearin' the Two Diamonds, ain't they?"

Hitch saw they fully intended to do it. He flashed into anger. "You're over the county line and know it. You can't do this."

Calmly the sheriff pointed to the four men bringing Hitch's cattle back. "Suppose you just watch me."

Irrationally then, anger drove Hitch into charging at the sheriff with his fists. He landed a blow that brought pain to his own knuckles but sent the sheriff staggering back. He sensed a quick movement behind him and tried to turn. Something struck him across the back of the head and sent him to his knees. He crouched in black, blinding pain. He sensed that Slant Unger had pistol-whipped him. He tried to push to his feet but instead went down on his stomach. Dizziness washed over him like a flood. The roaring in his head all but covered up the conversation above him.

"You oughtn't to've hit him so hard, Slant. You might've busted his head."

"He had his hat on."

"Lots of people look up to Hitchcock. They won't like us hurtin' him."

"A man that betrays the outfit he works for ain't much to worry about, to my notion. Anyway, this'll help teach them that nobody messes around with the likes of John Torrington."

"I got a bottle in my saddlebags, Slant. Go bring it here."

The sheriff helped Hitch to his feet, but Hitch was unable to stay there. He sank back to his knees. "Didn't go to do it like this," the sheriff said half apologetically, "but orders is orders, and I got mine. Here, have a drink of this." He held the bottle to Hitch's lips and tilted it. Hitch choked some of the whisky down. It set his stomach afire but gave him strength. The sheriff said, "It ain't exactly like we was takin' these cattle away from you. What we're doin' is sort of holdin' them in escrow till the court has made a final determination. You know what escrow means?"

Hitch wheezed, "You take them cattle back over that line and I'll lose them forever."

The sheriff didn't argue with him. He corked the bottle and started to place it back into his saddlebag. Then he changed his mind and put it into Hitch's hand. "Hell, you'll need this worse than I do. Keep it. Always kind of respected you, Hitchcock. Sorry things turned out thisaway."

Hitch attempted no answer.

The sheriff said, "Seems to me like you'd be better off if you went someplace else and started fresh. Be better for all concerned if we was to ride by your place sometime and find you'd pulled out."

It pained Hitch to talk, but he managed what he wanted to say. "You'll find me there."

He knelt, giving up for a time to the pain that all but blinded him, though he could see them driving his cattle away. He drank what was left in the bottle, hoping it would help. It didn't. He tried once to push himself to his feet, to get on the horse and go home. The last he knew, he was falling.

XI

HITCH WAS VAGUELY AWARE THAT HE HAD
lain there a long time. Some inner consciousness kept prod-
ding him to find his feet, but he resisted it as long as he
could, his head pounding. A thought came that perhaps the
sheriff had been right . . . perhaps that blow had fractured
his skull. He tried several times to bestir himself, and finally
he opened his eyes. It was dark; he had no idea how much
of the night had passed. He blinked, and gradually he was
able to see Walking Jack, standing there as if asleep on his
feet. At least the horse had not run away.

It took Hitch some time to get to his knees, for every
move brought blinding pain anew. He wanted to lie down,
to find oblivion and end the pain, but that nagging drive
would not allow it. He tried to get to his feet but could not.
He looked at the horse and tried to think ahead. He did not
know if or how he would be able to get in the saddle, but
he knew that first he had to catch the horse. He began crawling on hands and knees.

Walking Jack lifted his head, ears pointed forward in

doubt. He was not used to seeing a man move toward him on all fours. The horse tossed his head, trotted off a few steps, then turned again in curiosity.

Hitch stopped. If Walking Jack ran away, Hitch could lie here and die. He found voice. "Whoa, son," he rasped. "Be gentle now, son."

Jack watched him warily, but the voice was familiar. Hitch kept talking to him as he crawled. Jack seemed inclined to turn and run again, but the voice held him. Hitch reached cautiously toward the trailing reins, afraid his hand would frighten the horse and cause him to run. Jack held his ground, and Hitch's fingers closed on leather.

He stopped there a bit, breathing hard and painfully, resting from the exertion. He reached up and patted the horse's shoulder to set the animal at ease. Jack flinched but did not jerk away. Hitch rubbed the horse's foreleg and kept talking quietly until Jack seemed ready to accept him. He reached up and caught hold of the stirrup. Holding it, he slowly pulled himself to his feet and leaned heavily against the horse.

He thought of the whisky and wished he still had some of it for the momentary strength it might give him. He had also lost his hat. He kept leaning against the saddle, his hands on the horn. Presently he thought he might have the strength. He lifted his left foot and somehow fumbled it into the stirrup. He tried then to pull up and got about halfway before he slid down again. The left foot stayed in the stirrup, though, that much of a start for the next try. He waited and rested a minute, then tried it again. The third time he made it and brought his right leg across the cantle. Somehow he found the stirrup with his right foot.

"Old boy," he said, "don't you let me fall off again."

He considered tying himself into the saddle, but that was dangerous; cowboys lived with a fear of becoming entangled and being dragged to death. He knew it was up to him to find his way, for Jack was not yet used to the dugout camp. Turned loose and given his head, Jack would probably trail across to the W headquarters; Hitch was unlikely to be able

to ride that far. Hitch sagged over the saddlehorn but turned
Jack in the direction he knew led to the dugout. Every step
brought pain, but gradually it became blunted to the extent
that he was able to endure it. He clamped his teeth and made
up his mind he was not yet ready to die.

Much of the night was gone when he reached his dugout.
He knew he could not climb down. When he tried to leave
the saddle, he was likely to fall. What if he could not then
get up? He could lie here at the front of his own dugout
and be as helpless as out there on the prairie. The more he
considered it, the more convinced he became that it was
foolish to stop here. Farther on was help . . . farther on was
the McGinty place if he could stay in the saddle that long.
He turned Jack away from the dugout door. The horse
seemed reluctant to leave, for horses have the same resis-
tance to physical effort that humans do; he had expected to
be turned loose here. But directly Jack became resigned to
the notion that he was not through working. Hitch had the
horse moving in the right direction when he sensed consciousness trying to leave him, and the pain coming harder
again. He took a tight grip on the horn and hoped that if he
did lapse he would not fall; he had slept in the saddle many
times, some subconscious instinct keeping him astride.

By summoning all his will he retained enough consciousness to stay in the saddle and to give Jack some vague guid-
ance. It seemed they had been moving all night in Jack's
easy walk when suddenly they dropped into a familiar trail.

Hitch sensed when the horse stopped in front of the
McGinty dugout. It was still dark, but the east showed some
promise of morning light. He tried to call. "Rascal. Rascal
McGinty." There was no strength in his voice; he tried
again. The voice was little better than a whisper. He shifted
his weight and lost his balance. He grabbed vainly at the
horn but could not hold it. He slid down the horse's shoulder
and leg and piled limply on the ground. Jack stood a moment as if afraid he might step on Hitch, then pulled away
a few feet, looking confused. Hitch tried to crawl but could

not. He lay there and lapsed into either sleep or uncon-
sciousness, he did not know which.

After a long time he was aware of a woman's cry from
the flap of the dugout. He managed to open his eyes and
saw that the sun had just come up. Kate McGinty stood at
the dugout. "Hitch?" she called in surprise. "Is that you,
Hitch?" She rushed up the hewn-log steps. Hitch tried to
answer but could not bring out words.

"What's happened to you, Hitch?" she cried as she
dropped to one knee beside him. Her fingers gently touched
the back of his head where the pistol had struck him.
"You've taken a fall or somethin'. You been hit a bad lick.
I better get you inside." She looked around as if for help.
"Can you hear me, Hitch?" He nodded. She said, "There's
nobody here but me and the baby. Law and Rascal are gone.
I'll try to get you down these steps and into the house. Think
you can help a little?" He nodded again, though nod was
about all he could do.

She put her arms around him and lifted him up; she was
a strong woman to be so small. He tried to carry his own
weight but could not. He managed only to get a little movement into his legs.

It took them a long time to get down those steps, and he
was sure he cried out a time or two. But finally he was lying
on his stomach on a bed. Her fingers gently probed the
wound. "That's an awful nasty place," she said. "I'll have
to clean it up before I can even see how bad it is."

She poured something over it that burned like coals from
Trump Tatum's campfire. He passed out.

He awoke later to voices. Someone out front called, "You
McGintys! Anybody home?"

Opening his eyes, Hitch saw Kate sitting in a rawhide
chair beside the bed. She turned toward the dugout flap. The
baby began to fret at the disturbance. The voice came again,
"Rascal McGinty, you in there?"

A man pushed through the flap and stood in the gloom
of the tiny dugout, staring in surprise at the woman. "Mrs.
McGinty?"

Kate stood up. "I'm Kate McGinty, Sheriff. My husband is not here, and neither is Rascal."

A second man entered. The sheriff moved forward. "I got some papers for your menfolks, ma'am." He nodded toward the bed. "Somebody hurt?"

"It's Hugh Hitchcock. I found him lyin' outside when I went to feed the chickens. I don't know what happened to him."

The sheriff picked up the lantern for a closer look. He turned to the other man, rebuke in his voice. "Damn it, Slant, I told you you shouldn't of hit him so hard."

Kate's voice went sharp. "You hit him? But why?"

"He resisted a lawful and legal order, ma'am, but we didn't go to use him that badly. You reckon he'll be all right?"

Kate was indignant. "Hugh Hitchcock is a good and honorable man. He's not one to be clubbed thisaway. Now, what was this all about?"

The sheriff retreated a couple of steps in the face of her anger. "I served a court order on him takin' custody of his cattle. Same order I got here for your menfolks, an order for me to take all cattle in the LR brand into custody for the county court."

"So that's it!" She leaned forward belligerently, hands on her hips. "You stole Hitch's cattle and now you're here to steal ours. Well, Mister Sheriff, you've come too late. They're gone."

"We'll find them."

"Not in this county you won't."

The sheriff stared at her in surprise. "I'd sure give a pretty to know how everybody found out we was comin'."

Slant Unger said urgently, "Ol' John Torrington will nail our hides to the barn if we let them get away with them cattle."

"Your hide, not mine. I ain't workin' for him."

"The hell you ain't. Come on."

Kate McGinty followed every step of their retreat, her voice accusing. "You're thieves, is what you are. You talk about law, but the devil himself wouldn't have you. You won't catch Law and Rascal now because Hugh Hitchcock sent us word. You hurt Hitch and stole his cattle, but in the end he's beat you.''

Unger said, ''We ain't beat yet. You comin', Sheriff?''

The men went out through the flap and hurried up the steps. The baby was crying, disturbed by the sharp voices. Kate went to its crib and picked it up, cradling it in her arms and swinging gently to and fro, speaking softly and kissing its face. When the baby was quieted, she went back to Hitch. ''You heard?''

He nodded, though it hurt.

She said, ''When Joe Sands brought word, Law and Rascal and a friend of Law's started gatherin' cattle the quickest way they could. They drove them all night. By now they ought to be well across the county line. Ain't no way the sheriff can get our cattle now.''

If Hitch could have talked he would have told her that might not be enough. All he could do was nod.

He was awake at times, but mostly he slept, fighting through a recurring bad dream of John Torrington and Prosper Selkirk driving him out of the country with a long cutting whip. Late in the afternoon he awoke to noise outside and a man's voice calling, ''Kate, we're home.''

Horses trailed past the dugout and moved on in the direction of the corrals and shed. Presently he heard heavy spurs ringing to quick-paced footsteps. The flap pushed open and Law McGinty stood there, ''Kate, I see Hugh Hitchcock's horse out yonder.'' He saw Hitch then, lying on the bed, head bandaged. ''What's all this about?''

Kate told him, voice crisp with indignation. ''That sheriff said he would catch you too. Did he?''

''Not till we was ready to be caught.''

Rascal McGinty came in. He bumped Law in his haste to reach Hitch's side. He turned to Kate. ''How bad's he hurt?''

''I can't tell. They hit him with a pistol.''

Law frowned. ''He been here all day?''

"I found him when I went out this mornin'. He's been like this mostly, asleep or unconscious; it's hard to tell which."

Rascal bent low. "Hitch, you hear me?"

Hitch found a weak voice. "I hear you."

Rascal eased a little. "How do you feel?"

"How do I look?"

"Like pure hell."

Hitch nodded, letting that stand for an answer.

Kate had to explain it all again for Rascal. Rascal clenched his fists. "They get all your cattle, Hitch?"

"All I could round up in a hurry."

Rascal cursed. Kate glanced apprehensively at the baby, and Rascal told her it wasn't old enough yet to pick up the words.

"Ain't likely you'll improve much before he *is* old enough," she said reproachfully.

Law watched Hitch in silence. At length he said, "Me and you have had our differences, Hitch, but I owe you for sendin' Joe Sands. I owe you for what they done to you, too. If they hadn't been busy with you they'd of been after us a lot sooner. We wouldn't of got away with most of our cattle."

Hitch asked, "You *did* get away?"

Rascal said with angry satisfaction, "Got far across the county line before they come ridin' up wavin' their papers. We told them they was out of their county, and they said they hadn't seen no sign. But we was on the Matthews country, and the Matthews men rode up and gave witness to it. That sheriff, he backed off like a scalded dog."

"I'm glad, Rascal."

"It was you that done it for us. They probably drove your herd someplace to where somebody else picked it up before they come for ours. That gave us time." He put his hand on Hitch's shoulder. "You'll be needin' watchin' after till we see how bad hurt you are. Kate's the best watcher you'll nearly ever see. You got a home here, Hitch, as long as you need it.'' He glanced at Law as if asking him to make it plain.

Law said, ''Rascal talks for me too, Hitch.''

Hitch feared he detected reservation in Law's voice, but perhaps it was on his own part; he hoped so. He nodded his thanks and wished they would go away awhile now and let him alone. His head ached terribly.

Then he saw a third man, silently standing just inside the flap. Law said, ''Hitch, I believe you know Cato Bramlett.''

Hitch did. He knew Bramlett's reputation, too. ''I know him. I wish *you* didn't.''

He managed to raise up and eat a little supper. He found after a while that he was too weak to stay up, and he lay down again. Kate very carefully removed the bandage and cleansed the wound. ''It's swollen worse, Hitch, but I reckon that's to be expected. Been a full day now since it happened.''

Her hands were gentle, and he warmed to their touch despite the pain they brought. The warmth roused a vague guilt, for it was in his rigid code of ethics that he had no right to enjoy another man's wife, even to this innocent extent. He found her looking directly into his eyes, and for a second came a fear that she might read his thoughts. He quickly looked down. She said, ''I hope I'm not hurtin' you.''

He said quietly, ''You never hurt anybody in your life.''

Bedtime came with darkness, for nobody spent more money than necessary on kerosene for lamps. It was proposed that Hitch be left where he was and that Law and Kate could carry the baby crib over to Rascal's dugout and sleep there. But Hitch wouldn't hear of it. ''When I'm dead you can put me where you want me. I'm not dead yet.''

He had Law and Rascal help him to Rascal's dugout. They put him on Rascal's cot despite Hitch's protest that he could as well sleep on the floor. Rascal said, ''The cot is yours, so hush up about it. I've slept on the ground so much of my life that when I do sleep on a bed I feel like I'm puttin' on airs.''

Cato Bramlett followed silently, taking no part in helping Hitch, offering no conversation. He had a couple of blankets on the earthen floor. He pulled off his hat and boots and lay on one blanket in the rest of his clothes. He pulled the other blanket over him. He lay smoking a cigarette, the glow not strong enough to light his face. Presently Rascal was snoring.

Bramlett said, ''You don't like me, Hitchcock.''

Hitch did not feel up to an argument. ''You and me don't see noways alike.''

''Your way don't seem to've got you anywhere. They gave you a cow-puncher shampoo and took your cattle. They ain't took nothin' from me.''

''They'll kill you someday, and maybe everybody that's around you.''

Bramlett finished his cigarette in silence and flipped it into a corner, where it winked out. By his even breathing, Hitch knew he was soon asleep.

But Hitch could not sleep, not for a time. Maybe he had slept too much during the day. His head throbbed dully now but without the hard pain he had felt earlier. He decided that since he had not died by now, he would live. He would probably suffer through this constant headache a few more days, and he would probably have to avoid overexertion. But he would live, and if John Torrington thought he had run Hugh Hitchcock out of the county, he was in for disappointment.

By and by, lying awake in the close stillness and quiet of the dugout, staring up at darkness, he let his mind drift to Kate. He put the tips of his fingers to the side of his face where for a few seconds he had felt the gentle warmth of her hand. Now, unbidden, came the thought of her and Law lying in each other's arms, giving each other love in the bed on which he had lain all day. It was a tormenting thought, a corrosive one, and he tried to push it away. He tried to force his mind to better days when he had ridden with Charlie Waide on the W, when he had shared the genial pleasure of a cowboy crew before trouble came prowling these hills. But always the picture came back, relentless, and against his will he wished it were him instead of Law.

The life of a cowboy had its freedoms; it had its many compensations to help offset the grinding hardships; but always there was this dark and lonely side, this troubling deprivation that Hitch had tried never to allow himself to dwell upon. Now he was unable to put it aside.

Then came the ugliest thought of all: *Law is a thief. Kate might be better off in the long run if something happened to him. I'd be better off, too.*

He denounced himself in silence for his weakness, his selfishness. He had not realized this effect the McGinty place would have on him. He decided that if tomorrow he could stay in the saddle, he would leave here. He could not spend another night in this dugout, these guilty pictures burning into his brain.

He arose next morning when he heard Rascal stirring. He sat up on the edge of the bed, the small room seeming to reel. He put his hands to his head. Rascal, hat on before either his shirt or his britches, said, "Lay back down, Hitch. We'll fetch you some breakfast."

Hitch reached for his clothes. "One baby here is enough." It took some effort, but he got himself dressed, and he stood up bracing one hand against the dirt wall. In a minute he managed a thin smile. "I believe I'm goin' to make it."

"Don't rush anything."

Hitch swayed to the flap and pushed outside. He struggled up the steps by bracing himself, and he stood alone, testing his strength. He turned his head carefully, looking back at Rascal and finding that the cowboy watched him worriedly. "Looks like my head was almost as hard as Slant Unger's gunbarrel."

Rascal was in no mood to banter. "Don't you overstep yourself. I'd as soon bury my own brother as to bury you, Hitch."

Hitch's eyes burned as he realized Rascal meant it. He moved toward the other dugout in short, halting steps. The farther he went, the stronger he became. Rascal helped him down the steps and called, "Kate, you ready for us to come in?"

"Come on, both of you." Hitch realized Kate probably had seen them through the tiny window which sat at ground level outside the dugout, shoulder level inside.

The smell of fresh coffee was good, and Kate's smile glowed. She was scrambling eggs, something a man didn't often have on a ranch unless there was a woman to watch out for the chickens. "Set him down at the table, Rascal. Breakfast'll be ready directly."

Rascal pulled a chair away from the table for him, but it faced toward the bed; Hitch couldn't look at that. He moved around the table. "If it's all the same, I'd rather sit where I can look out the window."

Cato Bramlett came along and they all sat down to breakfast. It surprised Hitch how hungry he was. The men ate without talking, the forks and knives rattling against the cheap tin plates. After a bit the baby stirred, tiny hands reaching beyond the top of the crib. Law smiled at his wife. "He wants his breakfast too." She smiled back. "Well, he's not goin' to get it while you men are in here."

When he had finished eating, Hitch said, "Rascal, you got my horse up close? I'll be goin' home today."

Kate protested quickly. "You can't do that. Who'll look out for you?"

"Same one who always does, me. I've made up my mind to it, Kate. I'll be all right."

Rascal seemed about to make an argument but changed his mind, seeing that Hitch would not be argued out of it. "I might just go over there with you and spend a day or two."

"No need in that."

"May be some of our cattle strayed in that direction. It'll give me a chance to find them before the sheriff does. Could still be some of yours left in the brush too, Hitch."

"I'm countin' on it. One reason I want to get on home."

Law frowned as he rolled a brown-paper cigarette. "Didn't figure on you leavin' so quick, Hitch. There was some business we wanted to talk to you about when you felt better."

"Business?"

"Bunch of us come up with an idea. We hoped you might like to join in with us."

Hitch glanced at Kate. The baby was fretting a little more. Hitch said, "Let's go talk about it outside. Not everybody has had breakfast yet."

A couple of short benches stood near the front of the dugout; there the McGintys sometimes sat to enjoy the cool of the evening. Law motioned for Hitch to take one of them, and he took the other. Rascal slouched on the ground, and Cato Bramlett squatted, silently playing mumblety-peg with a pocketknife.

Law leaned forward, face earnest. "Them big ranchers have got it in their heads they're goin' to run this country with an iron hand, but there ain't no reason we got to back away and let them, Hitch. There's ways for the little man to stand up and fight, and to earn himself a place here as strong as anybody. We can't do it standin' alone. We all got to stand together."

"We stood together once," Hitch pointed out. "We lost anyway."

"We lost a battle, but we ain't lost the war. There's one thing them big outfits understand and respect: size. They're strong because they got lots of cows, and cows mean money, and money means power. We can have lots of cows too, Hitch, if all of us combine what we got."

"You're talkin' about a pool outfit?"

Law nodded. "We already got us a name and a brand for it. The Three Cs, Cowboy Cattle Combine. Them of us that got cattle, we're throwin' them in for their value in stock. Them that got some money saved up, they're buyin' stock and givin' us some workin' capital."

Hitch could see Law was excited over the idea, and he

thought Rascal showed a little of it, too. He frowned and pointed his chin toward the man tossing the pocketknife. "Is Cato a part of it?"

Bramlett looked up. "I got me an interest."

Law said, "So've lots of other people, Hitch. Ol' Fant Gossett over in town, he's put money in and helped us figure some of the legal points like gettin' us a charter for the corporation."

"Fant Gossett too." Hitch mused. "If Fant puts his money into anything, he figures on a return."

"He'll get it; we'll all get it. I tell you, Hitch, pretty soon we'll have us an outfit big enough to hold its own against Selkirk or Torrington or any of them. They won't stomp on no poor cowboy anymore."

"The big outfits won't recognize you. They won't accept your reps."

"We'll have our own roundups; we don't need them. We'll be out there first, and with that many cowboys huntin' for them, there won't be many mavericks get away from us. Give us a year, Hitch, and there'll be ten thousand cattle runnin' these hills with the Three C brand on their hide."

"Takes land to run cattle."

"Them of us that've got places, we'll lease them to the combine. But there's all kinds of open range out here. The big outfits got no more right to it than we have. We'll take our share. And did I say ten thousand cattle? Give us two years and it'll be twenty thousand, or thirty. It's cows that make a man rich in this country, and we'll have more cows than anybody. We'll show them big outfits that they ain't so damned much."

"Cowboy Cattle Combine." Hitch said it quietly, getting the taste of it and finding it a little bitter. "Sounds more like the Get Even Cattle Company to me."

Law grinned. "I hadn't thought of that, Hitch. It fits; by God, it *does* fit. I wish we'd called it that."

"John Torrington and them others, they'll call it a lot worse. You think they'll be standin' still while all this goes on?"

"He'll be jumpin' around like a chicken with its head cut off, but there won't be a thing he can do."

"Don't you ever bet on it."

Law gazed intently at Hitch. "We'd like to let you in on the combine."

"I ain't got much left. You don't need me."

"A lot of people look up to you. Some of them on the fence, they'd join up with us if they seen you do it. Anyway, we owe you for helpin' me and Rascal save our cows."

"I like to know my partners, Law."

"You know us."

"I know Cato Bramlett, too, and Fant Gossett." He caught a look of threat in Bramlett's eyes as the man let the pocketknife drop.

Law showed disappointment. "I wish you didn't feel that way."

"I wish I didn't have to. If I was you, Law, I'd take a good look at the people I was throwin' in with."

"I've had a good look at the people on the other side. I like my partners better."

Hitch shrugged. Law was a grown man. "How about you, Rascal? What's your feelin'?"

Rascal's eyes were narrowed. "They done us awful dirty, Hitch."

That, Hitch decided, just about told it all.

XII

BEFORE HITCH WAS FAR DOWN THE TRAIL HE knew he had bitten off a large bite, trying to go home. At least the other night he had been unconscious part of the time and had not felt all the jarring. With each step Walking Jack took, it felt as if the top of Hitch's head was about to come off.

Rascal McGinty said, "You want to turn back, Hitch?"

Hitch didn't shake his head; it hurt too much. "I've come this far."

He was grateful when at last they rode over the final hill and he could see his place below. Never had that dugout looked so good. But bitterness touched him as he looked down at the half-finished corrals where he had been working when Joe Sands brought him the news. It appeared he wouldn't need those corrals now.

Rascal hadn't been there in a while. He whistled. "You've put a right smart of sweat into this place."

"Maybe all for nothin'."

"You get down and rest yourself. I'll do up the chores."

There wouldn't be much to that. Hitch hadn't gotten himself a milk cow, though many settlers had done so, including the McGintys. He had gone so long at the W without the taste of milk that he had no use for it, not to drink, not even for making bread.

Rascal looked around curiously. "What come of the chickens you bought off of the Matthews?"

"I'm not around here enough to watch out for them. Seemed like every day or two I come up with one less. Sometimes I'd find a half handful of feathers, sometimes no trace atall. Them coyotes, they can sneak in here in broad daylight and raid you while you're lookin' off. Only got three or four chickens left. They're so wary that I can't even find their eggs. I wish the coyotes would get them too so I could stop worryin' myself over them."

"Messy anyway, a chicken is. I'd rather walk amongst cattle anytime than amongst a bunch of chickens. If it wasn't for Kate and her cookin', we wouldn't have a chicken on the place. She *is* a dandy cook, Hitch."

"I noticed."

"Kind of nice havin' a married brother. You get to be a bachelor and still have a woman do the cookin' for you. Ain't hardly any way to beat that. You never did have no brothers, did you, Hitch?"

"Got three, back home in South Texas. They've never come up here, though; I don't expect they ever will."

"Then you'll have to find a woman for yourself; you can't get by easy like I done. A woman sure does pretty up a place, Hitch."

"I noticed."

Hitch slept well that night and felt much better the next morning. He and Rascal ate an early breakfast, saddled up and began riding out his claim and the draws and swales around it that might conceal cattle he had missed in his hurried roundup the other day. Among other things he hunted for and finally found the hat he had lost where the sheriff had overtaken him. They stopped in the shade of a big cottonwood at noon to chew on tough jerked beef and

to rest awhile from the heat. Hitch still had a constant headache, but it was less than yesterday's.

They had gathered a small herd of cattle through the
morning and now let them drift and graze along the banks
of the creek where the cottonwoods grew.

Rascal said, "Twenty-two cows, fourteen calves is the
way I count it. They didn't leave you much, Hitch."

"They won't leave me these either if I don't drift them
out of the county before they make another drag through
here."

"We'll run them over toward the Matthews place, where
we took the LRs," Rascal said.

"We don't want to overstock that country. If it comes a
dry summer and a hard winter, we'll all be in trouble."

"Them few you got left won't overstock anybody, and
you're already in trouble."

Hitch kept looking back over his shoulder as they drove
the cattle, half afraid the sheriff would come riding along
about the time they hit the county line. But he didn't; he
was probably busy gathering in other "maverick" herds.
Late in the afternoon Hitch and Rascal turned the cattle
loose along a good creek and sat awhile to watch them drift.
Hitch hoped they wouldn't decide to drift back home.

The two men took advantage of range hospitality to go
over to the Matthews ranch, knowing they would be invited
to have supper and spend the night. The Matthews men had
been buffalo hunters a decade ago, coming here from the
Arkansas River country shortly after MacKenzie set the Comanches afoot in 1874 and forced them to the reservation.
When the buffalo played out, Walt and Ben Matthews laid
claim to one of their favorite hunting camps and took cattle
there. They were only a nuisance size to big companies like
the Figure 4 and Snaketrack, too small to consider as equals
but too large to push around. They ran perhaps a thousand
or fifteen hundred cattle, which was more than Hitch and
the McGintys and several other cowboy operators combined.
They had remained neutral and untouched during the strike;
they never hired more than a couple or three extra cowboys.

Their wives were fruitful, and they raised their own help.

The women's cooking was good and their sympathetic attention was pleasant, if only the youngsters' incessant running and shouting had not seemed to make Hitch's head hurt worse. Rascal took pleasure in watching the children, though. The older ones crowded around him and believed his outrageous lies.

"Hitch," Rascal said, "I hope Kate has a dozen kids. I expect Law'll be happy to do his part." He studied Hitch, frowning. "Did I say somethin' wrong?"

"Been a long day, and maybe I overdone it some. I'm goin' to find me a place to spread my blanket."

Next morning Walt and Ben Matthews suggested they had several days of work on which they needed help and offered standard cowboy wages if Rascal and Hitch would stay. Hitch figured they did it more out of sympathy than need; he declined. Rascal accepted.

"You sure you're able to be by yourself now?" Rascal worried.

"I'm all right."

"The cookin's good over here, and so's the company."

"I want to be home where I can think things out. I got some decisions to make, Rascal."

"You think some more about that combine deal. You'd be a good manager for the Three Cs."

"I'll study on it."

He did not have to give it much study; all he had to do was remember that Fant Gossett and Cato Bramlett each had a part in it. He regarded Gossett as a windbag and opportunist whose integrity was in serious doubt. He had no doubt whatever in regard to Bramlett's integrity.

He took his time going home, riding out some of the breaks in hopes he would find other Two Diamond cattle he had missed. He found one cow mixed with several carrying the Figure 4. One maverick heifer was running with the bunch. He knew within reason that she probably had been weaned by a Figure 4 cow, but there was no way for him or anyone else to prove it.

"One heifer," he said to himself. "They owe me a hundred times that many. But sis, you're a start."

He shook down his rope, touched spurs to Walking Jack and lined her out in a lope. He swung the loop over his head until he had her positioned just to the right and a few feet ahead of the horse. He sent the loop sailing around her half-developed horns and pulled up the slack. He slowed Jack gently, letting her reach the end of the rope without being unnecessarily rough. He flipped a little slack out to let it drop down over and around her rump, then spurred Jack away from her. The effect when he hit the end of the rope was to pull her completely around and flop her on her side hard enough to knock the breath from her momentarily. Hitch stepped down quickly with a short piece of rope, dropped the loop of it around one forefoot, then wrapped that foot and the two hind feet together before she had time to recover and get up.

The exertion was extreme for him, and he paused awhile, panting. When he had his strength again, he walked around and knelt by her head, turning it up and smelling of her breath. "No milk," he said in satisfaction. "Your ol' mammy has cut you off, all right."

To brand a calf that had milk on its breath was foolhardy for a mavericker; if that calf turned up following a cow that wore another brand, it was all the evidence needed to prove theft.

Hitch gathered dry wood from dead brush and built a small fire. Into this fire he dropped a cinch ring from his chaps pocket. Waiting for the ring to heat, he remounted and rode a circle, looking for sign that anyone was around. The fire was too small to create much smoke and draw attention, but there was always a possibility someone might ride by out of coincidence. Seeing no one, he went back. He cut a green switch from a tree and doubled it though the ring to hold it steady. Laboriously he ran his Two Diamond brand onto the heifer's spotted hide, pausing once to reheat the ring. Finished, he stepped back and dropped the ring into the sand, pushing it under with his boot to cool it. The stench of burned hair was strong. He dug out his pocketknife and notched her right ear with his own mark. Then he untied the rope and jerked it from her feet.

"Get up, sis. You belong to me now."

She was more frightened than angry and made no effort to fight him as she arose, hind end first. She trotted toward the other cattle, her hind end wobbling from partial cutoff of circulation while she had lain with her feet tied. Hitch poked his toe in the sand until he brought up the ring and found it cool enough to touch. He dropped it back into his chaps pocket, stomped out the little fire and remounted. He picked out his Two Diamond cow and the newly branded heifer from the others and drove them east, toward the Matthews country where his other remnants had gone.

He watched them trail away into the dusk after he turned them loose. Voice bitter, he said under his breath, "That's just maverick number one, Prosper Selkirk. You and John Torrington owe me a hundred more, and you're goin' to yield them up."

Hitch did not expect finding mavericks to be easy, and it was not. Main purpose of the big ranches' roundups was to brand the calves before they had a chance to become mavericks. Another thing, competition was keen, for many a cowboy left at loose ends by the strike had decided to go into business for himself. Hitch would get up long before daylight of a morning and ride to some distant point where he had not been, then spend most of the day combing the rolling hills and the draws and the creekbottoms for unbranded cattle. Many days he found none; other days he might find one or two. He found fresh brands he had never heard of, things like a Boxed Cross that he knew was probably a rustler brand purposely made out of the Figure 4; an RE connected, the R backward against the E and probably incorporating Torrington's Snaketrack; an arrowhead, this likewise fashioned out of the Snaketrack.

The boys have been busy, Hitch thought, *and they've been bold.*

Increasingly he saw the CCC, most often in combination with some previous-owner brand, indicating the owner had put his cattle into the pool. But Hitch also found it sometimes on yearlings that carried no other brand; these were mavericks someone had caught and claimed for the combine. If any combine stock had been sold to cowboys still working on the big ranches—which he suspected was the case—it would be particularly easy for these cowboys to put the pool brand on company cattle when no one was looking. That was exactly the kind of thing that had prompted the ranchers to invoke the no-cattle rule against employees. By now they probably were prohibiting any interest in the combine, too, but stock ownership might be hard to prove if a man choose to remain silent about it.

Three weeks of hard riding netted him only nine mavericks. At this rate he would never be even for the cattle they had taken from him, for as time went on the mavericks would be even harder to find; the competition was severe.

One day he came across a scattering of Snaketrack cattle along a creek and gently rode through them. The wagon crew had worked this area within recent weeks, for the calves carried fresh Snaketrack brands to match the ones their mammies had. Not a maverick in the bunch. But Hitch did find a single bull calf following a Figure 4 mother. This calf somehow had escaped both iron and knife; had he not still been following a plainly marked mother, he would be free for the taking.

In his bitterness Hitch considered the various dodges he had heard of for forcing a calf to be weaned. He had known of men burning the calves' noses, making it too painful for them to suck, or of cutting the hoofs to the quick to lame the calf temporarily so it could not follow, then running the mother to hell and gone; or simply shooting the mother and driving the calf away. Hitch discarded such notions out of hand, for these were cruel, and anyway he was not a thief. He had never branded a calf that was not a true maverick.

But damn them, they owe me.

Then came the idea, a hair brand. It was not quite legal,

yet it was not really illegal either. This was simply a brand made on the hair but not on the hide. Unless inspected closely, it would be regarded as a regular brand, and a company cowboy was likely to ride on by and give the calf no further attention. But through the long winter months the hair would grow out. By the time the calf was weaned there would be no sign of a brand, and the calf then would be a maverick.

The plan was so simple and easy that Hitch was surprised it had not come to him before. If the cow were a Selkirk, he could put a Figure 4 on her calf's hair; if a Torrington, a Snaketrack. Granted that other maverick men would have as good a chance as he to take that animal next winter or spring, at least he should be able to catch a good share of them. If he worked at it, for every two or three calves he hair-branded, he ought to be able to harvest one maverick later.

Even if caught, he could show that he had broken no law. The brand he placed on the calf would be the same one carried by its mother.

"Torrington . . . Selkirk," he whispered as he shook down his rope, "you'll pay me yet."

Catching the calf was easy, and he dragged it down into the brush where any chance rider was unlikely to see. He flanked the calf by hand and tied it, then gathered wood for a small fire and dropped in the cinch ring. He squatted on his spurs and studied the calf which lay vainly trying to kick. It bawled, and its anxious mother answered.

Ol' John Torrington would bawl too if he knew, Hitch thought. *Him stealing off of me was one thing, but me stealing off of him is something else.*

Stealing. The word did not sit easy. Hitch told himself that what he was doing was not stealing; it was simply recovering the equivalent of what he had lost.

But what he was doing here was the same, in effect, as what he had fired Law McGinty from the W for; he was artificially creating a maverick, knowing full well the brand its mother bore.

I don't know what's so bad about it anymore, he told himself in justification. *Everybody does it; the big take away from the small, and the small take away from the big.*

The cinch ring began to glow. Hitch tried to grip it in a green switch and burned his fingers. He dropped the ring into the dirt and shook his hand. He pushed the ring back into the fire to heat again. This time he got a heavier switch and a good hold. Carefully he ran the brand, burning the hair down to the hide but not marking the hide itself. He backed away a couple of steps to check his work. It looked good.

He castrated the calf and put the Snaketrack mark into its ear, knowing he could replace it later with his own larger one and no one be the wiser.

He stood up and looked at the brand again. Nobody would ever know.

A sobering thought chilled him. *Nobody? I'll know.*

This was the first time in his life he had ever stolen anything. *I never thought any man could force me to this.* He tried to shrug off the depression that came over him. *Hell, it's their own fault; they brought it on themselves. I'm only taking back what they stole from me.*

He tried to dismiss the doubts by telling himself there was a good chance someone would beat him to this calf anyway, as soon as it was weaned. The hair brand was no guarantee he would personally profit. But it was virtually guaranteed that Torrington would lose.

He reached for the tie-rope to let the calf up, but he could not bring himself to jerk the knot. He knelt, cursing himself for weakness and indecision. "Aw," he swore finally, "what the hell?" and dropped the cinch ring back into the fire. When it was hot he branded the Snaketrack well into the hide, where it would stay. He let the calf up and hollered "Git!", sending it running. "Git before I change my mind." But it was too late to change his mind.

"No charge, Torrington. But damned if I'll ever do it again."

He mounted Walking Jack, recoiled the rope and started home, hunched in anger at himself.

John Torrington, he thought, *you and Selkirk may break me; you may take away all I've got but one thing, and that's my pride. Be damned if I'll let you turn me into a thief.*

The incident left him in a ill humor for hunting cattle. The coyotes had finally gotten all the chickens but one hen, which relieved him of any worry about eggs. But they hadn't hurt his garden, and it needed tending if he was to eat this winter and not have to spend much from his meager bankroll. The garden work caught up, he went back to building his corrals. True, he had no cattle here now; he could not afford to bring any and risk their being taken into "escrow" like the others. But a man had to show faith in the future.

One day he looked up from digging postholes and was shaken to discover a man sitting on a blue roan horse, silently watching him from perhaps thirty yards. Hitch didn't know how long he had been there; he had been so busy cussing and fussing with rocks in the postholes that he hadn't noticed him riding up. He rubbed his sleeve across his face to stop the sweat from running into his eyes, and he tried to clear those burning eyes long enough to tell who the man was. He was no one Hitch had seen before. Hitch said, "Howdy. Come on over."

It had been a week or ten days since he had seen anyone. He hadn't realized how lonesome it would be out there by himself after working with a cowboy crew for years and having people all around him. He was ready for company. But the man just sat there.

Hitch thought he might not have heard, so he hollered again. The man still sat there staring at him. Though Hitch didn't know him, he became increasingly afraid that he knew the type. "Howdy," he said a third time, without eagerness now.

The sweat was running down his chest and back, the shirt sticking to him, but nevertheless he felt a hard chill. He saw the pistol in the holster at the man's hip, and the sun caught the shiny stock of a saddlegun in a scabbard under his leg. Directly the man touched spurs easily to the roan horse and moved up in what seemed like the slowest walk Hitch had ever seen. Hitch looked at that pistol and that saddlegun, and the thought kept running through his mind that his own saddlegun was in its scabbard in his saddle beneath the shed fifty yards away. He had never owned but one pistol in his life, and he had swapped that a long time ago for a pair of chaps, a good bridle and a saddleblanket. Those were much more practical for his use.

The rider came so near that with one good stride Hitch could have reached out and touched him; he wouldn't have made that stride for a thousand dollars. The man looked down at him with cold eyes the color of steel. His mouth lay flat and hard beneath a gray-salted mustache that curved grimly around its corners. A small badge shone on his shirt pocket. He said, "Whichaone are you?"

"My name is Hugh Hitchcock."

The man nodded. "Hitchcock. I remember. They said you was wagon boss for old Waide, had lots of men workin' under you. You was really somebody come." He looked over the dugout, over the still unfinished brush corrals, then back to Hitch in sweat-crusted old clothes patched and ragged. "The mighty do fall, don't they?"

Dread came to Hitch, dread like he had once felt when he had to enter a house where a man had died of smallpox. "What can I do for you?"

The rider said, "I'm the new deputy sheriff for this county. Name's Lafey Dodge."

The chill came again. Lafey Dodge had been mixed up in that Lincoln County trouble over in New Mexico. Some said he had been a friend of Billy the Kid, some said he had been an enemy. It didn't matter; neither way was any recommendation. It was said he hired out the use of those guns to whoever offered his price. He called himself a shootist, which was a way of saying he was an artist with a gun. He had the reputation of being an undertaker's friend.

His age surprised Hitch a little; he had not expected Lafey

Dodge to be a man this old. Dodge appeared to be in his fifties, and a little softness was pushing over his belt. But there was no softness in his eyes.

Hitch said again, "Somethin' I can do for you?"

"You could move out."

Cold sweat was breaking on Hitch's face. "This is my place."

"I know a couple of men who would buy you out. If I was you, I'd be in a notion to sell."

"You meanin' to threaten me?"

The man's expression never changed. "I never threatened nobody. I've never had to. I always been one just to state the facts and let a man make up his own mind whichaway he stands. The facts are that there's some people that don't cotton to a lot of squatters settin' theirselves down on the river."

"I'm no squatter. I got the papers."

"That makes you a higher-class squatter than some, but still a squatter just the same."

Hitch decided if Lafey Dodge intended to kill him now he would already have done it, for the man obviously derived no satisfaction from this talk. Hitch sized him as a cold, methodical man who took no pleasure in taunting or baiting. Whatever he came to do, he would do it without talk and fanfare. Dodge was unlikely to shoot an unarmed man; he had the reputation of staying close enough to the law that he could stay around and spend his money in the same place he had earned it. Hitch said, "We're all squatters in this world, when you look at it that way. The land belongs to the Lord; we just use it a little while."

"I wouldn't know about that. I just know there's some taxpayin' citizens worried about *this* bunch of squatters. The trouble with a squatter is, he don't generally have much of his own, so he uses that which belongs to the other man. Land, cattle, all of it."

"Has somebody accused me?"

"Can't say as I know. I was just sent here to deliver a

message. If they decide they got another message for you, I'll be back.''

Afterward Hitch thought of many brave things he could have told Dodge had he had the inclination, which he did not. He could have said he figured the big difference between Selkirk and the little people was that he was a big squatter and they were little ones. If the Figure 4 or John Torrington had had to keep all their cattle confined on the land their papers covered, they would not have amounted to much in the cow business.

But it seemed a waste of time to point this out to Lafey Dodge; he was not looking for that much information. Possession was nine points of the law, and his bunch had all nine.

XIII

LAFEY DODGE WOULD HAVE MADE AN EASY target, riding that blue roan horse away in no hurry at all, back turned as if he were trying to tempt Hitch to move toward his rifle. More likely, Hitch decided, he was walking that horse to give Hitch a long time to watch him and contemplate so he would not soon forget him. Dodge need not have troubled himself over that.

Hitch had to finish building those corrals, but now it was a nervous, unpleasant job. Because Dodge had caught him digging postholes the first occasion, each time Hitch went back to it he kept thinking he might look up and see Dodge there again on that big roan. He kept expecting to.

One day he looked up and saw a rider coming, and the breath caught in his throat. But he knew the horse, and he knew the man by the way he rode, shoulders cramped as if they hurt him with every step the horse made.

Charlie Waide.

Charlie was by himself, which didn't particularly surprise Hitch. What surprised him was that Charlie came at all. He hadn't seen the old rancher since he went to deliver the strike notice, and that had been three or four months. Charlie looked older now.

Hitch laid aside the "idiot stick" and raised his hand. "How do, Charlie? Git down."

Charlie dismounted as if it hurt him. The two men shook hands and went through the amenities, but they were awkward about it, like strangers cautiously making themselves known to one another. Charlie asked how everything was, though he could see for himself that prosperity had not found Hitch's address. Particularly he inquired about any aftereffects of the pistol whipping. Hitch asked how Charlie had been, and Charlie told him about all the trouble he had had lately with his arm.

"Come on up to the house, Charlie," Hitch said, "and I'll fix us some coffee." He had gotten in the habit of calling his dugout a house, something he had caught from Kate McGinty. Even yet, it was more camp than home.

Charlie Waide shook his head and dug into his saddlebag for a bottle of whisky. "Coffee don't do much for the pain." He passed the bottle, and Hitch took a shot of it, his first swallow of whisky in a long time. Charlie took a long, long drag like he was trying to find the bottom of the bottle. Then he squatted in the loose earth where Hitch had been digging. He rambled awhile about the fact that Hitch had done a lot to bring the place up, that his fences looked good and square, and that sort of thing. He expressed his regrets over the taking of Hitch's cattle and said there hadn't been a thing he could do.

Hitch said, "Anyway, I thank you for sendin' Joe Sands."

"If anybody ever asks you, it was a hoot-owl whispered in your ear."

Hitch decided Charlie was not here by chance; he had come for a purpose, and he was putting off talking about it as long as he could.

Charlie finally blurted, "Selkirk's got me by the short hair. Been talkin' about callin' in my loan. I reckon if he knowed that I told Joe Sands, he'd of called it already.''

Hitch let a long breath go out slowly. ''That's too bad.''

''He's been mad ever since the strike; says I didn't give him and Torrington enough support. If he calls that note, he'll bust me to a splinter.''

''That's rough, Charlie.'' Hitch wished he had stronger words of comfort, but that was all he could think of to say.

Charlie's eyes were bleak. ''Goddamn Yankees . . . they been after me all my life, seems like. Tried to kill me in the war; left me crippled. Been after my hide ever since I come up here and started spreadin' out and lookin' like I might overtake them. Don't seem like they can stand to see a native man pull himself up and amount to somethin'. They'll slap him down ever chance they get.''

Hitch knew that was more Charlie's prejudice than fact. John Torrington, for one, was a Texan, born in war and weaned on border troubles that had left him tough as a rawhide boot. But there was no gain in arguing with Charlie Waide. Hitch said, ''At least you'd be free of Selkirk then, free from all of them. Whatever you had left would be all yours; they couldn't touch you.''

Charlie nodded his gray head, and some of the old spark flickered in his eyes. ''That's the consolation; I'd pay them off and then I'd tell them to bend over and kiss my left hind cheek. At least I own a right smart of my own land, and some of them don't. From now on every dollar I lay my hands on, I'll use it to buy land with. One of these days that free-grass bubble will bust, and then we'll see who's who. We'll see how them damnyankees like havin' their faces rubbed in fresh doin's.''

The anger and the hate came boiling up. Hitch understood better than ever now that in a way Charlie had gone on fighting the war long after it had ended, and he seemed to think everyone else was fighting it too. He had kept trying to prove that even in military defeat he was still much of a man. He was trying in his off-center way to make up for the wound that had crippled him, to keep hurling defiance into the faces of old enemies who had long since forgotten the fight.

Charlie's voice was gritty. "By God, I'll whip them yet before I die."

Hitch managed a smile. "Charlie Waide, you'll never die. You'll just turn into an old gray mule and kick some *young* man to death."

That seemed to please Charlie; he eased a little. Presently Hitch told him, "They're a long ways from bein' whipped yet. They sent me a visitor the other day." He told about Lafey Dodge.

The news was no surprise to Charlie. "I swear to you, Hitch, I been no party to that. Old John Torrington was the one who wanted to hire professionals and break up the strike by force, only him and Selkirk wanted to make an assessment against all us ranchers to pay for the guns. I told them hell no, and some of the other ranchers done the same. Way I heard it, Torrington and Selkirk wound up havin' to pay for Lafey Dodge all by themselves. You know Selkirk; he got the sheriff to deputize Dodge so the county has to carry part of the load." Charlie poked aimlessly in the dirt. "You'll want to be careful of him, Hitch; he's a bad one."

Hitch said he had no intention of stirring Dodge up.

"If ever he comes after you," Charlie said, "don't be foolish and give him a chance. Take every advantage. Kill him any way you can."

He kept scratching in the dirt, and Hitch noticed he had made a Figure 4 brand, then altered it into a McGinty LR. Charlie said, "Ain't really you I'm so concerned about, Hitch. I feel like you'll take care of yourself the way you always took care of me. But I *am* worried about Law and Rascal McGinty." He looked off toward the McGinty claim, away yonder and out of sight. "You ever see them?"

"Sometimes."

Charlie frowned deeply. "I wisht you'd go talk to them. They wouldn't listen to me, I'm afraid. I try not to remember what Law done; I try to remember the good cowboy he used to be. I'm worried about him, Hitch. He's puttin' himself in shape to get killed."

Hitch stared.

Charlie asked, "Hitch, you bought any interest in that Three Cs outfit?" When Hitch said he hadn't, Charlie said, "That's good. But Law is in it up to his neck. Somethin' bad has got into that boy to make him throw in with the likes of Cato Bramlett. Law's been runnin' Figure 4 cattle down into the breaks and changin' them over to the LR. Been changin' the Snaketrack into one of them other pool brands."

Hitch shook his head, hoping Charlie wouldn't see that he already knew.

"He don't know it, Hitch, but Law's been watched. Remember, what John Torrington said about catchin' somebody and makin' an example of him? They got Law McGinty's name wrote at the top of their list. They're watchin' him, and sure as a spotted calf follows a spotted cow, they'll spring the trap on him. Then you'll know what they hired Lafey Dodge for."

Hitch sat on his heels, staring at Charlie's cattle brands in the sand. His hands were wet with cold sweat, but his mouth was dry.

Charlie said, "Maybe Rascal knows, maybe he don't. I don't believe he'd be a party to it, but he might know and not stop it. If he's around when they come for Law, they're liable to kill him for bein' in the way."

"I doubt Law would listen to me."

"Talk to Rascal then, if you got any feelin' for them boys and for that little girl over there. Make Rascal bend a gunbarrel over Law's head if he has to, but stop him. Them people want blood."

Charlie started to go, but he kept hanging back, wanting to say something more. "Worst day I've had since the war was the day you boys all up and left my wagon. Hitch, we still friends?"

The need for friendship was heavy in his eyes. Hitch said, "We'll always be friends, Charlie."

But somehow he knew it would never again be the same.

*   *   *

Hitch found Law and Rascal shoeing horses behind their shed. He didn't see Kate. She evidently hadn't been aware of his coming, and he was glad for that. She would ask the reason for his visit; he didn't want to lie to her.

The McGintys said they would finish the job in a few minutes and go "up to the house" for a drink. Hitch said, "I'm not here for social reasons. I got somethin' you-all need to hear."

They studied him curiously; the deadly seriousness of the matter must have shown in his face. Rascal said, "If it's Lafey Dodge you're talkin' about, we already seen him. He scared Kate half to death."

That, Hitch thought, was probably part of the strategy. Get a man's woman scared enough and the man was likely to leave. "Ain't Dodge I come about, at least not altogether." He didn't know how to phrase it gently, so he just threw it out there like a loaded gun. "Law, they all know you been swingin' the wide loop."

Color rushed into Law's face. "What you been tellin'?"

"I ain't told anybody nothin'." He recounted what Charlie Waide had passed on to him. Law appeared more angered than worried, but Rascal's face seemed to turn gray.

Law said, "If you're spreadin' stories, Hitch, you ain't no friend of mine."

"I came here because I *am* a friend."

Law's voice was angry. "Like hell you are. You better go!"

Rascal McGinty turned savagely on his brother. "Damn you, Law, shut your mouth and listen to somebody for once in your life!" He so startled Law that the younger McGinty rocked back on his heels, silent. Rascal said tightly, "Hitch, we're doin' all right; we don't have to steal . . . not from nobody. I got a little outside work with some of these little ranchers now and again, and if we're careful on what we spend we'll make it through. We don't have to steal."

Hitch had the feeling Rascal was talking more to his brother. Hitch didn't have to ask outright; he could read it in Rascal's eyes that he knew Law was guilty. Hitch said, "What you're doin' ain't necessary, Law. You got a start here, you and Rascal. Keep all your heifer calves and you'll be surprised how soon you'll have a herd as big as Charlie Waide came to this country with. You got no need to throw in with the likes of Cato Bramlett. This other way is slower, but it'll get you there."

"When?" Law demanded. "When I'm an old man with a beard down to my navel? I ain't waitin', Hitch. They owe us for what all they've done, and they'll pay. The Three Cs is goin' to have forty-fifty thousand cattle before I'm done. They'll wish they'd never tried to mess with Law McGinty. You can cringe and bow if you want to, but I'm standin' up and spittin' right in their coffee."

"In their eyes you're a thief."

"And in your eyes too, I suppose?" Law seemed to answer that question for himself. "I told you already, you better go."

Hitch wasn't ready. "Don't underestimate them, Law. They mean business; that's why they hired Lafey Dodge. You got a wife to be thinkin' about, and a baby."

Law flared, "I'll take care of my wife; I don't need you to help me. Seems to me like you been more concerned about her than you got any business bein'."

Rascal exclaimed, "Law!"

"It's the damned truth," Law said bitterly. "He wanted her himself, only I beat him to her. He knows he can't ever have her and it eats at him. Don't believe me? Look at his face."

In the moment before he turned away, Hitch knew his eyes betrayed him.

Rascal said reproachfully, "Law, Hitch come to help you."

"By makin' me out a thief? If you believe him, why don't you just go on along with him?"

Rascal's face was splotched, and for a moment it appeared he might strike his brother. "Hitch tells the truth,

Law. I've known it a long time. Now, I believe I *will* go with him.''

Hitch heard a sound, a tiny whimper. Turning, he saw Kate McGinty. The baby in her arms was making some soft noise, but Kate made no sound at all. She stared, eyes wide with hurt and surprise.

Hitch's mouth dropped open. He wondered how much she had heard.

She tried to speak, and her voice broke. Tears shining, she tried to say, ''I was . . . goin' to ask you-all . . . up to the house . . .'' She broke off and hurried back to the dug-out, crying.

Rascal silently riding beside him, Hitch left there feeling like a whipped dog.

Rascal didn't stay long; he found another short-term job at the Matthews place. Hitch bided his time, living out of the garden and off of stray beef, the custom of the country. He spent most of his days riding the Canadian River country in an almost futile search for mavericks.

The green grass made its seedheads and stood gold against the summer sun, then began to cure with all the strength that once made it the great buffalo range it had been for uncounted generations of Indian hunters, and the cow range it had lately become. The hot wind was always there, searching a man out wherever he went. It came sometimes like a friend and sometimes like it sought to punish, but always it came.

And one day as it came it brought the sound of running horses and turning wheels. Even before Hitch went to look, he thought he knew. He had sensed the inevitability of it that day Charlie Waide had talked to him.

Kate McGinty drove the wagon as if she were trying to wreck it. Her baby was tied in her lap so both her hands were free for the lines. She shouted at the lathered team, and as she rolled into Hitch's camp she was screaming.

''They're killin' him, Hitch! They're killin' him! Help me, Hitch, for God's sake help me!''

The team had stopped by the corrals, bellies heaving, their
mouths open and their nostrils flared. Kate's face was
flushed red. Even as she blurted the story, Hitch was throwing the saddle on Walking Jack.

"They came to get him, Hitch. They let me and the baby
go, but they cornered Law in the dugout. He's trapped."

"Where's Rascal at?"

"Gone on a job. You're the only one can help us."

"How many are they?"

"Seven or eight."

Hitch considered the odds and felt a chill. "They didn't
hurt you none, Kate?"

She shook her head. "Please do somethin' to help Law.
He can't stand against them long."

Hitch pointed east. "You know where Dan Truman's
place is, and the Matthews outfit just past it?" She did, and
he told her to go get Dan, get the Matthews men. "Get
anybody else in reach!"

He spurred Walking Jack into the hardest lope the horse
had struck in a long time. As he looked back he saw Kate
slapping the lines at the team, driving them into a run again.
She would likely kill them, or run them into the ground.

Hitch pushed the horse as hard as he dared, the hot wind
burning his face. Seven or eight men, and one of them certainly Lafey Dodge.

What in the world will I do when I get there? he asked
himself urgently, and he came up with no answer, no earthly
idea. All he could do was keep urging Walking Jack with
the spurs.

A sick feeling washed in his stomach; he had a fear that
whatever he did, he would be too late, and he dreaded what
he would find when he got there. He tried to think of something he could do, but he had no more plan when he neared
the McGinty place than when he had left his own.

He saw a lone horseman moving west, slumped in the
saddle. The rider spotted Hitch but kept his horse in a trot.
Angling toward him, Hitch recognized the sheriff. The lawman appeared badly shaken. He started trying to wave Hitch

back, but Hitch stayed on course and pulled Jack to a halt in the dry grass.

The sheriff said, "Hitchcock, go back to where you come from."

"What's happened?"

"I had me a prisoner. They took him. Don't go over there, Hitchcock. It'll already be too late."

"Law McGinty?" Hitch demanded, though he knew before he asked.

"I tried to arrest him and he got into his dugout. His wife and baby come out and then we tried to smoke him loose. Finally we brought the dugout down around him and drug him into the open. Then they taken him away from me, Dodge and them others."

"You mean you *let* them have him!" Hitch shouted. "What kind of a sheriff are you?"

"I'm an ex-sheriff, that's what kind I am."

"You're not a sheriff and never was. You're a coward."

"There's worse things than bein' a coward; there's bein' dead. When I taken this job they told me there wouldn't be nothin' to it; just a drunk cowpuncher now and then was all. They don't pay me enough to fight Lafey Dodge. If you're smart, Hitchcock, you'll wait a while before you go down there. Don't go amongst them while their blood is hot or they might do it to you, too."

Hitch stood in his stirrups, wanting to strike the man with all the strength that was in him. "If they've done what you say they have, I'll be in to see you, Sheriff."

"You better be quick about it. Soon's I can get my plunder together there won't be nothin' left but an empty office."

Hitch still had no idea what he was going to do, except keep riding. He spurred Jack into a hard run over the hill and down to the McGinty place, a cold knot drawn tight in his stomach.

He found what the sheriff had told him he would. The dugout lay in ruins, two ropes still looped around the center pole to pull it down. The dog had been killed. A milk cow lay dead in a corral gate, struck by a stray bullet. Hitch saw no men, but he quickly found the tracks of the horses. They led down to the river, where the trees were.

XIV

HITCH HAD NO PLAN; HE WASN'T EVEN thinking ahead now. He simply gave full rein to a cold rage that took over. He pulled his saddlegun out of its scabbard and rode in a walk. He saw the men clustered in the timber on the river, a couple on horseback, the rest afoot.

Hitch cocked the hammer back and kept riding. The tall cottonwoods swayed and threshed in noisy struggle against the high north wind. The men stared in morbid fascination at the result of their work and did not notice his approach. Lafey Dodge was the one Hitch watched closest; he stood on the ground. Old John Torrington, in the saddle, looked up at Law in satisfaction; this was not his first hanging. Slant Unger was also a-horseback and equally unmoved; whatever suited John Torrington was always all right with him.

But on the ground Prosper Selkirk was drawn up tightly, probably even trembling. It surprised Hitch that the man was here at all. Two Selkirk cowboys stood back to themselves as if ashamed. Tobe Ferris, Torrington's Negro cowboy, was the only man not looking up at Law. He stared at the ground; he might have been silently praying.

Ferris caught Hitch's movement from the tail of his eye and turned quickly. Hitch was almost close enough to have struck him with the gunbarrel. The other men turned then in surprise. Hitch was too choked to tell them to raise their hands. He motioned with the muzzle of the rifle, and they easily got his meaning. He held the saddlegun on the ready; in his rage it was all he could do to keep from picking one of them and shooting him. He glanced up and felt sickness come over him. He forced his eyes away from Law.

Lafey Dodge did not speak; he stared at that saddlegun. Prosper Selkirk was pale. John Torrington glared at Hitch with more impatience than fear. "This man was a thief," he growled.

Hitch's mind was afire with things to say, but he could not say them. He motioned the gunbarrel toward Unger, who was nearest the body. "Cut him down!"

Unger did not move. Torrington glanced at the hired gunfighter. "Do somethin', Dodge."

Dodge shook his head, not for a moment taking his eyes off the rifle.

Torrington growled, "Dammit, what do you think we're payin' you for? He don't know how to use that thing. He's nothin' but a cowboy."

Dodge said evenly, "That's the most dangerous thing there is, a mad cowboy with a gun in his hands. He'll kill somebody sure as hell."

Slant Unger said, "I ain't afraid of him," and spurred toward Hitch.

In cold rage Hitch shot him out of the saddle. He levered another cartridge into the chamber.

Unger writhed on the ground, clawing at a shattered arm. Dodge glanced down at him, then up at Torrington. "Goddammit, old man, I told you."

Hitch said to John Torrington, "*You* cut him down!"

Torrington looked at the smoking rifle and with care not to let his hand come anywhere near his gun, he fished a knife from his pocket. He cut the rope, and two men on the ground caught Law and laid him out on the grass.

The fallen Slant Unger began moaning. The sight of the blood brought Hitch to a realization of what he had done, and the bad position he was in. If Lafey Dodge was all his reputation implied, he could probably draw his pistol and kill Hitch any time he wanted to. Hitch's chance of bringing that saddlegun up to his shoulder and taking aim against a fast-draw man was not the kind a good gambler would bet his poke on. Hitch had shot point-blank at Unger without consciously trying. That he had even hit him in the arm was probably an accident.

But Lafey Dodge just stared at that saddlegun and gave it full respect. Gradually Hitch came to a conclusion that surprised him a little: at this moment, Lafey Dodge was afraid of him. He wondered if the man's reputation as a *shootist* might not be somewhat exaggerated.

Old Torrington's face was ablaze. "We're a legal posse, duly sworn."

"You ain't no court," Hitch told him. "You lynched a man without a trial. That makes every man here a murderer!"

Hitch watched all the men, but he continued to watch Lafey Dodge most. John Torrington had been a hellion in his day but was too old now to do much real fighting for himself. Prosper Selkirk's being here didn't seem to fit; best Hitch could figure, his and Torrington's presence was meant to make it clear that the big ranches' full weight was behind this. The other men were simply cowboys . . . two Selkirks, three Torringtons. Hitch knew them every one.

Dread was cold in his stomach as he faced the eight men. It was like having a wildcat by the tail and being unable to turn loose. If all suddenly came at him, he might have time to shoot one, but he would certainly go down.

They were not going to rush him, though. He saw in every face what he had seen in Dodge's. As a mob hanging a helpless man they were one thing, but facing a gun they were eight uneasy individuals, each pondering the awful possibility that he might personally be the next shot down.

Hitch had a strong feeling he was about to throw up. If he did, he wouldn't want these men able to take advantage of his helplessness. He motioned with the saddlegun. "One at a time, you-all drop your guns."

They did, until the turn reached Lafey Dodge. Hitch said, "Not you, Dodge. You keep yours." The men looked at him in surprise, but Hitch was afraid to let Dodge touch a gun, even to shed it.

"What you fixin' to do with them guns?" Tobe Ferris asked cautiously.

"I'll throw them in the river."

"Mine cost me better than two months' wages."

"Spend the next two months thinkin' about the man you killed here. Now all of you, get on them horses and move out."

He held the saddlegun aimed at them until they rode over the hill, Ferris and another man supporting Slant Unger. Hitch had seen a couple of saddleguns and wished he had made them leave those, but he had been afraid a man could pull a horse around to cover himself and bring a rifle into play. He had left well enough alone.

He considered the possibility that someone might circle back and try to pick him off. Gradually he decided they would not come back. They had done what they came to do. He slumped. Throat tight, eyes afire, he looked down at the cowboy he had known for most of ten years. "Law," he whispered half accusingly, "you never would listen to a man, would you?" He noticed for the first time that Law's britches were wet. He realized with sudden force what terrible fear the cowboy must have suffered in those last moments.

"Goddamn them!" Hitch cried. "Goddamn them all!"

It was more than an hour before Dan Truman got there. He took a long look at the collapsed dugout, then rode over to Hitch, standing beside the saddleshed. His face showed that he knew. "I'm too late."

Hitch nodded. "We're all too late." Dan dismounted. Hitch led him into the shed and motioned toward the corner where he had carried Law out of the sun, covering him with a tarp he had found there.

Awhile later the Matthews men loped in. Far behind them came Kate McGinty's wagon with a fresh team. Mrs. Walt Matthews was driving so Kate could hold the baby. As the wagon stopped, Hitch strode out to meet it. Kate McGinty sat looking at him, her face grave. In her eyes he saw that he didn't have to tell her anything. She slowly handed the baby to Mrs. Matthews. Hitch raised his hands to help Kate climb down. She leaned into his arms and sobbed quietly. He held her, helpless to speak. He knew not a word that could change a thing.

Finally she asked, "Where is he?"

Hitch motioned toward the shed. Kate reached up and took the baby from Mrs. Matthews. She started to go into the shed but stopped and looked back at the ruins of the dugout she had so carefully kept. Hitch helped Mrs. Matthews to climb down, and together the women went into the shed.

The men remained outside, silent and grim. At length Dan Truman asked, "What we goin' to do about this, Hitch?"

Hitch was a long time in attempting a reply. "What they done was murder in the eyes of the law."

"Anywhere else, but not here. So what do we do now?"

Hitch shrugged. "I don't know. We'll do somethin'."

Later, when Kate was composed, Hitch suggested they could probably all work together and raise the dugout's center pole so that it could be repaired and made livable again. Kate shook her head. "Thanks, but no. If we can rescue some things out of there that we need, that'll be enough. I couldn't stay on this place again."

Hitch thought he knew her feelings. There would be Rascal's dugout for a night or two, if she needed it. After that she would probably go stay with her mother. He said, "First thing we have to do is put Law decently away. Do you want us to take him to town?"

Again she shook her head. "And bury him in Boothill? No, Hitch, this is his place; I want him buried on his own land."

"All right. I'll go to town and find a minister, and get your mother. While I'm there I'll see what I can do to have justice done."

She reached out and touched his hand. "Don't get in any trouble."

Dan Truman said, "I'll go with you, Hitch. You ain't goin' there all by yourself."

They rode straight to the sheriff's office. Hitch had little hope of getting satisfaction there, but he would try. He stepped through the door and stopped short. In a rawhide chair, feet propped up on a desk, sat Lafey Dodge, the silver deputy badge catching light from the window. He held a pistol in his lap, and a cleaning rag. But Hitch suspected the rag was only to give him some apparent reason to have the pistol out. Every chamber was probably loaded.

Dodge said coldly, "Figured you'd be in."

Hitch's stomach drew up, much as when he had faced Dodge and the other men earlier. His saddlegun was out yonder on the horse, a safe place for it, beyond temptation. "Where's the sheriff at?"

"I gather there ain't no sheriff. Wrote out his resignation and left town. Want to read it?" Dodge paused. "Suddenly decided town life was bad for his health, which looks to me like a good idea for some others. Town's hard on a boy who's used to the good clean country air. Feller like you, out of the country, ought to come to town as little as he possibly can. *Never*, if he can help it."

Dan Truman demanded, "You takin' over the sheriff's office?"

"Reckon there ain't nobody else to do it. They'll have to call a special election to fill the vacancy. Looks like I'm all the law they got till then. Hope you boys don't figure on makin' no disturbance."

Defeated, Hitch went to Kate McGinty's mother. Her reaction was a bitter mixture of condemnation for "that wild boy'' and sympathy for ''that poor little helpless girl of mine.'' Hitch told her he would borrow a buggy from Edson Biggs, or perhaps Biggs would take her out there himself.

At the small adobe building in which Edson had set up his new banking business, Hitch reviewed what had happened. Depressed, Dan Truman stood in the open doorway, leaning against the jamb and smoking cigarettes as he watched the sparse foot and horse traffic moving up and down the dusty street. Edson said with sadness. ''Law didn't have to steal. I told him and Rascal if they wanted to borrow some money to buy cows, I could get it for them. But Law thought he could get big faster through the Three Cs. Maybe he figured that way he didn't have to pay anybody back.''

''He paid.'' Hitch held silent a while, his throat too tight for talk. Presently he said, ''We got to have a preacher. I never been much to go to church, but I was hopin' you'd know one.''

''Sure, Hitch. First thing a banker does in a new town is to join the church.''

Dan Truman came erect and threw his cigarette out into the street. ''Hitch, it's Rascal!''

Hitch jumped to his feet. ''My God! Where?''

''Headin' for the sheriff's office hard as he can go.''

Hitch passed Dan Truman on the plank porch and hit the street running. ''Rascal!'' he shouted. ''Rascal, wait!''

If Rascal heard him he gave no sign. He reined in at the front of the sheriff's office and dismounted. Even at the distance Hitch could see the pistol in his hand. ''Rascal!''

He lost a stride, expecting gunfire, expecting to see Rascal stagger back out that open door. But there was nothing. Rascal strode out again, the pistol still in his hand. By now Hitch was almost up to him.

Bitter tears flowed down the red face. ''Where's he at, Hitch? I'm fixin' to kill him!''

Lafey Dodge had left the sheriff's office. But it wouldn't take Rascal long to find him in this town.

Breathing hard, Hitch could barely speak. ''Rascal . . . wait up. We got . . . to talk to you.''

Rascal shouted, "You seen him, Hitch?"

Hitch held off answering until he had most of his breath. "You're no match for him. He'll kill you."

"Not if I get the first shot."

Hitch saw there was no hope of arguing Rascal down; he had gone into a fury that would stop for nothing except blood. Hitch grabbed the pistol and gave it a sudden wrench. Caught by surprise, Rascal reacted to the pain by loosening his hold. Remembering what Slant Unger had done, Hitch jerked the pistol from Rascal's hand, brought it up and fetched Rascal a hard blow on the side of the head. Even through the felt hat, it was severe enough to send Rascal to his knees.

I *fractured his skull*, Hitch thought for a moment, then decided he hadn't. He grabbed the cowboy to keep him from dropping on his face. Dan Truman caught Rascal's left arm. Edson Biggs came running, not far behind. He said, "He'll be sore at you, Hitch, but he'll be alive."

They lifted the half-conscious Rascal onto his horse, and they had to hold him on till they got him to Biggs's bank. There they cleansed the wound with whisky. Rascal would have to go back to the ranch in the buggy with Biggs and Kate's mother.

Hitch did not expect to see many people at the funeral. He assumed that most would take Law's death as a general warning and would want to avoid displeasing the powers responsible. The crowd surprised him, families arriving in wagons and buggies, single men a-horseback. Before time for the service he estimated between seventy-five and a hundred horses tied around the dugouts and down by the river.

Biggest surprise, perhaps, was the quiet arrival of Charlie Waide and many of the W cowboys. Some of the river settlers and veterans of the strike edged back uneasily to give them room. Charlie Waide stood by his horse until he picked Hitch from the crowd, then handed the reins to a cowboy and walked to meet Hitch. His eyes were bleak.

"I come to pay my respects to Kate."

Hitch pointed his chin toward Rascal's dugout. "She's in there, Charlie. I'll take you to see her."

Charlie hesitated at the steps that led down to the door. "I'd sooner take a whippin'." But he came on. The canvas flap had been laid open, and Hitch let Charlie go in ahead of him. Kate McGinty sat in a rawhide chair, her mother and some of the neighbor women clustered in painful silence around her. Charlie crushed his hat in his hands, plainly afraid of the reception. "Kate . . ."

"Mister Waide," she said in little more than a whisper. "I didn't expect to see you."

"Took me a while to get the nerve to come. Kate, I want you to know . . . I didn't have nothing' to do with what happened. Done all I could to stop it."

She nodded. "I knew that all the time. I'm grateful to you for comin'."

"Kate, if there's anything you need, anything at all . . ."

"What I need, there's no way to bring back. But I'll always remember that you asked."

Charlie turned to leave, avoiding Hitch's eyes. Kate said, "Mister Waide, one thing I want you to know. Law always respected you. Even after he left the Ws, he never had a bad word to say about you."

Charlie didn't look back. He went up the steps. Hitch followed him. Charlie walked a short way from the dugout, then turned to look back. "Hitch, I meant what I told her. If she needs the borrow of any money . . ."

"Sure, Charlie. But it seems to me like there's somethin' else that's badly needed here. What're we goin' to do about them that killed Law?"

Charlie clenched his fist. "You got to remember, Hitch, he was stealin' cattle."

"A man goes to jail for stealin' cattle: he don't get hung."

Charlie looked Hitch in the eyes, a warning in his voice. "You had judgment enough to know when the strike was over. I hope you still know when to turn aloose of somethin' you got no chance to win."

When the time came, Hitch and the other pallbearers carried the pine coffin out of the shed and up the slope to a place Kate had picked. There were Dan Truman, Edson Biggs, the Matthews men, the ever-complaining Asher Cottingham. The minister followed, Bible in hand as he walked beside the black-veiled Kate. She carried the baby in her arms. Behind them walked a solemn procession of people many of whom could not possibly have known Law McGinty but whose presence could be taken as silent protest against the manner of his dying. That the message would quickly reach Torrington and Selkirk, Hitch had no doubt. There were many people here whom he did not know; certainly among them must be someone who would report to the ranchers.

They set the coffin on the ground and waited for the crowd to work around in a circle. The minister bowed his head for a prayer, then raised his chin. He looked at the people.

"It is always painful for me to perform a service like this for one so young, for one whose life should have spanned far more years, who should have been allowed to live to see his children grow to manhood, who should have lived to see the seeds of his labor bear fruit and yield their harvest to him. It is always tragic to see a life cut down just as it has come to flower.

"But there is an element of even more tragedy here, for this man was not swept away by some illness over which no man had control, nor was he victim to some accident which no man could have avoided. No, he was willfully put to his death by plan, by men who assumed unto themselves a power which the Scriptures plainly reserve to God alone. Had Lawton McGinty died of illness, or of some accident, we could have consoled ourselves that God's will was somehow served. But the act of murder is contrary to the will of God. Therefore as we weep today we weep in double anguish, for this death should not have been. This fine young woman should not be dressed in mourning clothes, and this baby should not have lost a father it will never be able to remember.

"So we come here today to mourn for Lawton McGinty, but let us do more than simply mourn. Let us pledge ourselves to seek some way of assuring that no other widow shall be left mourning in this manner, no other child left fatherless. There was a time, perhaps, when we could have shrugged our shoulders and said this was simply a thing that should be expected on the raw frontier, that harsh conditions somehow justify harsh actions. But my friends, the frontier is gone. We are a civilized people now, with laws and courts and established methods of justice. There are still some among us who live by the old ways, and this is a shame upon us as much as upon them, for we do not have to allow it. We must rise up in righteous anger and declare to them that this shall not happen again, that we shall not be silent nor stand fearful in the presence of their power. We must show them that we have come into a new time, that we intend to see this land pleasing to the sight of the Lord, and bountiful in His service. We need not bow to anyone but God."

The hymns started then, and it seemed to Hitch they would never stop. He did not know the words to most of them, even if he could have brought himself to sing. He watched Kate and wished for her sake that the service were over. The baby cried much of the time, and Kate cradled it tightly to her bosom. Perhaps, Hitch thought, it was a blessing the baby gave her concern, for it kept her distracted and did not let her dwell entirely upon her grief.

Finally the last amen had been said, and the coffin was lowered slowly by rope. Friends filed by and dropped a little sand into the grave. People moved back down the slope without the order they had shown on the way up. A few women repaired with Kate into the dugout, and many of the people left. But many stayed, talking among themselves. They still simmered in the quiet anger roused by the minister's words.

Charlie Waide acted for a moment as if he wanted to say

something to Rascal and Hitch, but the words wouldn't come. Hitch asked, "Charlie, did you listen to what he said?"

Charlie frowned. "He's just a preacher, Hitch. A preacher don't have to answer for anything." Charlie climbed stiffly onto his horse, his cowboys trailing after him. Some of the other men gathered in awkward silence around the saddle-shed, staring at each other, staring at the ruins of Law and Kate McGinty's dugout.

Rascal wore a bandage around his head, as Hitch had done a few weeks earlier. He had withdrawn into himself and had spoken little, seeming like some wild creature wounded and bewildered and seeking solitary retreat in his misery. Now suddenly he let the grief begin to spill out in talk. He spoke to no one in particular, unless possibly to himself.

"Pa died first, and then Ma, and then it was just me and Law. He was a little dickens then, ten-eleven years old, and me just a button myself to look after him and try to raise him. Law would tag along behind me like a colt followin' after a grown horse, only I wasn't grown either. We wandered around a long time before we found us a place with ol' Charlie. Seemed like there was always a little hell in Law. It ain't like he meant no harm by it, though; he was always just funnin'. There never was no real harm in that button, just a little more than his fair share of hell, was all." Rascal's fists clenched, and he cried out in a pain that was close to tears. "They could at least of shot him instead of hangin' him thataway; that's no fit way for a man to die. Even a cow-killin' wolf is given that much of a show."

He looked around bitterly. "And where's the people at that got him into this mess in the first place? Where's Fant Gossett? Where's Cato Bramlett?"

Asher Cottingham spat. "Fant couldn't afford to shut down business. You know how it is with a rich fat man. Cato Bramlett slipped out of town in the night, headin' west. Figured he was likely to be next."

Rascal cursed Gossett and he cursed Bramlett. The men

listened, letting him work off the grief by talking. When Rascal was done they looked at each other uncomfortably. Rascal finally walked out to be alone awhile. Edson Biggs's eyes followed him. Sorrowfully shaking his head, Edson said, "Law was born twenty years too late."

Hitch asked what he meant by that.

"I mean that Law had a lot more in common with John Torrington and Prosper Selkirk than he ever realized. Old man Torrington, he's greedy after land. Selkirk is greedy after money. Law was greedy after cattle: he couldn't get them together fast enough. If he'd been here twenty years sooner, when all a man needed was a fast horse and a long loop, he'd have been as big today as John Torrington. And probably just as mean."

Rascal McGinty came back presently, subdued. All eyes went to him in silent sympathy. Dan Truman cursed under his breath and said, "Men, we got to do somethin'."

Hitch hunkered, eyes on the grieving Rascal McGinty. He had nothing to offer.

At length Edson Biggs spoke. "I've given this thing a lot of study, and I've got an idea. It's not a total answer, but it's a start. This county doesn't have a sheriff now; it has to call an election. The big ranchers'll hand-pick themselves a man. I doubt they'll go so far as to put up Lafey Dodge: his reputation would stir suspicion as far away as Austin. But they'll choose a man they can control."

A small rancher said, "That leaves us no better off than we've been."

"I said *election*, and an election is supposed to have more than one candidate. Why don't we put up a man of our own to run?"

Several men spoke at once with reasons that occurred to them on the spur of the moment. Edson let them speak their piece, then said, "I think the strike brought changes in this country that you-all haven't realized yet: I don't believe the big ranchers have, either. Most of the men who went on strike had always voted however the ranchers wanted them to. A lot of those men are still here in the county, and thinking for themselves now. Give them a man to vote for and I think they'll hand these ranchers a surprise.''

Hitch wished he had thought of that himself. The idea stirred him. The longer he mulled it over, the better he liked it. "You sayin' you'll run, Edson?"

Edson Biggs demurred. "Not me; I'm not the man for it. But I know a man who's been here a long time and won respect for a clear head and leadership. I believe if we put his name on the ballot he'll stand a good chance." Edson paused, looking at Hugh Hitchcock. "I'm talking about *you*, Hitch."

Hitch's mouth dropped open. "Edson, you've lost saddle, blanket and all."

"I don't think so. The sheriff idea came to me first, then I started trying to think of the men who would qualify. I kept coming back to the same one."

Hitch saw that hope had stirred among the other men. Dan Truman spat an oath that would curl mesquite bark. "He's right, Hitch. You're the one can do it."

Hitch swallowed, thinking of all the reasons he didn't want the job, and there were plenty of them. He pointed out that he had his place to worry about and work on, that he had never carried a gun in his life, except the one on his saddle. "What if I had to shoot somebody? I've never even shot *at* a man except a couple of Indians, and I never done *them* any harm."

Edson said, "There's already one too many *gun*men in this country. We want a man."

"Find somebody beside me."

Edson kept pressing him. "We need a man who'll stand up for the plain people and put a stop to the oppression we've had here. The only way to do anything about what happened to Law McGinty will be to get a sheriff who represents our way of thinking and not that of a few big outfits. Longer this thing goes on, the more chance somebody else will be killed."

Hitch said, "I'm no fair opposition to Lafey Dodge."

Dan Truman declared, "You won't have to face him by

yourself. Comes time, there'll be lots of men behind you.''

Hitch had reservations about that, remembering the strike.

Edson argued that Hitch could use the sheriff's salary to buy land and cattle and fix the place to his liking.

At length Rascal McGinty spoke, and everyone else stopped talking. ''Hitch, you listen to Edson; he's right. And remember you promised me that somethin' would be done about Lafey Dodge and them. It won't be unless you see to it that we have fair law in this county. I'm askin' you as a friend, Hitch. Run!'' He pointed his finger. ''One more thing: if you win you'll need a deputy. I want to be him. I got a sore head that says you owe me that.''

Even as Hitch argued, he knew they would pin him against the wall.

The minister said, ''Mister Hitchcock, I'll pray for you.''

Hitch said, ''You'd damn well better.''

XV

FILING FOR SHERIFF REQUIRED MORE PAPER-signing, it seemed to Hitch, than he had put into filing for his land. He couldn't put aside the nagging concern that he was making a mistake. He told Edson Biggs, "I never realized how much work a candidate does before he gets in office."

Biggs nodded. "More, like as not, than after he gets in office."

"I got a lot to learn. What I know about politics I could write on my hatband."

"Nothing to it," the banker smiled. "You just have to get more votes than the other man."

"Sounds easy."

"Just have to get out and see the people, that's most of it. Those who don't know you have to be given an opportunity to see you have an honest face. I'll go with you as much as I can and help you electioneer. When you have a banker with you everybody will give you a hearing. Some of them are borrowing from my bank and the others know they may someday want to."

When the legal necessities had been attended to, Edson suggested that he and Hitch have a drink to seal the commitment and bring good luck. Hitch observed that the drink would have done him more good *before*, but it was never too late. They walked into the Buffalo Bar, which charged more than Fant Gossett but carried a better grade of sipping whisky. Edson raised his hand in greeting to the saloon-keeper. "Tending bar yourself, Luke?"

Lanky, sad-faced Luke Gannaway wiped a damp cloth across the mahogany, then set up a bottle and two glasses. "Way business has fell off since the strike, I can't hire much help."

Edson said, "I'll buy *you* a drink too, Luke. We're celebrating a new candidate for sheriff."

Luke looked around as if to see who might be listening, but the three had the place to themselves. "Got him all signed up, did you?"

Edson nodded. Luke said, "Then I'll buy the drinks, and I'll join you."

That surprised Hitch a little, for the big ranch-cowboy trade was the backbone of Luke Gannaway's business. Luke poured the glasses full and raised one in salute. "Whup them good, Hitch."

When the glasses were empty, Edson poured them full again. "This is my round."

Gannaway's eyes narrowed in concentration on Hitch. "You really figure you got a chance, any chance atall?"

Hitch shrugged. "I don't know enough about . . ."

Edson put in, "He'll win it if enough straight-thinking people decide we've had all the big-man rule we need around here. There's a new day coming, and we'll do all we can to rush it along."

"Three months ago," Luke declared, "I'd of said you're crazy. I'll still say I don't think you got a Chinaman's chance, but I'm tickled to see you try. It'll take money to keep you runnin'. I ain't no Fant Gossett when it comes to that, but I'll chip in my share if you won't say where it come from."

That surprised Hitch again. He stammered that he didn't know, but Edson cut him off. "I'll be around in a day or two, Luke, and we'll talk about it."

As they walked out Edson said, "Feel better? You already have support you didn't know you had."

"One bartender. That's a long ways from prosperity."

Edson agreed that as soon as he could get ahead on some work at the bank, he would join Hitch to spend several days riding over the country shaking hands and drumming votes. Accordingly, he showed up at Hitch's dugout just before dark a few days later, still more cowboy than banker as he swung down from the saddle.

Hitch looked up from his wood-cutting, drove the ax deep into a chopping log and leaned on it to rest. "You bein' a financier," he said dryly, "I thought you'd be travelin' in a nice black buggy by now, or at least in a buckboard."

"I'm in business to lend money, not to spend it." Edson looked at the Spartan place Hitch called home. "Doesn't look like you've spent much either."

"It'll surprise a man how much he can get by without. I expect you're dry."

"You expect right. Coffee if that's the best you can do, stronger medicine if you have it."

"I've got it. I knew a money-changer was bound to show up."

They saw to the horse first, an unwritten rule of survival around any cowcamp. Edson untied a rolled blanket from behind the cantle of his saddle and unstrapped a pair of saddlebags. "Brought my own medicine," he said, hefting the bags, "just in case. But I'll drink yours first."

Hitch conceded, "You'll prosper in the bankin' business."

Hitch built a fire, pinched biscuits off of sourdough he kept in a crock, and put a small pot of beans on to reheat for the fourth or fifth time. "I got a slab of salt pork here that I traded off of a farmer up the river."

"After years around a chuckwagon, I can eat anything."

Hitch had seldom seen an old bachelor cowboy living alone who wasn't skinny as a whip-poor-will. After a few months of doing his own cooking, he knew why.

Edson said, "I don't suppose you've heard who the ranchers are putting up for a candidate."

"All I've heard out here is the coyotes howlin'."

"They're runnin' Dayton Brumley."

Hitch pondered that news without emotion. "I know Dayton. He was Figure 4 rep at our W wagon awhile. Him and Rascal McGinty like to've burned powder last spring. But he's always been a good honest company man."

"That's what they want, is somebody who'll do what he's told."

They ate in silence, Hitch pondering the campaign ahead and not caring for the prospect. "I been thinkin', Edson; maybe we ought to go by the McGinty place and have Rascal ride with us."

Edson frowned. "I was hopin' you wouldn't suggest that."

"Why not?"

"Rascal is a brother to Law McGinty."

"If it hadn't been for what happened to Law, I wouldn't be in the race."

"There's another side to it. Folks'll remember that no matter how much they regretted the way he died, Law *was* stealin' cattle. I wonder if Rascal being with you might not do you as much harm as it does good? Some people might take it as a sign that you condoned what Law was doing."

"Rascal's my friend. What kind of a man would I be if I denied my friends?"

"Not deny him, Hitch, just kind of stay away from him till this race is over with. Sometimes in politics a man has to compromise a little."

Hitch angered. "They'll take me as I am or pass me by. I don't intend to try to look different than I am. If they take me they'll have to take all them that go along with me, them that believe in me."

Edson shrugged. "A suggestion, Hitch, that's all it was. Let's go see Rascal."

Rascal was pleased at the invitation to go along. Hitch watched him shave a week's growth of whiskers at a tiny cracked mirror nailed to a log in front of his dugout. "Where should we start, Edson?" Rascal asked.

"Some merchants have a theory that if they can make a sale to the first customer who walks in, they'll do all right the rest of the day. Gets their confidence up. I'd suggest we take a couple of easy ones first to get everybody in the right frame of mind."

Rascal aimed the tip of his straight razor at Edson. "I know just the place for that . . . ol' Morey Shumm."

Morey Shumm was one of the many cowboys who had lost his job as a result of the strike. He had a small claim out in the middle of the rolling prairie, far from wood and water. Like Hitch's and Rascal's places, it was devoid of comforts, any indulgencies of personal pleasure. His water supply was in a barrel at the front of his mud-daubed dugout. From an ash-blackened pit and scattered pots and Dutch ovens a few steps from the dwelling, Hitch deduced that the man did most if not all his cooking outside rather than in the cramped quarters of the dugout. He was probably used to spending most of his time in the open anyway.

Shumm eagerly shook Hitch's hand. "Man alive, I sure was tickled when they told me you'd agreed to run, Hitch. I'd all but given up on any future for me in these diggin's. Ol' Torrington, he's been lookin' at me kind of cross, and I figured sooner or later he'd find some excuse to come and take me over. And if not him, then maybe Prosper Selkirk. You're the biggest hope we got. Maybe the only one."

Flustered, Hitch mumbled an acknowledgment of the compliment and wished he knew better what to say. Shumm didn't give him time to worry about it much.

"I bet you fellers are hungry, and I got fresh beef that was runnin' around yesterday on four legs eatin' grass. I'll get a fire started and we'll just have ourselves a feed."

As Hitch expected, Shumm kindled a fire in the outdoor

pit, using dried cowchips. He kept the beef hanging in the dugout, where it was cooler than here on top. Pretty soon he had sliced steak sizzling in deep grease and sourdough biscuits browning with glowing chips both under and atop the black Dutch oven that held them. "The beef's my own," Shumm said, "in case you're worryin'. Couldn't hardly feed a sheriff candidate stolen beef. Though I expect you ate more stray beef over at the Ws than you ever ate of Charlie Waide's."

Hitch only smiled. It was widely known that even the big ranches which protested about cattle theft were more likely to kill stray animals for meat than their own. It was said of many a rancher that the only chance he ever had of eating his own beef was in visiting a neighbor's wagon. To Charlie Waide's credit, Hitch remembered no time that Charlie had ever ordered the killing of a stray except those rare occasions when one suffered a broken leg in the roping and would otherwise have gone to waste. Waste was one thing Charlie Waide would not abide.

"Hope you fellers don't mind eatin' outdoors," Shumm said. He pointed his chin at his rough dugout. "Never have been able to get used to stayin' in a house. Place smells like damp earth all the time. Man wakes up in the night and it's pitch dark and like bein' in a grave. Found a rattlesnake in there with me the other day and almost decided just to give it to him."

Shumm had provided a scanty shade by building a small brush arbor, though he must have had to drag the materials for miles; Hitch saw no brush around here . . . nothing but miles and miles of wide open plains and summer-brown grass. If a cowboy wanted to nap in the shade he had to have a horse that would stand mighty still. Beneath the arbor Hitch saw a roll of blankets. Shumm must be sleeping outdoors, except perhaps when the weather was bad.

Shumm noticed that Hitch was looking his place over. "Ain't much of a layout, is it, Hitch?"

"No worse than mine," Hitch said, stretching it a little.

"No, it ain't much, but at least I got a toenail hold on

somethin' that belongs to me.'' Shumm looked across his
open land, and affection showed in his eyes. "I come up
here from the brush country, Hitch, where a man couldn't
see a hundred yards through the mesquite and chaparral.
First year or so up on these plains, I thought this open country would run me crazy. And this everlastin' wind . . . But
it grows on you. I can stand here on my own little parcel
of land and see two-three hours' ride in any direction. I can
see and count every cow I own, peart near. I loved a woman
once, Hitch, and I lost her. Now I've come to love this
country the way I used to love that woman. I'd hate to lose
it, too.''

Hitch knew some people would consider that Shumm
didn't have much here to lose, a poverty claim like this. But
those people never would understand that Shumm didn't
really live in this cheerless dugout, this crude cowcamp; this
was just a place to come for the night. He *lived* on that big
prairie, and there he spent the time that really mattered to
him. Some people would never understand the hold this land
could take on a man if he stayed rooted long enough in one
spot to develop a communion with the grass-blanketed earth,
to begin to feel and fall in with the rhythms of the changing
seasons. There was a pulse in this land, like the pulse in a
man, though most people never paused long enough to sense
it.

Shumm said, "Every man has a right to what belongs to
him. I got nothin' against Torrington and Selkirk if they
would just stay in their own yard. But me and you, we know
that ain't in their nature. They're *reachers*. That's why I'm
with you, Hitch. They'll have to break my leg to keep me
from votin'.''

Edson had been right; the visit to Shumm lifted Hitch's
spirits, made him feel better about the campaign. The reception was similar at the next couple of camps the three
men went to. But they came finally to a small ranch operated
by a man with whom Hitch had had a nodding acquaintance
the last two or three years, a man who reminded Hitch uncomfortably of Kate McGinty's late father. The woman and

four children were out hoeing a garden which appeared to be withering under the hot sun. The horsemen rode up to the smooth-wire fence that surrounded it, and all took off their hats.

"We're lookin' for your husband, Mrs. Free," Hitch said.

She pointed toward the house. "He's yonder, diggin' us a well. You-all be stayin' for supper?"

Hitch couldn't tell whether she really wanted them to or not. Playing safe, he said, "I reckon we'll be movin' on directly."

She appeared relieved, though she said, "That's a pity; there's aplenty for everybody."

Hitch doubted that; not one of the children showed much flesh. Mrs. Free herself was skinny as a cedar post. "We're obliged anyway, ma'am." He pulled away.

Free's oldest son, about twelve, operated a windlass, drawing up the dirt that Free dug from the bottom of the hole. Hitch winked at him, then leaned over the rim and called down, "Mister Free, it's Hugh Hitchcock. I'd be obliged if I could talk to you."

Hitch and Rascal relieved the boy and turned the windlass to draw Free to the top. The man, as hungry-looking as his family, had mud and dirt on him from his ragged felt hat down to his cracking old boots. He made a useless effort to brush a little of it off, then extended his soiled hand to Hitch. "You'll excuse my looks; I ain't on my way to church. I figure there's water down yonder someplace if I just go deep enough."

Rascal smiled. "You're liable to find hell down there if you go too far."

"I've found hell up here; that's why I'm huntin' water." Free wiped his arm across his sweaty face and pointed his whiskered chin toward a picket shack he had built of small trees, standing them up and lashing them tightly together to form the walls, the roof also of pickets, covered by dirt. "Cooler over yonder in the shade. You said you wanted to talk."

Free paused long enough to tell the boy he had better

move some dirt he had spilled too near the edge of the hole.
Hitch followed Free's example in squatting on the shady
side of the shack, his back against the rough wall. "You
may not have heard, Mister Free; I'm runnin' for sheriff."

Free showed no enthusiasm. "I heard. You're runnin'
against the ranchers."

"I'm a cowboy, Mister Free, not a politician. I reckon
you know why I decided to do it."

Free cast a quick glance at Rascal. "I believe I do. But I
also believe you might be mistaken in your thinkin'."

"How is that?"

"You've took on men like Torrington and Selkirk;
you've put the challenge to them. Anybody that backs you
up, it means *he*'s took them on, too. And anybody the ranchers think *might* back you, whether they really do or not.
That's a big thing for a man to have hangin' over his head
if he intends to stay in this country. A man wants to think
twice before he goes to angryin' up the likes of them, and
the power they got behind them."

"It's bad for anybody to have that much power over
somebody else, Mister Free. But if we don't make a stand,
they'll get even more powerful. We think we can draw up
the string on them."

"You *think?* You ain't real sure of yourself."

"We got no cinch."

"You sure don't. So what if you try and don't make it?
What happens to them that get their necks stuck out there
with you?"

"If a man believes in a thing strong enough, he takes a
risk."

"I've already took enough risks in this life, Mister Hitchcock. I got a wife and five kids that can't afford me to take
anymore. From now on anything I get my hands on, I'm
hangin' onto. I ain't takin' no chances of losin' the little I
got. Look around you; what do you see?" He didn't give
Hitch time for an answer, and Hitch didn't know what he
was expected to say anyhow. Free said, "It's damned little
better than starvation, but it's cost me and my family an

awful lot, and I got no wish to throw it away.''

"A man has got a responsibility to his neighbors.''

"He's got a lot more responsibility to his own family.''
Free's mud-smudged face furrowed deeply. 'I'll grant you,
there's truth in what you say; them big outfits have done
things I don't personally approve of. But on the other hand
I'm just a little feller, and them thieves, they steal off of me
just like they do off of the big ranches. Difference is that I
ain't big enough to protect myself. And even if people like
Torrington and Selkirk may step on me a little now and
again, at the same time they're protectin' themselves they're
protectin' me too.''

He looked regretfully at Rascal. "Sure, I was sore distressed about that hangin'. They oughtn't to've done it. But
I will say that some shady characters left this country right
afterwards, and I doubt they're ever comin' back. So you
see, I made some net gain out of what them ranchers did,
bad as I hated the way they done it. It helped me like it
helped them.'' Free pushed to his feet, indicating the visit
was over as far as he was concerned. "I'm sorry, Mister
Hitchcock; I'd like to help you. But things bein' like they
are, and us needin' law and order so bad, I just can't go
along with you.''

Hitch stood up, hands shoved deep in his pockets as he
tried to think what to say. "I can understand the way you
feel, Mister Free, even if I don't agree with you. Thanks for
listenin' to me, anyway.'' He turned to leave but couldn't.
There was one more thing that had to be said. "You mentioned about law and order. I notice that lots of people who
talk about law and order don't mean it for anybody but
themselves. When somebody was stealin' cattle off of Torrington and Selkirk, that was a crime. But when Torrington
and Selkirk stole mine off of me, they called that justice.
Someday they may come for yours, Mister Free.''

"Not if I make sure they know I'm on their side. This
country has got to have strong protection. If a few people
get run over in the process, they shouldn't of been standin'
there in the way.''

Hitch knew there was no point in staying around arguing over it; nobody's mind would be changed. He went to Walking Jack, mounted, then pointed. "I believe I saw another house over yonder-way."

Free nodded. "Elijah Neihardt. You'll want to talk with him."

Hitch rode off without looking back, Edson and Rascal silently flanking him. Edson had no problem reading his thoughts. "You can't expect to get them all, Hitch."

In frustration Hitch exclaimed, "Don't he know that Torrington and Selkirk are no friends of his?"

Edson Biggs shrugged. "He's like a child that hides behind his mother's skirts. He doesn't realize that if she makes a wrong move she'll step on him."

Rascal rode in brooding silence a long time. Finally he asked, "Did you-all notice the way he kept lookin' at me?"

Hitch glanced at Edson, then at Rascal. "I didn't notice anything." Edson looked down at the horn of his saddle.

Rascal said, "I seen it. He kept thinkin' to hisself, 'That's the brother of the man they hung for stealin' cattle.' "

"He never said any such of a thing."

"With his eyes he did."

Hitch said, "You're imaginin' things, Rascal," and looked to Edson for help. He received none.

They could hear angry shouting before they reached the Neihardt place, and Hitch thought uncomfortably that they might be riding in on some kind of fight. But through the dust he could see a man struggling with a pair of young mules, evidently trying to teach them how to work. One would pull ahead and the other balk or try to kick free of the traces. The man would curse and slap at their rumps with the reins and try again. Hitch looked at the piece of ground the stockfarmer was trying to break and wondered idly if it should ever be turned over by a plow; he seriously doubted it was cropland, and farming it might ruin it for the grass God must have intended it to grow.

Neihardt saw the visitors but gave the mules one more minute of disgusted effort before cursing loudly and bringing them around. He let the mules stand and blow while he walked toward the horsemen.

"Hugh Hitchcock," Hitch said, extending his hand. "I take it you'd be Mister Neihardt?" When the man nodded, Hitch introduced him to Rascal and Edson. Neihardt frowned, giving Rascal a moment of special attention, then turned to Biggs. "I believe I've seen you in town. Banker, ain't you?" When Edson said yes, Neihardt added frostily, "I doubt as you'd ever lend me any money. A banker never will loan a man unless he knows he don't really need it."

Edson made an effort to be pleasant. "You might be surprised. Come see me sometime if you're ever in need."

"I always been able to take care of myself." Neihardt turned back to Hitch. "You'd be the man that's runnin' for sheriff."

"Yes, sir. I came to ask you for your support."

Neihardt glanced again at Rascal. "And suppose you tell me why you think I ought to give it to you."

Hitch reviewed the same general case he had made to others before. Neihardt listened without comment, his eyes boring into Hitch. At length Neihardt said, "You come from the direction of Doug Free's. You talk to him?" When Hitch nodded, Neihardt asked, "What did he tell you?"

Reluctantly Hitch told the truth. "Said he couldn't support me."

Neihardt nodded. "Me and Free, we talked it over a couple days ago. I notice, Mister Hitchcock, you never said nothin' about the rustlers, though you done a lot of talkin' about how the ranchers had done wrong. Them cow thieves been more worry to me than the ranchers have; they don't respect no man, big or little. Awhile back they took off half the cows I owned." He turned his eyes to Rascal McGinty, though he went on talking to Hitch. "Seems to me like you ought to've said what you're goin' to do about them rustlers."

"Well, you know I'm against them. I'll do whatever I can to see that they're put a stop to."

"I always been a man to call a spade a spade, Hitchcock.

Seems to me like this man here is a brother to the man the ranchers hung for a cow thief; ain't that true?''

Rascal answered before Hitch could. "They *said* he was one. There never was no trial." Rascal's eyes hardened.

"There don't seem to've been no doubt that he was guilty. I judge this country is better off without him; better off than it might be with a sheriff who rides around the country with the brother of a known thief."

Neihardt never saw Rascal's fist coming. Suddenly the farmer was flat on his back, his hands up defensively, his nose bleeding. Rascal stepped forward angrily to grab him and pull him back to his feet, but Hitch and Edson caught the cowboy and shouldered him aside. "Damn you, Rascal," Edson said harshly, "you trying to get Hitch beat?"

"You heard what that farmer said!" But Rascal loosened a little. Hitch turned back to help Neihardt up, and the farmer angrily waved him off, rubbing his nose and cursing the three men the way he had cursed the mules, ordering them off the property and warning that he had a gun in the house. Rascal stood with fists clenched, ready to pursue the conversation, but Hitch and Edson pulled him to his horse. Red-faced, Rascal kept looking back as they rode away. He talked awhile, then muttered, then was quiet.

Hitch said, "Rascal, we come onto this man's place without any invitation. He had a right to say what he thought whether we agreed with him or not."

Remorse was beginning to set in on Rascal. It always did, after the sudden storm. Rascal said, "Well, I reckon I cost you a vote."

Hitch shook his head. "I never had *that* vote to start with."

Soberly Edson Biggs said, "By the time Neihardt gets through spreading the story around, it's likely to cost a good many votes."

"Depends on what his neighbors think of him. Way I sized him up, he ain't no easy man to be neighbors with."

Rascal watched their shadows reaching out across the thick turf of curing grass. "I tried to tell you somethin' while ago, Hitch, and you wouldn't listen. This goes to prove that I ain't doin' you no good. I'm goin' home."

"You're takin' it too personal."

"It is personal." Rascal lowered his head. "He's right about Law; I know that. But I still can't stand by and hear somebody else say it. So you give them a good fight, Hitch, and I'll see you about election day." Rascal shoved his hand forward, and Hitch took it unwillingly. Rascal turned to the banker. "Edson, you keep Hitch out of trouble." The cowboy struck out across the prairie, shoulders slumped in melancholy.

Hitch sat on Walking Jack and watched until Rascal was only a speck far out on the flat tableland. "Edson, I wouldn't of hurt him for the world."

"The *world* has hurt him, Hitch; you didn't."

For the next three days Hitch and Edson hunted out farms and small ranches, line shacks and cowboy batch camps all over the county. Hitch disliked the electioneering part; pleading for votes was somehow demeaning, a little like going from door to door and begging for money, though he considered his reasons worthy. It went against the grain for a man who had been self-sufficient since he was fourteen or fifteen. But the visiting itself was pleasant. It surprised him, meeting settlers he didn't even know were there. He enjoyed finding cowboys he had known and ridden with in years gone by.

The sedentary life of a banker had not yet set in on Edson Biggs; he rode as tirelessly as Hitch the long miles up and down both sides of the river, meeting people, speaking his piece. At one point Hitch suggested they were probably several miles across the county line. Edson said, "For all we know they may want to come over and vote with us. It's been done plenty of times in the past."

One day they rode onto range claimed by old Allie Clay of the Nine Bar. Hitch felt uneasy about being there, for he knew within reason that as a large rancher Clay had allied himself with Torrington and Selkirk even though Clay and John Torrington had feuded for years over water and grass.

But Hitch felt he had nothing to lose by talking to the old man; there was always the longshot chance that Clay might throw his support to Hitch simply out of enmity for Torrington. It wouldn't cost anything to find out.

Clay had had lumber hauled all the way from Colorado to build himself a house bigger than John Torrington's. Actually, he needed it, for he was married and had brought up a family, which his rival had never done. Mrs. Clay, a gray-haired woman of sixty, was lonely to talk to someone new, and Hitch could have spent the day at the ranch headquarters if he had been in no hurry. But as Edson pointed out in a whisper while the old lady went to fetch coffee, women didn't get to vote and they had better move on where the votes were. Mrs. Clay told them her husband was with his west division wagon and reluctantly bid them farewell, standing behind the oval glass window of her front door and watching them as long as they were in sight.

Clay should have built that house in town, Hitch thought, where she could see people. But these plains ranches were not established with a woman's comforts and needs in mind. Someone had said this country was fine for men and horses but hell for women and dogs.

About midafternoon they came upon a young cowboy having trouble drifting a string of Nine Bar cows and calves in his chosen direction; they were led by an old spotted cow of an independent longhorn strain that had never accepted man's domination. Their home was a brushy little header a couple of miles back, and she meant to return there, incidentally taking the others with her. She made a break past the cowboy, and he spilled a loop trying to rope her. Hitch shook his own rope loose from the hornstring and built a loop in it. As she came by him, he swung it over his head and sailed it out around her horns. He let her skid on her rump, then come over hard on her back. When she tried to rise up hind quarters first, Hitch brought her down again. The cowboy got off of his horse, a short length of rope in his hand. Kneeling on her shoulder, he tied the rope around one forefoot, then the other, bringing the feet close together.

He slipped Hitch's rope off of her horns and stepped back.

She got up slinging her head and wanting to fight, but as she attempted to charge, the hobbled forefeet crossed her up and brought her to her knees. She slung her head in anger and frustration, trying once more and going down again. A calf bawled, and she turned to see. She gave the men one more menacing look, then hopped awkwardly to her calf.

Hitch recoiled his rope and hung it on the hornstring. The little exertion had warmed and pleased him; he had liked the feel of the rope in his hand, the sudden violence of the cow at the end of it. It was a challenge he had always enjoyed as a cowboy, a man's prowess against animal strength, and the feeling of pleasure at a skill well learned.

The cowpuncher—a stranger to Hitch—raised his hand in belated greeting. There hadn't been time before. "That'll give ol' Sis somethin' to think about besides runnin' off. An outlaw like her ought to be sent up for beef."

Hitch said, "No, it'll be a sad day when all the wild things are gone." He introduced himself and Edson Biggs. "Whichaway's the wagon?"

The cowboy pointed. "Yonder. We'll be throwin' the gather down by the Kildee Lake. You lookin' for somebody in particular?"

"Allie Clay."

"He'll be with the gather. You-all had as well ride along with me if you'd like. You're a pretty good hand with that rope."

"Had aplenty of practice."

"I can tell that by lookin' at you."

Hitch didn't know if that was meant as an indication he was looking old. To a youngster like this one, seventeen or eighteen, he supposed he did, but the thought was not reassuring.

The lake was one of the playa variety so common on these plains, wide but shallow, fed by runoff waters in the rainy seasons and doomed to recede toward a stagnant center as heat and dry weather set in, its edges grown up in rank weeds and grasses that parched brown as the water gradually withdrew toward the middle. At this side of it, where Hitch knew buffalo must once have congregated by the thousands or tens of thousands, several hundred cattle were being gathered into a dusty, milling, bawling mass. He had to rein up and look. It was a sight he had watched more times than he could count, and he had not realized how much he really had missed it since leaving the W. It was a joy to watch, and yet it brought an ache as well, for he sensed that he would never be a part of this again.

He and Edson stayed back a little from the herd and the busy cowboys, because an outfit like this usually had evolved a place for everyone without new orders being given, and two outsiders unexpectedly riding in had no particular usefulness. They watched the cowboys and the cattle. The longing must have shown in Hitch's face, for Edson remarked, "Makes you want to go back, doesn't it?"

Hitch nodded.

Edson said, "Just remember that it was always for somebody else, never for yourself."

"I reckon that makes a difference. But I miss it all the same."

As the sun dropped down toward the brassy edge of the prairie sky, most of the cowboys rode away from the main herd, letting it spread some to graze. The smaller "stray" herd was moved farther to keep the cattle from coming back together. These would be the animals belonging to other brands; other ranches' representatives would periodically take them home. Seeing that most of the cowboys were on their way to the chuckwagon, Hitch and Edson followed along.

Old Allie Clay was taken aback, seeing them here. He shook hands civilly enough but without warmth, for he well remembered that they had been regarded as leaders in the cowboy strike. "I expect I know what you men come for. I'll have to say that I didn't expect it."

"We kind of surprised ourselves," Hitch admitted. "Maybe we oughtn't to've even come. But we wanted to talk to you. We wanted to let you know where we stand."

"I reckon I already know where you stand." Clay looked around at his curious cowboys, probably wondering if he was risking strike talk again by letting Hitch and Edson stay in camp. "We'll have us some supper, and then we'll talk. An empty stomach always distracts a man."

The cook was a red-faced fellow with all of Trump Tatum's irritability and only a modicum of his cooking ability. The beans had rocks in them, and the sourdough bread hadn't been given enough time to rise; it had been baked on the squat. But the meal beat the ones Hitch had fixed for himself, so he guessed he was ahead.

After supper he put forward his case. "I suppose this race has taken on a look of the big ranches against the little people, Mister Clay, but it shouldn't have. I'm not against anybody for bein' big; I'm only against people usin' power in an unfair way against other people who can't protect themselves. I've never heard anybody complain about you bein' unfair to neighbors, any more than I ever heard them complain about Charlie Waide. My bein' sheriff won't mean trouble for anybody except them that *make* trouble. And that includes cow thieves, Mister Clay. I hear some people sayin' I'll take up for the cow thieves, but you know me well enough to know that ain't so. I'll bear down hard."

"And you came here thinkin' I might come out in your favor?"

"I been hopin' you might."

Allie Clay smiled thinly. "It'd tickle me to do it. I can imagine what old John Torrington would say, how he would cuss. I'd like to be the one to tell him, so I could watch him go into a fit of apoplexy." The smile died. "The hell of it is, Hitchcock, that politics makes a man do things he never thought he would, makes him join up with people he'd rather crawl into a snakepit than be associated with. Like me and ol' John. I always figured you for a good man, Hitchcock, because Charlie Waide wouldn't of put up with you if you hadn't been. I take it you're honest, and I'd like to help you. But you can see how it is: we've all had sides chosen up for us whether we like it or not. We've had our friends picked out for us whether we like them or not.

"When you was a button, Hitchcock, did you and your friends ever have a cowchip battle? I did, lots of times. I always liked to find and throw the freshest ones, that hadn't been long out of the cow. Them kind, when you hit a man with them, they splattered. You got everybody around him. It's like that now; whatever you hit Torrington with, it's goin' to splatter. There's people yellin' for Torrington and Selkirk to be pulled down, but they'll pull down some of the rest of us with them if they do. We been dealt a poor hand, and there's nothin' to do but play it out and play to win. Some other time, some other situation, I'd support you and ask my men to support you. But the way it is . . . well, Hitchcock, that's the way it is."

Hitch nodded soberly. "I guess I knew all the time, but I thought I'd try."

"A *man* always tries, Hitchcock. We'll beat you, but nobody can take away from you the fact that you tried."

XVI

THOUGH HITCH DREADED IT, HE INEVITABLY
had to move his campaign into town, for that was where the
largest number of people lived. He found he disliked town
more than ever, and the thought that if he won he would
have to spend most of his time there was no comfort to him.

The place to see most people who came in was the saloon.
That, for most cowtowns, was the place to rest one's sad-
dlesores, to see one's friends and enemies, to swap off a
horse or to sell ten thousand steers.

Hitch made it a point to avoid Fant Gossett's place. One
night he sat in Luke Gannaway's Buffalo Bar, not drinking
but simply visiting with people who came in. Some were
cowboys from the big outfits, and they spoke to him self-
consciously, most of them, then pulled away. Eventually a
familiar face showed in the doorway. Dayton Brumley spied
Hitch and came on in.

"Howdy, Hitch. I'd like to have a drink with you. I'm
buyin'."

Hitch shook hands with his opponent. "I'd be tickled," he said, though he wouldn't.

Brumley signaled Gannaway for a bottle and glasses, and he motioned toward a small round table, shoving a brass spittoon aside with his boot. Brumley studied Hitch, troubled. "Hitch, we always used to be friends."

"Far as I'm concerned, we still are."

"I'm glad. I was afraid under the circumstances . . ." He poured the drinks but didn't pick up his glass. "This election, Hitch, you really want to go through with it?"

"Hell no, I don't want to. But I reckon I'm stuck."

Brumley raised his glass. "Here's to a clean race."

"I'll drink to that."

Brumley fingered his glass, frowning. "They're usin' us, Hitch, both of us."

Hitch tried to cover his surprise. "What do you mean?"

"People used you for that strike, and they're usin' you now. As for me, Prosper Selkirk has always used me, and now all the big outfits are doin' it. Difference between me and you is, Hitch, that I always knew."

"There's another difference."

"What's that?"

"I'm bein' used for a better cause."

Brumley shrugged. "Maybe so; I give up thinkin' a long time ago. I think me and you if we was smart would both pack up and leave this country and let everybody else fight their own battles."

"We won't, though, neither one of us."

"I suppose not." Brumley finished his glass. "One thing I promise you, Hitch. I'll do what I can to see that it's a straight election."

"That's all a man could ask for, Dayton."

Lafey Dodge stayed in town most of the time, walking up and down the streets in his dark, grim silence, making sure the voters fully recognized the power for which he stood. He never overtly threatened anyone; in fact, he had little or nothing to say. But his ominous presence itself was a threat, a reminder that the men who had always controlled the country intended to continue and that any who opposed them were likely to be quietly marked and their transgressions remembered, perhaps to be called up for accounting on some future day when all this foolishness was over and relationships had returned to normal patterns.

As the campaign went on, Hitch found himself increasingly discouraged. He was sure he had visited every little ranch, every dugout, every bonepicker camp in the county and for several miles beyond on all its perimeters. He had knocked on every door in town.

"Way I see it," he told Edson Biggs disconsolately, "I ain't got the chance of a three-legged rabbit in a wolf den."

"You've made lots of friends."

"I always been a good hand at countin' cattle, and I been carryin' a pretty good count of people in my head. Now you figure up all the big ranches, and you figure up the cowboys workin' for them. Then you add to that the people here in town who'll follow the ranchers' lead because they want to protect their trade or they got some other personal interest in keepin' the courthouse like it is. Tote them all up and you got defeat written there plain as daylight."

"Election's not over till they count the ballots."

"I've already counted them."

Two days before the vote, Hitch unexpectedly came face to face with Prosper Selkirk, walking self-consciously with Lafey Dodge on the street. Selkirk paused in midstride, blinking uneasily at the sudden confrontation.

Hitch nodded civilly. "Mister Selkirk." He neither spoke to nor looked at Lafey Dodge.

"Hitchcock," said Selkirk. Just plain Hitchcock, still no *Mister*. The two men looked at each other a nervous moment. Selkirk said, "I was somewhat impressed with you once, when you were at the W. I didn't think you would be dragged into this kind of mistake."

"Sir?"

"I know this is a free country and every man has a right, but I hate to see a man completely waste his time and energies and make unnecessary enemies in a hopeless cause.''

Hitch didn't intend to betray his lack of confidence. "We'll pretty soon know if it's hopeless."

"In spite of all that has happened, I've always had a certain respect for you, Hitchcock. My impression is that you entered the strike out of some misplaced loyalties and more or less against your will. I dislike seeing an honorable man hurt. I'd like to help you."

"You could start by releasin' my cattle from 'escrow.' " Hitch knew that was unlikely to happen; even if it did, it would be a hollow victory because the county had taken poor care of his Two Diamond herd. Thieves already had made off with most of it; those cows were probably far across the New Mexico line, beyond retrieving.

Selkirk said, "You can't make anything on that little amount of land you own. I'd like to buy it from you at a fair price. Even more than fair. With that money you might do better for yourself elsewhere."

"You makin' me an offer?"

"I would. But first I would have to ask what you would take."

"If I sold out, I suppose you'd want me to leave the county."

"You would have no reason to stay."

"That'd be an easy way for you to win the election."

"We'll win that election anyhow. The offer is made in good faith."

Hitch figured they didn't want him staying on even in defeat, a *reminder* to his backers and perhaps an encouragement for them to try another round. "And I'm turnin' it down in good faith."

Selkirk shrugged. "It's your choice. You may wish you had taken it." He walked away, his back stiff.

Lafey Dodge remained a minute, his eyes without emotion. "Sounded to me like the man made you a good offer."

Hitch tensed, searching the man's words for a threat but not sure he found one. "Me and you, we both know why he done it."

"His kind naturally thinks of money first. But always remember, if he can't buy you off, he can buy you killed."

A chill went down Hitch's back. "You'd be the one to do that."

"I'm just a workin' man. I do what I'm paid for."

After that encounter, Hitch had had all of town he could stand for a couple of days. He saddled Walking Jack and rode east to his own place. There he found a good many Snaketrack cattle grazing his grass and figured Torrington had his cowboys drift them there on purpose. Hitch circled them, bunching them the best he could, and pushed them off his land onto the Figure 4. *Let Selkirk wrestle with Torrington over the grass*, he told himself.

Resting, watching the cattle drift away, it occurred to him he had not seen Rascal McGinty since the cowboy had left him and Edson on the electioneering venture. It would be pleasant to ride over to the McGinty place and *augur* awhile, and not ask anyone for a vote.

He noticed many Snaketrack cattle grazing McGinty grass, just as they had been grazing his. *Greedy old bastard*, he thought, *won't even let our land alone*. He would help Rascal push them off.

But he found no one at home. Evidently Rascal had found temporary day-work somewhere. Disappointed, Hitch prowled around the little place, as if hoping Rascal might come riding over the hill. But he knew somehow that the cowboy wouldn't. Without wanting to, Hitch found himself looking down toward the river. He could see the tall cottonwoods rocking in the wind as they had done the day Law died. The memory came back in a rush that made him suddenly cold. He turned away, trying to shut it from his mind.

But the image would not go away, and now he looked toward the gentle rise where they had carried Law to bury him, safely above the occasional floods that sent angry red water sweeping this valley. He felt a compulsion to ride up there.

When he allowed himself to think about it, which was seldom, he felt guilt for the fact that just once—that night he lay suffering in Rascal's dugout—he had told himself it might be better for him and Kate if something *did* happen to Law. That unbidden thought had been on his conscience of late. It was as if, even for a moment, he had willed Law to die.

Dan Truman had put up a simple plank headboard with Law's name on it. As Hitch approached the grave he found the board lying flat on the ground. An angry thought came that somebody had contemptuously done it on purpose. But cowtracks on the mound made him realize that a wandering cow had knocked it down, or perhaps some itchy-hided bull trying to scratch himself.

Hitch dismounted and removed his hat, remembering Law in another time, a wild, impetuous kid who would ride anything that pitched or rope anything that would run. He began talking quietly, partly to himself, partly to the man who would never hear. "Law, I'd figured we'd set things right for what happened to you, but now it don't look like we can. Far as I can tell, we're beat at that election before we start. Don't look like there's any way to even the score except to take the law in our own hands the way *they* done, and you know that ain't our style. So it looks like it was all for nothin', Law. All for nothin'."

He stared at the cow tracks on the grave. "Don't look like you'll even have peace here till we put a fence around this place. I'll see what I can do."

He rode down to the shed and corrals. He found a stack of posts that had been cut for corrals but never used, and long branches cut for rails. He tied a rope onto several of the posts and snaked them up to the gravesite, then made several more trips dragging poles. When that was completed he got the diggers and began digging holes for the posts.

He was so absorbed in the work that he didn't hear the horseman until the shadow fell across him. He turned, startled, and his eyes went wide. Sitting on a big blue roan was the solemn-faced Lafey Dodge.

Hitch's heart hammered. He had no gun except the short rifle in the saddle scabbard, and Walking Jack stood tied fifty or seventy-five feet away. Hitch stood with the diggers in his hands and tried not to let his fear show through. At length he managed to speak. "Looks like you always catch me thisaway."

Dodge nodded. "I make a point of it. But don't worry yourself about the gun. I ain't here to kill you. Ol' Man Torrington just wanted me to follow along and scare you."

Hitch's tongue explored his dry lips. "You've done that."

"I been trailin' you at a respectful distance ever since you left town, curious to see what you was doin'. Thought you might be leavin' the country."

"Disappoint you that I didn't?"

"Some. I hate to fight a man I respect. Damned few men I *can* respect anymore."

"If I ran, you wouldn't respect me."

"A pity, ain't it? This way we're both in a bind." He nodded curiously at the grave. "What you fixin' to do?"

Hitch showed him the cowtracks. "I was goin' to put a little fence around it to keep the livestock out."

Dodge pondered a moment. "Good idea. I believe I'll help you."

Hitch stared, dumfounded. He was inclined to refuse but knew he was in no position to make an issue of it. "But you killed him."

"I take no pride in what happened to this boy. It was a poor piece of business."

"Then why did you do it?"

"It was a job of work. I always deliver what I'm paid for. I told Ol' Man Torrington I'd rather just shoot the boy; that's the businesslike way. Hangin' a man never went well on my stomach. The old man felt like folks wouldn't learn much from a shootin'. Hang a man, though, and they'll sure take notice."

Dodge hung his belt and six-shooter across a pile of posts not far out of reach. "I want your word you won't do nothin' foolish."

Hitch nodded, still surprised. "I'm in no hurry to get killed."

"See that you remember." Dodge picked up the diggers and attacked the soft earth with a vengeance. He dug a pair of holes, then Hitch took the diggers and started to move to the next post location. Dodge pointed. "Thataway would suit me better." Hitch's direction would have moved him closer to Dodge's pistol. Dodge tamped dirt around the two posts, spaced just far enough apart for the poles to wedge between them.

Sweat running down his face and soaking his shirt, Hitch paused in wonder. This didn't fit his mental image of a man coldly singleminded in Dodge's profession. "Dodge, I thought I had you figured. Now I don't understand you atall."

Dodge wiped sweat from his face onto his sleeve and stopped. "I don't know what you mean. I'm just me. I always been just me."

"You act like you've done this kind of work before. You didn't always make your livin' with that gun."

"I was a farmer once, a long time ago. The big war come on and by and by I was a soldier. Folks cuss the war, but them was pretty good days in some respects. There was room for a man to find out if he *was* a man. But finally the war was over and all of a sudden there wasn't no call anymore for Confederate soldiers. People was sick of the fightin', and of them that done the fightin'. A little while then I tried packin' a star for the State Rangers, but that was a carpetbag outfit of Unionists and scalawags that a man couldn't take no pride in. Besides, it didn't pay much; you had to steal most of what you got. So I become a free agent. Somebody wanted a man caught and was willin' to pay, I went out and caught him."

"Like you done Law McGinty?"

"A job of work, that's all it was. I never took no pride in the hangin'."

Hitch saw that Dodge had no remorse over the killing, only for the method. He said, "One thing always puzzled me a little. I can see *you* bein' there, and Torrington bein' there, but I never did picture Selkirk havin' the stomach for it.''

Dodge frowned. ''He didn't want to. Said he'd done his part by payin' his money in. But Ol' Man Torrington, he said it wouldn't mean nothin' if they wasn't both there. He cussed Selkirk for a yeller-legged pothound and browbeat him into goin' along. Selkirk throwed up his dinner after we left you and that boy down on the river.'' Dodge spat. ''Torrington's a mean one, but you got to respect him for his guts. Never could have no respect for Selkirk and his caliber. Them kind, they think when they hire another man to do a dirty job, they keep their own hands clean. Seems to me like I've made the biggest part of my livin' workin' for cowards.''

Together Hitch and Dodge finished the fence. If it was not a pretty job, at least it would keep the cows out. Someday somebody might put up a better one.

Dodge strapped his pistol back on his hip. His shirt was soaked with sweat, his hands and face grimy. ''You know, there's somethin' about work like this that sort of frees up a man's blood, makes him feel good. Makes him sort of wish . . .'' He broke off, perhaps not really knowing just what he *did* wish.

Hitch sensed that for a little while Dodge had reverted to a better time when a man's honest labor had counted for something. He sensed a vague satisfaction in Dodge, but it was a fleeting thing soon gone. Dodge drew the pistol, and Hitch's breath stopped. But Dodge only turned the weapon over in his hand, examining it. ''Almost forgot this gun for a while. Afraid we might've throwed a little dirt on it.'' He slipped it back into the holster. ''Well, Ol' Man Torrington will want to know if I scared you enough to change your mind about runnin' for election.''

''You scared me,'' Hitch admitted, ''but I ain't quit.''

Dodge nodded. ''That's what I told the old man, but he ain't much judge of people. You take care of yourself, Hitchcock.'' Lafey Dodge shoved a foot in the stirrup and methodically swung up onto the roan. He rode off, taking his time. He must have known Hitch could have gotten his saddlegun and shot him in the back, but Dodge neither hurried the horse from its easy trot nor looked around.

Hitch stared after him, his mouth open.

"Law, how do you punish a man who don't even know he's done anything wrong?"

XVII

ELECTION DAY. HITCH SAT IN A RAWHIDE-
bottomed straight chair in front of the Buffalo Bar, bootheels
hooked over the bottom brace, the top leaned back against
the adobè wall. Directly across the hoof-churned street stood
the little courthouse where the polls had been set up. The
saloon was not allowed to sell liquor during election hours,
but it would be considered cruel and inhuman to close the
doors and deny the visiting public a place to go and sit for
brief shelter from the hot summer sun. For the duration of
the day, at least, service at the bar would be limited to hot
coffee and cold lemonade, or water dippered out of a
wooden barrel.

Rascal McGinty strode up the dusty street and onto the
plank porch, slapping his dusty hat against his clothes. He
grinned. "Thought I'd wait till late in the day, but I couldn't
sleep, so I rode most of the night. Mind if I sit down with
you?"

Hitch gratefully shook hands. "Anything you want to do.
Where you been hidin'?"

"Had a short job drivin' some horses over east to Clarendon. Got back yesterday. You're winnin', ain't you, Hitch?"

Hitch didn't answer, and he could tell that Rascal could read the answer in his face. Rascal ran his sleeve over his forehead and into his red hair. "I swear, Hitch, but it's hot. Whose idea was it that they can't sell a man nothin' to drink?"

"State law. Politicians don't want people gettin' drunk and killin' anybody that ain't had a chance to vote yet."

Rascal said, "Hitch, you just got to win."

Hitch looked back toward the courthouse. "Don't count on it. Looky yonder." He nodded his chin toward a dozen riders. By the horses, some of which he remembered, he knew these to be part of Allie Clay's Nine Bar hands come to vote early. Dust on the trail behind them showed more were on the way. "I been sittin' here watchin' ever since the polls opened. Ain't seen many friends of mine ride in."

"Day's young yet. Things'll look different by sundown."

As the morning wore on, he saw little to change his feeling. In small bunches and big ones, cowboys drifted into town and tied their ponies around the courthouse, walking up to the steps with spurs jingling in lively concert. After they had voted, some hung around the courthouse to talk in the shade; others made for the saloons and were quickly disappointed to find the well dried up for the day.

A little before noon, Kate McGinty walked up the street toward him. He thought she probably would pass by him on some errand, and he watched her surreptitiously, still finding it difficult to look at her without an old tightness building in him, a sense of wanting and of loss. She came directly to him. He stood up as she neared, the front legs of the chair dropping noisily. He took off his hat.

She spoke first to Rascal, then turned to Hitch. "You've avoided us, Hitch. We haven't seen you much."

He tried to make light of it. "Women can't vote. Been doin' my visitin' with the voters."

"Well, you'll do some with us for a little while. We've

fixed a special Election Day dinner. Neighbor killed a couple of chickens.''

"Wait till tonight and I'll probably eat the neck."

"Come along, Hitch. You too, Rascal. The only thing poorer fed than a cowboy at a chuckwagon is a cowboy doin' his own cookin'.''

The attention of the women—Kate and her mother and a couple from a nearby house—was embarrassing. But Hitch ate his share of the chicken and watched Rascal hungrily stack bones at the edge of his plate. Rascal didn't leave the table until the baby awoke from its nap. Rascal seemed always to melt when he looked at his nephew. That baby had him tied in a helpless knot. "Look there at Punkin', Hitch," Rascal insisted, "don't you see the McGinty in him? Lookin' more like me every day."

"If so, God help him."

The women other than Kate busied themselves clearing the table. Hitch walked outside under a little arbor that substituted for a porch on the pitifully poor shack that Kate's mother called home. Out back, respectfully far from the privy, Hitch could see the blackened wash-pot that served as the old lady's only means of livelihood. Kate's coming here had given her some help but probably had not added greatly to the revenue.

"Kate," Hitch asked worriedly, "you made any plans?"

"Plans?"

"You said you didn't ever want to live out at the place again. You figurin' on stayin' here with your mother?"

She shook her head. "A while, maybe, but not forever. It's a strain on her, and the baby's sure no help."

"You got anywhere else to go?"

"Been thinkin' I might go to one of the cities and try to find me a job of work. I could cook in a cafe or sew or take in washin'. Bigger the town, the better the chance."

It hurt him to consider these alternatives. In time Kate would be another bitter, wornout woman like her mother. He said, "Don't be in too big a hurry, Kate."

"What do you mean?"

He knew exactly what he meant, but he couldn't say it in so many words. There hadn't been enough time yet since they had put Law in the ground. "Maybe somethin'll turn up here close by. Maybe if you'll stay around . . . somethin' else will come along."

She touched his hand, then pulled away. "Hitch," she said evenly, "I know what you're tryin' to say. Don't."

"I'm tryin' not to. But when you talk of leavin' . . ." His face burning a little, he looked straight into her eyes, trying to find an answer there.

Rascal McGinty stood in the door. Hitch didn't know if he had heard. Rascal said, "You ready to go, Hitch?"

Hitch nodded, giving Kate one more quick glance.

They thanked the women for the good meal, then walked together awhile in silence. Presently Rascal said, "I remember readin' somethin' in the Book one time, somethin' that if your brother dies, you should take his widow to wife. You ever read that, Hitch?"

Uneasily Hitch shook his head. "I always meant to read the Bible, soon as ever I had time."

"It's in there someplace. I done a lot of thinkin' on it here lately, since Kate and that baby been alone."

The town was filling up with cowboys, for once they had come to town and cast their votes they had no intention of leaving dry. Hitch took up his station in front of the Buffalo Bar, moving the chair only enough to keep it out of the afternoon sun.

The single bit of excitement came when most of the cowboys had found dinner one place or another and were sitting around in the shade to rest and belch. A lone cowboy in a hurry to get to town from some outlying camp, and probably not realizing the place was dry until the polls closed, carelessly dropped a match to the ground without being sure it was out and the stick broken. The sun-dried grass flared up. Jumping to the ground to try to stamp out the blaze, he let his frightened horse jerk loose and run away from him.

Sight of brown smoke a mile from town aroused the idle cowboys and brought a mass rush for horses. In a rain-shy time like this, a prairie fire out of hand might race for miles and miles, leaving the range a huge stretch of black ashes, useless for grazing next winter and possibly dooming hundreds or even thousands of cattle to starvation unless they could drift far enough south to find grass; even then they would be doubling the grazing load on someone else's range.

Hitch and Rascal had their horses in a corral, and it didn't take them long to saddle up. By the time they reached the blaze, they found a dozen or so cowboys had pretty well stamped and beaten it out. It had had time to spread only a hundred or so feet, leaving ragged fingers of black as it had raced along in the dry grass trying to build momentum and heat. Left alone in those first minutes, it would quickly have gotten beyond control except by major measures and an army of men. Old buffalo hunters said that in Indian times huge prairie fires occasionally swept across these vast plains, burning wildly until they finally reached a river. That was one reason so little brush grew here.

Slapping each other on the back, the smoke-smudged cowboys rode into town again. A thing like that made men thirsty, and they loudly propounded a view that the Election Day saloon rule ought to be suspended in return for the service they had performed for the community. But the law was the law, and most of them settled for cool well water.

As the afternoon passed, Hitch saw a few townsmen drifting in to vote, taking time away from stores, jobs or whatever they had to do. A few stray riders came in, people Hitch remembered from the strike and with whom he had visited to ask for votes. But they weren't enough; nowhere near enough. A time or two Edson Biggs came down from his little bank to sit with Hitch. Rascal would stray off restlessly. Edson said, "Don't give up. All the voters haven't been heard from."

"Some of them may not ever be. All those big-ranch cowboys sure don't encourage them none. And Lafey Dodge is no help to us, either."

"He may be more help than you think."

Dodge had been in strong evidence all morning, quietly walking the streets, gravely studying all who came into town. Now, in afternoon, he was back at it.

Hitch said, ''I'd just as well go home.''

Edson said, ''The polls are still open.''

John Torrington came in, flanked by a dozen or more of his riders. Slant Unger was not among them; his wounded arm was proving slow to heal, Hitch had heard. Torrington's gaze touched Hitch and then cut away. Torrington gave no orders; he simply dismounted, tied his horse and walked straight to the polling place. His men followed after him.

The stockfarmer Free came to town, riding a plowhorse. As John Torrington came out of the courthouse, Free met him on the steps. Nervously Free announced for everybody to hear, ''Thought you'd want to know, Mister Torrington; I'm votin' for your man Brumley. I've been tellin' everybody, I think he'll make us a good sheriff.'' Torrington did not reply; he only stared at Free as if he were a worrisome gnat. More nervous now, Free said, ''Just wanted you to know, Mister Torrington.'' Torrington only nodded at him, then came on down the steps.

Prosper Selkirk came with the headquarters contingent from the Figure 4. Most of the Figure 4 wagon crews had been in town since morning, but the headquarters men had probably been too closely under Selkirk's thumb to waste more of the day than necessary in town. Selkirk studiously avoided looking directly at Hitch as he rode by.

Rascal waited until the cowboys had all come back out from the polls. ''Well, Hitch, me and you ain't voted yet.''

Hitch let the chair go forward and arose, stretching his legs. ''Might as well. That's the only two votes we're sure of.''

Many of the cowboys watched in idle curiosity as Hitch and Rascal went up the steps and into the courthouse. Marking the ballot took only a minute; it seemed almost too simple for the importance it carried. Even so, Hitch had to wait some for Rascal. Together they walked out into the courtyard. Another set of horsemen had just arrived, Charlie

Waide in the lead. He looked dusty and tired. Limping beside Charlie, his leg mending, came Joe Sands. Cowboys from the other outfits were watching, and Hitch noted that Prosper Selkirk was, too. Hitch decided it was best to let Charlie make the first move.

Charlie took Hitch's hand. "Hitch," he said solemnly, "you know you're goin' to lose."

"I figure that."

"Then why keep on?"

"Why do some horses fight the rope even after they know they're caught?"

"I've always wondered." Charlie moved painfully up the steps.

Hitch turned his attention to Joe Sands. "What you doin' these days, Joe?"

Grinning, Joe glanced across the street toward Selkirk. "Watchin' out for greyhounds, mostly. Good luck, Hitch."

Late in the afternoon Hitch began to see what Edson Biggs had meant about waiting. The "little men," the stray cowboys left at loose ends by the strike, the handful of nesters all seemed to hit town at the same time. Almost in a body, as if by consent and perhaps for a measure of mutual protection, they advanced on the courthouse to register their votes. A string of them led by Edson Biggs marched up the steps past the lounging cowboys from the big ranches. Hitch could see John Torrington peering darkly at them from the wide-open doors of his favorite saloon. Beside him stood a grim Lafey Dodge. Torrington was talking to the old gunman, and pointing.

Edson Biggs came out presently and walked briskly over to Hitch. Edson was dressed now in a town suit and a derby hat; he already looked more banker than cowboy. "See what I told you, Hitch? They came."

"But not enough, Edson. Like I told you, I was always pretty good at countin' cows. I been countin' people all day. There just ain't enough."

His somber appraisal seemed to sap the optimism from Edson. Frowning, the banker took a cigar from his pocket, bit off the end, then forgot about lighting it. He walked away, the cigar still in his hand. Hitch watched him, idly thinking that Edson was beginning to put on a little weight; if he stayed in the banking business, he would probably weigh three hundred pounds someday.

Word quickly swept through the crowd when the polls closed, and most of the cowboys made a rush for the saloons. Hitch sat glumly and watched a dozen or so Figure 4 hands push into the Buffalo Bar. "Well, Rascal," he said quietly, "we done the best we knew how."

Rascal seemed finally to have come to the same conclusion as Hitch. "It ain't over for Lafey Dodge," he gritted. "Not by a damn sight."

Hitch glanced at him in quick concern. "Rascal, without the law behind us we can't do nothin'."

"I can do somethin'."

"You can get yourself killed, is all. Let him alone."

Presently Dayton Brumley came along smiling, carrying victory in the set of his shoulders. "Hitch, I'd be tickled to buy you a drink." He looked at Rascal, forgiving past differences. "And you, Rascal. I'd be right proud."

Hitch shook his head. "Another time. You got a victory celebration started in there, Dayton, and we'd be out of place. Another time, maybe."

Dayton nodded his understanding and went on in.

Lafey Dodge came along, walking by himself. He didn't go into the saloon, for the cowboys were never at ease in his company, nor he in theirs. He was a man long used to being alone. There was no mocking in his eyes; he was not a man for that. His brief gaze seemed simply to say, *I told you so*, without any reproach, and he went on. Rascal McGinty got to his feet and seemed inclined to follow. Hitch caught Rascal's arm.

"Come on, Rascal. Let's go someplace."

As they left the front of the saloon they could hear some of the Figure 4 cowboys addressing a toast to Sheriff Dayton Brumley. Hitch walked aimlessly down the street, the taste of defeat like ashes in his mouth, even though he had expected it. He gazed awhile at Fant Gossett's saloon, about the only one the big-outfit cowboys hadn't taken over, and he thought how much good a stiff drink might do him. But he didn't enter.

"Maybe we ought to go tell Kate we've lost," Hitch said. Loss of the election meant there would be no retribution for Law.

Rascal said, "You go tell her, Hitch; it's your place to do it."

Hitch hesitated about leaving Rascal, thinking of Lafey Dodge. Rascal read his worry. "I won't hunt no trouble, Hitch."

"I take that as a promise."

"It is."

It was a good way over to the shack, and Hitch could have saddled his horse again, but he preferred to walk. Walking sometimes helped work the anger and frustration out of a man. After a while he stood under the arbor, facing her, and he found again that he didn't have to tell her. She knew by his face.

"It doesn't matter, Hitch. Truth is, I'm glad."

"Glad?"

"I didn't want to tell you before, but I always hoped you'd lose. If you'd won you'd likely tangle with Lafey Dodge."

"It ain't right, us not able to do anything about Law."

"I can live with it, Hitch. Vengeance won't bring Law back; it's just apt to get somebody else killed . . . more than likely you. A man like Dodge always gets his wages sooner or later. Let somebody else pay him." She touched his hand, then beckoned with her chin. "Come on in. We'll have supper directly . . . what we had left over from dinner."

Hitch tried to smile. "I'll eat that chicken neck."

He sat down at the plain pine table to sip coffee from a tin cup. He watched Kate bustling about, and he watched the baby in the cradle Rascal had made for it, reaching up and grasping at the air, flexing its tiny fingers. For a while the simple comfort of this poor little house reached him

through the disappointment, and he felt almost content. The
sting of the loss was almost gone.

He became aware of voices outside, shouting his name.
Rascal burst excitedly through the door. "Hitch, they've
done with the countin'. You didn't lose after all. You won,
Hitch, you won!"

Hitch let the cup tip, and some of the coffee spilled.
"You're lyin'."

Edson Biggs came in behind Rascal. Outside, Hitch could
hear several more shouting for him to come on out and take
his victory. Edson reached into the pocket of his suit coat
and thrust a cigar at Hitch. "From now on you stick to
counting cows and let me count the votes. You won it by a
fair margin, Hitch."

Hitch pushed to his feet, looking back at Kate. To his
surprise he saw dismay in her eyes. Kate cried, "No, you
must be wrong!"

Edson was bursting with cheer. "The ranchers were
wrong, not us. A lot of their own cowboys voted for you,
Hitch; they don't like Lafey Dodge. Do you understand what
this means, Hitch? They've lost control of their own cowboys."

Kate cried, "No, Hitch, no."

Before he could stop them, the men outside surged in and
he found himself being rushed out the door. He glanced
back and saw the anguish still in Kate McGinty's face. Then
the men were sweeping him down the street in a loud, bois-
terous, shouting parade. They shoved him through the open
door of Fant Gossett's saloon. The broad-bellied Gossett
hove out from behind his bar, both big hands outstretched
in a wide, beaming welcome. "Hitch, boy, you come on in
this house. First drink for everybody is on ol' Fant Gossett.
I knowed all the time you was goin' to win; told everybody
you'd come through for us honest folks."

Next morning at eight o'clock Hitch was knocking on the
county judge's front door. Behind Hitch were Rascal and
Edson Biggs and several townsmen. The wizened judge

peered unhappily at them; his watery eyes indicated he had drunk quite a bit last night, and not for celebration. "What can I do for you?"

"The oath," Hitch told him. "You want to administer it here or do it down at the courthouse?"

Judge Wilkins looked like a man being led to prison. "Courthouse is the proper place. I'll get my hat."

They walked back down the street, the judge swept along unwillingly but without protest, for he had seen the handwriting scrawled all over the political wall. Additional spectators fell in behind the original crowd, swelling its size. The judge looked back once, plainly distressed, and afterward never looked any direction but straight ahead.

Prosper Selkirk kept a small house in town for his convenience when he had business here that kept him overnight. Hitch glanced that way and saw Selkirk soberly watching from his front door. *That's good*, Hitch thought; *I'll know where to find him easy.* John Torrington had left town last night shortly after the vote was counted, breaking short his cowboys' planned celebration.

Hitch's hand rested on a black-bound old Bible as he repeated the oath. When it was done the judge declined to pin the badge on him but simply placed it in Hitch's hand. Edson Biggs said, "Here, Hitch, I'll do the honors." He shined the star against his trousers leg, then pinned it on Hitch's shirt. He stepped back in satisfaction. "That's a sight I've wanted to see since the day we buried Law McGinty."

Hitch said, "You got a deputy's badge, judge?"

The judge rummaged around in a corner drawer and came up with one. Hitch said, "I want you to administer the oath to Rascal."

The judge argued, "You're legally entitled to do that."

Hitch stubbornly insisted, "I want you to do it." That was like rubbing salt into a wound, and Hitch did it with malice aforethought. Once Rascal was properly deputized, Hitch said, "Now, Your Honor, I have some complaints to file with you, and some warrants I need you to write out."

The judge knew what was coming. Eyes narrowed, he asked, "You know what you're asking me to do?"

"I'm on solid legal ground."

"There's no question of the legality. I'm thinking of the advisability. It wouldn't matter so much if they were simply cowboys, but substantial men like John Torrington . . ."

"He made a substantial mistake. I want those warrants, Judge."

He had some of them in his hip pocket when he walked up to Selkirk's town house, Rascal beside him. Dayton Brumley stood on the porch. As Hitch mounted the steps, Brumley moved to meet him, extending his hand. "Congratulations."

Hitch felt no animosity toward Brumley. "Hope it didn't hurt too much."

"Main thing hurtin' me right now is a headache from that *victory* party we was havin'. It ended kind of sudden."

"No hard feelin's, Dayton."

"Never no hard feelin's between me and you, Hitch." He glanced at Rascal. "Or us either."

Rascal shook his head. "That old roan cow died anyway."

Prosper Selkirk did not come to the door, but Hitch knew he was inside even before he asked Brumley. He knocked on the door and then walked in, motioning Rascal to stay on the porch. Selkirk sat at a table, some papers spread out in front of him. Hitch noted that a couple were upside down. "Mister Selkirk," Hitch said, "I've come to see you."

"Obviously." Selkirk's hands trembled a little on the table. "Sit down, Hitchcock . . . *Sheriff* Hitchcock. We have some things to talk about." He offered a drink, which Hitch declined. Selkirk didn't take one himself and probably wouldn't have even if Hitch had accepted. Hitch sensed that this would have been a subtle way of showing superiority. "Well, Sheriff Hitchcock," Selkirk said evenly, "the impossible seems to have happened, and I can well imagine the business that has brought you here. I've always believed you to be a reasonable man: I think we can come to some understanding.''

Hitch frowned. ''Maybe you ought to clear that up a little.''

''I realize now we made a mistake when we—the court, that is—confiscated your herd. I know now that you were not one of those who stole from us. I think I could prevail upon the court to release that herd to you.''

''There's no herd to release. Most of them've been stolen and run off.''

''How many have you lost?''

''Accordin' to the receipt I got, the county took eighty-four cows and fifty-seven calves and three bulls. How many of them are left we can't know unless we round them up and take a count. There won't be many.''

''I've always tried to be a reasonable man myself, Hitchcock, and a fair one. I'll buy your interest in those cattle. Whatever are left, we'll vent to the Figure 4; any loss will be ours, not yours. I'll pay you a decent price. What do you think they are worth?''

Hitch hadn't considered it, but he quickly priced the cows and bulls at fifty dollars apiece and the calves at twenty. He expected to haggle and finally settle for forty. Even that would have been forty dollars more than he had ever expected to recover. To his surprise, Selkirk totted the figures on a piece of paper, then wrote him a check for the whole amount. Selkirk wrote a bill of sale describing the cattle and the brand. ''There, Mister Hitchcock, and I hope you'll accept my regrets for a rather unpleasant incident.''

Hitch said, ''I got some Two Diamonds cattle that the county didn't seize. I want it wrote on there that all Two Diamonds not vented to the Figure 4 brand within thirty days revert to me; that'll protect me on the others.''

''Done,'' said Selkirk, and added that provision to the bill of sale.

Hitch took the check and signed two copies of the bill of sale, keeping one. ''I sure didn't expect this.''

"I daresay you didn't, but I've always been a man who faces up to his debts."

"I'm glad you feel that way, Mister Selkirk, because you still got another one to pay." He handed him the warrant.

Selkirk's face fell. "Really, Mister Hitchcock, I thought we had come to an understanding."

"I understand *you*. You thought you'd bribed me with my own cattle. Much obliged for the check. I'll deposit it with Edson Bigg's bank right away."

Quick anger showed in Selkirk's face. "I've been trying to understand that election. I think it was Charles Waide who put you across. Charles Waide and his men."

Hitch remembered the financial hold Selkirk had on Charlie. "It wasn't Charlie; he told me he couldn't support me."

"Then who was it?"

Hitch shrugged. "It's your right to ask for a recount."

"In the meantime, do you actually think you're going to put me in that dirty little jail?"

"No, I know you're not goin' to run off anywhere; you got too much at stake here. Judge Wilkins'll set bond for you. Knowin' him, I doubt it'll be much."

It was a long ride out to Torrington's headquarters. Hitch and Rascal moved in an easy trot to spare Walking Jack and that wicked mustang bay named Sweetheart. They came finally to the place. Four cowboys stood by the barn, watching as Hitch and Rascal approached. One came forward and volunteered, "The old man's up at the house."

Hitch asked, "What about Dodge?"

"Up there with him. You fetchin' warrants?"

Hitch nodded. The cowboy said, "I'm sorry it come to this for the old man. Lafey Dodge, now, I don't care nothin' about him; you can throw him in jail and forget what you done with the key. But I almost didn't vote for you, worryin' about the old man."

Hitch stared. "You voted for me?"

The cowboy looked around carefully. "A lot of us did. We want Lafey Dodge and his kind of trouble cleared the hell away from here. But don't you tell the old man."

Hitch edged his horse toward the simple two-room frame that the cowboys gratuitously called "the big house." If Torrington had ever married, no one knew of it. He spent so little time indoors that all he wanted of a house was something to keep the rain off, and that was about the most which could be said of this one. It was in nowise a match for the one Allie Clay had built. Hitch did not dismount. He sat in the saddle and called, "Mister Torrington!"

On second call the old man stepped out onto the little porch, the breeze lifting his short gray beard and ruffling his uncombed thatch of frosty hair. His eyes were defiant as a wounded hawk's. Lafey Dodge came out and stood on one side of him; the Negro Tobe Ferris stood on the other.

"Mister Torrington," Hitch said, "I brought some warrants."

The old man stared antagonistically without reply.

Hitch said, "I got warrants here for you and Lafey Dodge, for Slant Unger, Tobe Ferris and Hobson Clark."

The old man's jaw trembled in anger. "Warrants. *Warrants?* What right you got to be talkin' to *me* about warrants? Me, the first white man into this country with a herd of cattle? What right you got to be a-wearin' that badge?"

"You was there; you know how the election came out."

"You-all *stole* it, is what you done. You stole it from us that settled this country, us that built it and put all we had into it. Now all you people who waited till it was safe are doin' your damndest to take it away from us."

"Nobody's takin' away anything that's rightfully yours, but you can't take away what's rightfully somebody else's, either. It's not enough anymore that you was the first one here. There's other people now, and other rights. Time don't stand still for anybody. I'd of liked to've seen it stay just the way it was for us cowboys, but you didn't let it. It won't stay the same for you, either."

He saw no sign in Torrington's face that the old man understood what he was saying. Torrington never would understand; it wasn't in him.

"About those warrants, Mister Torrington . . ."

Tobe Ferris stepped down off the porch, face somber. His black hand reached up. "I'll take them. Mister John's legs is got too much of the miseries to be a-troublin' himself comin' down them steps."

Hitch said, "The warrants mean you'll have to come to town and make bond, Tobe. You understand?"

Tobe Ferris nodded. "Whatever Mister John says, that's all right with me. And somethin' *you* better understand. Ain't no no-count strikin' cowboy goin' to lay a hand on Mister John." Tobe's eyes carried a strong threat.

Hitch looked at Lafey Dodge for sign of trouble. Dodge gave none. John Torrington abruptly turned and walked back into the house.

As Hitch and Rascal rode away, Rascal said, "That old man don't know it yet, Hitch, but he's headed down the hill."

Hitch nodded. "Mean as he is, give him credit. He was a gritty old bastard in a time when grit was what it took to stay. The country needed him then. Without him, the rest of us wouldn't be here." Remembering Selkirk he said, "One other thing about the old man."

"What's that?"

"He might kill us off, but not in a hundred years would he ever think of tryin' to *buy* us off."

XVIII

THE DEFENDANTS ARRANGED TO MEET IN town and make bond together. Selkirk did most of the talking, John Torrington standing by in defiant silence, Lafey Dodge showing no emotion at all. The involved cowboys watched the two bosses and said nothing except to answer a brief question or two.

Hitch had not seen Slant Unger since he had put a bullet through the man's arm. Unger had lost weight and his face was pale, for he had not been outdoors much. The arm was still bound. Someone whispered that Unger's arm might be impaired for life. Hitch was uncertain whether to feel sorry for him or not; at least he was glad he hadn't killed him.

The attitude of the county judge and county attorney Zachary bothered Hitch. He had never paid much attention to legal matters and had not understood until now whose job it would be actually to prosecute the case. By his action, Zachary seemed more a defense attorney than a prosecutor.

"Now, Mister Torrington," the attorney said apologetically, pushing some papers forward, "we hate to trouble you with so much detail, but we must meet all requirements of the law. The judge and I agree that you and Mister Selkirk are men of substance who will not leave the county, so we have agreed that the bond should be set on a nominal level, a hundred dollars per man.''

That wasn't much, Hitch thought critically. Selkirk would let a thirty-dollar cowboy kill himself chasing a thirty-dollar cow, but he would spend a hundred on himself and never look back.

Judge Wilkins impatiently scanned the charges, reading glasses at half-mast down his nose. ''I've half a mind to throw this whole damned case out of court.''

Stubbornly Hitch said, ''Then I'll find me a court someplace that won't.''

The judge peevishly began to lecture him about contempt, but Zachary raised his hand. ''The sheriff has a point, your honor. It is to the advantage of all concerned to bring this case to trial and see it properly disposed of. If these men are found guilty, so be it. If they are not, a verdict of innocence in a proper court renders them free of jeopardy forevermore. Until we have such a verdict, this matter will always hang over their heads. Disgruntled persons and a hostile court could use it against them years from now.''

The judge frowned over his glasses. ''You got a recommendation?''

''Yes, that we convene a grand jury at the earliest possible date, have indictments drawn and call the case to trial. The sooner we finish the entire matter, the sooner this community gets back to normal.''

Judge Wilkins glared at Hitch. ''That would suit me better than anything I know . . . for things to be normal again.''

The legal manuevers left Hitch confused. The grand jury was called into session the following week and evidence presented. All defendants appeared, but none was called to testify. Selkirk watched the action with confidence. John Torrington's narrowed eyes focused on the window most of the time, his mind probably on the work he needed to be doing instead of wasting his time in this hot, cramped little courtroom. The grand jury signed the indictments as Zachary wrote them, and Judge Wilkins set trial for two weeks from Monday. "That," he pointed out to Prosper Selkirk, "should give you time to get a competent defense attorney."

Selkirk smiled without humor. "Adequate time, Your Honor."

After everyone else had filed out of the courtroom, Zachary took another look at the signed indictments. "Well, Sheriff, you've gotten everything you wanted so far."

"So far," Hitch said grudgingly. "But I get the feelin' you're about to drop a wagonload of rocks on me."

"We're interested only in seeing that justice is done fairly and impartially, to the least as well as to the largest."

"And then turn them all loose," Hitch said dryly.

Rascal McGinty waited for him at the door. Rascal said, "I don't understand what *indictment* means, Hitch. Ain't they goin' to jail?"

Hitch shook his head. "It just means they'll go to trial."

"But I thought *this* was a trial."

"This was more like the roundup, Rascal. The brandin' comes later. Only, I'm afraid somebody has run off with all the irons."

"There ain't no question that they done it. Why ain't they in jail?"

"The law is set up to make sure they get their rights."

"The law wasn't around to see that they gave my brother his rights. How come it's so bothered about theirs?"

Hitch shrugged.

Edson Biggs looked up from a ledger and flipped a black eye-shade out of his way as Hitch and Rascal walked into his small bank. "How did it go?"

Hitch said, "I get the feelin' it's *me* on trial, not them." He related what had happened in the grand jury session. "I always figured when a man committed a crime and the sheriff caught him, that was the end of it."

Biggs's brow furrowed. "One lawyer can turn loose more men than ten sheriffs can jail. Selkirk has already sent to

Kansas City for a good defense attorney. It'll be him against Zachary.''

Hitch gritted, ''And Zachary won't half try, so we already know how the trial will come out.'' He clenched his fist. ''What did we go to all this trouble for if nothin' is to come of it? How come me wearin' this badge? What good was it for people to vote for me if the court throws out everything I do?''

''We've made a start, Hitch. Regular elections come next year. Sooner or later Zachary and Judge Wilkins are bound to go down.''

''That's no help to us today.''

''But we've made a start, that's what counts. And if they can send off for a good lawyer, so can we. We can see to it that when the trial starts, Mister Zachary has help whether he wants it or not.''

Selkirk and several Figure 4 cowboys were in town to meet defense attorney Loring DeWitt as he arrived on the mail hack. Hitch watched curiously from across the street to see what caliber of man Selkirk's money would buy. DeWitt was something spectacular for a cowtown like this, his fine tailored suit dusty from the long ride but his dignity not the least impaired as he stepped down with a flourish. The whole town quickly knew he was there.

The special prosecuting attorney hired by Edson Biggs arrived on horseback from Austin so quietly that hardly anyone noticed him. His name was Allan Baucomb, and he put up in the adobe house where Edson lived. Hitch took him out to the McGinty place to familiarize him with the scene of the crime. Baucomb talked to a few people and stayed out of sight. Not until two days before the trial did the Torrington-Selkirk side even learn about him.

When Hitch introduced him to Zachary, the county attorney sat down heavily and stared like a calf knocked in the head. Judge Wilkins began leafing furiously through his lawbooks, looking for a way out. Baucomb calmly cited him page and paragraph, establishing his right to participate. Zachary immediately got himself a buggy and team and disappeared from town in a hard trot.

By nightfall Prosper Selkirk was in town. He wasted no time getting over to Edson's house and introducing himself to Baucomb. Resentfully glancing at Hitch and Edson, he asked Baucomb if the two of them might go somewhere in privacy and talk business. It occurred to Hitch that Selkirk might have brought someone with him, and if his talk with Baucomb did not end as he wished it, Baucomb might not get back. Hitch said, "Me and Edson will go have us a smoke, Mister Selkirk. You can visit *here* with Mister Baucomb."

Hitch and Edson did not stray much past the front door; they kept an eye on the house. In twenty minutes or so, Selkirk strode out stiffly and rode away in the Figure 4 company buckboard.

Baucomb explained, "Tried to hire me. Said he had a good attorney from Kansas City but thought it might be well also to have a man versed in Texas law. I told him it wouldn't be ethical for me to change now; I already had my clients."

Edson said, "We should've known he'd try to buy you."

Hitch frowned. "And now that he knows he can't, maybe he'll let Torrington use his ways. Mister Baucomb, you better not leave this house anymore unless some of us go with you."

Hitch did not sleep much the night before the trial. Court was set to convene at nine o'clock in the morning. Hitch lay on his cot listening to Rascal snore. All night Hitch mentally gave his testimony against a hostile judge, a hostile county attorney and defense attorney. By daylight he was up, poking a fire into life beneath the coffeepot in the office's small stove. He could hear horses moving outside, and he walked to the window. Against the glow of the eastern sky he saw half a dozen sleepy-looking horsemen riding up the street from the cottonwood-lined river, a thin trail of late-summer dust slow to settle behind them. At the head of the street were five or six more.

Gathering early, he thought.

By the time he had his clothes on and finished his first cup of coffee, he saw more riders in the street. He knew some of the faces, but mostly he went by the brands on the horses. Snaketrack. Figure 4. Rascal McGinty was up now and standing in the doorway, looking outside. He said, "Looks to me like Selkirk and Torrington must've sent word to every camp, every wagon. Looks like every man they got is in town."

Hitch worried, "I wonder if I got the authority to close all the saloons while court is in session?"

Rascal said, "You'd have to ask the judge. If he sees you want it, he'll probably rule against it on principle."

"Best leave well enough alone," Hitch nodded. He picked up his carbine; he had never gotten used to wearing a pistol. "You stay close and keep out of trouble, Rascal. I'll go see how Edson and Baucomb are comin' along."

Walking out into the street, he became uneasily aware that he had the full attention of every cowboy. None spoke to him, either friendly or otherwise; they just watched him. He tried to keep his step steady and even, showing no outward sign of the nervousness growing inside him. He knocked on Edson's door, and the banker hollered for him to come in. The two men were eating steak and eggs. Biggs motioned for Hitch to help himself. Hitch tried, but he couldn't get much breakfast down. "You-all looked outside yet?"

Edson said, "More people than the Fourth of July."

Allan Baucomb commented uneasily, "Surely they wouldn't try to disrupt a trial. It's to their interest to settle this right here rather than risk the outcome in a court where they lack influence." Baucomb was in his mid-thirties, wearing black muttonchop whiskers and a heavy mustache, already trimmed this morning. They gave him an appearance of severity. "Surely they are intelligent enough to recognize that, Sheriff. Selkirk, at least, if not Torrington."

Hitch abandoned any attempt at eating. He poured a cup of Edson's coffee, which he found weak to his taste, and stood in the doorway where he could watch the street. It was an hour now until time for court. The town was full of horses and men. Hitch finally mused, "We got a long ways to walk. Reckon we ought to get a buckboard?"

"It's not very far," Edson argued.

Hitch nodded toward the gathering cowboys. "Could be the longest walk any of us ever took."

Presently he sensed that something had happened, for word began passing down the street, and men started mounting their horses and riding toward the courthouse. "I reckon Torrington's here, or Selkirk. Maybe both of them. Right now might be a good time for us to go."

Edson went for his coat and Baucomb for his satchel. Hitch stepped out into the street, holding the carbine at arm's length, the other men stepping briskly to catch up with him. They began walking. They had not gone far before the horsemen started moving down toward them. Every few feet a couple of men would drop out, forming lines on each side of the street. Hitch glanced uneasily at Edson, then at Baucomb. "Boys," he said, "we're alone out here like a pigeon on a post."

They could have turned and run back to the house, but neither man beside him showed any disposition to do that. They kept walking. Whatever came, they would meet it head-on.

Hitch knew John Torrington by the way he sat straight and proud in the saddle, and Selkirk by the way he slumped in his. It struck him as it had before how ill-matched the men were to be caught up together like this. Lafey Dodge was there, too, on one side of Torrington and opposite Selkirk. Torrington reined in twenty feet from the three men afoot, as did Selkirk. By now their cowboys lined both sides of the street all the way up to the courthouse. Torrington spoke to Lafey Dodge, and Dodge pushed his horse forward in a walk. He gave a moment's attention to Edson and Baucomb, then nodded impassively at Hitch. "Mister Torrington says court's ready to commence. You ready, Hitchcock?"

"Ready."

Dodge pointed his chin at Baucomb. "I reckon that'd be the Austin lawyer."

"That's him."

"Mister Torrington says tell him he ain't needed up at the courthouse, or wanted."

Hitch's breath began to tighten. "He's got a legal right."

"I ain't a lawyer, and I ain't talkin' about *legal* rights; I'm talkin' about facts. He stays here. You come on, Hitchcock, so court can start."

Hitch's hands were turning sweaty against the carbine. Up and down the street, townspeople were beginning to come out cautiously, watching the horsemen. Hitch said, "We're all comin'."

"You'll be the only one that gets there."

Hitch knew Dodge was not making idle talk; that was not his way. Hitch's mouth was dry, his heartbeat picking up. He looked hopefully along the street for help from the people of the town. They watched, and a few might help if someone would but start. Nobody started.

Far up the street, Rascal McGinty came running, pistol in his hand. Hitch froze, not breathing. Lafey Dodge would kill Rascal as coldly as he might kill a beef.

He never had to. Some cowboy swung a loop and sent it snaking out to catch Rascal by both feet. Rascal sprawled. Before he could get up, a couple of cowboys had the pistol. Rascal was out of it.

Hitch trembled now; he was scared, and he knew he showed it. But he remembered that Law McGinty had been scared too. Hitch stepped forward, thumb on the hammer of the carbine. His heart was pounding. He stared straight at Torrington, and everything else seemed to blur away as if Torrington sat at the mouth end of a funnel. Hitch walked past Lafey Dodge, half expecting to be struck by Dodge's pistol, or shot by it. It didn't happen, for Dodge watched him in wonder. Hitch cocked the carbine hammer back with his thumb. As he walked up close enough to reach out and touch Torrington's leg, he swung the muzzle of the carbine up. He aimed it point-blank at the old ranchman.

His voice sounded like someone else's, and far away. "It's loaded, Mister Torrington."

Torrington glared down at him. "You think I'm scared of that?"

"You ought to be. I am."

The old man's mouth was hard and flat behind the gray whiskers. "What do you mean?"

"I mean I'm within a hair of shootin' you. I don't want to, but there it is."

"There's two dozen, three dozen men would cut you to pieces."

"That wouldn't put you back together."

The beginnings of uncertainty stirred in the hard eyes. "You ain't got the guts to shoot me."

"I don't know, Mister Torrington; I honestly don't know. I don't think either one of us really wants to find out. We're goin' up that street, me and Edson and Baucomb, and you're ridin' along beside us."

Torrington swayed, but he did not yield. "Like I said, he ain't goin'. If you ever intend to fire that thing, go ahead and do it now."

Hitch already had taken up the slack in the trigger. One tiny squeeze now and it would shoot. He didn't breathe. His hands were cold and wet; he could feel his pulse drumming against the wooden stock.

A commotion started at the upper end of the street, and he glanced that way, blinking, trying to refocus. A new group of horsemen came toward him in an easy trot, passing between the lines of Snaketrack and Figure 4 cowboys. There weren't as many of these as of the others, but there were a respectable twelve or fourteen. In the lead rode Charlie Waide.

Charlie reined up, his men coming about and forming a semicircle around Torrington and Selkirk, Lafey Dodge and Edson and Baucomb. Charlie gravely sized up the situation, then said, "We come to see that court starts on time. You ready, Hitch?"

Hitch lowered the muzzle of the carbine, his knees suddenly feeling as if they would give way. He wanted to smile, but it wasn't in him. He gave Baucomb a quick nod of summons. "Ready, Charlie."

Torrington's angry eyes bored at Charlie Waide. "This don't noways concern you, Charlie."

Waide's voice was even. "It concerns me, John."

Selkirk found voice. "Charles Waide, you're forgetting that I'm in a position to ruin you."

Charlie gave him a look of contempt. "You damn near did already. You damn near took away what self respect old age had left me. Let's go to court, Hitch."

Some of the townspeople were emboldened by Charlie Waide. Gathering in, they and the W cowboys formed a protective circle around Hitch and Edson and the lawyer Baucomb. Together they walked up the street to the courthouse, moving safely between the lines of cowboys. Rascal hurried up to join them, dusty and angry. Someone had given him his pistol back.

Few besides the veniremen could get into the small courtroom at first. Hitch stationed Rascal at the door to take up all the pistols and put them in a clerk's office; there wouldn't be a gun in the courtroom except those of the sheriff and his deputy.

When Judge Wilkins gaveled court into session, the eight defendants sat at a table in the front of the room. Selection of the jury took time, defense objecting to any cowboys who had participated in the strike, prosecution objecting to any who now worked for a big ranch. In the end the jury was made up mostly of farmers, of townsmen, of a few cowboys from small outfits which had not been involved. All in all, Hitch thought the opposing attorneys had obtained as fair a jury as could be gathered here. There was no way to obtain men who had no detailed knowledge of the recent months' events, or opinions about them.

Hitch studied the defendants' faces. Selkirk was ill at ease; this might have been the first serious situation he had not been able to buy his way out of. Torrington stared resentfully at the jury, shamed at having to submit himself to the judgment of ordinary men for whom he felt no kinship, no particular regard. Dodge seemed untouched and unworried. Slant Unger sat hunched, his good hand gripping his crippled arm as if it still brought him pain. Tobe Ferris was visibly disturbed, looking out upon the curious crowd, then back to John Torrington as if for assurance. The other cowboys were quiet and worried, a little at bay as they had been that day under Hitch's carbine.

County attorney Zachary made a brief introductory comment about the subject of the trial but carefully avoided any accusations. He stated several times that "you will hear it alleged that these defendants did willfully" do so-and-so, seeming to reflect some doubt on his own part, adding that "It will be up to you gentlemen of the jury to decide based upon clear evidence and upon your judgment of the circumstances leading up to and surrounding this case."

Hitch figured Zachary was giving them an out should they decide that Law had deserved killing. He thought it would have been more seemly for the defense, not the prosecution, to say so.

Kansas City attorney DeWitt laid out the groundwork for the defense: "Gentlemen, I have been here but a few short days, and already I am greatly impressed by the beauty and the bounty of this high-lifted land. I ask you gentlemen to gaze upon this man, this hardy pioneer John Torrington, who dared bring the first herds into this region before the dust had settled behind the horses of the wild Comanche. This man and the brave cowboys who rode beside him opened the way for all of you to share the vision with him, to make this no longer a wasted land grazed only by the buffalo and traversed only by the savage. I ask if any one of you would be here today but for the sacrifice and hardship endured by these intrepid men? I daresay you would not. So now that all of you have shared in some measure the fruits of his labor and the fulfillment of his brave dreams, can you now turn upon him and betray him to his jealous accusers?"

He gave the jury a long, challenging stare. "Consider

next the man seated beside him, Prosper Selkirk, who
brought to this area the capital it needed to nurture the
growth begun by John Torrington and the valiant men
around him; who brought business acumen and sound man-
agerial judgment for all those who wished to observe and
learn from it, and thereby profit this entire land. Let me
assure you that in the financial community from which I
come, the name of Prosper Selkirk stands high in honor and
respect.

"And lastly let us consider these gallant cowboys whose
loyalty has stood the test of fire, men who have ridden un-
flinchingly through summer heat and bitter cold, asking not
selfishly for themselves but rather selflessly giving their best
for the ranches they proudly serve, and for this region they
have helped to build. Slant Unger, once injured in a border
battle alongside John Torrington, now perhaps crippled for
life at the hands of a man more inclined to defend the
thieves among us than the upright and the builders. Shorty
James, Hobson Clark, Reston McPhail, loyal cowboys all.
And this black man Tobe Ferris, a credit to his race, in his
way perhaps the most loyal of all because once freed from
slavery he chose to remain the lifelong friend and aide of
his beloved master John Torrington when he might easily
have followed the blandishments of those hypocrites who
so often used members of his race for political purposes of
their own."

Hitch kept waiting to see what the lawyer would say
about Lafey Dodge. DeWitt never mentioned Dodge at all.
He passed over him as if Dodge had been one of the cowboys, as if the jury could not count and did not know him.

Allan Baucomb took over for the prosecution. "Sheriff,
would you please bring Mrs. Lawton McGinty into the
room?"

Kate waited in the clerk's office, face pale, her hands
nervously twisting a handkerchief until it had begun to tear.
Hitch said quietly, "Kate, it's time."

She looked up, tears in her eyes. "Do I have to?"

"I'm sorry, Kate."

"Revenge isn't important to me, Hitch. It never was."

"It's not just for revenge, Kate; it's to be sure no other woman is ever widowed here again the way you were."

"I don't know if I can stand up to it."

"You got friends in there, Kate. And I'll be there."

"If you weren't, I *know* I couldn't stand up to it."

Baucomb began with innocent questions about Kate's name and place of abode. She spoke so softly at first that the judge had to admonish her to talk louder. When she had eased somewhat, Baucomb gently led her into telling how Law had ridden to the dugout in a hard run, closely pursued, and had ordered her to take the baby and get away. When Baucomb was finished, Loring DeWitt began his cross-examination.

"Mrs. McGinty, I do not believe in the course of his questioning Mister Baucomb ever got around to asking you where you lived before you came to this region."

She told him East Texas, over in the blacklands.

"I have been told your father was a farmer."

"Yes sir, that he was."

"A successful farmer, would you say?"

"He never did have much luck."

"An unsuccessful farmer, then?"

"I suppose he was."

"It would be easy for an unsuccessful man, struggling, to be jealous of those who were doing better, would it not?"

Kate blinked. "I don't understand what you're tryin' to say."

"A man so afflicted might well pass that jealousy—that resentment—on to his children."

Baucomb stood up. "Your honor, I do not see that this has anything to do with the case at hand."

DeWitt said, "Your honor can see where it has *everything* to do with this case, can't you, sir?"

The judge nodded quietly. "Carry on."

"Mister Torrington and Mister Selkirk are considered successful men in this region. Might you, Mrs. McGinty, feel a little resentful over their success in view of the very little your own people have achieved?''

Kate sat looking at him, not knowing what to say. DeWitt gave the jury a long glance which said her silence showed she agreed with the truth of his statement. He went on, ''Since you have been widowed, Mrs. McGinty, what is the means of your livelihood?''

''I help my mother take in washin'.''

''The pay for such work is very meager, I would assume.''

''We eat.''

''But not very well, do you?''

Again she failed to answer him.

''It would appear you are again trapped by the *hard luck*, as you put it, which seems to have plagued your family all along. Hard luck which it would be easy to blame on someone more fortunate.'' He paused, facing the jury and allowing time for effect. ''I sympathize with your distress, madam, and I have no wish to prolong your ordeal here today. However, there are some points I feel we must clear up in the interests of truth. You testified to the identity of the men who rode up that day in pursuit of your husband. I must ask you if you are positive you recognized them.''

''John Torrington was there, and Lafey Dodge.''

''Did you actually see them?''

''Yes . . . yes, I think so.''

''You think so? You are not certain?''

''Well, Law said . . .''

''You did not yourself actually see them?''

''I saw them, only things happened so fast and I was so scared . . .''

''Then you cannot for a certainty say that it even *was* John Torrington or any of these other men sitting here?''

''It was them, all right. Everybody knows . . .''

''Not everybody, Mrs. McGinty, for even you yourself obviously do not. You are acting upon supposition, and supposition is notoriously unreliable. The facts are that you saw a group of men but in your very natural and understandable fear were never sure, even, who they actually were. They might have been anybody. And quite probably your resentment of men such as Mister Torrington and Mister Selkirk—successful where your kin never were—made it easy for you to tell yourself it was they you saw.''

Kate insisted, ''It *was* them; I know it was.''

DeWitt turned away a moment, then back. ''Now, Mrs. McGinty, I have another question . . .''

''It *was* them,'' Kate said again. The judge admonished her to speak only in reply to a question.

DeWitt glanced at the jury. ''Mrs. McGinty, have you ever known a man named Cato Bramlett?''

Lips tight, Kate nodded.

DeWitt said impatiently, ''I did not hear you, Mrs. McGinty.''

''Yes, I know him.''

''And did your husband know him?''

''Yes.''

''Are you aware, madam, of the reputation of this man Bramlett?''

Baucomb said, ''I object, your honor. Bramlett is not being tried in this court.''

DeWitt said, ''He *should* be tried in this court. I believe your honor will find that I am working toward a key point in this case if you will but allow me.''

''Objection overruled.''

DeWitt frowned at Kate. ''Again, Mrs. McGinty, are you aware of this man's reputation?''

''I've heard things. I never did like him.''

''But it would seem your husband liked him, for they had business dealings together. Is that not true?''

Baucomb stood up, and the judge cut him off. ''Overruled.''

Kate said, ''I don't know about their business. Bramlett was there three or four times, is all.''

''Three or four times?'' DeWitt made it clear he did not believe that. ''I submit, Mrs. McGinty, that your husband and Cato Bramlett were in league in a cattle-stealing enterprise. If this was done without your knowledge, then you are a naive young woman.''

Kate looked at the floor. Hitch thought across the room he could see her shoulders shake a little.

Baucomb protested, ''Your honor, Lawton McGinty was the *victim* in this case; he is not the defendant.''

DeWitt said, ''My reasons will become clear as the trial progresses. For now, however, I am through with this witness.''

Kate looked accusingly at Torrington and his group. ''I know they're the ones who killed Law.''

The judge told her she was excused; she could go on home.

''It was them. All the rest of this is just talk,'' she declared.

The judge said, ''Mrs. McGinty, the bench always tries to be lenient with a woman. Now will you please go home?''

Hitch met her at the courtroom door and walked with her to the outside door of the courthouse. She was still shaking.

''I'm sorry, Kate,'' Hitch told her gently, ''that you had to go through that. I hope it won't be for nothin'.''

She leaned into his arms a moment for strength, then pulled back, blinking away tears. ''I just want to see an end of all this.''

He heard a sound and turned to see Rascal, surprise in his face. Hitch watched Kate walk down the street, his heart heavy. Rascal McGinty said quietly, ''Hitch, they want you on the stand now.''

XIX

No doctor had seen Law McGinty to
certify his death. It was for Hitch to establish the fact that
Law had indeed died, and that he had been hanged. "And
now," said Baucomb, "would you simply recite for the benefit of the jury the events leading up to the final act of
violence which has brought us together today?"

Hitch reviewed Kate's arrival at his place, her near-
hysterical story. Attorney DeWitt arose when Hitch started
to relate what Kate had told him. "Your honor, I object to
introduction of hearsay evidence."

"Objection sustained."

Hitch rubbed his hand across his face and proceeded to
tell about rushing to the McGinty place, and about meeting
the sheriff on the way. The Kansas City attorney objected
again, and the judge warned Hitch against repeating any
statement the sheriff might have made to him, for this also
would be hearsay. Hitch gritted his teeth, then proceeded to
tell what had happened on the river.

Baucomb said, "Sheriff Hitchcock, would you please

point out to the jury the men you saw at the scene while Law McGinty's lifeless body was still hanging there?''

"Yes sir." Hitch began to point out the defendants one by one. "John Torrington . . . Prosper Selkirk . . . Lafey Dodge . . ." He named them all.

"There is no possibility of any mistake on your part?''

"No, sir. I had plenty of time to look at every man."

When Baucomb had finished his questions, DeWitt arose, giving Hitch a long, careful study. "Now, Sheriff Hitchcock . . . you *are* sheriff, I believe." When Hitch acknowledged that he was, the attorney continued, "But you were not sheriff at the time these alleged events took place. Therefore, Mister Hitchcock, upon that occasion you were merely a private citizen, even as I, or any of these good gentlemen in the jury. You had no legal authority to give commands, make arrests or use a firearm against anyone."

"I went there to stop them from hangin' Law. I was too late."

"You've spoken at length about this so-called hanging. Did you actually see anyone hang this man?''

"You mean to actually pull him up there? No sir, he was already dead when I got to him."

"Are you a physician, Sheriff Hitchcock?''

"No sir."

"Then can you say with certainty that this alleged hanging was even the cause of death? Might he not have been shot, stabbed or otherwise done to death? Might he not, for all you or I as laymen can know, have even suffered a stroke and died a natural death?''

"I saw the body. There wasn't a bullet in him, or a knife mark. They had him hangin' up there. He died from hangin', and that's a pure fact."

"Even if we specified that this is so, you have already stated that you did not see these defendants actually perform the act."

"They was there."

"Might they not have happened innocently upon the scene after someone else executed this cattle thief?''

Baucomb said, "Your Honor, I must object. The victim is not on trial."

"Objection overruled." Judge Wilkins tore off a chew of tobacco with his teeth. "Everybody knows he was stealing cattle."

DeWitt said, "Mister Hitchcock, I have heard a great deal of talk in the days I have spent here, but I do not propose to deal in someone else's suppositions. I want to know if you ever personally saw Lawton McGinty in the act of taking someone else's cattle."

Hitch glanced at Baucomb, and Baucomb objected that this was irrelevant to the subject at hand. He was overruled.

DeWitt pressed, "Well, Mister Hitchcock, did you?"

Hitch looked to Rascal, wishing he weren't here, glad Kate had gone home. Reluctantly he admitted he had once found Law changing the brand on an animal that belonged to someone else.

"Did you do anything about it, Mister Hitchcock?"

"I told him it wasn't right."

"That was all you did?"

"I wasn't an officer then."

DeWitt nodded. "This establishes beyond question that Lawton McGinty was a cattle thief. Now, Mister Hitchcock, do you know a man named Cato Bramlett?"

"I've run into him."

"Again, I hate to deal in suppositions, but I am told he is a notorious cattle thief."

"He has that reputation."

"Have you ever seen him in the company of Lawton McGinty?"

Hitch hesitated, wondering where DeWitt was trying to lead him. DeWitt pressed relentlessly. Hitch said, "Yes, I seen them together."

"And now, sir, have you ever heard of a Three C Cattle Company, also known variously as Cowboy Cattle Combine and Get-Even Cattle Company?"

"I have."

"Do you now or did you ever own stock in it?"

"No sir."

"Were you ever offered the opportunity of buying such stock?"

"I was."

"And why didn't you?"

Hitch was slow in deciding how to answer. "I didn't want any."

"You didn't want it because you knew it was a company of thieves, designed specifically to prey on the big ranches and take revenge for loss of the strike. Isn't that true, Mister Hitchcock?" When Hitch didn't answer, DeWitt said again, "Isn't that true?" Hitch gave no answer, but he knew everybody could read it in his face. DeWitt read it. "It is true, gentlemen of the jury." He paced a little, staring at Hitch. "Now, sir, you have already stated that you saw Lawton McGinty and Cato Bramlett together. Did you ever hear cross words pass between them?"

Hitch said he hadn't.

"Have you seen this Cato Bramlett at any time since the death of Lawton McGinty?"

Hitch hadn't.

DeWitt nodded. "I understand that no one else has. He has disappeared like a man in flight. Now the natural question which arises next is: in flight from *what?* Could it be, Mister Hitchcock, that he and Lawton McGinty quarreled over the division of spoils? This is known to happen among robbers. Could it be that he and some of his henchmen hanged Lawton McGinty?"

Hitch flared. "Now, you know better than that. We all know . . ."

DeWitt cut him off. "We all know you did not see McGinty hanged. You came upon Mister Torrington and Mister Selkirk and these other men at the scene and took it on circumstantial evidence that they had done it. In actual fact, you have no way of knowing it was not done by Bramlett and some of his robber band."

Old John Torrington began to squirm.

Hitch declared, "Lafey Dodge himself told me . . ."

"I did not ask you what Lafey Dodge told you, Mister Hitchcock. I asked you what you had seen with your own eyes. Your Honor, I am through with this witness."

DeWitt sat down, and immediately John Torrington went into a whispered argument with him.

Baucomb stood up. "Your honor, before you dismiss this witness I would like to ask counsel if he intends to have any of the defendants to testify."

DeWitt seemed glad to break away from the insistent Torrington. "In interest of time, Your Honor, and because of the constitutional guarantee that a defendant need not subject himself to the ordeal of questioning, we have agreed that these men will not be called to the stand."

"Then," Baucomb said, "since the question of Lafey Dodge's statement has come up and Mister Dodge will not personally testify so that we may explore the question to its full potential, let me ask Sheriff Hitchcock just what Lafey Dodge did tell him."

DeWitt protested that this would be hearsay. Baucomb countered that it was not hearsay in that it involved a statement by one of the defendants. Confused, the judge stammered. Hitch did not wait for him to make up his mind. "He told me they done it, Your Honor. He told me . . ."

Wilkins hammered. "Objection sustained. You will not answer that question, Hitchcock."

"I already answered it, Your Honor. I said Dodge told me they done it."

DeWitt protested angrily. Judge Wilkins threatened that if Hitch persisted in giving testimony contrary to the rulings from the bench he would be jailed for contempt. He told the jury it was to disregard what Hitch had said because this was inadmissible testimony; they were to forget they had heard it.

Hitch smiled thinly. He had made his statement, and the jury would play hell forgetting it, especially when DeWitt's and Wilkins's anger tended to underscore it.

DeWitt said crisply, "Your honor, I am through with . . . no, just another moment. There is something else." His eyes narrowed. "Sheriff Hitchcock, I believe you have a deputy. Would you mind stating his name?"

"Ra . . . Michael McGinty."

"I believe you were about to say Rascal. I would assume he is better known by this name than by Michael."

"Ain't many people know his real name."

"Do you know how he came to be called Rascal?"

"Can't say as I ever heard."

"Perhaps simply because the name fits, Sheriff. He is a brother to the cattle thief whose death precipitated this entire unhappy affair. Given the oath of office, you immediately hired the brother of a known thief. One might wonder about your loyalties, Sheriff. One might wonder about *you*."

Hitch pushed halfway to his feet in a flush of anger, then checked himself. Baucomb immediately lodged an objection, and DeWitt backed off, looking satisfied. He had made his point with the jury. "I withdraw the comment, Your Honor."

The prosecution called Charlie Waide to the stand. Charlie stiffened in surprise, then limped reluctantly up the narrow aisle to the front of the room. He took the oath and sat heavily in the witness chair. He glanced at Wilkins. "I don't know what I'm doin' up here, Judge. Ain't nothin' I can tell anybody about this case."

Baucomb asked a few questions to establish Charlie's identity and the length of time he had spent in this part of the country. "Now, Mister Waide, it is my understanding that shortly before the cowboys went on strike, you attended a meeting of ranch owners at the Figure 4 headquarters. Am I correct?"

"That's a fact: I did."

"Do you recall the tenor of the discussions there that day?"

"There was a lot of talk; everybody had somethin' to say."

"Do you recall a suggestion by John Torrington that perhaps the way to assert rancher control would be by way of a few hangings?"

"There was lots of things said."

"But specifically, do you remember such a declaration by John Torrington?"

Charlie watched the jury warily. "I remember somethin' like that."

"If my information is correct, you argued against the Torrington point of view. What was the nature of your objection?"

"Just that we don't need to do things that way these days. There's other ways now."

"Did you have any part—in the planning or in the act itself—in the hanging of Lawton McGinty?"

"No sir, I did not."

"Why not?"

Charlie's hands rubbed nervously against the arms of the wooden chair. "I always liked that cowboy. Contrary, but I liked him."

"What if you had not even known him?"

"It still wouldn't have been right."

"Some would argue that such a course is justified in the defense of one's property."

"We have laws now, and men to enforce them."

"Did you know that someone had designs against Lawton McGinty before the hanging occurred?"

Charlie thought over the question. "I went and told Hugh Hitchcock that he better talk to Law, that somethin' bad was fixin' to happen if he got caught changin' brands."

Prosper Selkirk gave Charlie a look of hatred.

Baucomb turned to the jury. "Gentlemen, Mister Waide is known to all of you as one of the 'big' ranchers. Despite this, you have heard him state that he does not subscribe to the notion that owning property gives a person a right to circumvent the due process of law. He does not believe that one man's property rights are superior to another man's right to life. And I do not believe you gentlemen subscribe to that theory either."

Baucomb indicated he was through with Charlie. Prosper Selkirk was whispering in DeWitt's ear. The defense attorney stood up. "Your Honor, I have a question or two for this witness."

Charlie's hands rubbed the chair arm faster.

DeWitt said, "Mister Waide, have you ever participated in the hanging of a man?"

Charlie Waide looked at the floor, face coloring. DeWitt repeated the question. Charlie said, "Yes, I have."

"Would you please describe the circumstances?"

"It was a long time ago."

"We would still be interested in hearing about it. For what crime was this punishment exacted?"

"One time was for murder. Another time was for horse stealin'; in them days takin' a man's horse could be the same as killin' him."

"More than once, then." DeWitt nodded gravely. "And yet now you declare such a thing to be wrong. What has brought the change, Mister Waide, a guilty conscience?"

Charlie's gaze was on the floor, his voice soft. "There wasn't no law then except what we made for ourselves. If we hadn't done what we done, them people would have overrun us. Even so, I ain't proud of it; I've woke up many a night rememberin' and wishin' it never had happened. Them days we had an excuse, of sorts; now there's no excuse at all."

Baucomb called Allie Clay of the Nine Bar to corroborate what Charlie had said about John Torrington's comments at the ranchers' meeting. DeWitt made some effort to discredit Clay by bringing out the fact that he had feuded with Torrington a number of years and thus was not an objective witness.

The prosecution had no further witnesses. The defense brought out several people to vouch for the character of first one and then another of the defendants.

It came time, finally, for the opposing attorneys to present their summations. Baucomb had entirely taken over the prosecution. County attorney Zachary sat alone in resentful silence. Baucomb approached the jurors.

"Gentlemen, I want all of you to take a long and careful

look at the defendants. Most of these men are simply cowboys, working for wages and doing the bidding of the men who pay their hire. It might be argued that since they were simply following orders, they should be held blameless. But obeying an order to rope a cow is one thing; blindly obeying an order to put a rope around a man's neck and to murder him is something else entirely. One does not surrender his conscience, his soul, when he accepts a job. Each of us is still a man, and individually accountable for his sins.

"Consider then the two men who ordered this outrage. Prosper Selkirk, an arrogant product of the Eastern financial community, a man to whom all things reduce to a question of silver and gold, to whom no man's rights are as sacred as his own quest for the dollar. John Torrington, a feudal lord, an anachronism in this enlightened time when the poor man's aspirations are to be valued as highly as those of the mightiest landholder.

"Now, the time has come for you to go and consider a verdict. We all know there is traditionally a certain amount of rhetoric and a certain amount of showmanship in a trial of this sort, but now let us put all this behind us and try to sift rhetoric from fact. And the facts in this case are plain. We will specify that Lawton McGinty was indeed stealing cattle from the two principal defendants. They wanted it stopped. They wanted it stopped in a manner so chilling that others tempted to steal from them would be afraid; that even honorable men who seek only their just rights would not dare press the matter, might even become discouraged and leave the country. Torrington and Selkirk wanted no interference. When interference came, they met it with savage force.

"And the principal instrument of this force was this final man you see before you, this Lafey Dodge. I ask you gentlemen to remember what your own feelings were when first you learned that Lafey Dodge was in the county. Was it not fear, was it not a cold dread? His is a name, his is a reputation that automatically brings this reaction. To this man this reputation is a tool of his trade, as your saddle or

your plow are the tools of yours. His gun and his loyalty
are for hire. He kills not in the heat of passion but in cold,
mechanical calculation. His is a legacy left to us by a lawless
era which, thank God, is over. Men of Texas no longer settle
their differences with guns in the streets. Men of Texas no
longer hire the services of mercenaries like Lafey Dodge to
do for them with force that which they cannot do for themselves by legal means. At least, *few* men do, and those few
men have outlived their natural time; they have not seen
that we have entered a new era of law, of justice, of human
rights. They have not learned that Texas has outlived the
swaggering arrogance of occasional large property owners
who would walk roughshod over smaller neighbors.

"Most of you here remember the recent cowboy strike.
Whatever your personal *opinion* of it may be, you will all
concede that it was an expression of popular resentment
against the same blind despotism which led to the hanging
of Lawton McGinty. Despite the transparent attempt of the
defense to lay a false trail, you and I and everyone else in
this courtroom know where the truth lies. With the profes-
sional Lafey Dodge to lead the way, they entrapped Lawton
McGinty; and even as the anguished cries of his unfortunate
young wife echoed in their ears, they did drag him away
and hang him without pity. Now, I have conceded the guilt
of the victim in taking these men's cattle. Nevertheless, his
guilt should have been determined by a jury of twelve men
in a courtroom, not by eight men on horseback beneath a
cottonwood tree.

"Remember this: if you free these men, it can all happen
again. If you free Lafey Dodge, you will be loosing a savage
wolf among you. All this can happen again, and next time
it can happen to an innocent man. As you deliberate, consider this: that innocent man may very well be *you*."

Whatever had stirred Torrington earlier, he was still dissatisfied when DeWitt pulled away from him and stood up.
DeWitt paced in deep concentration, eyes first on the defendants, then on the jury, "Gentlemen, at this point I can think
of many things that perhaps I should say; yet in retrospect

it seems to me that I have said most of them before. I would remind you first of all that the man over whom this ill-advised trial has been waged was—by the admission of his friends and the prosecutor himself—a thief. A low, common thief. I would remind you once more of the hardships and sacrifice endured by this fine old pioneer, John Torrington, and his faithful cowboys, in opening this region for settlement; of the vision of Prosper Selkirk in bringing needed capital into this area to allow growth and prosperity to be shared by you all.

"I would now remind you that you are charged to find these men innocent if you are not certain of their guilt beyond all reasonable doubt. I have shown that the charges against them are based upon suppositions, fed perhaps by the bitterness and jealous hatreds which some men . . ." he looked directly at Hitch ". . . have carried since the collapse of their abortive strike, that ill-conceived uprising of the lazy, the malcontent and the misled. Shall we perpetuate this petty legacy or shall we cast it away with the disdain which it deserves? Shall we listen to these mean and strident voices and persecute these men whose farsighted leadership and devotion have brought this region to where it is today, or shall we respect and honor these wise and good and gallant men and stand together shoulder to shoulder with them in building toward an even greater future?

"I submit again that no eyewitness has come forward. I submit again that these men are the victims of circumstance, that the hanging was done by parties unknown, very probably led by the notorious Cato Bramlett, and that . . ."

He never got to finish. John Torrington stood up angrily. "Goddammit. Judge, this has gone far enough. It's a damned lie, every bit of it!"

Judge Wilkins pounded the gavel. "John, you set yourself down."

"The hell I will. I paid enough money for this Kansas City lawyer to've bought me four good sections of land, and be damned if I intend to see all of it thrown away in a lie."

Attorney DeWitt grabbed the rancher's arm. "Mister Torrington, you're out of order."

Torrington shoved back. "*You'll* be out of order if you keep a-pullin' at me." Tobe Ferris arose as if to aid Torrington. DeWitt backed off, agitated.

Torrington looked at the jury, then at the bench, defiance in his eyes. "Judge, what he said ain't the way of it at all. It wasn't no two-bit Cato Bramlett that done the hangin' and I don't want him gettin' the credit for it. It was *us* that hung Law McGinty. We done it because he was a cow thief, and we done it as a lesson to anybody else who might be thataway inclined. Now if people get to thinkin' maybe we didn't do it, then all that is wasted, don't you see?" Prosper Selkirk sat stunned, face draining of color. Torrington turned to the jury, in no way apologetic. "We done it because a man ought to stand up for himself, not wait for some slow-footed court to do it for him at public expense. You think this country was built by tiptoein' lawyers and a shelf full of lawbooks? No sir, it was built by men with guts, men who done whatever had to be done and didn't fool around about it. It's been that way and it's that way now; it'll *be* that way as long as I got strength to climb into a saddle. And if it ever stops bein' that way you can mark it down that this country has gone to hell.

"Law McGinty was a damned thief; he needed hangin' and we hung him. Better to hang one man as a lesson than to wait and have to hang a dozen. That's why I couldn't sit quiet and let the lie go without bein' answered. I didn't enjoy hangin' that boy; anybody says I did is a liar. I wouldn't want to do it again. But I *would* do it if I had to, and these good men of mine would help me.

"Now, if times has changed so much that a man can't take care of his own troubles anymore, then I say Texas is the worse off for it. And if you folks on this jury think you got to punish somebody, don't you do it to these good loyal men here who just done what we told them to. They are not responsible. If you got to punish somebody punish me and Prosper Selkirk." He glared at the jury. "But I want you to know one thing: I ain't in noways sorry, and I ain't in noways ashamed. And remember this is still our country. You don't have to keep on livin' here. If we was of a mind to, we could put you out."

He sat down. Prosper Selkirk's face was hidden in his hands. The courtroom was in shocked silence a moment or two. The judge hoarsely read his charge to the jury, and the jury was led out into another room to deliberate. John Torrington sat at the head of the defendants' table, nervous as a wild stallion trapped in a pen. Prosper Selkirk's face was still half hidden. He did not look at anyone. The cowboys were quiet and troubled. Lafey Dodge stared at John Torrington, and Hitch thought he saw a new respect in the gunfighter's eyes.

Presently Judge Wilkins arose from the bench. "If counsels would like, I might find a bottle in my chambers." Baucomb, DeWitt, Zachary, and the judge disappeared together through a door at the rear of the room. That surprised Hitch. He would have thought the heated differences during the court session would preclude any friendliness between opposing attorneys. But, he decided, there was a lot he didn't know about law.

He had a notion the jury would deliberate a few minutes, then come back with its verdict. Hitch had no watch, but he judged after a while that the jury had been out an hour, and he saw no sign of stirring in that direction. He was beginning to ache a little from sitting so long, and he stood up to stretch. He glanced at the defendants and found none of them looking his way except Lafey Dodge. He couldn't read what—if anything—was in the man's thoughts.

Rascal McGinty came up from the back of the courtroom, his patience gone with thin. "Dammit, Hitch, how long does it take the jury to find them guilty?"

"We don't know that it will."

"What else can they do? You heard what the old man said. He pulled the cell door shut on himself."

Hitch shrugged.

Rascal said, "I still blame Lafey Dodge more than any

of them. He's the one who kills people for hire. Without him, they wouldn't likely of ever done it.''

"Main thing is to be sure it don't ever happen again. It's not as important to say who was to blame.''

"It's important to me,'' Rascal insisted.

Darkness came, and still the jury was out. Hitch could not sit long at a time now; a nervous prickling started in his rump every time he went to the chair. Mostly he paced the floor or stood leaning against the wall, watching the lamps and lanterns being lighted around town. The same uneasiness stirred most of the defendants. Half of them were up looking out the windows, the rest slumped at the table patting their feet, drumming their fingers, smoking cigarette after cigarette. Selkirk started to say something to John Torrington and the old rancher turned on him in fury. This day had done something to Torrington. It had humiliated him to sit here like a common criminal in the dock, to be stared at and speculated about by people whom he held in contempt.

The Negro Tobe Ferris stayed protectively near John Torrington, staring out at the onlookers with angry eyes that seemed to rebuke them for this disrespectful treatment of the old man. It struck Hitch that there was a faint resemblance between John Torrington and Tobe Ferris, despite the differences in their skin.

The judge went into the jury room several times, and always he came out impatiently shaking his head. Often Hitch saw him pull a heavy watch from his pocket and hold it out to arm's length, squinting to read it.

Much of the original crowd gave up and went home, though other people came in to take their places. Allan Baucomb sat down wearily beside Hitch. Hitch said, "Does it always take this long?''

"Sometimes.''

"Is that a good sign or a bad one?''

"You never know.''

Hunger gnawed at Hitch, but he had no intention of leaving so long as the issue remained in doubt.

The lamps had been burning at least an hour when word

came from the jury room. Judge Wilkins went out for a brief conference, then came back to the bench and rapped for order. "I will remind everybody that this court is still in session." The jury filed into place. The judge leaned forward. "Has the jury arrived at a verdict?"

A tall farmer designated as foreman stepped forward. "Like I told you back there, Judge, we been havin' some trouble. There's some says guilty, and there's some says we owe John Torrington too much to do this to him. We've talked and argued with each other till we're wrung out. We still don't come to any agreement."

"You're deadlocked, then?"

"Sure looks like it, Judge."

"What would happen if you took a little more time?"

"A fight, more than likely. Ain't been a man changed position in two hours."

The judge evidently had known this from his several visits to the jury room. "That being so, I declare that we've got a hung jury and this court is dismissed." He pounded the gavel.

The defendants looked at each other in confusion. Tobe Ferris whispered a question to John Torrington, and the old rancher stood up. "Judge, I'm figurin' on goin' home, and takin' my boys with me. Is there any reason I can't?"

Wilkins shook his head. "You're still under bond till there's a decision made on whether or not there'll be a retrial. That depends on the prosecution." He looked past the county attorney and fixed his gaze on Allan Baucomb. Baucomb said, "We'll have to take it under advisement, Your Honor."

The judge frowned. "Well, you know what *my* advice is. I rule that bond be refunded to those men and that if there's ever another trial—which I doubt—new bond can be set for them. Anybody wants a drink with me, they'll find me at the Buffalo Bar." He rapped the gavel one more time for emphasis and got up from his seat.

Some of the Snaketrack and Figure 4 cowboys began

crowding around the defendants, laughing and slapping them on the backs.

Hitch looked at the floor, his frustration sour as clabbered milk. To Baucomb he said, "I reckon we lost."

"Depends on how you look at it. Two years ago . . . *one* year, even . . . you would not have ever gotten them to trial."

Hitch said hopefully. "How about a retrial? Maybe next time . . ."

Baucomb shook his head. "You've made your point, Hitch, that's the main thing. Even a hung jury is a sign of change, and a warning. This thing would never be stood for again. In another year or two the whole bunch would stand convicted. I'm sure Selkirk realizes that. If the old man doesn't know it now, it'll soak in on him. What happened to Law McGinty will never happen again . . . not here."

Rascal McGinty's eyes were bitter. "Does this mean they don't even get punished?"

"They've been punished just bein' here," Hitch said.

As a deputy, Rascal McGinty had not had to leave his pistol outside. He drew it, his eyes afire. "Well, Lafey Dodge ain't gettin' away."

Before Hitch could move against him, Rascal leveled the pistol. Lafey Dodge, unarmed, stood rigid, almost resigned. Hitch leaped at Rascal, striking his arm just as the pistol fired. It made a thundering noise in the small courtroom. Black powdersmoke billowed in a choking cloud. Hitch wrestled Rascal for the pistol while men dived excitedly for windows and doors, under tables and chairs, behind the cold pot-bellied stove.

Hitch got Rascal down onto his back and drove his knee into the cowboy's stomach. Rascal relaxed his hold, and Hitch flung the pistol across the floor. Lafey Dodge stooped and picked it up in his left hand.

Expecting retaliation, Hitch shouted, "Dodge, don't you do it!"

Dodge made no move to aim the pistol at Rascal. He held

it out butt first. "Here, Hitchcock, I expect you'll want this thing. I've never killed a man for pleasure."

Hitch saw then that Dodge's right arm hung limp, blood beginning to soak the sleeve and run down his hand. Hitch glanced back at Rascal, expecting more fight from him. But Rascal had made his try and was through. He sat on the floor with arms tight against his stomach while he attempted to regain the breath Hitch had knocked out of him.

Hitch said to Dodge, "We'll get the doctor for you."

Dodge said, "I been hurt worse than this tryin' to open a can of tomatoes."

Hitch shoved Rascal's pistol into his own boottop and helped Rascal to his feet. "I'm takin' you to jail, Rascal, for your own protection."

Rascal made no protest. He still didn't have all his breath back. Hitch told the bystanders to get Dodge to the doctor. "I'll be along directly," he said. Hitch took Rascal to the jail and unlocked a cell. Rascal walked in without protest and sat on the iron frame meant for a cot. "Hitch," he said heavily, "he didn't get off scot-free. I drawed blood on him."

"You did that," Hitch admitted. "I hope you're satisfied."

"Not particularly, but I reckon I'm through. What you fixin' to do now?"

"Go see that Lafey Dodge gets patched up, then first thing in the mornin' ride along with him till I make sure he's plumb out of the county. Till he's gone, you're stayin' in here."

"Am I still your deputy?"

"I don't know. I'll have to think on it."

"It don't matter. I done what I wanted to be a deputy for. I drawed blood on him, at least." Hitch turned to leave. Rascal called him. "Hitch, you be careful with that Lafey Dodge. He'll kill a man as soon as look at him."

"I'll watch out."

"Before you go, Hitch, I got somethin' that needs sayin', somethin' I want you to think on."

"About Dodge?"

"About Kate. Ain't good, her bein' alone. I been thinkin' maybe after a proper time I ought to marry her myself."

Hitch made no reply; he didn't know how.

Rascal said, "But I can see now that I couldn't do it. I couldn't touch Kate in no way except as a brother. The time'll come when she'll need a man again, and not just a brother. I seen you two at the courthouse, and it come to me. You're the one to marry her, Hitch."

Hitch let go a silent sigh of relief. "It's a way too early for us to be talkin' thisaway. We need to wait a proper time."

"If you go with Lafey Dodge, you better think on it now. I don't want nothin' happenin' to you."

XX

THEY CROSSED THE WIDE, SHALLOW RIVER shortly after sunup, following the marker stakes to avoid the quicksands, then started across the rolling hills toward New Mexico. Lafey Dodge rode that big blue roan of his. Hitch rode Walking Jack. Dodge's right arm was tightly bound. Anger pinched his face.

"That son of a bitch Selkirk," he grumbled. "Still owes me a thousand dollars. You mark it down in your book, Hitchcock: a man like that ain't to be trusted."

"I never did."

"Give me an old fire-eater like John Torrington anytime. Bullheaded, stupid sometimes, but he's every inch a man. He's got his honor. If he's ever said he'll do somethin', he'll do it. Paid me all he had promised and a little extry besides. But not Selkirk. He says the whole thing turned into a fiasco and he didn't see where he owed anybody another nickel. That son of a bitch!"

Hitch listened without particular interest. He did not care whether Dodge was paid or not; he simply wanted him gone.

Dodge said grimly, "But he just thinks he's done with me. One way or another, he'll damned sure pay."

Hitch's eyes narrowed. "You wasn't thinkin' about comin' back and doin' somethin' to him, was you, Dodge? I could lock you up for makin' threats, but I'd rather just see you out of the country."

"No, I promised you I'd leave, and I'm like ol' John Torrington; I keep my word."

"Then I don't see how you'll make him pay."

"There's ways."

They did not talk for a while. Hitch felt no worry about treachery from Dodge. For one thing, Hitch had the man's pistol, and he did not intend to return it until he was ready to turn back. He looked at the cattle, most of them Torrington's, and at the dry, cured grass which blanketed the ground like some huge light-colored buffalo robe.

Dodge tried rolling a cigarette one-handed and spilled his tobacco. When Hitch started to help him, Dodge shook his head. "I got to learn or quit smokin'. This right arm ain't goin' to be much use to me for a while."

Dodge finished the cigarette and struck a match to it. He started to flip the match away and Hitch warned him to be sure it was out. "This country's dry enough to go up in smoke."

Dodge nodded. "Wouldn't want to hurt ol' man John." He pinched the head of the match between his fingers, wincing from the heat.

Hitch said, "Where are you goin' from here?"

"There's some good Mexican people over close to Anton Chico that I done a favor for once. Thought I'd stay with them till this arm's healed. I can't afford to be out in public as long as I'm in this shape. You ever see what a bunch of wolves will do to a crippled buffalo?"

"It's lucky Rascal didn't do a damn sight worse to you."

Dodge shrugged. "I reckon he felt like he had a right. You goin' to do anything to him for this?"

"Without you here to press charges, I don't suppose anything'll come of it."

"It's just as well. I never did favor jails much . . . for me or for anybody else. Tell him I hold him no grudge."

"When your arm heals, what then?"

"I don't know. By that time there'll probably be another job."

"Times are changin'. There may not be."

Dodge blinked, not comprehending. "There's always a job for a man that knows his business."

"Not if time runs out for his kind of business. And for yours, it's runnin' out fast."

Dodge still didn't understand. "I always gave a man his money's worth. There's always been more work than I could get around to."

Hitch saw that there was no reaching Lafey Dodge, no more than there was any real way to reach John Torrington. Neither had recognized a change since the Civil War.

It's a pity, in a way, he thought. *Somebody'll shoot him, more than likely, or put him away in a prison, and that's just another kind of death for a man like Lafey Dodge.*

They rode all morning. By now the Canadian River hills were behind them and the prairie rolled gently, solid dry grass as far as a man's eyes could see. Dodge pointed to some cattle. "That's the Figure 4 brand on those. Selkirk's, ain't they?"

"We been on Selkirk country since we come through that last set of breaks. It goes yonderway for half a day's ride. There's a little creek just ahead of us. We'll stop and fix us some coffee, then I reckon I'll turn back."

They drank the coffee and ate cold biscuits and bacon Hitch had brought along. Finished, Hitch said, "You take the coffee can and what food we got left. You'll likely need it."

Dodge nodded. Hitch rolled it up in a canvas sack and tied it behind Dodge's cantle, along with his bedroll and small warbag. The last thing he did was hand Dodge his cartridge belt and pistol. "It's unloaded," he said. "I figure you got cartridges someplace. I just don't want you usin' them around here anymore."

Dodge said, "I won't. I promise you I ain't comin' back."

"And you leave Selkirk alone, you hear?"

"I *didn't* promise you that." Dodge studied Hitch intently, not seeming to want to pull away. "There's somethin' been botherin' me, Hitchcock, somethin' I'd purely like to know."

"What's that?"

"If old Charlie Waide hadn't come along on that street when he did, would you of really shot John Torrington?"

Hitch pondered. "I'll never know."

"I'm bettin' you would have. And the old man thinks so, too. He'll hate you as long as he lives, but he'll never look down on you." Dodge shoved his left hand forward, offering to shake. "Been a pleasure to know you, Hitchcock."

Hitch hesitated, then accepted. "I'm sorry I can't say the same."

He sat a long time, watching Dodge ride away. He had a feeling Dodge meant to keep his promise about not coming back, but he felt compelled to stay and see him out of sight. After a long time, Dodge disappeared into the heatwaves that shimmered over the distant brown grass and that melted the vague horizon line into the clear summer sky. Only then did Hitch swing up into the saddle and head Walking Jack back toward town.

A long time later the prairie wind brought him the vague smell of something burning. He turned in the saddle and brought Walking Jack to an abrupt halt, wheeling him around. Light brown smoke billowed in the west, clouds of it climbing up into a sky of burnished brass.

Instantly he knew. "Lafey Dodge!"

Old-timers always remembered that fire as a curly wolf. With the north wind to push it and all those miles and miles of dry grass to feed upon, it swept across much of the Figure 4 range, taking out a big percentage of Prosper Selkirk's grass and leaving him without half enough for the next winter. It covered parts of John Torrington's and several other ranches, too.

The sight of such a fire strikes fear into the heart of a brave man, the angry smoke boiling higher than a circling hawk, the noise fierce as screaming eagles. All the animals flee ahead of it in panic. At night the bright red flames reflect on the rolling smoke above, invoking visions of the hell so dreaded by the believing man. Times when wind and ground conditions are right, a prairie fire can outrun a man afoot. This one swept over a nester's place north of the Canadian, and he saved himself only by jumping into his own well. Even so, he almost drowned.

Cowboys turned out from all the ranches, and many who were unemployed joined in, though they had nothing personal at stake. So did many of the people in town. It was not that they worried about Selkirk and the Figure 4, or about old John Torrington, but the fire was hurting other people. There was a danger that it could sweep on to God knew where if they did not stop it.

For a time Hitch found himself fighting fire side by side with John Torrington, and on either side of them were jobless cowboys set adrift after the strike. Some no doubt had been mavericking Torrington cattle, yet the old man asked them no questions and they asked him no favors. The rabbit and the wolf will run side by side to get away from a fire; human enemies will stand together to fight one.

Some of the men fought the blaze half out on the western line, then had to run for their lives when the wind whipped it around them and caught them in the middle. All the nesters who had plows went ahead of the flames and cut deep furrows. Hitch helped Charlie Waide kill a Torrington cow, split her open with an ax and flatten her out. Hitch tied onto one hind leg, Charlie onto the other, and they dragged the whole juicy mess up and down the front line of the flame, smothering it. Other cowboys were doing the same.

One way and another, after two days of fighting they

brought the blaze to a standstill. A rainstorm thundered
down from the north and finished putting out the fire, the
first minutes of rainfall sending clouds of steam rising up
from the hissing ashes.

The danger gone, from the east came the wagons and the
buggies and hacks, and women from the scattered ranches
and from town, bringing food and fresh water and pots to
boil coffee in.

Charlie Waide sank to the ground, totally exhausted. He
was holding the bad arm now. He had ignored it the last
couple of days and had forced it to do things certain to bring
him pain later. They watched John Torrington, weary and
bent but still riding up and down the line. His slicker had
been lost somewhere in the fight against the fire. The old
man still hoarsely barked orders, though the men were so
tired they did little but nod acknowledgement. They were
far more interested in the food and coffee.

Hitch said, "You know where we're at now?"

Charlie Waide looked around. "Figure 4."

"We didn't save much of Selkirk's grass for him."

Charlie shook his head. "He'll never make the winter out,
Hitch. Come spring he'll probably be broke flatter'n a
stepped-on centipede."

"He's got it comin' to him."

"But he'll take me out along with him. He'll have his
bank call me in."

"Why? That won't save him."

"I took your part against him. He won't let me stand
while he falls."

"I'm sorry, Charlie."

Charlie shrugged. "It'll hurt like hell, but they can't get
it all. I ain't so old and wore out but what I can't start fresh.
I'll beat them damnyankees yet."

"Sure you will, Charlie." Hitch stared at him, the words
coming easy but the doubt strong. "How about me goin' to
the wagon and bringin' you some coffee?"

Charlie looked, and his eyes softened. "Go to the wagon,

Hitch, but don't be in no hurry. Come back in your own good time.''

Hitch turned. He saw Kate there at the wagon, face smudged by smoke and ash. Through the ash, she was smiling.

Available by mail from

TOR
FORGE

1812 • David Nevin
The War of 1812 would either make America a global power sweeping to the pacific or break it into small pieces bound to mighty England. Only the courage of James Madison, Andrew Jackson, and their wives could determine the nation's fate.

PRIDE OF LIONS • Morgan Llywelyn
Pride of Lions, the sequel to the immensely popular *Lion of Ireland*, is a stunningly realistic novel of the dreams and bloodshed, passion and treachery, of eleventh-century Ireland and its lusty people.

WALTZING IN RAGTIME • Eileen Charbonneau
The daughter of a lumber baron is struggling to make it as a journalist in turn-of-the-century San Francisco when she meets ranger Matthew Hart, whose passion for nature challenges her deepest held beliefs.

BUFFALO SOLDIERS • Tom Willard
Former slaves had proven they could fight valiantly for their freedom, but in the West they were to fight for the freedom and security of the white settlers who often despised them.

THIN MOON AND COLD MIST • Kathleen O'Neal Gear
Robin Heatherton, a spy for the Confederacy, flees with her son to the Colorado Territory, hoping to escape from Union Army Major Corley, obsessed with her ever since her espionage work led to the death of his brother.

SEMINOLE SONG • Vella Munn
"As the U.S. Army surrounds their reservation in the Florida Everglades, a Seminole warrior chief clings to the slave girl who once saved his life after fleeing from her master, a wife-murderer who is out for blood." —*Hot Picks*

THE OVERLAND TRAIL • Wendi Lee
Based on the authentic diaries of the women who crossed the country in the late 1840s. America, a widowed pioneer, and Dancing Feather, a young Paiute, set out to recover America's kidnapped infant daughter—and to forge a bridge between their two worlds.

Call toll-free 1-800-288-2131 to use your major credit card or clip and send this form below to order by mail

---

Send to: Publishers Book and Audio Mailing Service
            PO Box 120159, Staten Island, NY 10312-0004

☐ 52471-3	1812	$6.99/$8.99	☐ 53657-6	Thin Moon and Cold Mist	$6.99/$8.99
☐ 53650-9	Pride of Lions	$6.99/$8.99	☐ 53883-8	Seminole Song	$5.99/$7.99
☐ 54468-4	Waltzing in Ragtime	$6.99/$8.99	☐ 55528-7	The Overland Trail	$5.99/$7.99
☐ 55105-2	Buffalo Soldiers	$5.99/$7.99			

Please send me the following books checked above. I am enclosing $_____. (Please add $1.50 for the first book, and 50¢ for each additional book to cover postage and handling. Send check or money order only—no CODs).

Name _____

Address _____ City _____ State _____ Zip _____

BOSTON PUBLIC LIBRARY

3 9999 05379 813 6

ESSENTIAL BIBLIOGRAPHY

Baines, J., J. Malek. *Atlas of Ancient Egypt*. Oxford -Nex York, 1980.

Christophe, L.A. *Abu Simbel, l'epopea di una scoperta archeologica*. Torino, 1970.

Curto, S. *Nubia*. Novara, 1965.

Emery, W.B. *Egypt in Nubia*. London, 1965.

Gardiner, A.H. *Egypt of the Pharahos*. Oxford, 1974.

Gohary, J. *Guide to the Nubian Monuments on Lake Nasser*. Cairo, 1998.

Porter, B., R.L.B. Moss. *Topographical Bibliography of Ancient Egyptian Hierogliphic Texts, Reliefs and Paintings*. 7 vols., Oxford, 1927.

Säve-Söderbergh, T. *Temples and Tombs of Ancient Nubia. The International Rescue Campaign At Abu Simbel, Philae and Other Sites*. Paris & London, 1987.

Siliotti, A. *Egitto Templi, uomini e dei*. Vercelli, 1994.

Taylor, J.H. *Egypt and Nubia*. London, 1991.

Vandier, J. *Manuel d'archéologie égyptienne*. Paris, 1952-58.

PHOTOGRAPH CREDITS

All the photographs in this book are by Alberto Siliotti/Archivio Image Service–Geodia except for the following:

Courtesy of UNESCO (Paris) in front flap (second photo above left), in back cover above right, pages 8, 20,

DRAWINGS

Stefania Cossu pages 4, 6 left, 6-7, 7 center, 7 right, 14-17 from a drawing by J.-Cl. Golvin/Geo, 22-23 from National Geographic Society.

Jean Claude Golvin/Errance Éd. pages 27, 32.

Elisa Martini pages. 6 above, 6 below center, 7 above, 7 below, 21 below from National Geographic Society, 23 right.

Boston Public Library

ABU SIMBEL
AND THE NUBIAN TEMPLES

EGYPT POCKET GUIDE

Alberto Siliotti

D0043101

THE AMERICAN UNIVERSITY IN CAIRO PRESS

Text and Photographs Alberto Siliotti
Drawings Stefania Cossu,
Jean Claude Golvin, Elisa Martini

General Editing Yvonne Marzoni
Graphic Design Geodia
English Translation Richard Pierce

Copyright © 2000 by Geodia (Verona, Italy)

This edition first published in Egypt jointly by
The American University in Cairo Press (Cairo and New York)
Elias Modern Publishing House (Cairo)
Geodia (Verona, Italy)

All rights reserved. No part of this publication may be reproduced or transmitted in any form or
by any means—electronic or photomechanical, including photocopying, recording, or storage in a
retrieval system—without the prior written permission of the publishers.

Created by Geodia (Verona, Italy)
Printed in Egypt by Elias Modern Publishing House (Cairo)
Distributed by the American University in Cairo Press (Cairo and New York)

Contents

Nubia

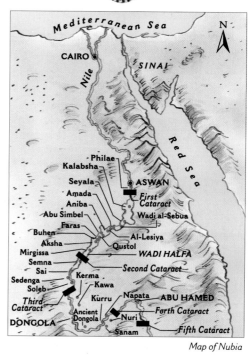

New Kingdom faience plaque representing a Nubian (Nubia Museum, Aswan)

*T*his vast region rich in gold and copper, lying between the First and Fourth Cataracts, was a passageway from Equatorial Africa and the Mediterranean for traders transporting spices, ivory, and other exotic goods.

Map of Nubia

The name 'Nubia,' which is probably derived from the Egyptian word *nbw* ('gold'), is applied to a large region between the First and Forth Cataracts of the Nile that is generally divided into two parts. The northern sector, bordered by the first two cataracts, is called Lower Nubia and was known in ancient times as *Wawat*; the southern area, Upper Nubia, was ancient *Kush* and is now part of Sudan.

Although Nubia was basically a desert region, it was always considered extremely important both for its mineral resources, especially the gold deposits of Wadi Allaqi, and as a link between Equatorial Africa and the Mediterranean. This is why Nubia was called 'the passageway to Africa.' Spices, ivory, gold, exotic animal skins, incense, and aromatic plants from the central regions of the continent passed through Nubia and were then sorted and sold in the great emporium of Aswan.

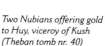

Two Nubians offering gold to Huy, viceroy of Kush (Theban tomb nr. 40)

Lake Nasser

*T*he second largest artificial lake in the world, Lake Nasser has been called 'the sea of Nubia.'

The waters of Lake Nasser form a great number of inlets known as khors

Lake Nasser, which was created between the First and Second Cataract as a consequence of the construction of the Aswan High Dam in 1971, extends from north to south for about 500 kilometers (380 of which are in Egyptian territory), with an average width of ten kilometers and a maximum depth of about 80 meters. The lake water is regulated so that it is 183 meters above sea level, 62 meters higher than the original level of the Nile River.

The volume of the lake has been calculated at about 132.5 billion cubic meters, and this large amount of water has provided irrigation for 8,000 square kilometers of land. The water of Lake Nasser has flowed onto the surrounding desert land, and in following the configuration of the terrain has created many bights and inlets of varying sizes. These are called *khor* in Arabic. The lake abounds in fish, providing about 50,000 tons annually to the more than 5,000 local

LAKE NASSER STATISTICS

Surface area: 5,250 sq. km
Total length: 496 km
Length of coastline: 7,800 km
Average depth: 60 m
Mininum width: 5 km
Average width: 10 km
Maximum width: 32 km
High capacity:132.5 billion cubic meters
Amount of water lost annually through evaporation: 6 billion cubic meters

fishermen. Lake Nasser constitutes an extremely interesting ecosystem with an abundance of

Lake Nasser viewed from a satellite

the only surviving specimens of Nile crocodiles (*Crocodilus niloticus*) in Egypt. These awesome creatures are sometimes more than 2.5 meters long.
In the surrounding desert, on the other hand, there is a population of dorcas gazelles (*Gazella dorcas*). There are also a great many interesting birds living in the Lake Nasser zone, which is home of the

Dorcas gazelle

most important population of aquatic birds in Egypt,

Original course of the Nile

First Cataract

NEW KALABSHA

Kalabsha

Qertassi

Beit al-Wali

Dendur

Gerf Hussein

Dakkah

Maharraqa

NEW SEBUA

Al-Sebua

NEW AMADA

Amada

Aniba

Toshka

Toshka New Valley

ABU SIMBEL

Ballana

fauna. The seasonal fluctuation of the water is about 10 meters. By far the most common fish is the genus *Tilapia*, which represents about 97% of the plentiful annual catch for local fishermen. Another important fish is the Nile perch (*Lates niloticus*). The characteristic inlets of the lake (there are about 80 large ones), bordered by the typical plants in this zone, tamarisk shrubs (*Tamarix nilotica*), are the habitat of

numbering approximately 200,000 individuals. Some of them are sedentary and nest here—for

Spur-winged plover
(*Vanellus spinosus*)

Nile perch
(*Lates niloticus*)

Tilapia nilotica

Nile crocodile
(Crocodilus niloticus)

example, the spur-winged plover (*Vanellus spinosus*) and the Egyptian goose (*Alopochen aegyptiacus*) —while others migrate to the region for the winter: the black-necked grebe (*Podiceps nigricollis*), the tufted duck (*Aytha fuligula*), and the white pelican (*Pelecanus onocrotalus*).

The tufted duck (Aytha fuligula) *flying and in the water*

Egyptian goose
(Alopochen aegyptiacus)

Black-necked grebe
(Podiceps nigricollis)

White pelican
(Pelecanus onocrotalus)

A khor *bordered by tamarisk shrubs*

Tamarisks (Tamarix nilotica)

Detail of a tamarisk flower

HISTORY

Origins

New Kingdom

Christian Nubia

Nubia Today

The UNESCO Campaign

Origins

Upper Paleolithic stone tool (Nubia Museum, Aswan)

Predynastic period ivory comb (Nubia Museum, Aswan)

Nubia had already been settled in the Paleolithic era, and important cultures rose up there in the fourth millennium B.C. The region did not remain isolated for long, since from the proto-dynastic period onward there was important and continuous cultural exchange with pharaonic Egypt.

Archaeologists have found stone artifacts in Nubia dating from the Paleolithic period, as well as numerous predynastic (Naqada culture) and protodynastic human settlements. The distinct development of the Nubian populations

Typical A-group grave (Nubia Museum, Aswan)

A-group cultures tumulus grave (left, a section; right, seen from above)

compared to classical Egypt has led scholars to divide them into two major groups: the cultures of the

Predynastic A-group pottery (Nubia Museum, Aswan)

so-called A-group, which takes in the period between the protodynastic age and the Old Kingdom (approximately from 3000 to 2150 B.C.), and those of the C-group, which correspond to the Middle and New Kingdoms (2100–1076 B.C.). The Nubian populations belonging to the A-group, whose economy was originally based on hunting and gathering, soon began to rear

Graffito of King Djer from Gebel Sulayman (National Museum of Khartoum)

livestock and cultivate cereal crops. However, Nubia remained isolated from the rest of Egypt, and the pharaohs of the first Dynasties sent expeditions there, as is testified by a

Models of Nubian archers found in a Middle Kingdom tomb (Egyptian Museum, Cairo)

graffito dating from the time of Djer—who was probably the second pharaoh of the 1st Dynasty (2920–2780 B.C.)—which was found on Gebel Sulayman, in the Second Cataract area, south of Buhen. During the Old Kingdom the pharaohs had firm control of the region as far as the Second Cataract and occasionally sent exploratory expeditions further south with the aim of exploiting trade and minerals in Nubia, as can be seen in the abundant use of Nubian granite and diorite in the monuments and sculpture of the reign of Khafre (4th Dynasty, 2520–2494 B.C.). Between the end of the Old Kingdom and the beginning of the Middle Kingdom (the First Intermediate Period, 2150–2056 B.C.), taking advantage of the internal disorder and weakened central government in Egypt, new populations settled in Nubia. They probably came from the region of Kordofan and are classified as members of the C-group. These warlike populations, who were expert archers, began to provide mercenaries for the armies of the different Egyptian governors, as documented by the models of Nubian warriors found in the tomb of an overlord of Asyut. The Egyptian pharaohs of the Middle Kingdom (2100–1750 B.C.) regained control of Nubia and built a series of fortresses, mostly in the Second Cataract region. The most grandiose of these is the one at Buhen, which was already a major trade center during the Old Kingdom. In this period the Egyptians spread their dominion even farther south, as far as the Third Cataract.

Headless diorite statue of King Khafre (Nubia Museum, Aswan)

New Kingdom

*B*y now an integral part of the Egyptian empire, which had extended its borders as far as the Fourth Cataract, Nubia greatly attracted the New Kingdom pharaohs, who built many temples and shrines in the region as a sign of their political and religious might.

An ushabti of Heka-Nefer, governor of Nubia (Nubia Museum, Aswan)

During the New Kingdom (1550–1076 B.C.), and in particular during the reign of Tuthmosis I and Tuthmosis III (28th Dynasty), Egypt extended its influence over Nubia as far south as the Fourth Cataract and built many cities there, including Napata. In this period the region was considered a province of Egypt, governed by viceroys who bore the title of

Colossus of Ramesses II from the Temple of Gerf Hussein (Nubia Museum, Aswan)

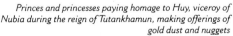

Princes and princesses paying homage to Huy, viceroy of Nubia during the reign of Tutankhamun, making offerings of gold dust and nuggets

'King's Son of Kush,' and many monuments were built in honor of the leading Egyptian gods and pharaohs. Certainly the leading figure in this flurry of architectural activity, the most grandiose expression of which are the temples at Abu Simbel, was Ramesses II.

Late Period

*T*oward the middle of the
8th century B.C. the
Kushite sovereigns who ruled
at Napata managed to extend
their power, first in the Thebes
region, and then over all of
Egypt. Thus began a new
dynasty of 'black pharaohs'
that lasted up to the Assyrian
conquest of Egypt.

*Stela commemorating King Piye (25th
Dynasty) (Nubia Museum, Aswan)*

*Taharqa, the leading 25th
Dynasty pharaoh (Nubia
Museum, Aswan)*

With the demise of
the New Kingdom
and the subsequent
political and military
instability and weakness
that characterized the
Third Intermediate
Period (1070–712 B.C.),
Nubia also went through
a phase of decline. This
ended in the 8th century
B.C., when the Kushite
king Kashta, who reigned
at Napata, asserted
control over Upper
Egypt. His successor, Piye,
marched with his army as
far north as Memphis,
leaving a granite stela
commemorating this
exploit in the Temple of
Amun at Napata.
This marked the begin-
ning of the Kushite
period, exemplified by the
inversion of traditional
roles in the relationship
between Egypt and Nubia,
and by the presence on
the throne of Egypt of
Nubian kings, who formed
the 25th Dynasty.
The most brilliant of the
'black pharaohs'—who, by
the way, did not consider
themselves invaders, but
the true successors of the
New Kingdom
pharaohs—was Taharqa
(690–664 B.C.), who
made a determined effort
to thwart the threat
posed by the Assyrian
army. The Assyrian ruler
Ashurbanipal, after allying
himself with Necho, king of
the city of Sais in the
Delta, and with his son
Psammetichus, finally
succeeded in taking
Thebes, putting an end to
the dynasty of Kushite
kings. The Nubians
retreated to Meroe in
Upper Nubia, beyond the
Fifth Cataract,
where they
reigned for nine
more centuries,
while Egypt
remained under
Persian
dominion for
three centuries,
after which it
was conque-
red by Ale-
xander the
Great and
ruled by the
Ptolemies.

*The Divine Adoratrice of Amun, Amenirdis,
sister of King Kashta (Nubia Museum, Aswan)*

Greco-Roman Period

Statue of a Roman legionary (Nubia Museum, Aswan)

*I*n the Ptolemaic and Roman periods, Nubia was the Dodekaschoinos, a region where the Meroites, Blemmyes, and Nobatae also made their influence felt.

The pylon of the Temple of Kalabsha, built during Augustus's time

the reign of Augustus. From the 3rd century A.D. on, Nubia become more and more influenced by the Blemmyes and Nobatae, warlike populations who came from the Libyan and Arabian deserts respectively and who were always in conflict for control of the region.

Bas-relief of Augustus in the Temple of Kalabsha

Under the Ptolemies the area between the First Cataract and the city of *Hieraskaminos* (Maharraqa) was included in the region known as the 'Dodekaschoinos,' a Greek word that means 'land of the twelve schoinoi' (a *schoinos* was a unit of measure of about 11 kilometers). This period also witnessed the rising influence of the Meroitic kingdom, the capital of which was Meroe (Sudan), as attested by the construction of the Temple of Dakka by the Meroitic ruler Arkamani in the late 3rd century B.C. When Egypt passed under Roman hegemony in 30 B.C., the Meroites and Romans vied for control of Nubia. The latter asserted their dominion and built many temples, especially during

Augustan age coin (Nubia Museum, Aswan)

Scholars have classified these peoples as members of a culture called the 'X-group.' They built the tombs found at Qasr Ibrim, Ballana, and Qustol, which date back to the 3rd to 6th centuries A.D. and are famous for their magnificent funerary goods. In 535, the Nobatae, led by their king Silko, routed the Blemmyes and gained control of Nubia.

GREAT TEMPLE AT ABU SIMBEL
Built by Ramesses II and dedicated to Amun-Re, Re-Harakhti, and the deified Ramesses II, this is the largest temple in Nubia.

TEMPLE OF AMADA
Built by Tuthmosis III and his successor Amenophis II, and later enlarged by Tuthmosis IV, this temple was dedicated to Amun-Re and Re-Harakhti.
The temple was moved to *New Amada*, 2.5 kilometers from its original site.

TEMPLE OF WADI AL-SEBUA
This temple, part of which was cut out of the rock, was built during the reign of Ramesses II and dedicated to Amun-Re and Re-Harakhti. It is more ancient than the temples at Abu Simbel. It was moved to a new site, called *New Sebua*, four kilometers further west.

SMALL TEMPLE AT ABU SIMBEL
Built by Ramesses II and dedicated to the goddess Hathor and the pharaoh's chief wife, Nefertari.

TEMPLE OF DERR
This temple, built by Ramesses II and dedicated to Amun-Re, is similar in structure and decoration to the one at Abu Simbel. Unlike all the other Nubian temples, it originally stood on the right (eastern) bank of the Nile. It was transported to the present site of *New Amada*.

CHAPEL OF AL-LESIYA
This rock-cut chapel was built by Tuthmosis III and dedicated to the Nubian god Dedun and to the deified Senusert III. It is now in the Egyptian Museum in Turin.

Nile

TEMPLE OF MAHARRAQA
Built in 30 A.D. by the Romans and dedicated to Isis and Serapis. It was moved to *New Sebua*.

TEMPLE OF DAKKA
Built toward the end of the 3rd century B.C. by the Meroitic king Arkamani, a contemporary of Ptolemy IV, this temple was dedicated to the god Thoth. It was enlarged during the reigns of the Roman emperors Augustus and Tiberius. It was moved to *New Sebua*.

TEMPLE OF GERF HUSSEIN

TEMPLE OF DENDUR

Greco-Roman Nubia

TEMPLE OF BEIT AL-WALI
This small, partly rock-cut temple
was built by Ramesses II and
dedicated to Amun-Re.
It was moved to *New Kalabsha*.

ISLAND OF PHILAE

N i l e

TEMPLE OF GERF HUSSEIN
Built by the viceroy of Kush, Setau, during the reign of Ramesses II and dedicated to the gods Ptah and Ptah-Tatenen, the goddess Hathor, and the deified Ramesses II.
The temple lies under the waters of the Nile, but a colossus of Ramesses II, which stood in the hypostyle hall, is now on display at the Nubia Museum, Aswan.

TEMPLE OF DENDUR
Built during the reign of Augustus Caesar and dedicated to Isis, as well as to the sons of a Nubian chieftain, Petisis and Pehorus.
It is now in the Metropolitan Museum of New York.

TEMPLE OF KALABSHA
This temple was built in the 1st century A.D. by the emperor Augustus and dedicated to the god Mandulis. It is the largest freestanding Nubian temple.
The Temple of Kalabsha was moved to the site of *New Kalabsha*; its gateway was donated to the German Federal Republic and reassembled in the Egyptian Museum, Berlin.

TEMPLE OF TAFFA
Two small Greco-Roman temples.
The north one was moved to the Netherlands and reassembled in the Rijksmuseum, Leiden.

KIOSK OF QERTASSI
Built in the Ptolemaic period and dedicated to Hathor, it was moved to *New Kalabsha*.

TEMPLE OF DABOD
Built in the 3rd century B.C. by the Meroitic king Adikhalamani and dedicated to the god Amun, it was enlarged in the Ptolemaic period and rededicated to the goddess Isis.-
Some bas-reliefs were executed during the reigns of Augustus and Tiberius.
The temple was moved to Spain and reassembled in a park in Madrid.

SANDSTONE QUARRIES

Christian Nubia

*F*rom the 6th century onward, Christianity grew throughout Nubia and lasted for eight centuries, until 1315, when the Arabs deposed Kerenbes, the region's last Christian sovereign.

Tenth-century fresco from the Nubian church of Abdallah Nerqe, which is now under water

Christianity spread rapidly in Nubia, as in other regions of Egypt. After the edict issued by the Byzantine emperor Theodosius the Great in 384 that made Christianity the official religion of the empire, the pagan temples were closed and pagan rites were prohibited, but the Blemmyes and Nobatae made repeated attacks against the Christian communities. In 543, Silko, the king of the Nobatae, converted to Christianity, which spread throughout Nubia from the 6th to the 10th century and was centered at Qasr Ibrim, which became the seat of the Nubian Patriarchate. Many temples—such as the ones at Wadi al-Sebua, Amada, and Beit al-Wali—were transformed into churches and decorated with new wall paintings, while new churches were built in Nubia, particularly in Qasr Ibrim and Faras, where cathedrals were erected. The one at Faras (now under water) was decorated with famous frescos that are now on exhibit at the Khartoum Museum, Sudan.

A Coptic priest (10th c.)

The remains of the large cathedral at Qasr Ibrim

Nubia Today

Nubian culture and identity—the characteristic decorated houses, music, dress, varied languages, and traditions—continues to live.

A Nubian girl

A characteristic mudbrick Nubian house

The creation of Lake Nasser not only caused the submersion of hundreds of archaeological sites, but numerous villages, built in the traditional Nubian architectural style, were also lost forever. Furthermore, the inhabitants were forced to move elsewhere. Some went to Cairo, others to Sudan, and many chose to settle around outskirts of Aswan, the chief city of Lower Nubia, in the hope of recreating their former life by keeping alive their cultural identity and maintaining their customs and traditions.

Today it is still possible to visit some typical Nubian villages around the High Dam and on Sehel and Elephantine Islands. The Nubia Museum, which opened in 1997, was founded with the aim of honoring Nubian culture and its artistic forms of expression.

Lyre player

A Nubian village near Aswan

The UNESCO Nubian Rescue Campaign

On 1 October 1965, at Abu Simbel, the huge, 16-ton face of one of the colossi on the façade of the Great Temple of Ramesss II, was removed

*T*he con-struction of the Aswan High Dam jeopardized the very existence of all the monuments in Nubia along the Nile. These treasures were saved by an extraordinary international campaignæ under the auspices of UNESCO, which included the Nubian temples as part of the world's cultural heritage.

*T*he worldwide campaign promoted by UNESCO to salvage the ancient monuments in Nubia—which, after the construction of the Aswan High Dam and the consequent formation of Lake Nasser, would have been swallowed up by the waters of the Nile—was a breathtaking race against time in which 51 nations participated with great generosity.

The official inauguration of the dam construction was held on 9 January 1960, and on March 8 of the same year UNESCO's Director General launched an appeal to all the nations of the world to save the Nubian monuments. The first

phase of this operation took place the following year, in 1961, when the German Federal Republic agreed to dismantle and reconstruct the large Temple of Kalabsha. This

This is how the temples at Abu Simbel looked before the construction of the Aswan High Dam

Section of the artificial hill with the Great Temple of Ramesses II

undertaking reached its successful conclusion in 1963, when the temple—which had been been cut into 13,000 stone blocks—was reassembled 50 kilometers away from its original site, at a place that was named *New Kalabsha*, on a rocky spur one kilometer from the Aswan High Dam. Next to the temple, the Egyptian Antiquities Organization placed the Kiosk of Qertassi and the rock-cut Temple of Beit al-Wali, which had originally stood a short distance from the Temple of Kalabsha. Later on, in April 1964, while the waters of the Nile were rising at great speed, the dismantling of other important temples was initiated: the ones at Wadi al-Sebua, Derr, and Maharraqa, and the tomb of Pennut at Aniba. At the same time, the Nubians who lived in the many villages on the banks of the Nile were being evacuated. The Temple of Amada, the most ancient in Nubia, could not be dismantled and rebuilt, because this

The Great Temple of Ramesses II was built inside an artificial hill

would have caused irreparable damage to the wall decoration. The solution, carried out by France and Egypt, with the technical support of the Institut *Géographique National of Paris*, was remarkable. The temple, 25 meters long and 10 meters wide, was lifted in one piece by a series of powerful pneumatic pumps and hoisted onto a specially built flatcar on railway tracks. It was then slowly hauled to its new home, named *New Amada*, 2.6 kilometers from the original site. The temple reached its destination, on higher ground, in March 1965 and maintained the orientation it had had on its former site.

The same year, 1964, witnessed the beginning of the salvage of the temples at Abu Simbel, the most grandiose monumental complex in all of Nubia. This was the most difficult, colossal, and painstaking rescue operation of all, given the size of the monuments: the Temple of Ramesses II alone has a volume of 11,000 cubic meters. Of the various projects proposed, the Egyptian government chose the one that would involve cutting the temple into

The UNESCO symbol

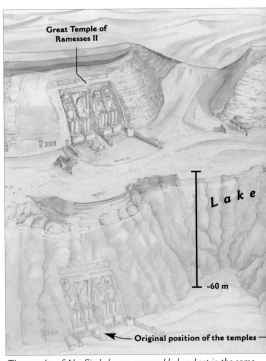

The temples of Abu Simbel were reassembled and set in the same alignment, in a higher position farther away from the water

The rising level (in meter) of the water in Lake Nasser

large blocks, some of which would weigh more than ten tons, and then reassembling them on a more elevated site. The Great Temple of Ramesses II and the Small Temple of Hathor and Nefertari were thus totally dismantled and rebuilt with the same alignment on an artificial hill 65 meters above, and

180 meters behind, their original position.

The reconstruction of Abu Simbel was finished in September 1968. By that time all the other Nubian temples included in the rescue campaign had already been transported and reassembled in higher positions. The Nubian Rescue Campaign ended in March 1980 with

Small Temple of Hathor and Nefertari

Nasser

NUBIAN MONUMENTS IN OTHER COUNTRIES

The Egyptian government was quite generous with the nations that had participated in the international Nubian Rescue Campaign: as a token of its gratitude, it donated four small temples to the countries that had distinguished themselves in this arduous and prodigious feat. The rock-cut Chapel of Tuthmosis III at al-Lesiya was given to Italy and was reassembled in the Egyptian Museum in Turin. The Temple of Dabod was donated to Spain and rebuilt in a park in Madrid. The Temple of Dendur was offered to the United States and is housed in a large wing in the Metropolitan Museum of New York. The Temple of Taffa was given to Holland and is on display at the Rijksmuseum at Leiden. Lastly, the gateway of the Temple of Kalabsha was given to the German Federal Republic and is now in the Egyptian Museum, Berlin.

TEMPLE OF DABOD

TEMPLE OF TAFFA

GATEWAY OF KALABSHA

TEMPLE OF DENDUR

CHAPEL OF AL-LESIYA

the completion of the salvage of the monuments at Philae, carried out by Italian engineers and personnel.

Overall, over twenty monuments—temples, chapels, stelae, and bas-reliefs—were saved. Unfortunately, not all the monuments could be rescued from the water. The rock-cut temple of Horemhab at Abu Oda and the Temple of Ramesses II at Gerf Hussein, as well as over 150 necropolises, disappeared under the water of Lake Nasser, lost forever.

THE SITES

New Kalabsha

New Sebua

New Amada

Dakka

Abu Simbel

New Kalabsha

*T*he Temple of Kalabsha, the Kiosk
of Qertassi, and the small rock-
cut Temple of Beit al-Wali were
dismantled at their original sites and
reassembled at New Kalabsha, near
the Aswan High Dam.

New Kalabsha viewed from Lake Nasser

Temple of Kalabsha

This temple was built
during the reign of the
Roman emperor Augustus
(27 B.C.–14 A.D.) over
the ruins of a temple
dating from the time of
Amenophis II (26th
Dynasty, 1453–1419
B.C.). Originally it lay
about 40 kilometers
south of New Kalabsha, at
the ancient Greek city of
Talmis, and was dedicated
to the god Mandulis, a
Nubian form of Horus,
and the goddess Isis.
The Temple of Kalabsha,

74 meters long, is the
largest freestanding
Nubian temple. It is
preceded by a large quay
that bordered the shores
of the Nile, which is
connected to a causeway.
One enters the temple
through the great pylon
that gives access to the
court, which in turn leads
to the hypostyle hall. The
temple was originally
enclosed by a double wall:
the first, which no longer
exists, took in a large area
around the cult buildings,
while the second wall
surrounds the hypostyle
hall and sanctuary, with a

*Detail of one of the many
bas-relief carvings that
decorate the walls of the
sanctuary: the god Mandulis
and the goddess Isis*

Plan of the Temple of Kalabsha

narrow passageway in between. The hypostyle hall, or *pronaos*, is supported by eight columns with campaniform capitals and is decorated on the outside with bas-reliefs depicting the emperor Augustus making offerings to various deities. In the northern portion of the façade there is a graffito

with a commemorative inscription mentioning Silko, king of the Nobatae, dating from the 5th or 6th century A.D., while on the second wall between the columns there are some inscriptions: two Greek texts and one in Meroitic script recording Kharamadeye, king of the Blemmyes, written in the 4th century A.D.

The pronaos gives access to the two vestibules and the sanctuary, all of which became a Christian church in the 6th century. The walls of the sanctuary are covered with lovely bas-relief decoration executed in a conventional style; they represent scenes of Augustus making offerings to a great number of gods. Outside, at the southwest

Façade of the hypostyle hall in the west part of the court

corner of the temple, are the remains of a chapel dedicated to the Nubian god Dedwen, and farther south there are a number of blocks with prehistoric graffiti and some bas-reliefs from the Temple of Ramesses II at Gerf Hussein, which is now under water. Lastly, immediately north of the entrance to the Temple of Mandulis, is a large stela of the pharaoh

The chapel dedicated to the Nubian god Dedwen

Psammetichus II (26th Dynasty) in a good state of preservation that commemorates and narrates his victorious military campaign in Nubia (593 B.C.).

Reconstruction of the Temple of Mandulis at New Kalabsha

The Temple of Beit al-Wali

Behind the Temple of Mandulis is the small rock-cut Temple of Beit al-Wali ('house of the governor' in Arabic), which was built by Ramesses II and dedicated to Amun-Re. Its original site was also Kalabsha. The rock-cut portion of the temple is preceded by a long

Plan of the Temple of Beit al-Wali

Labels on plan:
- The pharaoh makes offerings to Horus of Baki and to Amun-Re
- The pharaoh with Khnum and Satis offering incense to Amun-Re
- Niche with statue of pharaoh with Horus of Baki and Isis
- Niche with statue of pharaoh with Khnum and Satis
- Sanctuary
- The pharaoh with Hathor makes offerings to Horus of Buhen
- The pharaoh with Anukis makes offerings to Khnum and Satis
- Vestibule
- The pharaoh slays the Nubians
- The pharaoh slays the Libyans
- Forecourt
- Scenes of battles against Nubians
- Scenes of battles against Libyans and Asiatics
- Stone gateway with mudbrick pylon

Ramesses II carrying out a purification ritual

Ramesses II makes an offering of wine to Horus of Baki

forecourt that one enters through a stone gateway with carvings of royal cartouches. The walls of the forecourt have bas-reliefs illustrating episodes from Ramesses II's military campaigns against the Nubians and Ethiopians (at left), and against the Libyans and Asiastics (at right). The vestibule of the temple is supported by two columns. In the back wall are two rock-hewn niches with statues of the king together with some deities. The vestibule leads to the small sanctuary, whose bas-reliefs show Ramesses II making offerings to numerous gods.

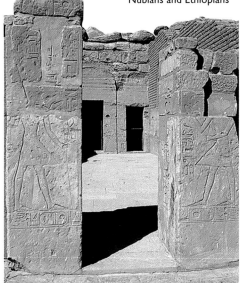

Temple of Beit al-Wali: the jambs of the doorway leading to the court

The vestibule of the Temple of Beit al-Wali

The Kiosk of Qertassi

Kiosk of Qertassi

A few dozen meters from the Temple of Kalabsha, on a slightly higher level, is the Kiosk of Qertassi, which was formerly situated 40 kilometers to the south. This small and delightful building consists of a single chamber that once had a sandstone slab roof. The ceiling was supported by four columns whose capitals are decorated with splendidly exe-

cuted floral motifs, while the portal is flanked by two Hathoric columns. The Kiosk of Qertassi was built during the Ptolemaic or Roman period and dedicated to Hathor, who was the patroness of mining and quarrying activities. Together with the temples of Dendur and Dabod, it was probably one of the stations along the processional route of the sacred boat of Isis.

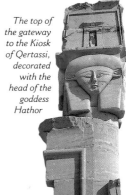

The top of the gateway to the Kiosk of Qertassi, decorated with the head of the goddess Hathor

New Sebua

The Temple of Wadi al-Sebua, preceded by an avenue of sphinxes

*T*hree temples have been reconstructed on the present-day site of New Sebua: the temple that originally stood at Wadi al-Sebua, the Temple of Dakka, and the Temple of Maharraqa.

The Temple of Wadi al-Sebua

rIn Arabic the name of this temple, which originally lay about four kilometers further east, means 'Valley of the Lions.' About half the temple is rock-cut. It was built during the latter half of Ramesses II's reign under the supervision of the viceroy of Kush, Setau, was dedicated to

Amun-Re, Re-Harakhti, and the deified Ramesses II, and was named 'Temple of Ramesses-Meriamun (*beloved by Amun*)-in-the-House-of-Amun.' The constructed portion of the temple, fronted by an avenue of leonine sphinxes (hence the name given to the temple by the locals), originally consisted of three pylons, only the third one of which survives, that led to three

The colossus of Ramesses II with his daughter Bint-Anath

courtyards.
In the first courtyard are six human-headed sphinxes wearing the double crown of Upper and Lower Egypt. The second court has a group

View of New Sebua   Temple of Dakka Dakka   Temple of Maharraqa

Plan of the Temple of Wadi al-Sebua

of four falcon-headed sphinxes also wearing the double crown; they represent different forms of the god Horus (Horus of Maha, Miam, Baki, and Edfu). The third (and only remaining) pylon is preceded by a majestic stairway and gives access to a terrace. In its original state this pylon was preceded by four colossi of the pharaoh.

Only one remains: Ramesses II is bearing a standard with the image of Amun-Re; next to him is his daughter Bint-Anath. The pylon is decorated with scenes of Ramesses II massacring his enemies of the north and south before Amun-Re and Re-Harakhti. This entrance pylon leads to a large court flanked to the east

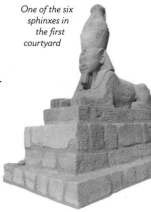

One of the six sphinxes in the first courtyard

and west by two colonnades, each with five Osirid pillars. The walls of these colonnades are decorated with bas-reliefs representing the king, followed by a procession of princes and princesses, in the act of making offerings to various gods (Re-Harakhti, Amun, Ptah, Horus, Atum, Thoth, Maat, Hathor, and Mut) and to himself, the deified king. A ramp leads from the court to the rock-cut part of the temple. This

Reconstruction of the Temple of Wadi al-Sebua during Ramesses II's time

Ramesses II

consists of a hypostyle hall with twelve pillars that is decorated with scenes of the king making offerings to different gods. The pillared hall is followed by a transverse vestibule flanked by two side chapels that gives access to the central sanctuary, which is also flanked by two chapels.

A human-headed sphinx

The avenue of sphinxes in front of the third pylon

The huge pylon of the Temple of Dakka is isolated from the rest of the construction

The Temple of Dakka

A few hundred meters from the Temple of Wadi al-Sebua, on the top of a hillock, stands the Ptolemaic Temple of Dakka, originally situated at the ancient Greek city of *Pselkis* ('scorpion'), where the troops of the Roman governor Petronius defeated the Ethiopians of Queen Candace in 23 B.C. It was dedicated to the god Thoth of Pnubs ('the sycamore tree,' the site of a still unidentified Nubian city), his consort, the lioness god Tefnut, and their son Arsenuphis. This temple originally stood forty kilometers further north, where it was built by the Meriotic king Arkamani (known by the Greeks as Ergamenes) in the late 3rd century B.C. The temple, the only one in Nubia oriented north–south, parallel to the course of the Nile river, was newly decorated by the Ptolemies and then enlarged during the Roman period with the addition of a pylon twelve

meters high. This pylon, which has rooms on its three stories that were perhaps used as storerooms, is distinctive in that it is separated from the rest of the

temple. The decoration on the outer side of the *pronaos*, which has a porticoed façade, dates from the time of Ptolemy VII. This hall is followed by a transverse vestibule

Plan of the Temple of Dakka

Pronaos of the Temple of Dakka

The Temple of Maharraqa

Situated a little lower than the Temple of Dakka, toward the banks of Lake Nasser, is the small Temple of Maharraqa, which originally stood about 50 kilometers further north, near the site of the Greco-Roman city of *Hierasykaminos*, 'the place of the sacred sycamore tree.' Construction of the temple was begun at the behest of Augustus and it was dedicated to the god Serapis (a hybrid god of the Ptolemaic period

decorated with scenes of offerings made by Ptolemy VII to various deities. The vestibule gives access to the chapel of the Meriotic king Arkamani, which was the first sanctuary in the temple and was decorated with numerous low reliefs. The present san-

ctuary was built during the reign of the Roman emperor Augustus, who had the original edifice enlarged.

The Meriotic king Arkamani making offerings to the god Harpocrates (Horus the Child) in one of the walls in the original sanctuary of the Temple of Dakka

The small Temple of Maharraqa

combining features of Osiris, Apis, and the Greek god Zeus) and the goddess Isis, but it was never finished. The edifice is almost totally lacking in wall decoration and consists of a hypostyle hall surrounded on three sides by a colonnnade with fifteen columns and a spiral staircase—the only example of this element in Egyptian architecture—that gives access to the terrace. Like the Temple of Wadi al-Sebua, this one later became a Christian church.

New Amada

*T*he site of New Amada boasts the most ancient temple in Nubia, flanked by the Temple of Derr and the rock-cut tomb of Pennut.

The Temple of Amada

The Temple of Amada

This temple, dedicated to Re-Harakhti and Amun-Re, dates from the 18th Dynasty, making it the oldest of the Nubian temples. The edifice was built during the reigns of three different pharaohs (Tuthmosis II, Amenophis II, and Tuthmosis IV— 1504–1386 BC) and was transported to New Amada, 2.6 kilometers from its original site, thanks to the intervention of France. Since the method of dismantling and reassembling the temple that had been adopted with the other temples in Nubia would have caused irreparable damage to the wall decoration, the Temple of Amada had to be lifted in one piece by means of a complicated hydraulic pump system and then set onto a specially built

View of New Amada

Temple of Derr

Temple of Amada

The pillared hall with proto-Doric columns, built by Tuthmosis IV

Amenophis II making the 'ritual run'

flatcar set on railway tracks. The temple was then transported to its new site at a maximum speed of 25 meters per day. Once it arrived it was situated 40 meters higher than its original position, while maintaining its original orientation. Tuthmosis III began construction of this small sandstone temple on a

was finished by Tuthmosis's son, Amenophis II, and then decorated by Tuthmosis IV with proto-Doric columns in front of the vestibule. This latter has scenes of Tuthmosis III and Amenophis III in the presence of Amun-Re and Re-Harakhti, as well as

Amenophis II making the 'ritual run,' and is flanked by two chapels. The vestibule gives access to the sanctuary, which has two small side chambers. The walls in the left-hand chamber are decorated with Tuthmosis II and Amenophis II making offerings to various gods, while the right-hand chamber has scenes of ceremonies related to the foundation of the temple.

Tuthmosis III before the god Re-Harakhti

site that was probably chosen because of a unique geographical feature: at Amada, the Nile makes a sharp bend and for a stretch flows southward instead of northward. The temple

Plan of the Temple of Amada

Year 3 inscription of Amenophis II; Amenophis on a boat offering wine to Re-Harakhti and Amun-Re

Tuthmosis III and Amenophis II before various gods

Side chamber

Side chambers

Sanctuary

Side chapels

Amenophis II makes the 'ritual run' in honor of Amun-Re

Vestibule

Tuthmosis III with Horus, welcomed by Re-Harakhti and Anukis

Portico

Tuthmosis III with Khnum, Re-Harakhti and Amun

Proto-Doric columns

Tuthmosis IV welcomed by Re-Harakhti, Amun-Re, and Isis

Hypostyle hall

Tuthmosis IV suckled by Hathor between Khnum and Isis

Stone gateway with mudbrick pylon

The Temple of Derr

This temple stands a few hundred meters from the Temple of Amada. Its original site was 11 kilometers further south. One of the many monuments built in Nubia by Ramesses II, this was the only temple in the region situated on the eastern bank of the Nile. The Temple of Derr was dedicated to the god Re and was similar in both structure and decorative program to the Great Temple at Abu Simbel, of which it could be

The pillared hall of the rock-cut Temple of Derr

Plan of the Temple of Derr

Scenes of offerings made by king to various gods and representations of the sacred boat

Remains of four statues

East side chamber

Shelf

Sanctuary

West side chamber

Ramesses II under the sacred tree and between the god Thoth, who is writing his name and holds the jubilee reed, and the gods Ptah and Sekhmet

Second hypostyle hall

Portico

Osirid pillars

First hypostyle hall

N

considered a simplified, reduced version. The temple, whose back portion was cut out of the rock, was originally called 'Temple of Ramesses-Meriamun-in-the-House-of-Re. The edifice was built to celebrate the first jubilee of Ramessess II, a feast that took place after the first thirty years of rule. The outer section of the temple consists of a first hypostyle hall with eight pillars that precede a portico supported by four Osirid pillars decorated with four colossi of Ramesses II; only traces of these statues remain. The rock-cut portion of the temple includes a second hypostyle hall with six pillars that leads directly into the sanctuary, without

Ramesses II under the sacred ished *tree*

a vestibule between them. The decoration in the hall includes scenes of the king making offerings to various gods, and other scenes connected with the jubilee ceremonies.

The most important of these latter is the one on the north wall representing Ramesses II under the sacred *ished* tree between the god Thoth, who is writing the pharaoh's

name on the tree and holding the jubilee reed, and the gods Ptah and Sekhmet. The sanctuary, flanked by two small side chambers, was decorated with four statues cut out of the back wall that are much like those in the sanctuary of the Great Temple at Abu Simbel. Only the lower parts of these statues have survived. On the walls are scenes of offerings made to the gods and representations of the sacred boat of Amun, which stopped at this temple during the religious ceremonies.

Tomb of Pennut

The small rock-cut Tomb of Pennut, a high official under Ramesses VI (1141–1133 B.C.) titled 'Deputy of Wawat and Miam,' was originally situated at Aniba, ancient *Miam*, the capital of Nubia, opposite Qasr Ibrim, about 40 kilometers south of its present-day site. It is the only Nubian tomb that was saved by the

UNESCO Rescue Campaign.

The tomb is extremely simple. It comprises a small offering-chapel; a rock-cut niche in the back wall that originally contained three statues, above the doorway of which is the motif of Re's sacred boat adored by two baboons; and the burial chamber. The wall paintings on the left-hand (west) side of the tomb

are connected with the Underworld, while those on the opposite side illustrate moments of the deceased's life.

Pennut, his wife Takha, and his six sons present floral homages to Re-Harakhti

The rock-cut Tomb of Pennut, with the central niche that was originally deocrated with three statues

Qasr Ibrim

*O*riginally Qasr Ibrim was a fortress lying on a massive headland that dominated the east bank of the Nile, while today it is an island in the middle of Lake Nasser.

The ruins of the Qasr Ibrim Cathedral

A Coptic cross

*Q*asr Ibrim, which means 'fortress of Ibrim' in Arabic, was the ancient Meroitic settlement of Pedeme ('Primis' in Greek). It is the only archaeological site in Nubia that, by virtue of its position, still stands above the waters of Lake Nasser. Although

The columns of the Cathedral

certain inscriptions concerning this site, which was of great strategic importance, date back to the period of Amenophis I (17th Dynasty, 1543 B.C.), the ruins we see today are mostly Coptic and are dominated by the large Christian cathedral, the seat of an ancient bishopric dating from the 7th century. In 1528 the sultan of Constantinople, Selim I, decided to establish an Ottoman military garrison on the site, and the descendants of the

soldiers lived there until 1811. At the foot of the headland are rock-hewn shrines dating from the 18th and 19th Dynasty and dedicated to the pharaohs and various gods. The chapels were later removed; one was reconstructed and is in the Nubia Museum at Aswan.

Abu Simbel

General view of the two temples at Abu Simbel

The explorer G.B. Belzoni (1798–1834)

*I*t was at Abu Simbel, the most famous site in Nubia, that UNESCO carried out the most spectacular of its rescue campaign operations by salvaging the temples.

The Great Temple of Ramesses II at Abu Simbel was discovered in 1813 by the famous Swiss Orientalist and traveler Ludwig Burckhardt, who is also credited with having found the city of Petra in Jordan. However, four years passed before anyone could enter the temple, because an enormous pile of sand almost completely covered the façade and its colossal statues, blocking the entranceway. This feat was achieved by the great Paduan explorer Giovanni Battista Belzoni, who managed to penetrate the interior on 4 August 1817.

A colossus of Ramesses II

The temples of Abu Simbel during Belzoni's time (1817)

Façade of the Great Temple of Ramesses II

The Temple of Ramesses II

The Great Temple at Abu Simbel, which took about twenty years to build, was completed around the year 24 of the reign of Ramesses II (which corresponds to 1265 B.C.). It was dedicated to the gods

Cartouche with Ramesses II's throne name, User-Maat-Re

Amun-Re, Re-Harakhti, and Ptah, as well as to the deified Ramesses himself. Four colossal 20-meter statues of the pharaoh with the double crown of Upper and Lower Egypt decorate the façade of the temple—which is 35 meters wide and is topped by a frieze with 22 baboons,

worshippers of the sun—and flank the entrance. This latter is crowned by a bas-relief representing two images of Ramesses worshiping the god Re-Harakthi, whose statue stands in a large niche.

Ramesses II's chief wife, Nefertari

The god is holding the hieroglyph *user* in his right hand and a feather (Maat, goddess of truth and justice) in his left: this is nothing less than a gigantic cryptogram for Ramesses II's throne name, *User-Maat-Re*. Next to the legs of the colossi there are other statues no higher than the pharaoh's knees.

Ramesses II worships the god Re-Harakhti, who is holding the user and maat hieroglyphs

Plan of the Temple of Ramesses II

These depict Nefertari, Ramesses II's chief consort, the queen mother Mut-Tuy, princes Amenhirkhopshef and Ramesses, and princesses Bint-Anath, Nebttawi, and Merytamun. The temple is complex in structure and quite unusual because of the many side chambers. The hypostyle hall (sometimes also called *pronaos*) is 18 meters long and 16.7 meters wide and

Ramesses II at the Battle of Kadesh

is supported by eight huge Osirid pillars depicting the deified Ramesses likened to the god Osiris, the god of the Underworld, to indicate the everlasting nature of the pharaoh. The colossal statues along the left-hand wall bear the white

Ramesses II

crown of Upper Egypt, while those on the opposite side are wearing the double crown of Upper and Lower Egypt (*pschent*). The bas-reliefs on walls of the pronaos depict battle scenes in the military campaigns the pharaoh waged. Much of the sculpture is given over to the Battle of Kadesh, on the Orontes River in present-day Syria, in which the Egyptian king fought against the Hittites. The most famous relief shows the pharaoh on his war chariot shooting arrows against

Detail of one of the colossi of Ramesses II with the crown of Upper Egypt

The large hypostyle hall in the temple with its huge Osirid pillars

his fleeing enemies, who are being taken prisoner. From the hypostyle hall, one enters the second pillared hall, which has four pillars decorated with beautiful scenes of offerings to the gods. This hall gives access to a transverse vestibule in the middle of which is the entrance to the sanctuary. Here, on the back wall, are rock-cut sculptures of four seated figures: Re-Harakhti, the deified Ramesses II, and the gods Amun-Re and Ptah. Re-Harakhti, Amun-Re, and Ptah were the main divinities in that period and their cult centers were at Heliopolis, Thebes, and Memphis respectively. The axis of the temple was positioned by the ancient Egyptian architects so that twice a year—October 20 and February 20—the rays of the sun worshiped

The sanctuary with the statues. From left, Ptah, Amun-Re, the deified Ramesses II, and Re-Harakhti

by the 22 baboons would penetrate the sanctuary and illuminate the sculpture on the back wall, except for the statue of Ptah, the god connected with the Underworld, who always remained in the dark. It is quite logical to assume that these dates had some relation to a great event, such as the jubilee celebrating the thirtieth anniversary of the

pharaoh's rule. In fact, according to calculations made on the basis of the heliacal rising of the star Sirius (*Sothis*) and inscriptions found by archaeologists, this date must have been October 22. The image of the king was thus enhanced and rivitalized by the energy of the solar star, and the deified Ramesses II could take his place next to Amun-Re and Re-Harakhti.

Ramesses II making offerings to Re-harakhti (left) and Amun-Re (right) on the pillars in the vestibule leading to the sanctuary

The Temple of Hathor and Nefertari

The Temple of Hathor and Nefertari, also known as the Small Temple, was built about one hundred meters northeast of the Temple of Ramesses II and was dedicated to the goddess Hathor and Ramesses's chief consort, Nefertari. This was in fact the first time in ancient Egyptian history that a temple or cult edifice was dedicated to a queen. The rock-cut façade is

Queen Nefertari

Plan of the Temple of Hathor and Nefertari

decorated with two groups of six colossi that are separated by the large gateway. The statues, slightly more than ten meters high, are of Ramesses II and Nefertari. On either side of the portal are two statues of the pharaoh, wearing the white crown of Upper Egypt (south colossus) and the double crown (north colossus); these are flanked by statues of the queen and the pharaoh. What is truly surprising is that for the only time in Egyptian art, the statues of the king and his consort are equal in

Façade of the Temple of Hathor and Nefertari

size. Traditionally, the statues of the queens stood next to those of the pharaoh, but were never taller than his knees. This exception to such a long-standing rule bears witness to the special importance attached to Nefertari by Ramesses II, who went to Abu Simbel with his beloved wife in the 24th year of his reign.

As at the Great Temple of Ramesses II, there are small statues of princes and princesses next to those of their parents. In this case they are positioned symmetrically: on the

The goddess Hathor on one of the pillars in the hypostyle hall

south side (at left as you face the gateway) are, from left to right, princes Meryatum and Meryre, princesses Merytamun and Henttawi, and princes Rahirwenemef and Amenhirkhopshef, while on the north side the same figures are in reverse order.

The plan of the Small Temple is a very simplified version of that of the Great Temple. As in the Temple of Ramesses II, the hypostyle hall or pronaos is supported by six pillars; in this case, however, they are not Osirid pillars depicting the king, but are decorated with scenes with the queen playing the sistrum (an instrument sacred to the goddess Hathor), together with the gods Horus, Khnum, Khonsu, and Thoth, and the goddesses Hathor, Isis, Maat, Mut of Asher, Satis, and Taweret; in one scene Ramesses is presenting flowers or burning incense. The capitals of the pillars bear the face of the goddess Hathor; this type of column is known as Hathoric. The bas-reliefs in the pillared

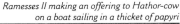

Ramesses II making an offering to Hathor-cow on a boat sailing in a thicket of papyri

The hypostyle hall has six Hathoric pillars

The rock-cut sanctuary and the two side chambers are connected to the transverse vestibule and are aligned with the axis of the temple. The bas-reliefs on the side walls of the small sanctuary represent scenes of offerings to various gods made either by the pharaoh or the queen. On the back wall, which lies to the west along the axis of the temple, there is a niche in which Hathor as a divine cow seems to be coming out of the mountain: the goddess is depicted as the Mistress of this temple dedicated to her and to Nerfertari, who is intimately linked to the goddess.

hall illustrate the deification of the king, the destruction of his enemies in the north and south (in these scenes Ramesses is accompanied by Nefertari), and the queen making offerings to the goddesses Hathor and Mut. The hypostyle hall is followed by a transverse vestibule, access to which is given by three large doors. On the south and north walls of this chamber there are two graceful and poetic bas-reliefs of the king and his consort presenting papyrus plants to Hathor, who is depicted as a cow on a boat sailing in a thicket of papyri. On the west wall, Ramesses II and Nefertari are making offerings to Horus and the divinities of the Cataracts—Satis, Anukis, and Khnum.

The gateway

Nefertari tenderly embracing her beloved husband Ramesses